DECEIVING THE DUKE

Gems of London
Book One

Elizabeth Ellen Carter

ARE YOU SIGNED UP FOR DRAGONBLADE'S BLOG?

You'll get the latest news and information on exclusive giveaways, exclusive excerpts, coming releases, sales, free books, cover reveals and more.

Check out our complete list of authors, too!

No spam, no junk. That's a promise!

Sign Up Here

www.dragonbladepublishing.com

Dearest Reader;

Thank you for your support of a small press. At Dragonblade Publishing, we strive to bring you the highest quality Historical Romance from some of the best authors in the business. Without your support, there is no 'us', so we sincerely hope you adore these stories and find some new favorite authors along the way.

Happy Reading!

CEO, Dragonblade Publishing

Additional Dragonblade books by Author Elizabeth Ellen Carter

Gems of London Series
Deceiving the Duke

Heart of the Corsairs Series
Captive of the Corsairs
Revenge of the Corsairs
Shadow of the Corsairs

King's Rogues Series
Live and Let Spy
Spyfall
Spy Another Day
Father's Day (A Novella)

The Lyon's Den Connected World
The Lyon Sleeps Tonight

Pirates of Britannia Series
The de Wolfe of Wharf Street

Also from Elizabeth Ellen Carter
Dark Heart
Warming Winter's Heart

The essence of lying is in deception, not in words.
—John Ruskin

To my beloved Duncan who believed in me
when I didn't believe in myself.

Acknowledgements

A big thank you goes to my amazing publisher Kathryn Le Veque and editor Scott Moreland for giving me the space and time to help me find my mojo again. Much love to the lovely, supporting authors of Dragonblade Publishing.

PROLOGUE

Glasgow, Scotland
March 1818

D ID IT ALWAYS *rain these days?* Endless gray misery had fallen from the sky in ceaseless fashion; weeks and weeks and weeks of it.

Ruby McAllister drew her attention from the window behind the solicitor to look at the man himself. His face lay in shadows, like the day outside.

How apt.

So much of what she thought she knew had turned out to be wrong, obscured, hidden from her. Sins of omission by her dear late papa were now laid bare.

For the past twenty minutes, she had listened in silence as the solicitor told her how much was left from the sale of the family estate, Strathaird, the only home she had ever known.

The man set down the piece of paper he referred to and raised his head, his widow's peak pronounced. The rim of his glasses glinted silver in the watery light that filtered through the window.

"We were pleased to get a good price for the estate and managed to negotiate the debts. There is a tidy little sum ye could live modestly on, if ye're canny about it," said Mr. Jameson Burns.

"We would be only too glad to honor yer father's memory and manage it on yer behalf. Start with purchasing a small cottage, outside Elderslie, perhaps?"

Burns slid the paper across the oak desk toward her.

The residue of the estate.

Ruby barely glanced at it.

The sum that remained was only a fraction of what it *ought* to be. The estate was well-managed and reasonably prosperous. It *ought* to have remained hers, but for the debts.

They were the fault of one man.

And that man was *not* her father.

Ruby looked down in her lap. The yellowed envelope in her hand stood out starkly against her black mourning gown.

She took a steadying breath.

"Before we conclude business, Mr. Burns, I wish your opinion on this document I found among my father's papers."

She hated the way her black-gloved hand shook as she handed over the old folder with its handwritten sheafs of paper.

He would think it was distress, or ignorance that caused the tremors.

By God, it was *not*.

It was cold black fury.

The middle-aged man frowned slightly as he opened the folder. He adjusted his glasses, sat back and perused in silence.

She listened to the muted chatter of Mr. Burns' clerks in the room next door, the dull splatter of rain on the window panes, and the mechanical tick of the mantel clock, counting down the seconds until they turned to minutes.

The document was a contract for a substantial share of Skye-Heath Textiles, Scotland's most profitable textile mill. The finest linens were produced there, along with the most sumptuous woolen cloth. Only a fraction of it was sold in Scotland, or indeed in Great Britain for that matter. Most of went to the very corners of the empire and beyond – even to America.

Skye-Heath had made its owners, the Musgrave family, very

wealthy indeed.

She herself owned Skye-Heath linens for the tables of Strathaird – *had* owned, she corrected herself bitterly – and not less than three of her winter gowns were made from the softest wools from that mill.

"A *thirty percent* holding, Mr. Burns," she said at length. "I know little of the law, sir, but I do know enough to be aware this contract was notarized and sealed. It ought to be delivered upon."

Behind the contract were pages and pages of drawings – of spindles, bobbins, heddles, cogs, and wheels, along with good-ness-knew-what, all drawn in ink by her father and annotated in his meticulous copper plate.

She only had an inkling of how important the innovation depicted here was. It was simply enough to know that William Gregory Musgrave, Duke of Auchen, thought enough of it to give her father a such a large stake of his mill to possess the design for this device.

Ruby made note of how Burns' lips pressed into a tight line as he stared at the document. Still, he said nothing.

She resisted the urge to twist her hands together.

"There is no accounting for it in the estate's records," she pressed.

The fact that he hadn't simply skimmed through the file and handed it back to her with blithe indifference told her all she needed to know about its contents. His legal opinion would only cement her own.

The Duke of Auchen was a *thief*.

After a moment, Burns closed the folder and sat back in his leather chair. He removed his glasses and placed them on the folder.

"I was yer father's solicitor for thirty years and, aye, a friend," he started. Ruby sensed what his choice of words presaged. She felt ice freeze across her chest, although the room was warm enough thanks to the cheery little fire in the grate. She, too, sat back, spine erect, anticipating what was to come.

"Now, as yer legal advisor, I suggest ye forget ye ever saw this contract."

The chill spread through her veins, stealing her blood's warmth to turn her cold fury hot. She opened her mouth to speak, but Burns shook his head.

"There'll be no satisfaction to be gained in pursuing this matter."

Ruby pointed to the file, anger making her arm shake. "That man *defrauded* my father."

"Now, Lady Ruby—"

"*It is there in the duke's own hand! I wish* you to pursue the matter. The money he owed our family will be enough to buy back Strathaird."

The only answer was a slow, sorrowful shake of the man's head.

"Ye canna accuse a duke of impropriety! The contracts were signed twenty-five years ago. Who's to say there is not another bringing the partnership to a close?"

No!

Ruby breathed in deep, the warm air thawing the frost in her chest just a little. She lifted her chin.

"Do you truly think it likely?"

Burns dropped his hands to the desk, his forearms resting on either side of the folder, reminding her of the *lions couchant* found on the Duke of Auchen's crest.

"Leave it and be content. It's what yer pa would have wanted for ye. There's nothing to be gained frittering away what ye have left on a fool's errand, even if ye did have legal standing, which, in this humble solicitor's opinion, ye do not."

Ruby swallowed against a lump in her throat. The discovery of the contract was the sole spark of hope that sustained her in the weeks following her father's death. Now that, too, was snuffed out.

"I cannot let it lie." She could find pride in the fact that her voice did not quaver too much. "Not without knowing the truth."

Burns shook his head slowly. "Then I canna help ye, lass. Only the duke himself can. And if ye think he's the type of man to defraud yer father of such a sum, do ye think he'll take notice of a slip of a girl with no resources of her own?"

THE SOLICITOR'S WORDS played over and over in Ruby's mind as she left the office and headed out into the street. She walked without coherent thought. Eventually, she found herself standing before her father's neatly tended grave.

With an umbrella in one hand to keep off the steadily falling rain, she bent down carefully to place a small posy of snow drops on the grave.

"There were no other papers, were there Father?" she whispered. "Surely if there were, they would have been with the original contract."

It seemed even the cold, gray stone bearing her father's name wept as she now did.

"You deserved so much better than this."

No one can help you. Only the duke himself…

She rose and squared her shoulders.

Very well then.

She would see the Duke of Auchen personally – *and* make him pay.

CHAPTER ONE

Glasgow, Scotland
March, 1818

D ESPITE THE AMOUNT of light spilling through the windows, the rows of numbers on the page blurred before him. Seth Musgrave closed his aching eyes a moment to fight a niggling headache.

He could make the excuse that the headache was caused by the loud rhythmic clacking of the looms on the factory floor beyond this room, but he knew better than to lie to himself.

Seth reached blindly toward the silver-rimmed spectacles at his right hand. There was no shame in needing optical aids, so why did he resist wearing them until his hand was forced?

The voice of his father came unbidden into his mind.

You weak, useless boy! Wear those things and you'll ruin your eyes for good. They're an unmanly contraption.

Seth gritted his teeth to silence the voice. During his early boyhood, he thought he *was* stupid and lazy, as his father so often claimed. If only the old man knew how hard he worked to keep up with his lessons. What he could not see, he had to ask and remember. Failure to meet His Grace's exacting standards resulted in lessons being learned at the end of a leather strap.

He was ten years old and still barely able to read when his

schoolmaster suggested he might need glasses and arranged for a visit to an optician. It had been a revelation. Colors and shapes which had been soft and indistinct came to him with sharp clarity. Letters of the alphabet had subtleties he'd never before known.

But by then, it had been too late. His father was convinced beyond persuasion that his son and heir was a simpleton, fit only for menial work rather than more elevated pursuits. The duke would not fund a place at university as his peers enjoyed. Instead, Seth was put to work at the age of twelve in his father's textile mill.

And every living moment since, Seth dedicated to defying his father's low expectations of him.

Exhaling a breath, he opened his eyes. After a moment, the black ink before him resolved into solid shapes neatly printed on the page.

A man in his position should have a clerk doing this work, but Seth always found deep satisfaction in working with figures. They were the abstraction of the bricks, mortar, looms, and wool that he could build on, improve upon, and make his own.

Now, he was ready to open his *own* mill – in competition with Skye-Heath Textiles.

The edge of a smile touched the corners of his lips.

Let's see what his father thought of *that*.

A knock on the office door interrupted his thoughts. The sound of the looms grew louder and then softened as the door closed. A man strolled in without waiting for leave.

"Ain't ye ready yet?" the visitor asked cheerily. "We're supposed to be heading out to look at the new property today."

Seth frowned a moment, taking in the blurry shape of a stocky man with short black hair. He set down his glasses once more. Roddy McClane, his foreman, man of business, and friend, fell into focus just in time for Seth to witness a grin and a shake of his head in friendly exasperation.

"Ye spend several thousand pounds on a pile, and ye've forgotten about it? Must be nice to have money."

He accepted the tease from Roddy with the tolerance born of long friendship.

"I left the purchase of a house in *your* hands," Seth countered. "I've been more intent in getting Habetrot Textiles up and running."

"Aye, ye will like this place. It's just a couple of miles away from the new mill site. Very pretty."

Seth felt the numbers call to him again.

"I'm sure it is," he muttered, turning back to the ledger. There was still much to do before they could start hiring workers.

"Ye dinnae get out of that easily." He heard Roddy pick up his coat from the hook. A moment later, he felt the weight of it on his shoulders.

"Out in the fresh air'll be good for ye. No good being cooped up indoors all the time."

Seth exaggerated a put-upon sigh. "Well, if you say I must see it, then I must."

He closed the ledgers and rose to his feet to put the coat on properly. He hesitated over whether or not to take his glasses. In the end, he did, slipping them into their case and then the pocket of the pea green coat.

There was really no need for him to visit the property. As far as he was aware, he'd signed all the legal documents required to own it. And, as far as the vendor's solicitor was concerned, the house had been bought in a company name that had nothing to do with the textiles industry. Seth suppressed a wry grin.

No need to tip off the old man that his son was setting up in opposition to him.

The carriage waited at the front of the building; the coach-man rugged up against the ceaseless drizzle. Inside was warmed by hot coals in a brazier box, an unnecessary but not unwelcome indulgence.

Did Roddy think him still an invalid?

The big man said nothing.

Just as well. Seth had spent too many years being thought of as feeble. At the age of thirty, he thought he had done enough to set that opinion aside and, yet, it hadn't been enough. Even the limited correspondence with his father revealed his sire's low opinion was unchanged, even now.

Still, he could hold his own – and he'd needed to in the early days. The son of the mill owner being sent to labor alongside the workers did not sit well amongst the working men. Seth proved himself in words and deeds – and, occasionally, with fists.

No one ever said a word against him again after they witnessed him single-handedly haul a bale of wool which weighed two hundred pounds as if it were an ounce.

He would defy any and all expectations of him.

Seth pulled himself out of his musings to pay attention to the view through the window as the carriage turned down an elm-lined drive.

The day's drizzle had finally come to an end, although the skies remained overcast. Enough softly filtered daylight remained to see that this was quite a substantial estate.

Before the road dipped down into a glen, Seth caught a flash of color in further out fields thriving with crops and, between them, sheep grazing at will on the luscious emerald green pastures.

Catching his eye before it disappeared among the trees was a deer – a big one if he figured right – quite possibly a stag.

Once through the wood, the estate opened out into a park into which was set a manor house, a gothic-looking structure with aspirations to be a castle. The building itself was four stories of gray stone. Conical roofs of slate topped tall narrow turrets.

It was a home fit for an earl, which he imagined Roddy had intended when he bought it.

"What is the name of this place?"

"Strathaird. The owner died leaving a small mountain of debt."

"The place looks well cared for."

"Aye, whoever was managing the place has done a good job

of it. From what I was told, the old laird sunk just about every spare penny into tinkering with mechanical whatnots. After he passed on, the place had to be sold to clear the debts."

"Remind me again how much this place set me back?"

Roddy named a figure. Seth let out a low whistle.

"I *have* been generous, haven't I?"

"Och, just wait until ye get a gander at her. This is the place for a man of yer status. Fit enough for a duke."

Seth knew that, one day, he would inherit the title – and the responsibilities that went with it. He glared daggers at his friend, who knew when to shut his trap, and he did so now.

He set thoughts of titles aside. His father was a big, braw man who bent the world to his will. He would outlast the bloody lot of them. Besides, Seth considered that the Duke of Auchen's cruelty and indifference to him was a blessing in disguise. He had been forced to work out for himself what kind of man he had the potential to be, without the crippling weight of expectation on his shoulders.

The carriage rolled to a stop at the bottom of a set of wide steps leading up to a double oak door set into an arched recess.

Seth emerged from the carriage and took a step back to run his eyes over Strathaird. It was even more imposing up close, with the gray stone competing with the sky to see which was the most austere. Off to one side of the building, a small door was set into a wall, which he suspected led of a sheltered garden. Bare branches, newly budding, reached heavenward.

Fruit trees? He hoped so.

The doors to the main house opened. He and Roddy climbed to the top of the steps to meet the butler, dressed formally in his kilt and sporran. In the entrance hall, on the stairs and landing, waited all the indoor servants, forty in all, dressed in their black and white uniforms.

"Laird Musgrave, welcome to yer new home. I'm Jackson, the butler, and it will be my pleasure to show ye about. Ye'll be right proud of this place. Never will ye find a group of servants as dedicated to their tasks."

Seth nodded to the cook and housekeeper, the senior of the servants, who stood nearby.

Interesting.

The butler was working hard to establish the credentials of the staff. Did the man think he would dismiss them? He supposed it wasn't an unrealistic expectation that a new owner would want to bring in his own servants. But that wasn't him.

Good Lord, he lived in a modest townhouse in Glasgow. He could count on one hand the number of servants he had and still have two fingers free.

Seth nodded then drew the attention of the staff to himself. He was not as broad as William Gregory Musgrave, the Duke of Auchen, but there was enough of the old man in him – his height for one – to make his presence felt.

"Strathaird is a credit to you all," he said, trying to make eye contact with each and every servant among the arrayed crowd. "I have no desire to make great changes as long as the place is, and remains, as well run as it appears."

He turned to Jackson. "Show me the place I intend to call home."

The butler led them through into the great hall. With its oak paneled walls and large stone fireplace, it appeared to be the oldest part of the property.

Seth and Roddy trailed as Jackson led them to the library. Seth breathed in the aroma of inks, glues, and paper that was particularly strong here.

Could one fall in love with a room? If such a thing were possible, then Seth had found not only his home, but his heart also. It was as though the world outside had disappeared. He saw himself here in the depths of winter, warmed by the fire, a glass of brandy in his hand. He was transported to the height of summer where the French doors leading out to a small terrace would be flung open wide to let in the breeze.

An almost preternatural shiver went through him. There

were some people who believed they lived more than just one life. He didn't think that was true, but it was interesting to entertain the thought. Was his reaction because of a ghost perhaps?

Now that would be *particularly* interesting...

It was only when he had been shown the grand dining room that another thought occurred to him. The house was furnished. Was there no one to inherit? Did the previous owner have no family? There seemed something rather sad about such a legacy falling out of a family.

What does it profit a man to gain the whole world, but lose his soul?

He shoved the aphorism out of his head the moment it appeared. An inheritance presupposed someone to inherit, and that meant family. If *his* were any guide, perhaps the owner had been better off after all if, as he imagined, they died alone.

Still, a degree of curiosity remained as they climbed up to the first galleried landing where there was a drawing room and a morning room as well as the master suite.

"And this was the McAllister family," said Jackson, directing their attention to a row of family portraits hung along the landing. "Will ye be wanting us to take them down, sir? I imagine ye'll be having some portraits of yer own."

They'd stopped before a portrait of a young woman, only a little older than a girl. Dark curly hair framed her face. Bright brown eyes with a keen expression looked out from the canvas. The portrait appeared to have been painted in the walled garden; the subject was posed by a rose bush with pale pink flowers in bloom. The contrast of colors was striking.

Again, a feeling struck him once more, as though he knew this place – *knew her.*

Seth leaned in to read the words engraved on the brass plaque attached to the gilded frame.

"Lady Ruby McAllister on her sixteenth birthday, 1811."

She would be aged twenty-three now, he calculated, and most likely wed. *If* she wed. Perhaps she had died, and that was why there was no one to inherit.

No doubt he was being feeling just a wee bit sentimental, but it seemed wrong to completely erase a house of its history. To pretend it had no past before now.

Could there be any harm in embracing this family instead of the one he'd been born into? Was that foolish? His father would certainly think so.

Damn the man.

Seth came to a decision.

"No, leave the paintings where they are."

Early May, 1818

SETH HEARD RODDY the first time, although he pretended he didn't over the clatter of the looms.

He watched the workers attend their tasks and made notes, looking for ways to make the production of cloth not only more efficient, but also safer. Mechanical looms had done a lot to increase efficiency, but they were also dangerous. Rapidly moving parts were responsible for terrible injuries if workers allowed their attention to lapse.

The big Scotsman put a hand on his shoulder and yelled in his ear.

"There's been another letter from London for ye."

Seth shrugged the hand off his shoulder and followed Roddy out of the factory.

"Is it from anyone I know?" he asked as they walked.

He'd posed the question, but he already knew the answer. He'd seen the letter on his desk when the post was delivered this morning. He recognized the seal on the back as belonging to his father's solicitor.

"Avis and Turner, solicitors in London."

He supposed he couldn't put it off. Seth headed back to his

office. He glanced at the offending missive on the table, picked up his spectacles with an angry swipe, and put them on his nose. He broke the wax seal and scanned the document while Roddy waited expectantly.

"It's the duke. Apparently, he is gravely ill, and this is a summons to attend him without delay."

"I'll make arrangements for a carriage to take us down to London."

Seth shrugged. "Don't be in such a hurry. I refuse to be at that man's beck and call."

"Yer old man could be dying."

Seth skewered his friend with a look. Roddy offered an insolent shrug.

"All righty then, so ye dinnae like the man. But when he kicks the bucket, yer the next Duke of Auchen, ye ken."

Seth dropped the letter which fluttered down to his desk. "I know. You keep telling me. And my father spent my entire childhood telling me I was a failure of a son and unworthy to be his heir. This," he said, pointing down to the letter, "is likely to make that all official, so why would I waste my time and my coin just to learn my disinheritance is official?"

"Well, ye willnae ken for certain unless ye go, will ye?"

Seth had no answer for that. He looked down at the missive once more. Of course, Roddy was right. He wouldn't be honest with himself if he refused to admit that he wasn't at least a little curious. It had been fifteen years since he'd seen his father. Despite the *froideur*, Seth had to acknowledge there was still a young boy living inside him who yearned even now for his father's approval.

He looked up from the letter. Roddy's face was in sharp relief. Seth removed his glasses, but not before noticing a victorious look on his friend's face – he saw the war that raged within him and had guessed at the victor.

Roddy already turned toward the door. "I'll arrange for the carriage in the morning and start with yer packing."

"With any luck, the old bastard will be dead before we get there."

"Aye." Roddy looked back and flashed a grin. "We can all live in hope."

CHAPTER TWO

Late May, 1818

"You're fair of form and face, and still have the title Lady Strathaird, if not the lands. It's not too late to enter the marriage mart if you've a mind to."

Ruby hugged her cousin around the shoulders while the woman's hands busily worked at the lacework machine.

"Yes, but not so young and not so wealthy as to catch the eye of a man who can help me buy back Strathaird."

Frances, older than her by fifteen years, sighed. Her husband was a sea captain, and they had spent more of their married life apart than together. Not blessed with children, Frances had turned her skills to sewing and had become a sought-after dressmaker under the embellished name of Madame Francine Dumont.

"There's plenty of work with my girls if you want it. Plenty of money to be made as a mantua maker in London."

Ruby sat on down on the upholstered chair opposite and watched her cousin work. It would take her a year to be half as skilled as the youngest of Frannie's apprentices.

"You are a lamb," she answered. "I promised I wouldn't be a burden on you, and I intend to keep my word. In fact, I have an interview today with a man who *will* help me purchase back

Strathaird."

Frances peered up expectantly over her half-rimmed spectacles.

"What *exactly* are you up to, Ruby McAllister?"

"I have an appointment with the Duke of Auchen."

The lace bobbins stilled. Ruby knew she had her cousin's full attention.

"Do you now? You're going to march right up to the man who you claim stole from your pa, a duke no less, and demand that he put the past to rights?"

Ruby was aware of heat rising up her cheeks.

It had seemed like a straightforward enough plan on the two-week journey from Glasgow to London. But now to have someone else speak it out loud, she had to admit it somewhat lacking in practical detail.

Still, she had not come all this way for nothing. Ruby leaned forward and whispered urgently.

"I have had copies made of the designs and the contract, and they are held with a solicitor here in town. Once I show the duke what I have, he will not be able to deny it. Should he refuse, then I will instruct my man to make the scandal public."

"*Ruby...*"

The tone of voice might quail Frances' seamstresses, but it would not work on her.

"Fear not, Cousin, I know what I'm doing. By all accounts, the duke is a hard man, but not even *he* is above the law. I will settle for nothing more than a legally binding acknowledgement of my father's invention and a settlement for the money Papa ought to have earned as his one-third share partner in Skye-Heath Textiles."

Frances pinned the length of lace in place. Her fingers, showing early signs of arthritis, popped as she stretched the hands out over her lap.

"If the duke is as hard you say, then what makes you think the family will let a McAllister through the door?"

"I can guarantee that His Grace has not lost a moment's sleep over defrauding our family. And I doubt he'd even recall the name McAllister. But to be sure, I'm using mother's maiden name. Campbell."

Frances wiped her hands down her skirts and picked up the bobbins once more.

"It's a vain hope that you'll change your mind?"

Ruby gave the woman a level stare.

Her cousin sighed once more and returned to her work, dexterous hands picking out the pattern laid out on the cushion.

"Well, you've attained your majority and with a bit of careful management, you're not exactly a pauper," she said. "But just consider whether the risk is worth it. If the duke catches on to your scheme, you'll be on a prison ship bound for New South Wales before you can catch a breath."

"I know what I'm doing."

Ruby hoped she sounded more confident than she felt.

Yes, she was aware of all the things that could go wrong should she fail.

"So, when is your appointment with the duke, then?"

"At eleven o'clock today."

"You will take care won't you, love?" The worry was clear in Frances' voice. "The first hint of your scheme unraveling, you'll come here? You'll always have a home with Angus and me."

Ruby got to her feet once more and wrapped her arms around her cousin.

"Bless you, Frannie. I promise I won't let you down."

THIS WAS NOT the first time Ruby had seen Glencoe House, the grand London home of the Musgraves, but it was the first time she had been through its gates. In the month she had spent in London, Ruby had traveled across the city to stand outside the home most days. Sometimes for hours.

It was said King James of Scotland, the uniting king of Great Britain, played there as a child. She knew every stone and every corbel on its façade. Indeed, she, with her meager drawing skills, had even sketched it in her book as the distinctive decaying smell of the Thames came to her on the breeze.

Ruby forced a stiffness in her spine to hide a shudder at the imposing edifice, and clasped the leather portfolio that contained her father's design sketches and the contract to her chest.

For this interview, she wore a plain dark blue dress, minimally adorned. Her hair was pinned back severely and hidden under a plain bonnet.

Out in front of the house, below the sweep of stairs up to the door, a carriage was being unloaded of its trunks.

Ruby fell in behind a footman who had one such case on his back and followed him up the dozen steps that led to the entrance hall.

Inside, an angry voice made its way down from the gallery above.

"How long has he been like this?"

The reply to the question was indistinct.

Despite the number of servants bustling about, none questioned Ruby's presence as she stood there, taking in the voices and her surroundings.

The subsequent question was louder than the first. The stomping of feet indicated that its owner was approaching the stairs.

"And you didn't think to get him a nurse?" the man demanded.

This time, Ruby could just make out the reply.

"My Lord, we *have* tried. None have stayed more than two days!"

The two men reached the top of the stairs. Ruby could now see them clearly. One was immaculately dressed, with a posture absolutely correct and military-like in its bearing. She took him immediately for the butler.

The other man was younger, travel-stained and scruffy, his light brown hair blown about as though he had driven the carriage she'd seen outside, rather than ridden within it. Still, there was no mistaking his features. This was Lord Seth Musgrave, Earl of Glenuig, the Duke of Auchen's son.

He was shockingly handsome.

Ruby pushed *that* thought down as far as it would go. Now was not the time to be distracted by prettiness. But the pounding in her chest didn't abate; if anything, it increased. She feared her plans to beg an audience with the duke were all to naught in the face of whatever drama was going on before her.

The two men reached the landing and noticed her for the first time.

"Who are you, Miss?" the butler asked.

But her eyes were held by the earl who bore such an intense look that it made her wonder whether he possessed the power to make her burst into flames.

The lie was out of her mouth before she could give conscious thought to her plan.

"I am the new nurse."

The earl's tense posture softened a little. He continued down the stairs.

"There you are, Stewart," he called behind him, "a problem solved. Speak to Roddy about where to forward my things. I'm going into town. I'll not spend another moment under this roof with that man."

The earl came to a halt before her. He was taller than she expected.

"What's your name, Miss?" His tone was softer, indeed kinder than the one she'd heard from the top of the stairs.

She dropped a belated curtsy.

"Campbell, sir."

Again, the lie came easily.

"You're Scottish?"

Ruby nodded.

"Perhaps that's been the problem all along," he said as he smiled. "No English woman could ever put up with such an obstreperous curmudgeon."

The full softness of his mouth thinned. Kindliness leeched from his expression until it was hard once more.

"I wish you luck in your assignment, Nurse Campbell. You will need it."

Musgrave stalked away, out the doors, and down the outside stairs as though the house contained the plague. Ruby and the butler looked at one another.

"I'm surprised the agency sent another one. They vowed they would not after what happened last time."

Ruby accepted the butler's scrutiny, waiting for him to identify her as a liar. Instead, he introduced himself. Then he added, "You are aware, Nurse Campbell, that this will be a live-in position?"

"Aye, sir," she said, adding a little Scottish brogue to her voice. "I'm fully aware of my duties."

"Well," the man said, looking her up and down, "I expected someone older, but never mind, you appear to be strong enough. If you don't mind some plain speaking, the duke is an exacting man who does not suffer fools or idlers. You will take your instruction from Dr. Brooks. He will be paying a call this afternoon. If he approves of you, then you will be expected to start in the morning. Satisfactory?"

Ruby gave an emphatic nod.

What a stroke of luck!

Nevertheless, her heart pounded. She was in the lion's den now and getting in was solely the product of good fortune and timing. Now, what if the duke recognized her somehow? Her father's eyes, perhaps. Would he see through her at first sight?

"The duke is resting quietly at the moment," the butler continued. "If he is awake, you will be introduced, but you will say nothing otherwise."

Ruby placed her leather folio on a side table and untied the ribbon of her bonnet. She took it off and laid it top.

Stewart remained where he was, frowning at her.

"You'd best be showing me about so I'll not waste your time or mine," she said briskly.

The man's expression changed slightly, a furrowed frown lightened a touch – not approval, of course, but certainly containing less hostility than a moment before.

Ruby climbed the stairs after the butler, noting the house was very near silent now. Perhaps she had been living too long in Frances' company, with people coming in and out at all hours, to make this observation. Still, in a house of this size, she would expect to hear the sounds of servants working on this floor. Even the most discreet and deferential of staff would have to make *some* noise.

Glencoe House was as quiet as a tomb.

Ruby pressed the thumb of her gloved hand into the palm of the other, a lifelong habit to focus herself when under stress. She forced her breathing to slow. It would be no good if she fainted within sight of her goal.

"I will see if His Grace is amenable to seeing you. Wait here until I fetch you."

Ruby was certain that the duke wouldn't be amenable to anyone under *any* circumstances.

"Very good, sir," she answered. Her voice was curt, but at least it didn't quaver. That would be enough for now.

Stewart walked down the wide hallway then turned left into a smaller passage and disappeared. The quiet house fell to complete silence. Even the sound of her booted heels was muffled by the long oriental rug that ran from one end of the landing to the other.

She paced along the length of it, examining each of the portraits that lined the wall. The Van Dyke beard and stiff lace ruff of a seventeenth century ancestor stared down at her fiercely. The light reddish hair marked him as a Musgrave.

The next portrait showed the apple hadn't fallen far from the tree. The current duke was tall, powerfully built. *Imposing.* The engravings she had seen of him in a periodical didn't do the clan justice.

Ruby got to the end of the hall where an arched window let spill a shaft of light. It illuminated a small group portrait. This one was more recent compared to the others, painted within the past twenty or so years judging by the gown worn by the woman.

She was a beauty. About Ruby's own age, mid-twenties, a slim figure underneath the light muslin gown in white, decorated with gold hail spot embroidery and gold brocade ribbon at the sleeves and under the bust.

The woman's hair was light brown, and the painter had captured a slight curl to it.

Standing at the woman's side, looking exceedingly shy, was a boy aged not more than ten. There was something subtle about the way the child was standing, closer to his mother than the man who stood on his other side.

The man was the duke, of that there could be no doubt. Again, what the artist captured was interesting. The child's face was more inclined to his mother's. Her hand sat protectively on his shoulder.

The duke stood face on; his shoulders squared to the viewer. A man standing apart from his family.

Ruby looked back to the little boy. His soulful blue eyes dared her to see his unhappiness.

The butterflies which she thought were under control took wing again.

She recalled what she had read of the family. Georgiana Grey, married to the duke for ten years, bore him three children; only the one survived infancy. A further miscarriage was to take Georgiana's life.

Was she so caught up in her own desire for justice that she couldn't see that there was more than just the monster she had made in her mind of the duke? Here was a man who had a wife and a son. She knew from her diligent research that he did not wed again, obviously feeling no obligation to provide a "spare" for his heir.

But that wasn't to say the man was chaste. Rumor went that there had been a longstanding mistress, but it would appear the man did not intend to make an honest woman out of her.

From somewhere in the cavernous house, Ruby heard a door close and the march of well-ordered footsteps that belonged to the butler.

She returned to the spot where he had left her. It would not be good for him to think that she had some particular curiosity about the family.

"The duke will inspect you now," he instructed. "You know your orders. Only speak when spoken to and answer his questions clearly and distinctly. No muttering, no prevarication. His Grace finds that annoying above all things."

A simple firm nod was her answer. The man led her down a smaller hall. Less grand than the galleried landing but, still, full of furniture and fine porcelain figurines that seemed to be more of a feminine taste.

Stewart rapped on the door once. A bark that might have been "Enter" came in response.

Here it was, the moment of reckoning. The devil himself, incarnated in the flesh of a duke.

Ruby pressed her thumb into the palm of her other hand to cover her nervousness.

You can do this. You've prepared for this. This man has no power to frighten you.

She crossed the threshold and stepped into a large airy bedroom. That was a surprise. Ruby wasn't sure what she was expecting. A dungeon for the dragon perhaps?

Instead, the curtains were drawn back, letting in plenty of light on this fine spring afternoon. Large windows that opened out onto a balcony were propped open. The breeze carried in the scent of flowers from the garden she assumed was somewhere below.

This seemed all wrong. In the gothic novels she had read, such inauspicious meetings should take place in the dark in the middle of the thunderstorm, not on a very pleasant day.

At first, Ruby thought she might have been taken to the wrong room. The man who sat in a chair by the window was wan, his hair gray and frame lean, *nay*, nearly emaciated. If this was the Duke of Auchen, he no longer looked like the man in the portrait.

Stewart stepped forward.

"Your Grace, I'd like to introduce you to Campbell. If Your Grace approves, she will be your night nurse."

Ruby wondered if the man was asleep but, after a moment, he shuddered violently.

"Well? Don't just stand there gawping like you've never seen a dying man before! Step forward. Let me take a look at you!"

His body may have been frail, but the duke was still in fine voice. *This* was the creature she had come to do battle with, not the elderly vulnerable man whose body he inhabited.

She lifted her chin in a small measure of defiance and did as he asked. When she was confident that he could see her clearly, she curtsied and answered, "Your Grace." It was out of politeness if nothing else.

His blue eyes met hers and held. She wouldn't back down. Let this be the first of many battles between them if necessary. This was a war she *did not* intend to lose. Brave words, but there was still something akin to fear that ran through her. Regardless of his physical state now, the duke was a villain who stole from her family. He would be made to pay.

"I imagine you're capable enough, so I suppose you'll do. The doctor will give you some stuff-and-nonsense about giving me incessant draughts and potions, but you are under *my* orders. Do you understand?"

She nodded once.

His wrinkled jowls rose to a snarl. "Cat got your tongue?"

"Your Grace may have a good many opinions which his physician is unlikely to share. If it is all the same to you, I prefer to keep my employment by keeping my patient alive."

The words were out of her mouth before she could censor herself. She resisted looking at the butler. No doubt, his face would betray horror at a servant speaking in such a manner. She kept her eyes on the old man instead.

The moment stretched on until the duke barked out a laugh which turned into a hacking cough.

"You'll do, lassie, you'll do."

CHAPTER THREE

A PROMISE IS *a comfort to a fool.*

Seth wasn't sure where he had heard the proverb, but it was particularly apt now.

He found a quiet corner at White's and sat himself down.

As an earl, he should have been able to walk through the place as though he owned it, but he was as unknown as a pauper here in London. To his embarrassment, he had to be hastily vouched for and sponsored by a couple of his father's peers who were surprised to even see him.

In fact, one of the old men confessed to Seth that he was sure he'd been told that the Musgrave heir died years ago.

A footman placed a glass of whisky at his elbow.

Seth sipped the amber liquid gratefully and pretended to look at the newssheet filled with words that would not remain in focus. He reflected on how woefully ill-prepared he'd been for his return to Glencoe House. He had been left gasping for breath, nearly drowning in a flood of memories that swamped him the minute his carriage rolled onto the grounds. Once again, he was an awkward and diffident ten-year-old boy returning home from school in trepidation.

Inwardly, he anticipated his father's brutal censure. A braw man, big in stature as well as temperament. That's who he remembered. What he hadn't anticipated was how wizened and

ELIZABETH ELLEN CARTER

frail the old man now looked.

Cancer.

He knew nothing of the disease, this invisible David that cut down a Goliath of a man, only that it had taken from the man's frame but left his mind – and temper – intact.

So, was this to be the fate of the man who made every waking moment of his childhood a terror?

The temptation to tell the duke exactly what he thought of him had been strong. He wanted to mete out humiliation, to make him feel a tenth of what *he* had suffered. But that would make him the same kind of bully as his father, and he'd spent his entire life making sure he was the exact opposite.

He might have found it within himself to talk to the man with a small measure of politeness as custom dictated, except his father had spoken first.

"You're still a weak one, aren't you?"

He'd managed to hang on to his temper until he'd left the room, but couldn't help taking it out on the butler, snapping angrily at him over his father's emaciated state as if he hadn't wished him dead already before he left Glasgow.

Once again, he felt the burden of inadequacy. This man was his sire. He should have ensured he knew of his father's condition. He ought to have made a greater attempt at reconciliation.

Seth downed the remaining whisky in one swallow. It seared his throat and cauterized his memories. No time for feeling sentimental now.

The only oasis of calm in the entire house had been the new nurse, apparently unshocked at what she'd walked into.

Nurse Campbell, that was her name. What must she think of the Musgrave family?

Seth shook his head and left his empty tumbler on the table. He had an appointment with the duke's man of business and the family solicitor.

No doubt, he would be pushed into spending more time in London when he'd much rather return to Scotland and work on making his own fortune. Work had started on building Habetrot Mill before he left.

Thinking of it gave him a momentary calm and a sense of pride. He'd sunk a large amount of money into an iron frame for the structure, iron beams to support the roof. Habetrot would be fireproof, not like other mills that had burned to the ground. It would be a safe place for his workers, a model even for the textile industry. The looms would be the very best, with the ability to produce more intricate designs more quickly. And it would be successful.

The liquor soured in his stomach abruptly. When he inherited, he would be expected to give up his enterprise. A peer of the realm might invest in particular industries, but no man of quality was expected to get his hands dirty.

Furthermore, as the Duke of Auchen, he'd also be expected to find a wife and produce an heir.

Could he renounce the title on his father's death?

He allowed himself to entertain the thought some more. Such a thing might be possible, and the Crown might welcome the return of the lands and the income back into its royal coffers. But a little voice whispered – it might be the chance to prove his old man wrong.

He'd been written off as a scholar, but he proved himself able and capable of turning his hands to books as well as things mechanical. The old man had no expectations of him as a member of the nobility. Perhaps he could prove him wrong there as well...

Unbidden, he recalled the nurse standing alone in the entrance hall once more. The young woman had cut a solitary figure. Did she know what a hell she was entering? He pondered whether he ought to ask after her, but then he recalled the quiet determination on her attractive face. Yes, his eyesight might not be perfect, but he recognized pretty features when he saw them. No, she didn't need his help. This Nurse Campbell seemed unflappable.

I suppose one would have to be as a nurse.

He mentally saluted her, wishing her Godspeed on her task, all the while acknowledging the nagging feeling that not everything is what it seemed.

A rather uncertain footman approached. "My Lord Glenuig?"

Seth blinked at him a moment before it dawned on him that *he* was the Earl of Glenuig. He nodded. The footman looked relieved.

"A carriage awaits to take you to your appointment, My Lord."

A carriage? The solicitor couldn't be any more than three blocks away. If he were at home, and the weather as fine as it was in London today, he would walk. But he supposed that it was not the right thing for an earl to do.

He tipped the doorman and, scanning along the line of waiting hackneys and carriages, spotted a carriage with the duke's own livery.

How did...?

The door opened. To his surprise, Roddy beckoned him from inside. Seth joined him.

"We cannae be having the future duke going 'round in a renter, can we?" Roddy slapped the roof of the carriage, and they started moving. "Yer old man has no use for it. And the one we came down in is good enough for the country, but it will nae do for the city."

Seth slouched in the deeply studded tan leather upholstery.

"I had no idea that you had pretensions to grandeur."

"Nae me, ye daft bugger. Ye're the man who's going to have to get used to the pretensions. And judging by how grave the old duke looks, ye've nae got much time to turn yerself into a gentleman now, have ye?"

"You're enjoying this way too much."

Roddy grinned.

"It's nae every day, yer best friend becomes a duke."

"I'm not a duke yet."

"Ye will be."

"No, I'm not. My father is damn Mephistopheles, and he'll live on forever."

RUBY SETTLED INTO a routine at Glencoe House. Her day would begin at noon with a briefing with the doctor who now came every other day. She would report on what occurred overnight, and he would tell her the course of treatment he recommended.

She had won the good doctor over quickly with her observations – little more than changes in breathing, color, demeanor.

The gray-headed physician looked over her notes again and added his signature.

"There's little to be done but to keep him comfortable and out of pain."

"Will the duke recover from his malady?"

The doctor shook his head gravely.

"I've told him to put his affairs in order and call for a priest if he is so inclined."

Ruby couldn't help the lift of an eyebrow. Dr. Brooks chuckled.

"You're right. The duke's own stubbornness will keep him alive longer than any of my potions. When it comes time for the Angel of Death to take him, he won't go easily. I've never met such an argumentative individual in all my days. It's been my experience that the pain is worse when there is unfinished business. I believe the duke will have an easier time of it if he attended to his affairs."

Ruby nodded gravely.

"Yes, unfinished business has its way on taking its toll," she answered.

Unfinished business indeed.

The doctor stood and finished buckling his satchel.

"I've spoken to the butler. There is no need for me to stop by so often, but he is to call on me should the duke's condition worsen."

After the doctor's departure, Ruby returned upstairs with a footman in tow. He carried a small tray of food. It was little more than delicacies. The duke's constitution was not up to eating a full meal. Ruby had seen him pick at a plate, angry and disgusted by turns, and at other times he'd become so listless that he couldn't eat at all.

And, each day, Ruby warred with herself.

She'd felt the natural compassion that one ought in seeing one of God's creations suffer. Then she'd remembered how the duke had behaved to other people in his prime. Should he be absolved from all the things he did to cause misery, not only her family but also undoubtedly to others?

Five days as nurse to the Duke of Auchen, and yet she had not broached her own grievance with the man.

What of his son, Seth Musgrave, Earl of Glenuig? Well, it seemed there was to be no help from that quarter either, not after the conversation the housekeeper had with her over supper.

The elderly woman had taken such a shine to Ruby that, within days, she had told her all about the sensitive young boy who struggled to please his father and was so coldly rejected after the child's mother died.

"The duchess was the only one who really had a care for the lad. And he loved her, too. But after she passed on, poor dear, it only got worse between the duke and his son," the woman had told her.

The estrangement had lasted nearly twenty years.

No, there was no love between father and son. On the relationship between the duke and the late duchess, the housekeeper would not be drawn.

As cold as the duke was, he did love his wife, Ruby suspected. There were reminders of Georgiana Musgrave everywhere – her portrait in the gallery, the distinctly feminine touch in some of the rooms, a choice of porcelain to complement the décor. Ruby was sure the duke himself possessed none of the refinement necessary for the task.

Perhaps that was the key.

Ruby stopped by the woman's portrait, leaving the footman to attend the duke alone. A moment later, two more footmen arrived bearing a tub accompanied by half a dozen maids with ewers of hot water and a couple more footmen with buckets of cold water.

Georgiana Musgrave looked down at Ruby, sightless across time.

An idea occurred to her.

If she could soften the duke with memories of his wife, then perhaps it would make him more amenable to the notion that he should right his wrongs before he had to account for them to Saint Peter.

How might the duchess have managed her husband? Ruby studied the portrait closely, hoping the artist had captured her personality as well as her beauty. Georgiana would not be intimidated by the duke's bluster. She would not be argumentative, but she would be firm. Quiet and resolute. What could she find out about this woman? How could she turn this to *her* advantage?

DAYS WENT BY and no one gave any thought to the new nurse and where she had come from. One week become another, until the weeks became a month, and Ruby found herself waiting in the hall once more for the duke's ablutions to be completed.

Once again, she was drawn to the portrait of Georgiana Musgrave. The artist was an exceptional talent. The more she looked at the painting, the more it called to her. She didn't know why, but today the light fell on it just so, highlighting the gold ribbon on the duchess' dress. What she thought had been random patterns were actually a repeating motif – golden apples and what appeared to be horses.

A most unusual design to be sure. Was it a flight of fancy

from the artist?

The parade of footmen emerged from the corridor. The duke's elderly valet nursed him by day, then bathed and returned the man to his bed where he would sleep for two hours before Nurse Campbell was expected to attend him. Her role was as much companion as it was nurse, writing his dictated letters if he was in the mood. Sometimes reading aloud if he was not, which was most of the time.

When the sun went down, the duke would sleep again for a short time, only to wake again late in the evening clutching his gut in complete agony.

Ruby would prepare the draught of opium the doctor prescribed and wait until the spasms subsided, after which he would fall into a slumber from which he would emerge just as the sun was dawning, and just as irascible as ever.

Those hours, she had to herself.

For the past month, Ruby had ingratiated herself with the servants. The butler had spent the first two weeks checking on her twice a day. After the third week, when he could see her bearing the duke's temper with equanimity – and showing no signs of quitting – he would only drop by to take his leave at the end of each day.

For the past week and a half, the hours between ten o'clock at night and five o'clock the following morning had been hers alone.

In the duke's rooms was a writing desk, usually kept locked, but not today. Stewart had been distracted by the demands made by His Grace, who happened to be in an even more vile temper than usual. Ruby watched the poor servant depart without locking the desk drawers as was his custom.

And she didn't say a word.

Somewhere in the house, a clock struck eleven. That would be the last of the chimes until morning.

The duke did not stir.

Temptation proved too much. Ruby rose from her chair and picked up a lamp.

On the desk, there was a sheaf of documents in a folder. The Duke of Auchen had ordered them to be left for him to review in the morning. Perhaps among them would be a good place to start.

She opened the folder and drew the lamp nearer.

The very first sheet read: Last Will And Testament of His Grace William Gregory Musgrave, Duke of Auchen.

I, Duke of Auchen, being in sound mind and perfect health of body, thanks be to almighty God, do make and ordain this my last will and testament in the form following…

I give and bequeath my only legitimate son, Seth Arthur Musgrave, in addition to all that is due as Earl of Glenuig, the sole ownership of Skye-Heath Textiles, the mills, and all associated patents…

At that moment, the duke drew in a shuddering breath. Ruby glanced back, her heart pounding as she waited for the demand for an explanation of what she was doing.

The old man slumbered on, but she knew it would not be long before his pain asserted itself.

With great reluctance, she slipped the parchment back into the folder and went over to a console table which now resembled an apothecary. The duke's stomach pains would worsen over the course of the next hour. As she began to prepare his opium sedative according to the doctor's instructions, she considered the document she had just begun to read.

The duke could not die until his will was changed to acknowledge her father and remedy his wrongs. Ruby grimaced. That her ministrations were not altruistic panged her conscience a little.

Seth Musgrave, Earl of Glenuig.

Now there was a mystery. She knew virtually nothing about him beyond what the housekeeper had told her. It was almost as though he had disappeared at the age of ten.

He was never mentioned in the society pages. Almack's had no record of him attending, neither did White's. Admittedly, she had not given the heir much thought since her focus had been on the duke himself.

The old man spoke in his troubled half-sleep, a single word – was it "hell" or a longer word cut short by the moan that followed?

He groaned secret agonies of the body and, no doubt, of the mind. Perhaps of his soul, too, a portent of the hell that awaited him.

Was that where he was now?

Ruby hurried with the mixture and went to his side. She laid a hand on his shuddering arm, stilling it.

"Shhh, I have something to ease you."

He seemed to focus on her voice. His breathing, which had been erratic, came in deeper. Ruby's hand slipped down to his wrist. His pulse pounded wildly.

"Helen! Don't leave me, don't leave me…"

The groans increased in frequency and pitch until they became a keening wail.

His head thrashed about. If she tried to spoon the medicine, he would wear more than he swallowed. She prepared a syringe with a portion of the mixture and depressed the plunger into his open mouth. The risk of his choking was more preferable than the hurt he might do himself in the throes of his agony.

She held her breath as the duke coughed wetly. He let out several hoarse, heaving breaths before the rise and fall of his chest became more even once more, and he appeared to drift off to sleep.

As she moved to lift her hand from his wrist, she found it firmly grasped by the duke. For a frail man, delirium made him stronger than she realized.

"You've come back to me, my beautiful Helen."

His eyes were open. They were wide and bright with delirium.

Not knowing what to say, and with her own heart pounding, Ruby manufactured a smile.

"That's right," she soothed. "I'm here."

"I've missed you, darling girl."

The man obviously saw someone else when he looked up at her. Not his nurse. Not his wife Georgiana. His mistress? She shuddered. If he started recalling intimacies, she had no wish to be here.

"Shhh, Your Grace, I'm not going anywhere," Ruby said in the hope that the words would seep through.

It pained her to add a touch of tenderness to her voice, but it seemed to comfort him. The grip on her wrist eased.

"I wish to give you the rest of your sleeping draught."

"Why would I want to sleep when I can talk to you?"

A shudder went through her. The duke heard her words, and understood them, but he truly was talking to a different person entirely. Most odd. Most odd, indeed.

"Helen? Why is it so dark in here?"

She touched a spoon to his lips, and he accepted the medicine as meekly as a child.

"You need to sleep. Close your eyes once more, and you will see me properly."

He did as instructed. She watched the rise and fall of his chest, satisfied that he was on his way to sleeping restfully.

Ruby left him a moment and went into the anteroom that served as her private night chambers. She made a note of the time she gave the medicine to the duke and, in her own personal diary, she made a note.

Who is Helen?

If she was a mistress, the woman was very discreet. There was no mention of anyone by that name and if anyone would have been prepared to deal in gossip, it was the housekeeper.

In pencil beneath her question, she wrote the name *Seth Musgrave*. She ought to find out as much about him as she knew about his father, because when the duke died, the only hope of recovering Strathaird would be in that man's hands.

CHAPTER FOUR

T WO PEOPLE WHO hated each other could reside under the same roof quite adequately – provided the roof was large and the dwelling beneath it even more so.

If Seth framed it in his mind that this was an academic exercise, he could just about swallow his pride and accept living at Glencoe House. Besides, renting in London was expensive – *damned* expensive – something he hadn't considered before.

He was not wealthy – not yet anyway. Fortunately, he was a man of simple tastes. He could live quite well in Glasgow, but here in London? It would take the better part of a month to arrange letters from his bank to draw on a line of credit here – and he didn't intend to stay that long.

So, he set himself up on the opposite wing to his father. It was quite a decent apartment he was forced to admit. Over two floors, it was a house-within-a-house, connecting to the greater portion through doors on two levels. It even had its own external private entrance, and Seth intended to make good use of it.

He settled himself at a table in his bedroom. From a newly purchased parcel, he pulled out a large swatch of Joseph Jacquard's fabric, examining the intricacy of the pattern.

This was the future of textile making. James Watt's engine coupled with Jacquard's punch cards. If there was also a way to safely and quickly change patterns, they could win back half a day's set-up for each new design.

There would be some safety measures to be employed as well. The record at Skye-Heath was excellent, but not perfect. No family should fear sending their loved one off to work.

Seth examined the schematics for a new loom. It was good – faster and safer than the existing ones at Skye-Heath. If things went to plan, one weaver could safely supervise four looms at once. The opportunities for expansion were endless.

How much easier it would be to use the resources of his father's company to introduce such innovations, but why should he bother when he was a mere employee there?

How ironic. His father thought to hide his deficient son where he wouldn't be an embarrassment, giving him a menial job at the mill. Did the old man know how well he had done there? That he had climbed the ladder to manage it? Did he even remember he owned a textile mill? If he paid attention to the dividends that dropped into his coffers every quarter, then His Grace ought to know that it was his own son who brought him such a tidy sum.

The title and the lands were entailed. As the old man's only legitimate son and heir, they would come to him regardless. But he would give them up in a heartbeat to attain full control of Skye-Heath.

But Seth was under no illusion. His capricious sire could bequeath his business interests to whomever he wished. In the rarefied air of the aristocracy, business interests were simply rich men's toys, something to amuse themselves when the turn of a card or the bloodlines of a stallion were not enough to hold their interest.

Well, not to Seth Musgrave.

Textiles were everything to him.

A rap at the connecting door started him from his musings. He swiped the glasses from his face and set them down. If it was a summons from the duke, his eyes would need time to adjust without correcting.

He set aside his work and listened to a muffled conversation between Roddy and the butler. He opened the connecting door which led to his bedroom and sloughed off his comfortable well-worn woolen shirt for one of linen.

Clothes maketh the man…

Now his father wanted to see the man who maketh the clothes.

He closed his eyes and worked a cravat from memory. With his blurred vision, the mirror was not his friend, but he'd long perfected the technique by feel alone. As a youth, it had taken twice as long as it ought to learn to tie a barrel knot in a tidy fashion, but he'd gotten there.

Why the hell did his father's approval mean so much to him after all this time? He should know better than to consider whether or not he was held in someone's good graces.

He hid a wince just as Roddy entered with all the formality of a valet.

"My Lord," he said in his most correct English. "His Grace, the duke, wishes an audience with ye at yer earliest convenience."

Hell, he wished his friend hadn't done that. It simply served to make him feel more on edge. With a curt nod of acknowledgement to Roddy, he followed the duke's butler out of his apartment, entering the house along the main gallery on the first floor.

He hadn't paid much attention to the portrait gallery when he first returned to Glencoe House. Just keeping his composure at being under its roof was enough.

Now the portrait of his mother stared out at him.

As a man, Seth more resembled his father. But as the boy he was when that portrait was painted, he was very much his mother's son.

He barely recognized himself – on the outside at any rate.

The weeping of a small boy at the loss of the only one who loved him tugged at his heart still. He swallowed hard against a tightness in his throat.

As he looked at the portrait, he sensed, rather than heard, a person behind him. He expected a footman. Instead, it was a slender woman in a plain dark blue dress, her pale face made even more so by the white cap that covered her hair. Dark lashes that framed brown eyes regarded him gravely. His eyes traveled down to her mouth then back up to her eyes which fluttered almost nervously several times before she lowered her head. What that suggested of the woman's own thoughts was beyond his ken.

"Your father wishes to see you, sir."

The curtsy came a moment later, an afterthought, it would appear.

Seth had forgotten the nurse was Scottish. She was younger than he first recalled. And after four weeks, she was still here, which, he understood from the butler, was some kind of record for nurses to his father.

Something about her nagged at him, although he couldn't explain what. But there she was waiting for some kind of an acknowledgement.

"Lead on, Nurse Campbell. Let's see if this interview can be brief, as it will not be pleasant."

A tic upwards on her lips suggested a sense of humor, although there was nothing in her manner which was not very proper, very correct.

His father's suite was light and airy. The smell of roses wafted through the window. It was something that had surprised him the day he arrived. It surprised him still.

His father's bed was empty. The sound of fabric rustling drew his attention to a wingback chair angled to give its occupant both a view of the room as well as the gardens down below.

Seth remained at attention while Nurse Campbell silently poured a glass of cloudy liquid into a glass. Lemon barley water, his keen nose informed him.

The shock of first seeing his father so weak and emaciated was no less shocking on his second visit. Hair that was once the fire of Scotland was now dull and gray. His expensive clothes hung on a withered frame.

"You came back," said the duke. "I thought you'd run off like the sniveling weak-willed, half-blind coward I always said you were."

Seth ignored the shocked gasp from the nurse who had the good sense to remain out of their eyeline.

"I'm disappointed," Seth responded calmly. "*I* came back hoping to see you laid out in your death shroud, old man."

Another sharp intake of breath from the nurse, but a spark lit in his father's eyes. On another man, it might look like respect. Seth knew better.

A silence dragged on and, with each second, Seth wondered how long he'd be able to stay in the same room. He forced a lid on his roiling gut.

But this was part of the game, wasn't it? A game of brinksmanship. If he walked out now, it would prove his father right.

Damn the man.

Abruptly, the duke rapped the tip of his cane so forcefully on the floor that it no doubt marred the board beneath the rug. He shouted, "Stay right where you are, Campbell!"

Seth squeezed his hands together behind his back to avoid an involuntary jump. As frail as the man might appear, he still had a brutally strong voice.

"I didn't give you permission to leave, did I?"

How did the nurse take this?

The young woman was frozen at the threshold of an antechamber. No doubt she'd been trying to discreetly leave what was supposed to be a private interview.

This time, her impeccable manners failed her. Seth read the contempt on her face as clearly as if she had expressed it out loud. Once more, their eyes met, and something like an understanding passed between them.

Seth kept his voice calm and authoritative. "Nurse, give my father and I a few minutes alone, will you?"

The woman bobbed a curtsy and closed the door after her.

Seth turned his attention back to his father. The spark in his eyes turned to flame at having his orders countermanded.

"Find a backbone somewhere in the Highlands, did you?"

"And so much more, Your Grace. If this interview is to be a recitation of my shortcomings, then I'll take my leave of you now and wish you a short journey to hell."

"You'd enjoy that, too, my boy, wouldn't you? Rob me of everything worthwhile in this life and steal from me even now."

Seth quirked an eyebrow. He ignored the veiled accusation in the first part – the fact his father blamed him somehow for the death of his mother was old news. But as for the second part – "steal from him even now"? The only thing he could mean was Skye-Heath.

On that, he would not stay silent. The duke wanted to un-nerve him, goad him. When he was younger, he had been successful at it.

But not now.

Seth steeled his voice.

"You've seen the books. Increased dividends in the five years since I became manager."

He didn't know the exact numbers for certain, but the flicker across the old man's face told him his father knew he spoke the truth.

"Would it kill you even quicker to thank me for the work I've done in *your* business?"

The duke shook his head. "You were paid to do a job, were you not? You've remunerated yourself quite well out of it."

Then his expression changed, almost softened.

"Your mother coddled you far too much."

The change of subject nearly made him dizzy. "And you were far too harsh," he countered.

Seth cursed his father once more. Then he cursed himself. The old man never changed; he only changed tactics. No longer could he use his size to intimidate, so he employed other, darker methods. Build up to a high dudgeon, and then hit him with a low blow.

His mother.

Unexpectedly, the duke whispered, "I want to see her again."

The longing in his father's voice surprised Seth and softened his heart. Many things separated father and son, but the love for one woman – wife to one, mother to the other – was a connection not so easily severed.

"Well, that's not up to us, is it?" Seth replied softly. "Only God Himself determines that."

The duke rallied. His face that had been pallid became puce.

"I want to see her grave! I want to see home…"

It was an understandable request; one a loving son would move heaven and earth to grant his dying father. But he was not a loving son, and his father was far from loveable. The idea of making the long journey from London to Scotland with an invalid was distinctly unappealing – and yet Seth felt compelled to provide some kind of conciliatory sop to him.

"I'll speak to the doctor. I'll make that promise and no more."

He turned on his heel and stalked from the room. That was as much as he could bear for today.

RUBY HAD NOT closed the door completely. She had watched the exchange from her little anteroom.

There was no love lost between father and son. Could the earl become an ally in her quest? Or did the apple not fall far from the tree, no matter what differences there were between them?

One thing she knew for certain was it would be to her advantage if a trip to Scotland took place – if the letters of patent existed, they would be somewhere at the Skye-Heath Textiles or at the Duke of Auchen's ancestral seat, Castle Glenuig, in Glasgow.

Ruby watched the younger Musgrave pivot on his heel and walk out of the room. She quietly re-entered and continued about her tasks as though the entire conversation had not taken place.

"Well?"

Ruby paused from picking up the morning newssheet which lay discarded by the bed.

"Don't play coy, Girl. I know you heard every word."

"I am paid to take care of you and to mind my own business, Your Grace."

"Humph! A politician's answer. The old goat of a doctor will refuse me permission to travel. You and my son will convince him otherwise."

"Even if it means hastening your death?"

"Do you think it is *death* that I fear? Some accounting to Saint Peter? Stupid girl! *Running out of time* is what I fear. There's too much bloody work to do to stop my idiot son ruining everything I worked for."

Ruby tamped down her desire to retort. Everything *he* worked for? Built on the back of *her* father's invention? Increased dividends year-on-year? One-third of that belonged to her father who might still be alive if not for this man.

"Give me your word that you will make the doctor kindly disposed to the idea," the duke demanded.

"I'm afraid that is something outside of my control."

"You will do it, or I'll have you out on your ear!"

She cast him a baleful look, but he was seated with his back to her so the gesture was wasted. After a month as his nurse, she was beginning to understand the tide of his temper – the ebb and flow of his mood – and what foul temper was governed by his disease and what was his own natural tendency.

His threats bothered her less and less, although he could catch her off-guard at times.

"I will speak to the doctor and do my best to persuade him."

The answer satisfied him and with nothing more to rail against, the duke slumped in his chair and closed his eyes. His vitality was all for show. He rallied if there was an argument to be had, and that was all.

Convincing the doctor was one thing, but she would need young Musgrave on her side if she was to make that happen. Did the earl mean it when he said he would speak to the doctor in favor of the trip? She ought to speak with the earl first to try to come to some consensus.

The duke now slept and if he did so without a soporific, he was not in too much pain.

She left the room and looked down to the end of the corridor and the connecting door to the wing that the earl had claimed as his own for the duration of his stay. She approached and rapped on the door.

It opened after a moment, but it was not the earl who stood there, rather it was his manservant, a stocky fellow with black hair. She had seen him about the house a few times. He was not liveried like the rest of the servants, nor was he dressed as fine as a guest.

Should she curtsy? She decided against it.

"I wish to speak to the earl."

"The e–?" he hesitated a moment. "Oh, the *earl*."

His manner changed and became more formal. "I'm afraid he's gone out, Miss."

"Oh..."

"I can tell him ye called by."

She nodded and started to turn away, but not before she noticed the man frown.

"It'll help if ye give me yer name, lassie."

Ruby hesitated, and it didn't go unnoticed by the man. "Campbell... His Grace's nurse."

The man nodded, and his expression became less serious. He performed an elaborate bow, at the bottom of which she caught sight of a wide grin.

"Roddy McClane at yer service, Nurse Campbell. I've been a friend of the earl before I even kent he was an earl. If there be anything at all ye need from His Lordship, ye can come to me."

A genuinely friendly face!

She returned his smile.

"Do ye have a first name?" he asked.

Could there be any harm in sharing a first name? It wasn't so uncommon to be particularly memorable.

"Ruby."

CHAPTER FIVE

"H ELEN…"
The whispered voice started Ruby of out of her half-doze by the fire. She was awake immediately, and on her feet, ready to prepare a further dose of laudanum, but the duke's eyes were closed and the lines on his face didn't seem anymore furrowed than they usually were. His breathing was easy.

"Helen?"

The voice was stronger, and it had an unmistakable question in it.

"Yes, my… dear?" She hesitated over the word, but once said, the duke let out a sigh.

"Our son has returned home. What think you to that?"

Ruby thought of the woman in the portrait, a protective hand on the young boy's shoulder.

"I am very pleased."

She held her breath, waiting for a reply, waiting for the duke to fully waken and demand to know why she was speaking to him. But he seemed to remain in a deep sleep.

Outside in the corridor, there was a creak of a floorboard.

Who would be awake at this time of night? Most of the servants had already retired. Those that were about would have no cause to be in this part of the house.

With one glance back at the duke, she left the room and

caught sight of a man rounding the corner and walking out onto the gallery where he was silhouetted in moonlight.

The man remained with his back to her, but he paused. He'd obviously heard her leave the duke's room.

"You wished to speak to me, Nurse Campbell." The earl's voice sounded tired, even resigned. Her heart went out to him in sympathy.

"You father wishes to go to Scotland."

"And what my father wants, my father gets."

She frowned. "You don't sound best pleased with the notion."

Seth Musgrave turned to face her. "He's sent you to advocate on his behalf? That's a novelty. I think it's the first time that he's simply not ordered something and had it done immediately."

She ventured a couple of paces closer. It would not do to have their conversation overheard.

"Is that why you're here? Because he ordered you to come? Is there no familial bond?"

"Not on my part, and I suspect not on his either."

Musgrave shook his head as though recognizing he had said too much.

"Well, he ought to be pleased he has an advocate in you," he said. "Or is there another reason for your interest?"

Ruby's heart pounded. It had been a mistake to give her first name to Roddy McClane. Had it sparked a memory? She tamped the thought down. How could he possibly know the McAllister name?

Before she could answer, Musgrave shook his head, as if dismissing his own question. He spoke. "I saw you today. You have no great love or loyalty to my father."

"I prefer to keep my employment, sir."

A perfectly true statement.

"That raises another question. I contacted the agency. You're not who you say you are."

A chill flooded through her being. Ruby brought her hands together, pressed her thumb into the palm of the hand opposite in her habit to cover her nervousness.

What could she say to that?

Nothing. So that's exactly what she said... not a thing.

Her stomach sank further as, step by step, he closed the distance between them until he was standing before her. If he stretched out an arm, he could touch her. She should move away, but found she could not. All she could do was look away from his cat-like stare.

"Who are you *really*, Nurse Ruby Campbell?" he whispered.

She felt a soft touch of his fingers under her chin, then it firmed as he urged her to turn her face and look at him once more. Now he was the merest handspan away. Awareness of him grew and, unbidden, she recognized the stirrings of desire. The thought of a kiss from him caused her lips to tingle. His eyes swept down to them, and they parted of their own accord in anticipation.

Then his eyes met hers.

"You don't strike me as a fortune hunter. In fact, I think you loathe him as much as I do. Is that the case, Nurse Campbell?"

"My reasons remain my own, sir." She was grateful her voice held strong and not wavered.

"Do you take me for an idiot like everyone else does?" he asked. "If you do, you'll be sadly mistaken."

His words, though softly spoken, carried restrained anger. Ruby's mouth dried.

"I'll ask you a second time. Who are you Ruby Campbell? And what are you doing here?"

She took an intake of breath then released it with a juddering exhale.

"My father died last year and we were broke. I had to sell my home. I decided to come south to... make things better."

All perfectly true statements.

"Why come to London?"

"I have a cousin who's a seamstress. But I couldn't live off her. I have my pride. And I heard you needed a nurse."

You yelled so loud, everyone within a mile could have heard it.

"I can nurse," Ruby continued, her voice stronger. "I tended my late father. I knew I could nurse yours. He hasn't thrown me out yet and I haven't quit. Ask the others. I do the job. Just you try finding someone else who will."

She watched him consider her words weighing each one to determine whether or not she was telling the truth.

"There's still something not right about you," he said after a moment.

He's going to dismiss me!

She couldn't let that happen, not now. Panic welled through her being.

"What? That I'll put up with the duke?"

Her words came out angry instead of fearful, which took Musgrave aback for a moment. He folded his arms and regarded her thoughtfully.

"I don't disbelieve your story, Nurse Campbell, but I don't think it's the full one. You're hiding something."

"My reasons are my own."

"I ought to dismiss you."

Ruby raised her chin, her eyes meeting his without wavering, silently daring him to, even as all her insides trembled.

He let out a snort of laughter. "You do have your pride, don't you?"

She held her breath.

Musgrave's sensuous lips twisted in faint amusement.

"So what are we to do about our patient, Nurse Campbell? *Ruby?* Since he has us both dancing to his tune?"

She licked her lips, trying to formulate an answer – difficult, when all of her senses were attuned to the man before her.

Ruby felt the exhale of his breath on her skin. She watched, mute, as he shook his head as if *he* were the one caught in a spell. He stepped half a pace away from her. It felt like half a mile.

The intimacy of the moment vanished.

"Meet me in the drawing room at one o'clock tomorrow

afternoon," he said, his voice at a normal volume instead of a whisper. No longer were they conspirators. For some reason – for all kinds of reasons – the thought was disappointing. "We'll face the doctor together. A united front will overcome the worst of his objections. What say you?"

"I agree, sir." Ruby was surprised to find her voice.

She remained where she was and watched Musgrave descend the stairs to the ground floor.

"I wish you an easy night with your patient," he called back up to her.

She stared into the dark void after him, until the sound of footsteps stopped. She listened. A sound of a door – the library perhaps – opening and closing before the house fell to silence once again. She wrapped her arms around herself to ward off a sudden chill.

Or was it dread?

What on earth was she thinking? Entertaining the thought of kissing an earl, the son of the man who had stolen from her family? It was foolish in the extreme, yet there was no denying how her body reacted to his nearness.

He *saw* her, she knew that.

But could he see *through* her?

"WHAT'S THE MATTER with you this morning?"

Ruby wrenched back the curtains, letting bright sunlight spill into the room. Her eyes watered with the brightness. She blinked them rapidly to clear them, taking a deep breath to wake herself up.

"Cat got your tongue?"

She turned to the duke who fixed her with a rheumy gaze.

"No, sir."

"Then speak when you're spoken to, you stupid chit! I asked you a question!"

"The doctor is coming today. The earl and I will speak to him about the trip to Scotland."

"The earl and I? The earl and I?" he mocked. "Does my imbecile son require a nurse to hold his hand?"

His venomous outburst set off a series of uncontrolled coughs.

The words rankled more than they ought. She had witnessed the bitterness between father and son. Still, she wondered at the temptation she felt to defend the man from his father. She poured a spoonful of cough elixir into a glass and stirred it while the duke fought to bring his breathing under control.

She handed him the glass. As he drank, Ruby used the opportunity to rein in her anger by chiding her patient.

"You know the doctor will raise objections. You may have gone a lifetime bullying people to get your own way, but that's not how civilized people go about things."

The duke shoved the glass back into her hand.

"What would *you* know about civilized people?"

"I know how to be civil, and perhaps that's enough."

The duke barked out a laugh. The animation in his face told her he enjoyed their sparring.

The man threw back the covers and struggled to seat himself on the edge of the bed. He reached forward for his cane and pounded it on the floor beside him.

A mere moment later, a footman hurried into the room. The young man glanced at her for silent instruction. Ruby simply nodded in the duke's direction.

"Hot water, now! I don't trust my stupid son or this strumpet to do as they're told. I'll speak to the doctor myself. Don't just stand there gawping, get me dressed."

Seth was on his way down to the dining room for breakfast when he caught a glimpse of Ruby as she left his father's room.

She looked exhausted.

He considered calling out to her with the excuse of asking after his father, but he did not. The memory of last night and the lingering scent of lavender from her skin had stayed with him.

She was a mystery to him and therefore intriguing, a puzzle to be solved. The fact that she was damned attractive beneath her plain clothes and severe manner was something else which added to her allure.

She's dangerous.

He wasn't sure where *that* thought had come from, but it stuck. He watched her leadenly climb the stairs up to the servants' quarters.

And why wouldn't she be tired? It was morning now, and she had been there when he was summoned to see his father yesterday. That would have been – what? Two o'clock in the afternoon?

She'd been caring for his father for at least the past sixteen hours. Just one-half of an hour in his father's company would have *him* feeling murderous.

So why did she do it?

She was his nurse, yes – but not one who had been employed through the agency. She just walked into Glencoe House, and no one seemed to know where she had come from.

But her arrival appeared to have been governed by Providence's hand, and that she took on the duke's furnace-like temper, and was still here after a month, meant no one cared to look too closely. Not even the doctor could be induced to express any curiosity about who she was.

Seth took the stairs two at a time. Should he investigate more? Or take this woman on face value?

Yesterday, he thought he was sure of his answer.

It was his responsibility as both son and earl to ensure that his father had the best of care.

And yet, he felt some sort of strange connection with her. She saw through the duke as clearly he did.

Furthermore, he found himself attracted to her, and that was something he couldn't even explain to himself.

Last night, he had been drawn to the portrait of his mother. Perhaps he had been tired, or Nurse Campbell had caught him off-guard in a sentimental moment, but none of that could explain how in the moonlight of the gallery he had come so close to kissing her.

He shook off his musings. His father wanted to go to Scotland, *he* wanted to go to Scotland, and Nurse Campbell appeared to want to go to Scotland – so off to Scotland they would go.

Was she homesick?

Was that why he felt an urge of tenderness toward her?

He shook his head.

He could very well be as stupid as his father claimed.

Seth entered the dining room. Roddy was already there, tucking into his breakfast. His friend raised a hand in greeting and continued chewing. The lure of hot food brought him to the sideboard. He speared a pork sausage from the silver-plated food warmer and spooned a generous helping of scrambled eggs onto his plate.

A trip to Scotland and the close quarters that would entail would give him an excellent excuse to find out more about how Ruby Campbell came to be here in the first place.

He managed to get down half of his food before Roddy spoke.

"I got the drawings back from the engineer. He says the idea should work. Where did ye get the notion? I thought the only weaver using punch cards in such a fashion was that Frenchman, Jacquard."

Seth slurped down a mouthful of tea before answering.

"I came across some diagrams years ago when I was clearing out old papers in the mill archives. Most of the drawings were completely impractical, but the design for a loom that could allow weavers to make intricate patterns without error was intriguing. I had no idea at the time whether such a machine was possible or simply some man's flight of fancy. I imagine the idea had been discarded as impractical. In fact, I nearly forgot all about it until I found them again when we were drawing up plans for Habetrot."

"Well, I'll tell ye, I'm looking forward to going back to Scotland. London's a wee too crowded for my tastes. I bet ye'll be best pleased to be going north, too."

"You're right. I've had enough already. I'm champing at the bit to see the progress on the building."

"Och, we'll be home before ye ken it," said Roddy, his eyes gleaming in anticipation.

Seth shook his head, taking no pains to hide a grimace of displeasure from his friend.

"I wouldn't count on being in such a hurry. The duke will be accompanying us."

CHAPTER SIX

"THE TRIP WILL likely kill him."

The doctor's pronouncement was unequivocal. Ruby watched the earl's reaction. He folded his arms in an insouciant fashion.

"Better that he dies on the way to his ancestral home than here in London."

"My good sir! My job is to rob St. Peter of the pleasure of this man's company for as long as possible!"

The doctor's face had turned red. Ruby rose to her feet. She feared the man might be in danger of a stroke.

"I fully understand your concern, Doctor," she said. "Perhaps it is best that the duke hear from you directly. A more authoritative verdict than ours is sure to persuade him."

The change in the man's expression revealed everything she needed to know. The doctor was afraid of the duke's temper.

She felt Musgrave's presence at her shoulder. She didn't need to see his face to gauge the expression on it. She imagined it would be a lot like the one in the portrait upstairs – implacable. Resolute.

The doctor gave them both a put-upon look and addressed his next remarks to the earl.

"Very well – but he goes without my blessing, and you be sure to tell him so. I'll give Nurse Campbell a list of the medicines the duke will need to take, and enough to ensure he can travel as pain free as possible. I will give you the name of a physician I can recommend in Glasgow."

"You've been more than fair, Doctor. Thank you." Musgrave's quiet authority seemed to mollify the man.

"And you be sure to tell His Grace so."

The doctor left the drawing room. Ruby looked to the earl.

He seemed unworried by the unusual interview. He even smiled at her. Once more, warmth bloomed in her chest. How was it that a man as handsome as he, the son of a duke, an earl in his own right, lived the life of a bachelor? Surely, some woman had caught his eye?

"I want to speak to you, Miss Campbell."

The fact he called her "Miss" should have alerted her, but she missed it.

"I want to thank you for your service. I will arrange to pay your fare to anywhere in the country as well as a full month's wages in advance."

He was dismissing her?

Dreams of restoring her father's legacy vanished before her eyes. The abuse she had endured from the ailing duke for the past month had all been for nothing. She wasn't aware she was shaking until she felt the touch of his hand to her elbow.

Ruby didn't object as he guided her to a chair and urged her to sit, concern on his face writ large.

"Have I done something to displease, Your Lordship?"

He frowned.

"No, of course not. On the contrary, I can't think of anyone who would put up with my father's behavior with the amount of forbearance you've shown. But I know you're not happy here. I thought that if it is fare home to Scotland you seek, then I…"

His voice trailed away. Ruby realized that he was just as uncertain as she was. His vulnerability and willingness to show it opened something in her that she was starting to long for – a connection, an intimacy.

"I have to stay," she whispered.

He crouched down and leaned in until his face was only a few inches away.

The uneasiness in him had vanished, replaced with something hard, unyielding. The change in manner surprised her. Tension thickened in the air like gathering storm clouds. Ruby found herself alert feeling an instinctive threat.

From the man before her?

No.

Then someone else?

His softly spoken words were urgent as though he feared being overheard.

"I can get you out of here. Enough money to get home and get by for a few months. I can help you find new employment. Don't become a prisoner to him. Heaven knows how long he'll live."

His blue eyes were stormy, and Ruby yearned to reach out and touch a finger to his brow and ease the lines there.

She offered him a shy smile, touched by his thoughtfulness.

"And what of you?" she asked, her voice as low as his had been. Once more, the feeling of intimacy created tingles in her chest. "Are you no less a prisoner of your father than I am as his nurse?"

"Ties of blood oblige me to him. It doesn't have to be this way for you."

"Would you subject another woman to his capricious temper and cruel words?"

"I would nurse him myself."

Ruby rose from the chair, shaking her head. He rose with her.

"Your father has little time left. I want to stay. I *need* to stay."

"Why?"

"Does it matter?"

"It does to me."

Ruby could see that it did. But what answer could she possibly give him? There could be no denying his success in operating

Skye-Heath, but the mill's success was also a direct result of her father's invention. She had to force the duke into rectifying this injustice. After the man died, there was no obligation for the son to right his father's wrongs.

Musgrave had rightly taken her silence for refusal. He continued.

"I can't ask you to do that. Our journey to Glasgow will take more than a fortnight, possibly three weeks. It is no easy trip for a woman. There will be few comforts, little privacy."

"I am the duke's nurse. Where else should I be?"

Ruby found her hands enclosed by his.

"So, you're an angel? Putting up with the old man's abuse out of your divine good nature?"

Ruby blushed. "No, far from that."

To her surprise, he lifted her hands to his lips.

"Your reasons are your own... you've told me. I hope that one day you'll trust me enough to tell me... as a friend."

She squeezed his hand in silent response. It would be so easy to give in now and tell him everything, but who knew how much time the duke had left? This was her only chance to restore her father's legacy.

"TELL ME ABOUT the mill."

The duke was having a bad night of it. Ruby had given him the maximum dose of laudanum that the doctor had recommended. He was drifting in and out of consciousness, his pain acute.

"The mill... the mill... why do you want to talk of the mill, Helen?"

"Because it is yours, and soon you will see it again."

"Oh, if it pleases you to, bring our son. It's time he learned how the world works. I fear he is an idiot. I was translating Latin at his age. He's barely able to read. The quality of his penmanship is appalling. Don't you agree?"

She had responded whenever he asked for Helen because answering him as her seemed to give him some comfort. But she had always believed he thought himself talking to a mistress or lover.

Did he call his late wife by the name of Helen? Why was that?

At last, she thought to answer. "I fear you are too hard on him, Your Grace."

"I have displeased you. You call me by my title," he wheezed.

She started. Her use of his title was a slip of her pretense, but that the duke thought ill of Seth as a boy saddened her. He was not an idiot. In fact, everything she had seen and heard suggested something quite to the contrary.

"Helen, don't leave me. Keep talking to me. As horrid as I am, you love me, I know you do, and I am selfish enough to do anything I can to keep you with me. Tell me I've vexed you."

"Shall I read to you?"

"Poetry…"

Even as he spoke, sleep claimed the duke, dragging him into a deep, drugged slumber.

Ruby took a lamp and wicked it low. The house was silent. By her reckoning it had to be about one o'clock in the morning.

Poetry…

She would never have believed it of the man. Poetry? The language of lovers? The man didn't have an affectionate or feeling bone in his body.

She sighed and got to her feet. Soon, they would begin their journey to Scotland. If reading to the duke gave him some measure of peace as they traveled, then it was a little enough chore to find a couple of books to accompany them.

The library at Glencoe House looked impressive when she happened to catch a glimpse inside. Whether it truly earned that status or was simply designed merely for show, she did not know.

Ruby ventured downstairs.

The house was dark apart from a spill of light from the half-open library door. On nearing, she heard the scratch of pen on paper. She peered in. At the desk was a man. Judging by the breadth of his shoulders, it was the earl, the light brown color of his hair turned golden in the lamplight.

She couldn't help the spearing tenderness that struck her at that moment. *Seth...* she saw the boy as well as the man. But more than that, she felt from him an aching loneliness that stretched on for years.

Her own soul resonated with it.

He straightened in his seat and rolled his shoulders. Reflections of lamplight filled the edge of his spectacles, a lock of wavy hair low on his brow.

Ruby felt the irrational temptation to sweep it away from his eyes. She closed her eyes. Her plans did not include tender feelings for the son of her enemy. She drew in a deep breath and lightly rapped on the door to announce her presence.

"The patient worse than usual tonight?" he asked even before she entered.

Had he seen her lurking?

Seth took off his glasses and placed them on the desk. Ruby took it as permission to enter.

"You're the only other person awake at this hour, so it didn't take much of a deduction," he continued, seemingly reading her mind.

"When your f..." It didn't seem right to call the man a "father" when he'd been nothing of the kind. "When the duke is restless, he finds comfort in being read to. He concentrates on my voice, and it seems to help him overcome the pain."

"Then by all means come in and make a selection."

She offered a brief curtsy. For some reason, that elicited a smile.

"There's no need for such formalities when we're alone. My father is a stickler for such things, but I am not. Here, let me set another lamp so you can see properly."

She approached the desk and glanced down at the papers there – drawings, lots of them. She recognized the complex web of warp and weft threads suspended on a loom.

"You recognize what this is?"

Ruby started.

"I… ah, yes… my father took an interest in textiles and how machinery operated. He would show me how each pattern would be set up."

She made the mistake of looking into his eyes. He was interested in what she had to say, and she'd said too much.

Thank goodness it was he who broke the spell by priming another lamp. Apparently, he was uncomfortable as she with this new intimacy.

She took the second lighted lamp from the desk and picked the farthest corner of the library to conduct her search.

Poetry. Perhaps the duke had a romantic soul after all – presuming he had a soul.

As she browsed the titles, she listened to Seth returning to his work. The pen scratching on paper and the whispered sigh of pencils as they shaded in his diagrams.

This was ridiculous! Mooning over a man who could mean nothing to her.

She grabbed a book, only glancing at it, intending to return directly to her patient. It was a book of poems by Pierre de Ronsard. With her focus on the door, she did not hear her name called.

A touch on the arm stilled her.

"Don't go… not yet."

She *should* go. Oh, how she should go. But she made the mistake of looking at the earl… *Seth.*

Those eyes seemed to see deep into her soul and found its twin in the loneliness.

He must have heard the answering call because he removed the book from her hand and placed it on the small side table by the door. His face was half in shadows, but she could see his eyes clear enough. They searched her face and seemed to know what was in her deepest heart.

He lowered his lips to hers slowly, giving her time to escape from him if she wished.

But she didn't wish.

Her eyes fluttered closed as his lips met hers. Never had she felt such emotion in so small a touch. She could taste the isolation, the need. She responded with a need of her own.

Seth responded by sliding his arms around her waist and pulling her into his embrace.

The kiss was all too brief, but his hold lingered. She had no idea how much she craved his touch until that moment.

SETH FELT THE tension leave his shoulders as soon as their lips touched. He was right! Ruby wanted him. For the first time that he could recall, he went with his instinct, and it didn't steer him wrong.

It gave him an unexpected elation.

He had experienced desire before and anticipated that kissing Ruby would be pleasant, satisfying. What he didn't expect was a spear through the wall around his heart that opened it up to golden sunlight.

His lips left hers. He didn't expect more, didn't deserve more, wasn't sure he could cope with more... soon perhaps, not now. It was enough to just hold her. Whatever there was between them was fragile and he feared too easily broken if he rushed.

Even now he second guessed himself. He was destined to be a duke, expected to make a titled match. But he didn't want the title, so why would he care for one in his wife?

Wife.

He released her, gently alarmed at the direction his thoughts had taken him so quickly. Her eyes were wide, and he read the question in them.

Why had he done this?

He had no answer to give her.

"I… I should return to my patient," she said.

He couldn't do anything else except nod and step away. She gave him one last glance before taking her book and disappearing upstairs. To the lion's den. And she went there willingly.

That rankled. The instinct to protect her was strong – but *she* didn't need protecting and certainly not by someone like him. And now she would accompany them all the way to Glasgow. Three weeks at close quarters.

Part of him anticipated it with pleasure. Not only was she beautiful, she was intriguing. He wanted to know her even though he recognized full well it could never work, could never last, between them.

But if, for some short time, they could find mutual comfort in the face of a common enemy, it would be worth it.

Wouldn't it?

CHAPTER SEVEN

O VER THE COURSE of the week, Ruby had glimpsed Seth and his friend supervising modifications to the duke's liveried berline coach.

It was a magnificent vehicle, one befitting an aristocrat, all gloss black and a crest painted in gilt and vibrant colors on the door. She wondered what the duke would think, having a carpenter remove the expensive Moroccan leather seats and the luxurious woolen carpets.

But the truth of the matter was the Duke of Auchen was much too frail to sit up for the journey. She had pointed out that it would be better if he reclined, propped up on pillows to allow him to rest as much as possible.

Seth didn't question the suggestion. He and Roddy sketched out plans and worked alongside the estate's carpenter. She hadn't been sure how they might make something suitable, but today Roddy had come to fetch her to see how a coach might be turned into a bedroom.

"Shall we take a closer look and see if it meets with your approval, Nurse Campbell?" Seth Musgrave's manner was all perfectly correct except for the glint of mischief in his eyes, drawing her in as a conspirator, a confidante.

It was dangerous.

Why had he kissed her? Had it been a spur of the moment

action, an acknowledgement of a brief mutual attraction, and that was all?

The man had been in a remarkably cheerful mood all week. She suspected it had less to do with the kiss and more to do with the fact that here, among the workers, the Earl of Glenuig felt at home.

Just as she neared, two men and one of the stableboys were wrestling a small mattress into the carriage. When they were done, she stepped forward with Seth to peer inside.

The formerly well-appointed interior had been stripped to basics, the upholstery removed so that the seats were reduced to mere benches. A shallow, open-topped box had been installed by the carpenter lengthwise between the front rear facing bench and the back bench. The mattress sat within the box to form a bed for the duke.

On the side from which she and Seth looked in, the front and back benches of the once capacious coach had just enough space remaining for two other passengers to sit on basic leather cushions across from one another, knee-to-knee.

"'Tis lucky ye're a slip of a girl," Roddy observed. "Someone much bigger'll have a much harder time of it."

Ruby stepped up into the vehicle, using the leather strap. The carpenters had not left any space to waste. The space beneath the bed was now given over to storage for bedding and securing the apothecary chest containing the duke's medical supplies.

"It is still not too late to change your mind, you know." Seth's words were said lightly, but she knew he remembered their whispered conversation in the duke's study.

"I may be a wee slip of a thing, My Lord, but you forget I'm a Glasgow lass. Traveling with a duke in a fine carriage, why it will be like floating on a cloud!"

Roddy laughed at her brave front. Seth managed a smile, and that was enough to warm her within.

In truth, she did not underestimate the trek. The journey from Glasgow to London had been an exhausting ten days, sitting shoulder-to-shoulder with half a dozen passengers in a coach that had seen better days.

Making the return journey in the luxury of a duke's finely sprung coach would be slightly more comfortable, if no less arduous.

It would not be the only vehicle accompanying them. Seth's own coach would make the journey and a wagon would follow along stowing much of the equipment needed to suit the duke's condition – his own bath, even a bed complete with mattress and bedding should that at a coaching inn be too inadequate.

The duke had protested loud and long about the inclusion of a bath chair, but it was included nonetheless.

More than four hundred miles at being in such close quarters with Seth...

That was going to be the most uncomfortable part of the journey.

THE CHIMES MARKING eleven o'clock echoed through the house followed by the footfalls of the butler silencing the bells and making his final rounds.

They were to leave early tomorrow. She would not sleep tonight.

Her own days had been filled with preparations for moving the patient. She had spent a full day with an apothecary to prepare various medicines – one to dull the pain but not the senses for during the day, an analgesic with a sedative to help him sleep at night and another to deal with the onset of nausea which seemed to come more frequently these days.

She wrote everything down in the journal despite the fact she had been given the list. If she kept busy during these quiet hours, her mind wouldn't return to Seth and his kiss.

He had described her as an angel. Ruby knew better. She was now a trusted member of the household, but she had inveigled her way into it with her scheme to make the duke pay his due to her father. It made little difference that those plans had so far fallen by the wayside.

She let out a soft sigh. Now, she was planning the greatest deceit of her life – none of which might have happened if she allowed herself to be distracted by the presence of Seth Musgrave.

Ruby closed the journal and turned to the book of poems she had taken from the duke's library. She opened it and reread the inscription.

To Georgiana, my beautiful Helen of Troy,
On our first wedding anniversary
From your beloved Uilleam

Helen – it was the duke's private pet name for his wife, and no one seemed to know of it, not even the duke's own son.

In his drugged tangles with Morpheus, the duke imagined he was speaking with his wife – his much beloved wife.

And now his wife was speaking back…

SETH CURSED HIMSELF.

The thirty-mile journey from London to Stevenage was the worst. It should have only taken half a day but, as it was, the Musgrave party didn't arrive until well after dark.

He had underestimated the logistics and his father's ill health. Worse still, he had underestimated the man's pain-induced rage.

How did Ruby put up with such a foul-tempered bastard with all his spite and venom? Seth cocked an ear and concentrated on the noise from the upper floor of the inn.

No – there he was, yelling his displeasure while the footmen scrambled up and down the stairs to assemble the bed. Seth couldn't make out the specific words, but Ruby was up there copping the brunt of it.

Roddy stepped alongside him, a beer in each hand.

"Here, ye'll be needing this," he said. "And I be thinking the lassie upstairs deserves something stronger."

Seth accepted the ale and welcomed the malty taste to rinse away miles of dust – *and* they had been traveling on the turnpike. He shuddered to recall how much slower and rougher the journey would be the further they traveled away from London.

Anxieties that had lain dormant since leaving home now thrummed through his veins. He thought he'd long conquered that.

Apparently not.

Seth drained the ale and shoved the empty vessel into Roddy's hands.

"I'm going to go upstairs, tie the man to his bed, and stick a rag in his fat gob."

He got no further than up three steps when the shouting stopped. A moment later, the door to the duke's suite opened, and four footmen nearly stumbled over themselves to leave. Seth was forced against the wall as the young men passed. He then looked back to Roddy, who had a comical expression on his face.

He entered the room and found it an explosion of clothes and linens strewn about. In the middle of the bed sprawled his father, his eyes half-shut, chest heaving.

Seth searched out Ruby and found her backed against the wall, her face pale, dark curly strands of hair awry from her chignon. Her lips were pressed to a thin line, dark circles under her bright, clear eyes. And, worst, a distinct red mark blooming on her cheek where she had been struck.

Disgust coiled in his belly. He turned toward the bed, ready to mete out the same treatment, dying old man or not.

"He meant no harm," said Ruby. "He was in a lot of pain and distress and so was flailing about. I managed to give him a draught." Her voice sounded as exhausted as she looked.

Turning and seeing her face again didn't lessen his anger.

"When was the last time you slept?"

She started as though she had, indeed, been asleep on her feet.

"Not since yesterday, there was too much to do to prepare. Hopefully, tomorrow's journey will be better." Her voice was dull, adding to his conclusion that she was utterly exhausted.

Seth had hoped to make Stamford by tomorrow, but that was unlikely. They'd barely covered thirty miles today, and Stamford was another sixty miles further still.

It would be a close-run thing as to whether this trip would kill the duke or whether Seth would strangle the old man before they'd even crossed the border.

"Don't whisper behind my back!" the duke slurred.

Seth approached the bed.

"No one is whispering. You yell so much that you fail to hear anyone speaking at normal volume. I have half a mind to turn our party around and have you committed to Bedlam."

The duke choked out a laugh.

"You don't have the bollocks to do it. I'd have more respect for you if you did."

That seemed to exhaust the man, or perhaps it was the elixir Ruby had managed to pour down his throat. Seth watched him close his eyes and fall into a drugged slumber.

He turned back to Ruby to find her unmoved from the spot by the table.

"Go downstairs and see Roddy. He'll arrange a room for you."

Ruby shook her head.

"You need sleep, and it is clear you've had none. I insist."

She offered him a tired smile.

"You're not going to go far if you couch your requests in such reasonable tones. Not according to your father, at any rate."

"My father can go to the devil for all I care."

She cocked her head, her dark eyes held him still. "But that's not true, is it? You *do* care."

Her words hit the mark. But that was something best not discussed with her – with *anyone*.

How could it be possible to love a parent who shared no love with his child? Duty? Obligation? He wished he bloody well knew. All the times he'd failed, he saw the scorn of his father condemning his uselessness. All the times he'd succeeded, he longed to rub his father's nose in it.

Yes, he damn well cared. But for the life of him, he couldn't fathom *why*.

Ruby seemed to understand.

Would she help *him* understand?

Seth stepped forward, heedless of proprieties and who else might enter the room, to enfold her into his arms. He thought she resisted at first, but when she said nothing, he realized that she was stiff with tension that had nothing to do with him and everything to do with his volatile temper.

"You ride in my coach tomorrow. And I'll nurse Father tonight. Just leave me with the instructions of when he needs his medicine," he whispered into her ear. He felt her relax, leaning into him. It felt good to be needed.

"No, I'll stay. His pain is often worse at night, and the mixtures have to be handled with care."

"Then may I keep you company?"

He felt her hesitation. They had not been alone together since that night in the library when he'd kissed her...

He withdrew from their embrace and set a grave expression on his face. The look of confusion in her eyes threatened his resolve before her expression righted itself, and she became the very proper Nurse Campbell once more.

"No, My Lord. You have challenges of your own to keep our party moving. I will rest in good time."

That was a door slammed firmly in his face.

He gritted his teeth. Message received and understood.

Just as he turned away, Ruby reached for his hand, and he was lost in her eyes once more. Her hand squeezed his.

"Thank you," she whispered.

He returned the squeeze and nodded his head silently.

"I'll leave you in peace."

He shut the door and returned downstairs to the dining room where he found Roddy and the coachman poring over a map.

"How's the wee lassie?" Roddy asked.

"She seems to be bearing up well."

"Aye, *she* might be, but I don't know about the rest of our party."

Seth nodded wearily "If today was such a trial, I don't know how we'll stand another three weeks of this. At this rate, it will take us five days to get as far as Sheffield."

The portly coachman set down his tankard and pulled his considerable girth upright.

"What if we just traveled the highways and nae go into towns other than to reprovision and get fresh horses?" the coachman offered. "We got means to camp on the side of the road. I dinnae mind telling ye that turning down some of them country roads gets my heart pumping. Axle deep in mud, I've been. Nae keen to do that with a duke's own coach."

Seth looked down at the map, the lines and shapes blurred as though it had been left out in the rain. Without his glasses, he could make no qualified judgment. He'd dismissed the idea of traveling by canal. While it would have been a gentler ride, he'd calculated that it would take longer still to get to Scotland – every lock was time wasted, the routes were indirect, and they would still need to transfer between disconnected portions by coach. Looking at the old man, Seth wasn't sure he had that much time left.

"Then that's what we'll do. We can start away early each day while the duke still sleeps and travel some through the night where we can."

CHAPTER EIGHT

RUBY PICKED UP a piece of embroidery and lowered herself into a chair beside the sleeping duke. She had hoped the evidence of the glancing blow to her cheek struck while her patient flailed would go unnoticed.

But Seth noticed.

One part of her heart leaped at witnessing his gallantry. To have a chivalrous knight as her champion reached a part of her that she didn't think she possessed. She prided herself on being the practical one in her family – a necessity as her father slipped further and further into his own little world in his last few years.

But a door had been opened a crack. Someone wanted to care for her. It shocked her to realize how much she wanted it, too.

She had distracted herself from those thoughts by completing her early evening routine of tidying the sickroom, keeping it clear of clutter, and giving some more medicine to the now quiescent duke.

He slept solidly, but in the early hours when his dreams began, he would ask for his beloved Helen – and she would be there to answer him.

But she couldn't do that if Seth was there. And she would be lying if she said her conscience didn't bother her.

It did. For what she had begun to consider doing was wrong, so very wrong.

How much easier it would be to tell Seth everything. He would make it right. She knew – hoped – he would understand, but this was not his fight. It would also set father and son further apart.

And Seth loved his father. That was beyond doubt. If there was a chance at reconciliation before the duke passed, Seth should take it – not for his father's sake but for his own. Ruby knew what regret was. There was so much she wished she knew about her mother and her father, and now it was too late. She would never know. She desperately missed them now.

"Drowning, alone."

The muttering began as it done every night for the past six weeks.

"I only see one fire."

Hallucinations? Or simply bad dreams?

Did he imagine hell, or something else?

The muttering continued. Nonsensical words, or so it seemed.

Ruby stood over the man and took a deep breath.

"Uilleam?" she whispered. And waited.

Would the duke awaken and berate her for the familiarity, or would he believe his beloved Helen was speaking to him?

The duke's breathing changed but, still, he did not awaken.

She wondered if this was the only chance she would get. She ignored the pricking of her conscience and began an experiment.

"There's not much time before you join me, but… *beloved*, there are things you need to put right."

The old man's breathing hitched before releasing into a low groan.

"You've not always been upright in your dealings, have you? I fear for your immortal soul, Uilleam. How can you be with me in the hereafter? I fear for *you*."

The groans increased; the sound more tormented. The duke started stirring on the bed. Unintelligible mutterings became words, whispered and indistinct.

Then she saw the duke emerging from his slumber like a man struggling up from beneath the waves to take his first breath of air after nearly drowning. Her heart pounding, Ruby sat down and picked up her needlepoint.

"Helen!"

This time, there was no mistaking it. The duke had called out the name and now was wide awake.

Ruby watched him out of the corners of her eyes as she calmly put down her sewing, then rose to pour him a glass of water. The duke struggled up into a seated position with a groan. His face was flushed, but his eyes were bright and alert.

He eyed the glass of water with contempt.

"Pah! I wouldn't piss in it. Give me a proper drink – whisky."

"Whisky interferes with your digestion, Your Grace."

"You will do what I say, Girl!"

"Calm yourself, sir. We are in a public inn. People are asleep."

"I will not calm myself. I will not be patronized by a chit!"

She readied herself for the string of invectives he would unleash her way. There was a strange sort of comfort in the predictability of it. When he lashed out at everybody in equal measure, it revealed he was in a great deal of pain. When his barbs became pointed and personal, she knew he was not in pain, but was simply being very, very vindictive.

As a result, she was careful to remain the cool, aloof nurse, unafraid to assert herself for her patient's good.

"Why can no one follow orders around here? Insubordination in every single one of you! I'll have you out on your ear before morning, do you understand me?"

The bedroom door swung back on its hinges and violently slammed into the wall. Ruby suppressed a squeal. The embroidery loop slid from the chair and clattered to the floor. Seth filled the doorway. In him at that moment, Ruby had a sense of what the duke must have been like in his prime – mesmerizing, magnetic, and with power barely constrained.

He wore only a nightshirt and yet seemed far more commanding than if he had been dressed in the most expensive superfine wool.

"What the *hell* is going on in here?" he demanded of his father.

Ruby spoke first. "His Grace has awoken from a bad dream and in pain, My Lord. I was about to prepare a draught."

Seth did not answer, but his look told her she was not believed. Instead, he addressed the man on the bed again.

"Do you forget that you're a gentleman, sir? Rank or not, illness or not, you do not speak like that to anyone, let alone a lady."

"A lady? A lady?" the duke mimicked. "Is that what she is? Fool! She's a jumped-up little slut with only slightly better manners than a gutter-bred lightskirt."

Seth crossed the room in two steps and had the duke hauled up by own nightshirt before Ruby could even draw breath.

But now at least the room was silent as the two men glared at one another, panting as though each had run a mile. Ruby had to own to feeling as tightly wound.

"Your Grace! My Lord! Cease this immediately!" she called. "This is a sickroom, not a tavern to brawl in."

The men paid her no heed.

"So that's the way it is?" the duke asked softly.

Seth's lips curled into a sneer. "I have no idea what you're talking about, *Father*."

"Do you not? Perhaps the meager intelligence I credit you with is too much."

Seth let go, letting the old man flop on his back onto the mattress. That set him into a fit of uncontrolled wet coughing. Ruby went over the medicine chest and pulled out a bottle containing a cough decoction – one that would also help him sleep.

"I'll play your game no longer," Seth said grimly. "I'll spit into your coffin, then dance on your grave when the time comes – and at the rate you're going, it will be sooner rather than later."

"You own nothing that I haven't given you," the duke rasped. "Your name, your title, your occupation, your wealth... *you* belong to me."

Ruby turned in time to see a slow bitter smile grow across Seth's face.

"I wouldn't be so sure about any of those things," he said.

Ruby put a hand on Seth's shoulder and urged him out of her way. She poured a spoonful of liquid into the bowl and touched it to the duke's unprotesting lips, still aware Seth stood so close behind her that she could feel the tension thrum through him.

With the task done, she turned to face the earl.

"He will sleep again soon," she said.

It was hard to resist the urge to touch him, to calm him, as he had comforted her after the duke's violent outburst this afternoon. His gaze fell on the mark on her cheek once again, then returned to her eyes.

"I will stay until he does."

"I will not have you two staring at me like buzzards on a carcass," the duke rasped.

Seth rolled his eyes and looked at his father over Ruby's shoulder. "Fine. Close your eyes, and you won't see us."

Ruby choked back a laugh, and she found the duke staring at her instead of his son. There was something unnerving about him when he did that, as though he could see into her soul.

Heat bloomed in her chest and spread outward.

He knew! The duke knew of Seth's regard for her.

Knowing she watched, the duke smiled slowly, smugly, then closed his eyes.

"Read to me."

Ruby frowned.

"What would you like to me to read, Your Grace?"

"Anything! Your voice is enough to put any man to sleep. I pity the poor fool who takes an interest in you."

Seth had positioned himself at the end of the bed, arms folded. She exchanged a glance with him before reaching for the book she'd brought with her from Glencoe House.

"What have you got?"

"A book of poetry, Your Grace."

"Then read it. Perhaps my ignorant philistine son will learn something of the finer arts."

Ruby returned to her seat. Would the duke say something about the choice of work? Would Seth?

She drew another deep breath and opened the volume at random.

> *Among love's pounding seas, for me there's no support,*
> *And I can see no light, and yet have no desires*
> *(O desire too bold!) except, as my vessel tires,*
> *That after such dangers I may still reach port.*
> *Alas! Before I can offer my prayers ashore,*
> *Shipwrecked, I die: for I only see one fire*
> *Burning above me, one Helen who inspires*
> *My vessel to seek its death on reefs so dire.*
> *Drowning I am alone, my own self-murderer,*
> *Choosing a child, a blind boy, as my leader,*
> *So, I ought to shed tears, and blush for shame.*
> *I don't know if my reason or senses guide me,*
> *Steering my boat, but I still know it grieves me*
> *To see so fair a harbor yet not attain*

The medicine had its effect. The duke slept on his back, open-mouthed, breathing in rhythmic snores that would last for hours.

As she read, Seth had sat down in the chair across the bed from her, a shadow in lamplight. Slowly, she closed the book and gently set it on the small table beside her.

"You should leave, My Lord. It will be another long day on the road tomorrow."

Seth remained as still as a statue. Had he also fallen asleep?

She recalled his flash of temper when the duke had insulted

her. Did he truly hold her in some special regard?

One part of her hoped he didn't – for his sake, as well as hers. Much of his father's present cruelty might be attributable to the pain of his illness, but not all. If the duke suspected anything tender between them, he would delight in being especially cruel.

Seth quietly rose to his feet.

"A word outside, Nurse Campbell."

She wondered at his formal speech a moment, then recognized that Seth was no fool. His father could be foxing, only feigning sleep, in order to eavesdrop on their conversation.

In the hallway, faint sounds from the dining room downstairs made their way up toward them.

"I've come to a decision. I'll care for my father during the daylight hours. You'll be made as comfortable as possible in my carriage. I'll also ensure that you have a chaperone in the evenings you attend him."

No, no, no, no!

She had to be *alone* with the duke overnight. He *spoke* to her then. He might be persuaded to do the right thing if, in his delirium, he believed he was speaking to his dead wife.

Seth's mother.

Ruby tamped down her nagging conscience once again.

"My Lord, you are very kind but –"

"Seth."

She frowned.

"I've not been known by any title since I was ten when my father threw me out of the house. I'm Seth to those I'm close to. Or Musgrave, if you prefer it. But please stop calling me 'My Lord'."

"Your father would beg to disagree. He already considers me impertinent because I speak my mind when the occasion calls for it.

"Surely you don't intend to seek his regard? You heard what he called you just before."

"I did." She shrugged. "He said I was little better than a

whore."

Her frank assessment appeared to take him aback.

"No gentleman could ignore a slur on a lady's character."

"I think you value me too highly. I'm just a nurse."

"You are far more than that to me."

Those simple words sent heat through her veins. She was grateful for the cover of darkness, lest he see how her cheeks flamed.

"Oh, Seth…"

He touched a finger to her cheek, and it was all she could do to stop herself sighing at the tenderness of it. He stepped closer.

"Don't tell me you don't feel this… thing… between us. You look at me as if you know exactly what I'm thinking, and I can see what hides behind those eyes of yours."

The heat dissipated, replaced by a tremor instead.

"I hope that is not true," she answered. "I see how you look at me – as an angel, a saint – but I'm none of those things, and if you truly knew me, then there would be no kindness in your eyes. I am vain and selfish. But I would do anything to keep you so kindly disposed to me."

Seth pulled her into his arms and swooped down. She was ready for him, opening her mouth, ready for a deeper kiss.

Her arms wound around him. As he shifted to bring his lips to her neck, she sighed into his ear and his embrace tightened.

"You are destined for great things, Seth," she whispered. "There are expectations, responsibilities, opportunities."

"What does any of that matter when I have you in my arms? What do I want with more?"

He didn't wait for a reply. He renewed his attention to her neck, her ears where the kiss sent shivers through her. She clung to him, aware of how her body reacted to his nearness.

Even as she reveled in his kisses, she closed her eyes to prevent the prick of moisture falling down her cheeks.

It was a folly, a magnificent folly. He wanted her, desired her, and, God help her, she wanted him just as much in return.

CHAPTER NINE

T HE CARRIAGE JOSTLED, the wheels going over a particularly bad rut in the road. Seth braced his legs to steady himself. He glanced to his father beside him. The man slept as he had done since setting off early this morning.

Seth looked up from the papers on his lap. The landscape outside was a blur of greens – the dark green of the trees, a softer green on the meadows and a yellower green on what he presumed were pasturelands.

If he took his glasses off, he could see outside more clearly. But if he did that, he wouldn't be able to see the papers on his lap, and they were more fascinating than the passing view.

They were plans for the new loom in the new mill. *His* mill. The one he was getting off the ground with his own earnings.

He'd had them drawn up but not gotten a chance to closely study them back in London.

He'd found the original illustration three years ago when preparing to dispose of some archived records. A single fantastical drawing. The design was brilliant, hinting at a simple change to how the punch cards were used that might increase the speed and efficiency of the loom dramatically.

But vital details were missing. Seth had gone back through every piece of paper in the old records personally to ensure there was not more. There wasn't.

So, the details he painstakingly tried to recreate with the help of Roddy. And before him in these new plans lay the hope that this loom could work.

He could hardly fathom the notion that his father had seen this concept and discarded it. He shook his head.

Well, it was just like him, wasn't it? Throw away something that didn't immediately appear to be useful. Like his own son.

The day he'd found the illustration was the day his plan was born. He had lived like a hermit, a monk, to scrape together every bit of funding he needed to build his own factory and put this loom in it. He'd even gone so far as setting up his own company with Roddy as his proxy to ensure his father didn't get wind of it.

And now, day-by-day, they moved ever closer to Scotland. The one thing he wanted more than anything was to see the look on his father's face when he was wheeled into a productive, new factory which was not Skye-Heath, but *his* mill.

We'll see what the old man thinks of that.

Seth supposed it was a petty notion, and in vain, too – his father would not live that long. Nonetheless, perhaps he might confide it in Ruby. After all, it was clear she had secrets to hide, a mission of her own that somehow involved his father. And, from what he had seen, it didn't seem to be money she wanted. Nothing so far betrayed her motives.

Perhaps they ought to join forces. He smiled to himself.

Then before he could entertain the idea further, he heard his father awaken. He watched the duke struggle to pull himself up into a sitting position in the jostling carriage.

Should he offer to assist? Seth dismissed the thought as soon as it occurred to him. If William Musgrave wanted help, he could ask for it.

Seth slipped the plans back into their envelope.

"You! An ugly face to wake up to instead of a pretty one," the duke rasped. "What a disappointment."

"Finally, something we can agree on, Father."

"Where is she?

"'She' is the cat's mother. If you're referring to Nurse Campbell, she is riding in the other carriage."

"Don't patronize me, Boy. Why is she not here to attend me?"

"Because I ordered her to rest."

"Who the hell gave you the right to do that? She's *my* nurse. I will give her orders."

"Nurse Campbell is asleep, or at least she ought to be. She tends you during the night. The very least you can do is let her sleep through the day."

"And what happens if I'm in pain? You're as useless as tits on a bull."

Seth let the insult slide. His father had gone from being pale and slightly disoriented to having a strong color in his face. Ruby was right, after all. His curmudgeonliness seemed to give him something to fight for.

"Your nurse has left medicine should you need it and instructions on how to administer it."

"Ah! Do you think I'd trust you with that task? You'd poison me – and deliberately I might add. You can't wait to get your hands on your inheritance, I expect. Well, you might get the title, but you shouldn't count on everything coming your way."

"At least you're crediting me with guile. From you, I'll take it as a compliment."

"You shouldn't. And you still have weak eyes. Why do you wear those damned spectacles things? They make you unmanly."

"They help me to see things more clearly. I suggest you try it. You would benefit from clarity of vision for once in your miserable life."

There was no rejoinder. Seth suspected the exchange had exhausted his father.

He removed his glasses, if for no other reason than to see his father in focus – the ill-kempt gray hair, the gaunt cheeks. He owned a measure of pity for the dying man. Soon, in months, or even just weeks, the man would be gone to meet the One who could not be bullied, carped, or cajoled into acquiescence.

What would life be like then? Seth worried that, deep down, the death of the duke would still leave a scar. But if his father could see Scotland one last time, get his final wish to see the grave of his wife, then perhaps there might be a chance for some kind of *rapprochement*.

"If the weather holds, we expect to be in Doncaster the day after tomorrow," Seth told him to fill the silence.

"Have we passed Grantham?"

"Not yet. Another coachman and postilion will be meeting us on the road just outside the town. They'll take us on to Doncaster. We'll stay there overnight and then head to Leeds. I'll decide then whether we continue by carriage or go on by canal."

Seth braced himself for an argument. He didn't get one.

That was a surprise.

Instead, his father looked thoughtful, rather like he was considering the distances and time himself.

"The canal will take too long. This isn't a bloody pleasure jaunt. I could have hired a coach to get me to Glasgow in two weeks."

"I can get you there in another seven days if you don't complain about the pace and the lack of amenities for Your Grace. What is it to be?"

The duke turned to face him properly. Seth could see the first glimmer of fear in his eyes.

"Get me to Scotland soon, Son. That's all I'll ask of you."

RUBY SLEPT, ALTHOUGH she didn't expect to. Seth's carriage was smaller than the ducal carriage, and more or less comfortable though not luxuriously appointed. She could just about stretch her full length across the seat and be nicely cocooned in a swaddling of blankets.

The swaying lulled her to sleep like a baby in a cradle. How long she slept was a mystery. The leather blinds had been lowered, keeping the carriage in semi-darkness. She fancied that if she breathed in deep enough, she could identify the cologne Seth wore.

Ruby stretched and hauled herself upright. She reached across and opened the blind to see the sky tinted gold. It was late afternoon. How far had they come today? She had not been called on to aid the duke, so she presumed the man fared well under his son's care.

She stifled an open-mouthed yawn and looked about the carriage. It seemed Seth and his man used the vehicle for business.

Textiles. A collection of fabric swatches lay discarded on the bench seat opposite.

She wished she could get another look at the plans for the loom he was examining in the study those few days ago in London. Was there anything of her father's invention in it?

Her eyes fell on a piece of paper peeking out from under the pile of swatches. She lifted the fabric away and found a sheaf of papers half-spilling out of a folio.

Giving herself the excuse that she was simply tidying up, she opened the folio and picked up the first piece of paper in it. It appeared to be an order for materials – wool, cotton, silk...

To a woman working at home on a piece rate, it would seem an enormous amount. For a textile mill, it was a very modest order. But this was not an order for Skye-Heath. The company was Habetrot Textiles.

Why would Seth have an order for another company in his possession?

Habetrot Textiles. She smiled.

Every Scottish child knew of Habetrot and her two companions. Weavers all of them, each with a deformity which highlighted their industry – the pendulous lip from wetting the thread, the swollen foot that worked so long at the treadle, and the enormous thumb from teasing out the flax.

Ruby reached for another document. This one was an order for building materials. She read further. It was for a building of some kind with iron columns instead of stone or wood. She searched through some of the other papers and found one with an illustration of a water wheel, and another that showed the workings of a steam engine that would power the Habetrot looms.

Why did Seth have all this?

A cold chill went through her despite the warmth of the day. Was this *espionage*?

It was not without precedent. Everyone knew of John Lombe.

The story went that the Derbyshire weaver's son had inveigled his way into an Italian silk weaving factory. He'd made copious notes about the spinning machines and returned to England to set up his own factory.

But the tale didn't end there. It was whispered that the King of Sardinia ordered a beautiful woman to travel to England and join Lombe's household. While there, she administered slow-acting poison, and Lombe was dead at the age of twenty-nine.

Was Seth looking for a similar way to crush his rivals? He didn't seem like a man who would use underhanded means to increase his business.

But his father had.

Ruby sighed and sat back on the seat. She closed her eyes for a moment against the beginnings of a headache.

How well did she *really* know Seth Musgrave, Earl of Glenuig?

The truth of the matter was that she knew him not at all. Not really. A few shared kisses and embraces. And yet...

No. The man she had come to know these few weeks was nothing like his father, which was why it was even more important to have the duke admit his wrongdoing himself.

She pushed her disquiet over the Habetrot documents down

as, outside, the coachman called to the horses. The carriage lurched as it slowed. Ruby tidied the papers and slipped the folio back under the pile of swatches – and hoped Seth and Roddy didn't notice anything amiss.

She straightened herself and reached into a little wicker basket for a comb and a spritz of lavender water to refresh herself.

Oh, to stretch her legs would be heaven after being so long confined. She did not wait for a footman to aid her from the carriage. She pushed the hinged step down with her foot and exited herself as soon as the vehicle rolled to a stop.

They had been on the road for several days now, and each time they stayed at a coaching inn. But today, they stopped on the roadside where fields and rolling hills pointed the way to woodlands in the distance. She stretched her arms and breathed in deeply. She smelled sun-warmed green grass and the little hint of sweetness from berries that were ripening somewhere nearby.

She got out of the way of the men tending the horses. Another small group attended the wagon, unloading poles and canvas to set up a campaign tent in the field beside the road.

She spotted Seth and Roddy in conversation with the chief coachman.

"Are we not going on to Grantham this evening?" she asked.

The men gave her a nod of acknowledgement then Roddy and the coachman excused themselves, leaving her standing alone with Seth.

"We're going to send a man into town to bring fresh horses here. We can be on our way in the ducal carriage hours earlier than if we stayed in town. The other men can break camp after we leave and follow behind. At the rate we're traveling, they'll catch up within two hours and, in another two, they'll be far enough ahead to prepare camp and ready for the next change of horses."

Ruby nodded her understanding.

"How is the patient?" she asked.

"Mercifully for me, he's asleep."

Seth moved past the carriage. Ruby fell in step with him, away from the sounds of the camp.

"He's not looking well," Seth continued. "I swear he's hanging on out of sheer stubbornness. He's desperate to see home once more."

The inflection in his voice caused her to look up at him. He *was* worried about his father.

"And what of you? Are you looking forward to going home?"

He shrugged a moment and offered a self-deprecating smile which made her heart increase its beat.

"I am. But if I tell you the reason, you might think less of me."

His eyes, the color of which matched the skies above, seemed to hold her in some kind of spell.

"That would never be the case," she whispered.

"Thank you."

Two small words but they seemed to mean a lot to him. For some reason, they meant a lot to her, too.

They walked on a few more yards away in silence until the sound of the wrens in the nearby blackberry bush were louder than the sound of the camp.

She wondered if she should ask him about the papers she had seen in his carriage, but to do so would expose her prying through them. She had no desire to deepen any doubts they had of each other. Then Seth answered her unasked question anyway.

"I am starting my own mill."

But the way he said it made it sound like a shameful confession.

"It is a venture my father doesn't know about. I placed an order for the material needed for construction just before leaving for London. It will be unlike anything else in Scotland. It will be safer, more productive." As he spoke, he warmed to his vision for the business. "I hope, when we return, that work will have started on cutting a channel from one of the burns that feeds the River Cart. We'll be using a water wheel to power the looms at first and then making them steam powered… I'm sorry, I must be boring you."

For the first time since they had met, Ruby could finally tell the truth.

"No, not at all. In fact, I find it fascinating."

Seth shook his head, "You are the most remarkable woman I've ever met."

CHAPTER TEN

RUBY TURNED AWAY from him once more. She seemed uncomfortable with praise. And yet, she remained beside him. So, he would take that as an indication that she didn't find his manner completely repugnant.

He had welcomed stretching his legs. He'd lasted exactly three hours in his father's company before he persuaded the most taciturn footman he could find to sit with the man for a while.

Even riding postilion was more enjoyable than sitting with his father. But the silence between himself and Ruby was more uncomfortable. They'd come to a stop by a blackberry bush in full fruit. He plucked a handful of berries as he searched for something to say to her.

"You mentioned your father was in trade."

Now how had he remembered such a thing? The truth of the matter was he was scrambling for any conversational gambit to learn more about Ruby Campbell.

He popped one of the berries in his mouth before he could say something foolish. The dark, delicious fruit, warm from the sun, burst in his mouth as he bit down on it, the flavor sweet.

He held his hand open to offer one of the five berries still in his palm. Ruby shook her head, but at least he got a smile from her.

"He was a well-respected man in our community," she began

at last. "Some called him laird, but he was no one of consequence. He loved understanding how things worked. And he was never afraid of getting his hands dirty."

She paused in her telling. Seth wondered whether that would be all. The smile returned, apparently recalling a fond memory. He hoped she'd continue.

"One day, our butler discovered that my father had disassembled the entire workings of a longcase clock. The poor man nearly had a fit. My father looked up at him, calmly as you please, and said to let him know when it was four o'clock precisely because he intended to make sure the clock chimed on time."

This time, Ruby looked at him directly. The tease of her smile was remarkable. Not only was she interesting, she was *beautiful*. Seth felt anticipation building in his chest.

"Well, the butler was even more horrified," she continued. "'But sir!' he said, 'that clock doesn't have a bell!'"

Seth burst out laughing.

It was a laugh that began gut deep and welled up until it spilled over. The voice of his father warned him that it wasn't seemly to show his emotions too easily, and judging by the expression on Ruby's face, she didn't expect her tale to receive quite such an uproarious reaction.

Her look of confusion was soon replaced by another that, if he was not so out of touch with the female of the species, he would have said looked remarkably like warmth.

"I think I'd have liked your father," he said, recovering himself.

He waited for the shutters to come down on her expression again and, indeed, he saw the hesitancy there, a slight furrow of the brow as she considered something, then it faded.

"I think he would have liked you, too."

He offered her the berries once again. This time, Ruby took one from his hand and popped it in her mouth.

Was he now on firmer footing with her? He hoped so. But he knew better than to take anything for granted, so he said nothing and allowed them to walk a little further on before turning and looking back at the camp.

There, he could see two footmen gingerly placing the duke in his bath chair in the shade. The man looked all skin and bones.

Ruby had apparently noticed what had caught his attention.

"Why do you stay with him when it is clear you hold each other in disdain? You could have refused his request and returned home."

Seth shrugged.

"I intend to show him I am not the useless, disappointing failure he supposes of me."

Ruby gasped, but he didn't look at her.

He couldn't, not if he might see pity there. Instead, he kept his eyes on the man who he loved and hated in equal measure; the man who had betrayed him, and who he was planning to betray in turn.

Only Roddy knew of his plans, but Ruby would be the only one to *understand*.

"I suppose my motives for returning *are* selfish ones. My father thought exiling me to work in his mill was a punishment. Instead, I found my vocation. The looms fascinated me. It seemed a miracle that so many strands of cotton or wool or silk could be turned into yards and yards of fabric. So, I made it my business to learn everything, from the carding through to selling the finished goods.

"When it became obvious my father cared little about the business other than his quarterly dividend, I took over the running of it. I made sure I returned him a profit, and he never interfered in how I ran things. And he has no idea I plan to open a mill of my own, in my own name."

He dared a glance at her then.

"Why would you walk away from a business you made a success of? You're his son, an earl, his heir. I still don't understand why he treats you this way."

"I wear glasses. My father sees that as a weakness."

"They're hardly anything of the sort."

"My need for correction put me behind in my schooling. And once my father had determined I was a dunce, there was nothing to change his mind, not even my mother."

"She was your greatest advocate?"

Ruby had put her finger right on the bruise. After more than twenty years, it still ached.

He couldn't answer. He'd never spoken to anyone about his mother.

Once her body had been laid into the ground, he had been whisked back to school, back down to London where no one knew or particularly cared for his grief. He threw himself into not only catching up with his school fellows, but working even harder to best them and prove himself.

And even that hadn't been enough.

He felt the touch of her hand in his. He returned the squeeze, but then let go. This was too raw. He slammed the door on his emotions for his own protection.

"Well," he began hoarsely, "who needs an advocate when you can stand on your own two feet? Isn't that right, Nurse Campbell?"

THE CHANGE OF mood was so abrupt, Ruby thought she'd dreamed the entire encounter. Brutally snapped back into wakefulness, she watched Seth take a few paces away before he turned back to look at her.

"May I escort you back to camp?"

Ruby shook her head.

"I wish to walk a little more."

Seth simply nodded. His eyes seemed haunted, lonely. He turned back to the camp. She watched him square his shoulders and move briskly toward a group of men to help erect another tent.

Ruby turned away and walked several dozen yards beyond a curve in the road. Out of view of the encampment, in long grass off the road, she attended to her most pressing needs. But mostly, she needed a few minutes of solitude.

What was happening was perilous. She never counted on developing such tender feelings for Seth. But here he was, exchanging confidences with her as though they were already lovers.

Lovers.

Her body reacted to that thought, recalling the feel of his arms around her and the devastating power of his kisses.

He had opened himself up to her, trusted her. Surely she could trust him with her secret in return?

How lovely it would be to unburden herself to someone who understood only too well what a scoundrel the Duke of Auchen was. And to think she was becoming sentimental and feeling sorry for the man.

She worried a stone from the road with the toe of her boot until it loosened. She kicked it. A stolen fortune and a stolen childhood – how *dare* he? How dare that man pretend to be so put upon by fate? Did the villain know how many lives he had ruined?

Ruby began to walk back, and the edge of the camp came in sight. As she drew nearer, she heard the duke's raised voice. Where was Seth?

She quickened her steps.

No. Now was *not* the time to tell Seth. After they got the duke safely to Scotland – then she would confess all.

She took a deep breath and headed toward her obstreperous patient.

"You!" The duke saw her and raised a bony arm in her direction. "Do I pay you to gambol through the meadow like a goat? No, I don't! I pay you to tend me, you stupid girl!"

The men about shared sympathetic looks in her direction, but

Ruby kept her focus on the duke.

"Do you wish for anything, Your Grace? Are you in pain?" she responded with exaggerated kindness.

She was pretty sure he was not. He was not due for another dose of his medicine until after he had eaten. "Are you hungry? If it is the latter, I shall find you something to eat since I believe supper is some time off."

"I don't pay you to patronize me either," the man sneered. "Make yourself useful and bring me a dram of whisky – and not adulterated with that poison Dr. Brooks gave you."

She dropped an exaggerated curtsy and left to prepare him a whisky tonic – ground spices – cinnamon, peppercorn, clove, cardamom, ginger and nutmeg. He might object to the additions, but they eased his cough and helped stop the tremors he would acquire when the evening became cooler.

They'd been blessed with fine weather over the past few days, and this evening was shaping up to be the same. The lowering sun cast golden rays against the blue-gray sky, silhouetting a horse and cart ambling up the road. Roddy and a couple of other men went out to greet the party.

They came from a nearby inn with food and drink for the evening. Roddy had everything organized with military precision. She had never given any thought to Seth's friend. Had he been in the army? How did he come to work for Seth?

Ruby turned her attention back to the duke. He had settled down after she had given him the dram. Now, he was *too* quiet. She picked up a lighted lamp and raised the wick. The chimney filled with light.

The duke was awake. He seemed aware of what was going on, yet offered no criticism of how the camp was arranged. He hadn't even complained about the spices she had added to his whisky. She suspected he would if he had the energy. No doubt, he would complain about the size of the fire, the quality of the food, or the off-tune whistling from one of the men.

His end was near. Did he sense it?

Seth approached. "Has His Grace eaten?"

"He has. I've asked the footmen to have him returned to the carriage to sleep."

"Once he's bedded down for the night, we'll get some sleep also. I want to be on the road at first light."

"How soon do you think we'll be in Glasgow?"

"Seven days if the weather remains dry. If not..." He shrugged his shoulders, then nodded over to his father. "It depends on how stubborn *he* is."

Ruby nodded, glancing at the duke. The man hated being talked about as though he was not there, but yet now he said nothing.

That worried her more than his temper.

"Helen?"

Ruby started awake from a doze but, grateful Seth's offer to have her accompanied during her night watch had gone by the way, she found the presence of mind to answer as if she were the woman who the duke believed himself talking to.

"Yes, Uilleam?"

"It's dark in here. I cannot see you."

"I am here."

"Speak to me, dear Helen. Speak to me so I know I'm not alone." There was an edge of panic in his voice.

Ruby hesitated. This was her chance. She could speak empty words of comfort, or she could use the opportunity to press her father's cause.

"Do you remember a man called McAllister?" she whispered.

Silence from the duke. She prompted further.

"He came to speak to you about the mill."

"Yes. I remember. He had an invention..."

Ruby's pulse quickened.

Yes... yes...

She forced serenity into her voice against rising excitement. "That's right, Uilleam. I remember you were impressed by it."

She bit her lip and waited. There came nothing but labored breathing and more silence. She pressed.

"You never fulfilled your promise toward that man, did you, Uilleam?"

He groaned.

A lantern, its wick low, stood on the narrow seat opposite her. She raised the wick and felt a pang of guilt for pressing on as she had. The duke's face shone with sweat. His face was contorted in pain. She reached below the bed to her apothecary box and rapidly prepared him a sedative.

Her hands shook as she spooned the liquid slowly into his mouth to ensure he didn't choke. The glass was finished before the groans subsided.

Soon after, the duke fell into a deep sleep.

Ruby thought nothing of his condition until the morning when the most she could rouse from him was a semi-conscious state.

"Your Grace! Your Grace! Wake up," she called out.

The door to the coach opened. She was hoping to see Seth. Instead, it was one of the footmen.

"Get the earl, now!"

The young man disappeared in a rush. With hands shaking, Ruby wet a cloth and wiped the duke's face and down his arms to his hands. She picked up his wrist and felt his racing pulse through her fingers.

The carriage tilted on its suspension. She didn't need to look round to know who it was climbing up.

"How long has been like this?"

She bit back a sob before Seth could hear her. "Since last night. I thought nothing of it, only that he was sleeping well, but I can't rouse him now."

Seth's hand rested on her shoulder.

"I'm sure you've done all you can."

Ruby chanced a glance back. He'd not shaved yet this morning. His shirt hung open and loose. In his haste, he'd not even dressed properly. He seemed to thrum with energy, like a bow string pulled tight.

His hand moved from her shoulder to her cheek where he stroked it. When he took his hand away, it was wet with tears. Her tears.

Worse – she didn't even know for whom she shed them. For the duke? For Seth? Or was her pity just for herself?

He leaned closer. In her distress, Ruby thought he was going to kiss her, but Seth reached past to where his father lay, mouth open. Only the slightest rise and fall of his chest indicated that the man lived.

Seth stared into his face for a moment, then looked back to Ruby.

"I promised I'd get him to Scotland," he whispered harshly. "And by God, I'm going to keep my word."

CHAPTER ELEVEN

T HE NEXT DAYS passed like a nightmare. Coaching stops were a blur, kept as short as possible, often only long enough to change the horses and that was all.

Ruby's every waking moment was spent sitting beside the duke, watching for any sign that the ailing man was slipping further from this life into the next.

With his sharp tongue and cruel words quieted, she saw him once more as a fragile, dying creature, deserving of her pity as well as her nursing care. As much as she hated him, she did not want him to die before his time.

Before getting what you want out of him...

She shoved the sour voice of conscience down. She had worked toward this for six months, endured the toil of his care for two. She had promised on her parents' graves that she would see the duke pay for his deceit.

Too late, it was all too late...

Two days became three, and the duke's condition did not change. He seemed caught between two worlds. He breathed without too much difficulty and swallowed when she spooned food into his mouth, but he did not respond to questions, nor offer any words of his own. Her self-reproaching conscience punished her, saying it was she who had pushed him to the edge.

Seth was worried for his father, too. He didn't say it, but she witnessed it in his face whenever he came to check on them – which was often.

Strange how love and hate were so intertwined.

She tried reading to the duke from the book of poetry but, in the end, could not. Nor could she endure endless hours in silence. So, she spoke quietly about her childhood and her father, how clever he was, and how hard he worked.

She had no idea if the duke could hear her, but the more she spoke about the man she had loved and admired, the better she felt. If nothing more happened, if the duke passed away, at least he would have heard about her father, even if he never knew it was Jacob McCallister.

Then, having run out of words to speak, Ruby found herself singing a folk song her father used to sing to her as a bairn. Much later, when she was older, she would hear her father singing to himself as he tinkered with his inventions. If she closed her eyes, she could imagine herself back at Strathaird on a fine summer's day, walking out to the part of the old stable block where Father had his workshop...

There once was a troop o' Irish dragoons
Cam marching doon through Fyvie-o
And the captain's fa'en in love wi' a very bonnie lass
And her name it was ca'd pretty Peggy-o

"Papa?" young Ruby called softly.

She slipped around the door, smiling at the fact her father hadn't heard her.

There's many a bonnie lass in the Howe o Auchterless
There's many a bonnie lass in the Garioch
There's many a bonnie Jean in the streets of Aiberdeen
But the floower o' them aw lies in Fyvie-o

She watched him hunched over a lathe, rocking back and

forward, and singing in time with the foot treadle he worked while fashioning something important. Ruby loved watching him work when he wasn't aware of it. She would admire this man she loved with all her heart, and try to puzzle out his task, trying to see the world as he saw it.

"What are you making, Papa?"

He did not miss a beat. The steady motion continued.

"I want to see if the shape of the shuttle will make a difference on how quickly and easily a pirn can be replaced when it needs refilling."

"Why, Papa?"

"Because it will make weaving cloth faster, and so weavers won't have to use their teeth to remove the pin."

Ruby ventured closer to get a better look.

So focused was she on what her father was working on, she didn't see how close she had come to the flywheel. She gasped as she was violently pulled away from the spinning disc. Immediately, she burst into tears.

"Papa! I'm sorry! I'm sorry!"

"Ruby, my lassie, you need to take care!"

She accepted her father's comforting embrace.

"You're a curious girl, and I like to encourage that in you, but workshops are dangerous places; mills, too. I've seen little boys not much older than you lose fingers on the looms. I don't want such a thing to happen to you."

Her hiccoughing sobs subsided. She nodded against the flannel of her father's shirt. He held her away from him so she could see his face.

"Now then – dry those tears."

He brought his hand to her cheek – a tender gesture, one that told her more than words how much she was loved.

Strange how his touch still felt warm and real after all these years…

"Time for real rest, Sleeping Beauty."

Ruby started awake. The man before her was not her father,

but Seth, leaning toward her from the facing seat.

He peered at her through his glasses, the silver wire framing his blue eyes. A skilled watercolorist couldn't have hoped to capture their hue.

Ruby scrambled to a sitting position, ignoring the racing of her heart. Her neck ached from slumping in her seat.

"It can't be, not yet, we're still moving," she protested.

Seth laughed. "You slept through an entire change of horses."

"You must think me very derelict in my duties," she answered, smoothing down her skirts for want of something better to do than just stare at him.

"I think you work too hard for too little rest and too little compensation."

Her eyes fell away from his. "My service is its own reward." She hated the lie the minute it left her lips.

She wondered if he believed it, especially when the silence lengthened for a moment before he chose to change the subject.

"Does my father's condition improve or does it worsen?" he asked, nodding toward him.

Ruby turned to her patient. He lay unmoving apart from the rise and fall of his chest and a twitch behind closed eyelids.

"It has not changed."

Seth nodded.

"We'll be home soon."

It was a prayer and a wish at once. Seth rapped on the roof of the carriage and a small hatch opened over his head.

"As fast as the horses will take it, Henry."

"Aye, Yer Lordship."

Ruby heard the coachman yell "hei" to the horses. The carriage lurched, throwing her forward. Seth caught her by the elbows, his touch firm but gentle. She was aware their knees touched, and she wished for nothing more than to be pulled into his arms and held. As though he'd heard her wish, he pulled her into his arms and onto his lap.

She put her arms around him and rested her head against his

shoulder. They stayed that way for a little while, the rocking motion of the carriage soothing. She took comfort in just being held, knowing that, in turn, she was providing solace to someone who needed it just as much.

"I don't know what I would do without you, Ruby," Seth whispered.

She closed her eyes and sighed against the eddy of warmth that filled her ear.

"When I feel overwhelmed about my father's care, you are there, stoic and calm. I'm beginning to fall in love with you."

"Oh, Seth," she whispered.

"Tell me, what can I give you in return?"

"Just hold me."

That was all she dared ask. Her emotions ran close to the surface. In this man, she had an ally, a friend. She dared not hope for more. It would be impossible. She could be nothing more to him than a temporary diversion. And yet, she could not deny the fact that now that she was in his arms, she wanted to stay there forever.

"What will I do when you go?" he whispered.

"Let's not think about it. Not now."

She placed a kiss on his cheek now bristled with stubble. He turned his face, and her next kiss was on his lips.

The truth of the matter was she didn't *know* what she was going to do after the duke's death, even if there was any hope at all of seeing justice for her father.

It certainly wasn't going to get Strathaird back into her hands.

Ruby gave herself into the kiss, and Seth didn't seem in any hurry to conclude it. His hands slid from her shoulder to her waist, the tips of his fingers brushing the side of her breast as they passed. She sighed with the unexpected pleasure of it, but knowing this had to stop, had already gone too far, not least of which because the duke in his sickbed might awaken at any moment.

WHO WAS HE kidding when he told her that he was *beginning* to fall in love with her? He was already in love – as near as he understood it to be. All he knew at that moment was that being with her was right.

The more he held her, the more he wanted her, to lose himself in her. He wanted to understand her, know her thoughts and desires and fulfill them in every way possible.

Although she had not returned his sentiment in so many words, the fact that she sat on his lap, matching his kisses enthusiastically, had to count for *something*.

He wasn't too much like his father to admit he was scared of how he felt. What did it say about him that the only woman to this point who had touched his heart and soul was his own mother?

He had to stop.

Fortunately, Ruby made the decision for him, breaking off the kiss and touching his cheek as he had done to her. Still, she made no move to leave his lap. Indeed, she remained in his embrace and seemed to be in no hurry to leave it.

"What are we to do?" she whispered.

Five simple words, but the question asked was not to be answered so simply.

Every mile traveled brought them closer to Scotland.

Every minute that passed brought his father closer to the end of his life, and there was so much unfinished business between son and sire.

And what of the future? He struggled to think beyond his responsibilities in the here and now, let alone taking on his father's mantle as duke. Everything he had achieved in his life was done to prove to his father that he was worthy of the man's regard. What did it really profit him if his father died without seeing what he had accomplished, and without hearing the words he desperately wanted to hear?

Well done, my son.

Seth realized that he hadn't given Ruby an answer. *What are we to do?* He embraced her and kissed her hair.

"We take each day as it comes."

THREE DAYS LATER, Ruby watched impassively as the servants from Castle Glenuig carefully stretchered the duke out of the coach.

She couldn't muster the energy to do more than feel a wave of relief that the ultimate responsibility for the duke's care lay in others' hands again.

The doctor already waited at the door. He was large man with a full salt and pepper beard. Another, younger man stood alongside him. An apprentice, she assumed.

She was startled out of her stupor by a passing footman. Ruby turned to reach back into the carriage for the apothecary's case when Seth reached over her to take the heavy box himself.

Good.

In her state, she was sure she would drop it. She still had enough presence of mind to keep the journals that chronicled the duke's condition from sliding off one of the seats. She clasped them to her chest and followed the others inside.

Together, the group trudged upstairs following the footmen and the retinue of servants.

She was conscious of how exhausted she was, yet Seth seemed utterly unaffected by their journey, though tension radiated from him. It galvanized the lethargy from her bones and gave her the energy to carry on.

By the time she'd climbed the flight of stairs and found herself in the ducal suite, the doctor and his assistant were hovering over the man, making a thorough examination of their patient.

"Ye're the nurse who accompanied him?" asked the gruff doctor.

Ruby nodded and found her voice. "I am." She handed over the books to the assistant's outstretched hands. "And this is the record of his care since I was employed."

The man seemed surprised and the curtness in his manner softened a little.

"An estimable job, bringing His Grace back to Scotland. I'm sure his family is grateful for yer service, Nurse…" he flipped the cover of the book to read her name. "Campbell."

Just like that, she was dismissed. The apprentice began reading out the entries of medicine doses from the beginning while the doctor examined the contents of the apothecary box.

Ruby offered a belated curtsy. She glanced to Seth who remained in the room, his arms folded, silently watching. Despite his show of energy, she could see the exhaustion in his eyes. The stubble on his cheeks had grown another day, deepening the planes of his cheeks, and making him look every inch a Scottish warrior as his forebears would have been.

She slipped out of the room.

A maid hovered outside the door.

"Nurse, we have a room in the servants' quarters set up, and –"

"No."

The maid swallowed her words at the earl's interruption. He filled the doorway behind Ruby.

"Miss Campbell is a guest. Prepare one of the rooms for her then come find her downstairs."

The maid gulped again, curtsied, and ran off.

"You don't have to do this," Ruby protested.

Seth shook his head.

"No arguments. You at least deserve a good night's rest for everything you've done."

She wished she could argue with him, but every limb was leaden, even forming a coherent sentence was now beyond her.

She nodded her acquiescence. He found the energy to grin, obviously pleased to have gotten his way with little argument.

CHAPTER TWELVE

A SHORT WHILE later, Seth watched Ruby wearily follow the maid back upstairs. and his heart went out to her. She would rest now. He would make sure of it.

Roddy approached. "Where do ye want me to put yer kit?"

He had been a stalwart support these past two months, but the man was chafing at having to remember his manners and his role of manservant in this setting.

Seth caught the butler's briefly scandalized expression before the man righted it. "And prepare another guest room for your friend, My Lord Musgrave?" he asked.

Seth nodded in the affirmative and addressed his next comments to Roddy. "Take your rest while you can get it. Tomorrow, we get back to work."

Roddy flashed him a grin.

"Right ye are then!"

As for himself, Seth ignored his own exhaustion and forced himself to find a second wind, drawing it from the buzz of activity in the house as the servants moved with alacrity to accommodate the return of the long-absent duke and his much longer absent son.

Having things to do kept the memories of his childhood at bay.

Being the one to give orders, and have them obeyed, gave

him a bulwark against the uncertainty he felt at being addressed as "His Lordship".

With his instructions being carried out with the efficiency an earl might expect, Seth now found himself alone in his father's study with an unrequested tumbler of whisky left for him on the desk.

He savored a mouthful of the fiery liquid, and considered what lay ahead. It wasn't just Roddy who was itching to get back to the mills. There was so much to do if they were to open Habetrot before the end of autumn. They had to talk to the dyers, spinners and weavers at Skye-Heath to see who would be willing to follow them there.

With his new process installed on the looms, he would specialize in making fine quality shot silk at a much more affordable price, undercutting Skye-Heath for the custom of the growing well-to-do merchant class as well as the aristocracy.

Once achieved, he would rub his father's nose in it if the man still lived. Either way, the duke could go hell with his blessing.

The best laid plans of mice and men often go awry.

Seth curled his lip and shook his head at the thought which had randomly appeared.

Well, thank you very much Robby-bloody-Burns.

After such a long and hard journey confined in a carriage, Seth could no longer bear to be indoors. Even Castle Glenuig felt suffocated by his father's presence.

He slugged down the remains of the whisky and went in search of space and solitude in the grounds.

All of his adult life, Seth had armed himself in preparation for the day when he would slay the dragon. Now, fully girded, sword in hand, he'd found his enemy was nothing more than a tiny lizard, unable to cause any harm.

What surprised him most of all was acknowledging in his heart that he didn't actually *hate* the man.

He felt *sorry* for him.

Seth was disappointed and a little ashamed of himself. The

plans had made so much sense when played out in his mind. He had rehearsed them, again, again and again. All the players knew their lines and when the curtain came down, the audience would rise with thunderous applause.

Now his plans for revenge seemed pointless. His father was too weak to see his *coup de grace*. Judging by the weighty looks from the doctor and his assistant, the Duke of Auchen was as good as dead already.

He might not even get his dying wish of seeing Mother's grave.

A sharp pain pierced Seth's chest. He fought it. He was a grown man; he shouldn't feel a child's despair at his mother's loss – but he did.

He glanced toward the house searching for the window to his father's suite. He half-wondered whether he should call on him. He decided against it.

It was three o'clock. The sun wouldn't be down for hours yet. Seth found the door into the walled garden. Despite the fact that it was summer, most of the raised garden beds lay fallow.

Across from him were apple trees, espaliered along the inside walls. They were still tended, at least.

That made him unaccountably glad. He approached the nearest tree, pleased to see it bearing unripened fruit. He recalled that, unusually, these apples would not ripen red. These were dark yellow in color, turning to orange when they fully ripened.

Seth smiled to himself. He hadn't thought of those apples for years. He was transported back to being a child walking hand-in-hand with his mother. His poor eyesight had not been recognized then. Indeed, he hadn't known any different, but seeing these beautiful blurred globes of golden yellow, he'd rather fancied they were actually made of gold, and that's how his father's fortune was made.

It grew on trees.

Seth approached the orchard. Leaves that had blown in from the woods outside these walls were desiccated and crunched underfoot.

A small water fountain made in the style of Grecian urns that should have provided cool relief from the summer heat was green with slime from years of disuse.

How long had it been since anyone but the gardener had stepped out here?

The only indication beyond the espaliered trees that the garden hadn't been completely abandoned was that one of the beds, which would once have had exotic ornamental plants, had become a secondary kitchen garden.

But at least the apples were well-tended.

He remembered asking his mother about them. She told him a tale, but he couldn't remember a lot of it – something about a man who had been given a golden apple by the gods to present to the most beautiful woman in the world.

Something like that. He couldn't quite remember.

Seth wrapped his hand around one of the part-ripened fruits and tugged. It fell into his palm. He ran his hands over its smooth, unblemished skin.

His father must have thought a lot of his mother to indulge a fancy for an exotic variety of apple such as this. Did he love her so very much? Was there a time when he was a better man?

These were the questions he couldn't ask his mother. Soon, he would not be able to ask his father. Did the romantic fool who performed such an elaborate gesture still exist inside the husk of the bitter man in the suite upstairs?

Seth sniffed the fruit, then took a bite. Because it was not ripe, there was tartness as well as sweet.

Much like Miss Ruby Campbell.

He'd be lying if he said she hadn't occupied much of his thoughts during their journey.

Her secret past for one. The truth was he knew as much about her past now as he did months ago. And nearly everything he knew about her came merely from observation.

There was much to admire – for instance, a steady calm to the point of being quite unshakeable even in the midst of his father's tirades. She was kind and intelligent, with a good practical common sense that he preferred.

And yet she had the manner of a gentle-born woman... the daughter of a laird, or so she'd told him.

Still, the honorific was used with such abandon in Scotland that it might mean something, or it might not.

What might it be like to take Miss Ruby Campbell as his lover? An image flashed in his mind of her naked body wrapped around his. He'd already tasted her kisses. There was a passion beneath the surface of the starched cap and severe dresses that he wanted to explore.

He wandered aimlessly through the garden and, unbidden, found the handful of apple a poor substitute for the handful of breast he would rather be touching.

He allowed himself to indulge his fantasy for a while. What harm could there be in it? He'd lived like a monk for months. Desired passions of the flesh he had subsumed into passion for his new mill. But still, a man had needs, and he'd neglected them, pushed them aside – until he'd set eyes on Ruby.

He glanced toward the house and imagined sneaking into her room, awakening her with kisses, touching her, feeling her warmth, the silky feel of her skin beneath his fingers, seeing her respond to him. Seth felt the beginning of an erection against the fall of his breeches.

Dangerous thoughts, man. Dangerous thoughts, indeed.

RUBY PRESSED HERSELF closer to Seth, his lips masterful on hers. His hands loosened the stays at her back. Clever fingers trailed fire down her arms and across her neck where he tugged down the yoke of her dress. She gasped at his boldness. The blue of his eyes glittered as though he'd already won, though she had not said a word. His touch disarmed her. His look challenged her to tell him to stop, but she wouldn't. How could she when he made her body feel so alive? And when his lips followed the trail of his fingers, she was undone. She wanted him…

Something intruded in her dream. Ruby kept her eyes closed to hold on to the vision before it disappeared and the whispers of feminine voices pulled her from her slumber. Her eyes insisted on remaining resolutely shut, but she must have sighed or shifted or something because the voices stopped.

She opened her eyes reluctantly.

Two housemaids stood a respectful distance away from the bed and curtsied, one and then the other.

"We're sorry for disturbing yer rest, Miss," said one.

"But His Lordship said to let ye sleep as long as ye wanted to. But it's the middle of the morning now."

Ruby shook her head and sat up in bed. It was one thing to dream of Seth in the privacy of her own thoughts, another to be reminded that he was not only a man, but "His Lordship".

"That's fine. I ought to be up anyway," she said. There was a little matter of the real reason why she was here – not just tender feelings for a soul who seemed as lost as she was. "Is there any word about His Grace?"

The two maids looked to one another. Ruby's heart sank. Had he already passed away?

"No, Miss," answered the elder of the two, "no words that we've been told."

Time to pull yourself together, Ruby.

"And His Lordship?"

"He's somewhere about the house, I think."

Ruby pulled back the blankets and set her feet on the floor. No sooner had she done that than the two maids began attending to their tasks. One drew open the curtains, filling the room with light, while the other poured the ewer of still steaming water into a bowl before departing with an uncertain curtsy.

She had to smile at that. No doubt, word had gotten around that the earl had ordered a servant be given a room befitting an honored guest. Indeed, the dark blue gown which served as her uniform while in the duke's service had been hung up to air. If she wasn't mistaken, it had also been sponged down while she slept.

Ruby smiled to herself as she unplaited her hair and ran her hand through it to loosen the dark curls until they tumbled over her shoulders and down her back.

Ah, the maids had even laid out her comb on the dressing table.

It had been such a long time since she'd had servants waiting on her. Not since she'd left Strathaird.

She picked up a comb and began drawing it through her hair. What she wouldn't give to see her beloved home again.

It might not have been the biggest estate in Scotland, but it was home, and luxurious nonetheless. She loved roaming the woods that led to the waterway known as the White Cart. Ruby and her cousins spent summers exploring the woods and tramping along the banks.

It was a place Seth would love.

The lavender-scented soap brought back memories of home; the feel of her hands as she washed became a physical reminder of Seth's embrace. She savored the arousal even though it remained unfulfilled.

What to do?

Was it wrong of her to try to get back that which had been taken from her? She was a Scotswoman, entitled to use the title of Lady Strathaird. She ought to have the land and the home to go with it, too.

If Seth could see Strathaird as she did, he would understand why she worked under an assumed name. She supposed he'd guessed much of her story. What harm could it do for him to learn of the rest – especially now that the duke was unlikely to recover from his travel north?

William Gregory Musgrave would die never knowing that she knew of his deceit. He would die, and she would be left in no better state than she was when she first lost Strathaird.

She reached for the plain blue gown with distaste. She was

sick of wearing the damned thing. She dreamed of wearing fashionable clothes again. All of her wardrobe, apart from three plain dresses, had been left in the care of Cousin Frances in London.

She would write and let her know they had finally made their destination, and give her an address to finally write back. Ruby missed her. They'd shared every confidence – until now. She didn't dare commit to paper an accounting of the kisses with Seth Musgrave. It was a complication she was still trying to figure out for herself.

She hadn't meant to fall in love with him. But he was kind, honorable, a sensitive soul, and she had fallen for him.

Did he feel the same about her? Or were his feelings merely that of the fellow traveler who would part at the first fork in the road when the path that had led them to this moment ran its course?

She put on the wretched blue dress and worked on pinning her hair, watching her reflection in the mirror as she did so. Lady Strathaird became dutiful Nurse Campbell once more. Regardless of her personal feelings, she had forged for herself an obligation to the duke to care for him. To make his final days comfortable…

RUBY SOUGHT OUT a late breakfast from the kitchen, ate quickly, then made her way to the duke's room on the same floor as her own. An older woman sat in a chair in the room, looking out of the window and idling away the hours with her knitting. She hadn't heard Ruby's entrance and stood in surprise when approached.

"Och, ye're His Grace's nurse!"

Ruby put a finger to her lips to quiet the woman, lest the duke awaken.

"Has there been any change to his condition?" she asked, keeping her voice low.

The woman shook her head. "The doctor's potion has kept him quiet. I havenae had to give him anything."

"Does he show signs of distress?"

"No, Ma'am."

"Very well. You may go."

The woman looked at her uncertainly, no doubt wondering whether the younger woman before her was in any position to give orders. But, nevertheless, she did so, perhaps persuaded by the authority with which she had been dismissed.

When the door closed behind the woman, Ruby ventured closer to the duke. His face was flushed, but he seemed to be breathing evenly and presumably without pain.

She found the book of poetry on a nearby console table, drew a chair near to the bed, and began to read.

So often forging peace, so often fighting,
So often breaking up, and then re-forming,
So often blaming Love, so often praising,
So often searching out, so often fleeing,
So often hiding ourselves, so often revealing,
So often under the yoke, so often freeing,
Making our promises and then retracting,
Are signs that Love strikes at our very being.
A sign of love is this loving inconstancy.
If in a moment feeling both hate and pity,
Vowing, un-vowing, oaths sworn and un-sworn,
Hoping that's hopeless, comfort that's comfortless,
Are true love signs, then our love's of the best,
Since we are always at peace, or at war.

"Helen…"

The word might have easily been a groan, but Ruby was so used to his voice by now that she recognized it. She hardened her heart, remembering her task, yet grieved also for the pain in the man's soul.

"I am here, *Uilleam*."

His next words were indistinguishable from groans. She set the book down and leaned in closer.

"We'll be together soon," she said softly, "but you know what you must do, don't you? There are things you need to put right before you go, isn't that true?"

His groans became breathless pants.

Ruby whispered into his ear. "*Uilleam*, shhh, shhh. All will be well. Listen to me. When your soul and your conscience are at ease *then* we will be together again."

The duke groaned, so she did not hear the door open – but she heard it close.

She started and looked up.

Standing at the door was Seth, peering at her through his reading glasses.

CHAPTER THIRTEEN

*H*AD HE HEARD *her?*
     Ruby held her breath. It seemed that even her own heart stopped beating. She watched him cautiously, but Seth's attention was fixed on his father's pallid face.

"Is he…?"

She looked back at the duke. His chest rose and fell almost imperceptibly. She turned back to Seth, started to shake her head, then stopped, concerned that it would be misinterpreted.

Ruby let out a ragged breath. "No, he's still with us."

Seth ventured further into the room and nodded at the book in her lap.

"You read to him? Even though he can't hear?"

She shook her head. "That's where you're wrong. I believe he can hear – especially when I read something he likes."

He was close enough to reach down and pick up the book from her lap. The intimacy of the action set her heart beating again, now in triple time.

He opened a page at random and read, frowning, then turning the book over to read the spine.

"Poetry."

The word was said flatly.

"Yes, poetry."

Another voice spoke those words.

Ruby started. So, too, did Seth. The duke's eyes were open, looking brighter than they had been in days.

"Pearls before swine," Seth offered.

Ruby gasped at his unkind comment, but saw the duke's mouth split into a grin.

"You still here, Boy?"

"Just until you're dead, old man."

The duke appeared to rally.

"You'll not be rid of me so easily."

Ruby rose to her feet to leave the room.

The duke turned his head. Indeed, his face seem livelier, more suffused with color.

"No home to go to, Campbell?" he sneered. "Hanging around here like a stray cat?"

She glared at the man openly, which seemed to delight him further. She dropped a reluctant curtsy before leaving by the closest door.

She'd walked to it without thinking, her heart still pounding from Seth's surprise arrival and the duke's unexpected lucidity. Look well if it was a closet.

It was only after the door was closed behind her that she realized she'd entered another bedroom, darkened by heavy, sage green drapes that covered the windows and protected the room and furnishings from the sun.

Through the closed door, she could hear the muffled conversation between father and son. Mostly son. But the tone seemed civil enough.

There was another door she assumed led out onto the passageway. But instead of exiting by it, she crossed to the windows and drew back the drapes to let in just enough light to see.

The room was slightly smaller than the duke's suite, and feminine in nature.

Fit for a duchess.

Standing opposite the door through which she'd entered, the canopied bed was the largest single piece of furniture in the room.

The outer bedcurtains were a green, a shade lighter than the curtains, and lined in a rose-pink silk.

The nightstand beside it was made of a golden-colored wood – cherry wood, most likely.

Ruby grazed her fingers along the wall coverings – large swathes of watered silk in the palest mint green were set into white-painted timber panels.

Would the silk have come from Skye-Heath's own mills?

A large gilt mirror, elaborately carved, stood over a dressing table. Atop the dressing table were porcelain trinket boxes, hand painted with garlands of flowers surrounding a cartouche featuring a monogram – the initials GCM.

This had been Georgiana's room.

Two tall armoires drew Ruby's attention next. She approached the closest of them. It was unlocked. Inside, a rainbow of silks and satins lay unworn. Prickles went up her spine. She felt watched.

She looked around. There was no one here but her.

Then she noticed. The furniture was not covered with canvases. Nor was it covered in dust. Although Castle Glenuig's owner was long absent, and this room's occupant long dead, it was tended as if master *and* mistress were due home at any moment.

Ruby took a deep breath. She closed the wardrobe door to gaze about the room once more. The woman who once slept here had passed away, but her life cast a long shadow over the two men in the room next door.

Ruby ought not be so curious.

But she *was*.

All she knew of the late duchess was gleaned from the recollection of the housekeeper in London – and what Ruby had discerned from Georgiana's portrait in the gallery – a forthright and beautiful mother, protective of her child, and resolute enough to withstand the duke's formidable temper.

She believed the duke had listened to her, respected her, and even loved her in his own way. Now he wanted to be reunited with her.

Ruby found herself in front of the unlocked armoire once again.

Did Georgiana keep the gown she was painted in?

Curiosity got the better of her.

She opened the wardrobe and ran a hand through the dresses – wool, muslin, silks – until her fingers fell upon the white and gold gown from the portrait.

She drew it out to better look at it. It was indeed as glorious at the portrait artist depicted, his attention to detail a testament to his talent as an artist. The gold lace and ribbon on the dress had not tarnished with age. Looking closer, she saw the trim, with its intricate repeating pattern of golden apples and the horse, was not natural but made deliberately "blocky" as one would expect from a Trojan Horse.

Helen.

She raised the garment to her nose and fancied she could smell the sweet scent of lilac. A wash of guilt poured over her, as though Georgiana's disapproval made itself known to her from the world beyond.

Her hand shook as she refolded the gown and put it back.

She had been a fool to believe she could bend the duke to her will. The longer she kept up her deception, the harder it was to tell the truth.

Ruby could still hear the sound of Seth's voice in the room beyond. She returned to the door and opened it a little, peering through.

"A priest would be of more use to you than a lawyer," he said.

The duke's voice was muffled.

"All right, all right. I'll send for him." Seth shook his head. He must have caught her watching out of the corner of his vision. His expression softened a moment.

"In that case..."

He sat up formally and raised his voice, intending she should hear.

"Nurse Campbell, will you join us please?"

That was her cue. She straightened her shoulders, set a level look on her face, and re-entered the room.

"My father believes himself well enough recovered from the journey to attend to business."

"Yes, My Lord," she replied.

"I wish you to ensure he is not too exhausted to see to his visitors."

Ruby dropped a curtsy. Everything in Seth's manner told her this was all a piece of theater played out for his father's benefit.

She knew it. And judging by his raise of an eyebrow, he intended that she know it.

Did the duke realize also? Perhaps not. His eyes grew heavy lidded. Exhaustion was clearly written on his face. Although his eyes now closed, he still had enough presence to speak.

"You will wake me each morning at eleven o'clock promptly, Nurse Campbell. I will be dressed and sat at my desk no less than half an hour before any appointment. I will not see a man on business in bed like an invalid."

"Yes, Your Grace," she answered.

That was enough to exhaust him and for sleep to claim him for certain.

She glanced to Seth who nodded toward the door of the duchess' bedchamber.

He closed the door after her and despite the largeness of the room, it seemed somehow smaller, more intimate with his presence.

"I haven't been in this room for twenty years, but it is exactly as I remember it," he said quietly.

Ruby watched him move around the room, reverently touching the furniture. He stopped at the dressing table and picked up a little ceramic dish. He removed the lid and sniffed at the contents.

"Even after all this time, it still smells of her. I half-expect her to walk in and sit down at her dressing table."

"Your father never changed the room," Ruby observed.

Seth looked back, giving her a considering look.

"Why is that, do you think?" he asked.

Ruby needed something to do while she considered her reply. The curtains. She opened them a little wider and looked down into a walled garden.

"It's not for me to say," she replied as she shrugged.

"Come now, Nurse Campbell. In the past couple of months, you have spent more hours in his company than I have in the past twenty-five years. *You* tell *me*."

Ruby pressed a thumb into the palm of her other hand and considered her answer.

"He loved your mother."

She heard Seth set the perfume pot onto the dressing table and approach her at the window.

Tell Seth all. Do it now.

She breathed in deep. "I need to speak with you."

He stood behind her and touched a hand on her shoulder, his fingers spread. They trailed down her back then up to her shoulder again, then down her arm.

She sighed.

"You can speak with me now."

She tried to steady her wits, looking for the words to begin, and turned to face him. That was a mistake. All the words she wanted to say evaporated like mist before the sun.

His face was a mix of curiosity and concern, but all she wanted to do was kiss him.

Dear Lord, what was wrong with her?

She breathed in the scent of his cologne, felt the warmth of his body as he stepped closer. His hands on her elbows drew her closer to him. What she wanted to say refused to come to her lips.

A heat rose through her, memories of her dream came to the fore, but he was here in front of her. *Real.*

No, this couldn't be real.

Ruby swayed toward him, but he'd already met her halfway. His lips, full and warm, touched hers. She sighed, opening her mouth to him, tasting him as he deepened the kiss.

"I want you, Ruby," he whispered, raining kisses on her face. "Tell me you don't feel the same as I do."

She hardly caught the words over the beating of her heart. Yes, she wanted him, but she wanted lots of things – her family home returned, her father's invention recognized... but she also wanted Seth's passion.

How easy it would be to give up. To give in to him.

"Tonight. Midnight." The two words were prized from her chest.

His warm breath tickled her ear, sending a shiver through her.

"Meet me in the library," he said.

She didn't trust herself to speak. She nodded her assent and watched him withdraw, not through the connecting door to his father's suite, but by the one out into the passageway.

He turned and offered her a slight bow.

"Until then."

SETH HOPED THAT the rather pleasant arousal that grew from the stolen moment with Ruby would last beyond closing the door to his mother's apartments, but one glance at the closed door to his father's suite brought him achingly, frustratingly, back to the present.

The man was toying with him.

A demand for a lawyer – in order to make changes to his will, no doubt – was nothing more than mendacious capriciousness from a man without human sensibility and feeling.

But he was nothing if not a dutiful son, so he would do what his father asked.

Seth entered the library, taking less care than usual in pulling the door to – it wasn't quite a slam, but it was firm enough to warn anyone within listening distance that this was not a good time to disturb him.

He settled himself at the desk and pulled a monogrammed sheet of paper from the compendium. He reached for his spectacles, charged the pen with ink and swiftly wrote the letter, preparing an envelope while the ink dried. He would instruct the butler to send someone to deliver it right away.

A stack of correspondence awaited his attention on the desk. He'd had few moments of his own since he arrived at Castle Glenuig. No sooner had they arrived than the estate bailiff requested an audience on a matter of business. The butler, too, wanted to know if anything was to change.

How the hell was he supposed to know? As far as he was concerned, the estate just *ran*. Who did they think he was? He was just Seth Musgrave. He was as far from the Earl of Glenuig as any man could possibly be.

Some part of him wished his father would live forever, leaving him free to chart his own course without the responsibilities of his office.

Seth opened the letters that awaited and scanned through their contents. There was nothing of any great urgency. Besides, he had his own business to run. And there was the nice little estate just a mile or so away from the site of the new mill that he'd barely set foot in.

He set down his glasses and rubbed his eyes.

You weak useless boy!

The voice of his father echoed through his mind. He worked his jaw. He never needed his father from the age of ten, so why should he need him now? The truth of the matter was his entire life was all about making his own way in the world without wealth or connections. All it would take was for Habetrot to have a strong first year in business.

Seth folded the spectacles and put them in their box. He

couldn't wait to get out to the mill site. If construction had advanced well in his and Roddy's absence, they would be ready to start work before the end of the year.

And that just left him with thoughts of Ruby. His only consolation would be having her back in his arms at midnight tonight.

She intrigued him, reminding him very much of a rose – beautiful in a formal, disciplined way, protected by thorns to prick the unwary.

He trusted his instinct when it came to her. Setting aside the secret she held, he saw nothing that made her untrustworthy. And he wasn't so stupid after all or lacking in curiosity about his father's nurse that he hadn't made some inquiries about her before they'd left London. They had come up empty. Not a soul had heard of her.

He'd spent yesterday evening in the library here looking for anyone by the name of Campbell. Roddy would also return from business today with word about whether any man named Campbell who was the right age to be Ruby's father was ever on the payroll.

Perhaps he would even ask his father's solicitor to make further inquiries.

Or he could ask her tonight – that is, if she didn't tell him first – if they weren't preoccupied doing other things.

He'd almost forgotten what it was like to savor making love to a woman, to bring her to the heights of passion while he found his own release.

"All work and no play makes Jack a dull boy" Roddy was always at pains to remind him, though he was sure he wasn't speaking of the play Seth now had in mind.

He had always dismissed Roddy's suggestion, claiming he couldn't afford to be distracted while he worked on the mill's particulars. And now? His interest in Ruby wasn't a distraction at all. In fact, being with her was like finding a safe port while the tempest of his life raged about. Sometimes when he was with her, he actually felt at peace – something he'd not experienced in years.

Since childhood, so much had been taken away from him that he only trusted what he could make with his own hands and buy with his own money. But he could not make a family on his own. And, as far as he was aware, he was his father's heir and would thus be expected to sire an heir.

A son necessitated a wife, a woman who, if she did not love him, at least found him tolerable enough to share his bed.

As for his part, a woman who was fair of face and figure was preferable, but not his sole requirement. She would have to have common sense, an inquiring mind, opinions, and perspectives of her own.

Although his current pool of prospects was limited, the only woman he could really see himself with was Ruby.

And *she* wanted to speak to *him*.

He didn't know if that was a good thing or a bad thing.

A sharp rap on the door pulled him from his musings.

He called enter, but Roddy was already halfway into the room.

"There's a been an accident."

"Where?"

"Habetrot."

CHAPTER FOURTEEN

S ETH'S STOMACH FELL to the floor and stayed there.
"What's happened? When?"

"The men were erecting some of the roof supports an hour ago when one of the cast iron columns gave way…"

Seth clenched his fists to hide his shaking hands.

"How bad is it?"

"Well, the roof's down. And two men are trapped. The others are trying to get them out."

Seth got up and had advanced no further than the hall when he saw Ruby descending the stairs, carrying a small medicine chest. The staff was aware of the new mill site, and news of the accident had spread quickly through the house, it would appear.

Roddy went over and acknowledged Ruby with a nod.

"I brought what I thought might be needed – bandages, tinctures."

"Thank ye for the offer of help, Miss. But there's no time to harness up a gig."

"I've already ordered a horse saddled for me," she replied.

Seth drew breath to comment on her response, but Roddy beat him to it.

"Ye ride?"

Ruby ignored the question and followed a footman who announced the horses were ready. Outside, three saddled mounts waited for them. She shoved the box in the footman's hands and opened it so as to distribute its contents into the saddlebags.

The mill was a half an hour ride if they cantered. He needed to be there quicker than that. He mounted and set the horse at a gallop with Roddy right behind him.

Every step of the way, Seth cursed himself.

This accident was his fault.

He'd insisted on iron columns over the usual wooden ones as a safety measure against fire. The friction of the machinery, the gossamer-light threads and dust that danced in the air were ready ignition sources – not to mention the hazard of the open fires that provided warmth and light.

At Skye-Heath, buckets of sand were never any further than three feet away from any worker's place at the machines. At the first sign of smoke, the loom was shut down and dousing became urgent. If a fire broke out and flames caught the timbers, the whole building could be alight in minutes.

He'd hoped to make Habetrot a safer place. Well, his "cleverness" might very well have resulted in the deaths of two people.

He glanced back just once. Ruby was gamely keeping up with them only a short distance behind Roddy, no mean feat on a horse unknown to her. Yes, she could ride.

Coming over the hill, down into the valley, his worst fears were realized. Broken iron columns spread out like ribs against the graying sky. If it rained, the disaster would be further compounded.

He coaxed more speed from his horse and pressed on regardless.

The foreman must have spotted them. He jogged up to meet him. Seth dismounted and covered the distance between them at a run.

"How bad is it, Jimmie?"

The man was ashen-faced, his mouth set to a grim line.

"I dinnae ken what happened," he said. "The roofing was going on just fine when one of the columns couldnae take the weight of the cross beam."

"Do you know if the trapped men live? Have you reached them?"

"We got one out already. He's hurt, but he'll be all right. The other is well under it, though. We can hear the laddie, but we've got our fears for him."

"Show me where he is."

The man looked at him oddly a moment, as if surprised he wanted to go into the wreckage, then turned to lead him back to the site.

Close up, the tangle of the fallen framework was even more chaotic. Seth observed a dozen men trying to lift a heavy iron beam without success.

On the edge of the collapse, a small group clustered around a man sitting on large slab of stone that would have become part of the walls. A makeshift bandage covered a wound on his head. Blood had already seeped through the bandage, leaving rust-colored streaks down his face, and the way the man also clutched his arm and grimaced suggested the limb was broken.

He and the trapped man were not the only causalities. Other men bore nasty scrapes and black bruises.

Seth approached the bandaged man. "Who's still under there, Mackenzie?"

"Fergus, My Lord," the man gritted out through his pain. "He was right beside me when the whole thing came down."

Roddy arrived carrying the saddlebag with Ruby at his heels.

"I'm going to leave you in good hands," Seth told the injured man. "We're going to get Fergus out."

Mackenzie gave him a weary nod of the head.

Seth forced bile back down in his stomach as he took in the twisted mess of iron. The beams had to weigh four tons if they weighed an ounce, and now they lay in a jumbled pile of metal and stone.

Behind him, Seth heard Ruby call for fresh water and wood for a splint.

Below, the shouts of the workmen became louder, quickly followed by anguished cries. Seth and the foreman jogged closer.

"We can hear him all right."

Seth frowned. "Sounds like he's in a lot of pain."

The foreman cupped in hands and yelled down to where others had clambered under the debris. "Can ye spot where he is?"

Another man yelled back.

"Aye, he's about eight feet in, but his legs are trapped bad."

"Has someone sent for the doctor?" Seth asked.

"Aye, he's on his way."

Well, there was a blessed relief.

Roddy slapped him on the shoulder.

"Let's see if we can use a fulcrum to lift the beam up and drag the poor soul out."

"Good idea," Seth replied. "Do it. I'll go in to free Fergus."

"Ye canna do that," said the foreman.

"Why?"

"Ye're a lord."

"Yeah, well this lord helps them that help themselves."

Seth stripped off his coat, dropped it on the ground, and rolled up the sleeves of his shirt.

"Help Roddy get more men together to find another beam to use as a lever. Order the others to start bringing some stone and bricks through to prop up the beam. That might give us a chance to get Fergus out with his legs intact."

Jimmie wasn't happy with his orders – that much was obvious – but he went and did it anyway.

Seth was under no illusion about the risk he was about to take crawling under that mess. One misstep, and there could be two bodies under the girders instead of the one.

What would his father make of that? His only son and heir dead, and His Grace still alive to learn of it. How ironic.

Seth shook off the grim thought. He took a deep breath and readied himself to head down into the rubble.

"Seth!"

He exhaled and turned to where Ruby was now making her way toward him. His name on her lips alone was enough to push the maudlin thoughts aside. Her face showed its concern, not just for the circumstances, but for *him*.

Seth readied himself for an argument with her about going in to rescue Fergus. Instead, she handed him a small corked vial and a hip flask.

"The whisky should dull the pain enough if he is not badly injured but, in case he is, the vial is a dose of laudanum. Don't give it to him unless his circumstances are dire, since we do not know what his injuries are."

Worry was etched deep on her face. He wished he could give her comfort, but he had none for himself, let alone another. He risked brushing her cheek with the back of his hand, instead.

"You shouldn't have come here," he told her softly.

"I can do more good here than I can by at your father's bed-side. There are men who need tending of their wounds..." She hesitated. "And I would feel better knowing for myself that you are safe."

Despite the misery of the moment, his heart swelled at her words. Had they been alone, he would have taken her in his arms. Instead, his eyes held hers for a moment before he turned away and headed toward the tumble of girders and columns.

The sounds of distress from the trapped man cut him to the quick. Seth clambered over the tumble of masonry until he found the location where the worker lay. He cleared away broken bricks so as to slide underneath a large girder, slithering several feet until he reached the injured worker.

"Easy there, man. We're going to get you out."

Fergus turned his head to look him, controlling his pain by breathing harshly through gritted teeth. He said nothing, but gave a curt nod.

"I can give you something for the pain. Whisky will go down smooth but it won't take away the worst of it. Or I can give you laudanum. It'll work quicker than whisky, but it tastes like shite."

Fergus sputtered out a laugh that turned into a low moan of pain. He sucked in another mouthful of air and rasped, "I wouldnae be a Scotsman to refuse whisky."

Seth grinned at him and flipped the silver cap on the flask. He guided Fergus' hand to it. The man took too large a gulp and offered up a choking cough.

"Easy there, take it easy. I fancy a dram of that myself, so take care to leave me something for when we get you out."

Fergus nodded valiantly. "Get on with it or I'll make ye no promises."

"We're going to raise the girder and pull you out. Ready?"

"Ready as I'll ever be…"

Seth shimmied back out until he could stand. He raised an arm at a signal across to Roddy. "Heave!" The grunting yells of the men on the other side of the fulcrum revealed the vast strain of the load. The heavy iron beam lifted an inch or two. Men scrambled to chock the beam against it dropping again…

Seth crawled and slithered through to Fergus again. He grabbed the man by the shoulders and tugged. The trapped man screamed in pain. Seth left him to crawl back out.

"Give me more height," Seth yelled.

"I'm not sure we can!" Roddy responded.

"For God's sake, try!"

Seth lay back down on the ground and shimmied part way back in.

Heave!

The beam lifted another inch and debris shifted. Seth could see now that everything below Fergus' knee was surrounded by fallen masonry. Likely the leg was broken. Seth squeezed his eyes shut a moment, then opened them as wide as he could if that alone might be enough to bring the scene before him in sharper focus.

If he could get closer, he could clear away some of the debris at the man's foot and free the trapped limb. But he couldn't pull him out at the same time.

He looked back and saw another man peering through the wreckage at him.

"You! Come and help me! Pull Fergus free when I give the word."

The man gamely crawled forward and grasped under the trapped man's arms.

Heave!

The load shifted a little more. Seth squirmed in down to Fergus' leg. He reached in as far as he could and pulled the shattered masonry away.

"Now, Man! Pull him out" he urged, and the worker grasping Fergus heaved on him.

Fergus screamed in pain as his bloodied and damaged foot emerged. It was worse than Seth had imagined, even seeing it with the blurred vision of his poor eyesight. Seth looked away and told the other man to drag Fergus out, following in the trail of blood from his crushed foot.

"Get out, Musgrave!" Roddy yelled. "We cannae hold this!"

Seth scrambled as quickly as he could, but was not completely clear before he felt something strike his head.

Then everything went back.

CHAPTER FIFTEEN

THE DOCTOR HAD arrived and seemed pleased to have an extra pair of hands to assist while he examined the injured men. Ruby was glad for her task. It gave her something to do other than fret over Seth.

Still, she listened as she bound wounds and cleaned deep grazes, holding her breath a moment as she heard the yelled command to heave. She breathed a little prayer each time – for Seth and for the man he risked his life to help.

Cheers erupted, drowning out Fergus' distressed cries as he was freed from the rubble.

Thank God, they're safe.

She turned in time to see the load shifting.

"Get out, Musgrave! We cannae hold this!"

Ruby found a scream trapped in her throat. She ran, pushing her way through the crowd of men who gathered.

"Turn him over!" one of the men called.

"Carefully!" Ruby yelled.

She reached Seth at the same time as Roddy.

"Is he all right?" the man asked.

Ruby looked down. Seth's eyes were closed. He was pale. He looked *dead*. She fought a wracking sob, and dropped to her knees to place shaking fingers to his neck. His pulse beat strongly.

"Yes," she breathed.

Seth's brow puckered, and his eyes opened.

"It would take more than a falling brick to knock some sense into me," he groaned, offering them both a lopsided grin. He struggled to sit up, but Roddy laid a hand on his shoulder to prevent him from rising.

"How's Fergus?" Seth asked.

"In a bad way," Roddy answered. "The quack's arrived with his dog cart, but we dinnae want to take him too far."

"Maybe to Strathaird?"

The name on Seth's lips was a bolt of lightning through Ruby's heart.

"You know it?" she asked, incredulously.

Roddy gave her a peculiar look and seemed ready to answer when Seth interrupted.

"Yes, I know it. Here, help me up."

Roddy gave Seth a disapproving look that Ruby herself couldn't match, but nonetheless offered his hand. Seth got to his feet and wobbled a moment, gripping Roddy's shoulder to steady himself.

Seth finally acknowledged her presence, giving her a lingering look as though he needed to reassure himself that she was there.

She might have thought it just her own flight of fancy, but he brushed her cheek gently with his hand, once again.

"Thank you," he whispered.

Ruby knew in her heart of hearts he didn't mean simply for her presence here today. An answering blush and a nod were the only replies she could give. Seth straightened himself up and limped off in the direction of the men who had formed a makeshift stretcher for the stricken man.

Out of the corners of her eyes, Ruby saw Roddy shake his head after Seth. The man folded his arms and gave her a direct look.

"If ye dinnae mind me saying, Nurse Campbell, ye seemed to go right peculiar when Musgrave mentioned Strathaird. As if ye seem right familiar with the place. I thought ye were from a different part of Scotland. I ken well that Campbell's not a name from around here."

She didn't answer him, *couldn't* answer him. She walked back to her medicines and bandages with Roddy as her silent escort.

"I have family nearby," she said softly, praying Seth's friend would ask no more questions.

He didn't. Instead, Roddy gave her another evaluating look before going over to where Seth stood with the others while the doctor tended Fergus. The man screamed abruptly.

Ruby turned away quickly, hiding her shaking hands. In fact, everything seemed to shake. Although she was a nurse of sorts, she knew she could not witness the tending of serious injuries.

The stream nearby beckoned, the cheery sound of a cascade drawing her away from the sound of Fergus' distressed cries.

She knew this place.

She used to ride out here with her father on his good days. They would picnic under the willow tree on the opposite bank. If they took the path south through the trees, they would cross back onto McAllister lands, and the house itself only a quarter of a mile beyond the woods.

The urge to see home felt like an ache.

She could volunteer her services to the doctor if her stomach could take it. But what if she met Strathaird's new owners? How could she face them in the house she once possessed and so desperately wanted to bring into McAllister hands again?

Ruby breathed in deep, closing her eyes – *all these questions and no easy answers*. The beginning of a headache made its unpleasant self known to her. She tried to distract herself by listening to approaching footfalls.

She opened her eyes and found them on Roddy. She didn't know him well, but everything she had seen of him had given her the impression he was an amiable and generally cheery man. Now his face wore a grave expression, making him seem much older than he was.

"Come now, lassie. Time to get ye back to the duke."

She cast a glance in the direction of the doctor's wagon, partly hidden from view by a willow tree. "Shouldn't we wait for Seth – I mean Lord Musgrave?"

She prayed Roddy didn't notice her familiarity. If he did, he kept it to himself.

"He's going straight to Fergus' family."

"The poor man's condition?"

Roddy shook his head. The mute answer told her everything.

FERGUS' CONDITION GREW worse on the one-mile journey to the village of Strathaird. His broken leg and crushed foot had been bound, his bleeding bandaged, but he began to cough up blood the moment they'd cleared the woods. The doctor ripped open the injured man's shirt.

Seth witnessed the purple and black bruise, the width of the beam, across Fergus' chest. And a heaviness settled on his own ribs.

This was all your fault.

The little voice in his head sounded so much like his father.

"Jimmie," he yelled to the man ahead of them. "Find Fergus' wife."

"Wait!"

Seth turned back to the doctor who shook his head.

"No need to hurry now. He's gone."

The words speared Seth's gut. Guilt must have spilled over into his expression.

"Ease yerself, Lord Musgrave. There was nothing more ye could have done."

Seth gave a curt nod and turned away to gain control over his emotions.

There was much more I should have done.

The design of the building was his. He did it differently because he didn't want to do anything the same way his father did.

And now look at what resulted.

Seth's head was pounding by the time they neared Fergus' cottage.

They were only a dozen yards away when the man's young wife, heavy with child, ran out and looked up at him with worried, questioning eyes.

Seth swallowed against the rock in his throat.

"Mrs. O'Donnell," he began. "I'm sorry, but…"

Her eyes fell away from his and took in the cart behind him, where her husband's body lay. She let out a heartrending scream, the likes of which Seth had never heard before and, he hoped to God, would never hear again.

Fergus' three children, aged between three and six, by his estimation, ran out at the sound and began to wail, too, at their mother's distress. One of the village women shepherded them away from the scene.

Two men took the litter inside the cottage, which Seth observed was little more than three rooms.

Someone had placed a stool by the litter, and Fergus' wife – widow – lowered herself onto it. She picked up her husband's hand and held it.

Seth stood in the doorway. The woman, engulfed by her grief, did not look up. He stepped forward…

"There was an accident at the mill site…" Seth began. It pained his throat even to speak. "We tried but…"

He didn't think he could feel any worse than he did at that moment, but he was wrong. Mrs. O'Donnell raised her face to him, tears streaming down reddened cheeks, strands of brown hair escaping the scarf she wore tied around her head.

"Three bairns, another on the way, and no means to support us," she said against hiccoughing sobs.

It didn't feel right to stand, as though he were lording over her. His desire was to crouch down so he could meet her eyes, touch her arm in consolation, but his instincts warned him that such familiarity would not be appreciated. He spoke the next words softly and respectfully.

"I promise you, Mrs. O'Donnell, you have my word that you and your family will be taken care of... I..."

The woman's tears became wracking sobs. "We have little enough, and now ye've taken my Fergus away from us!"

An older woman bustled past him and wrapped her arms around the grieving widow. "Now, Mary, dinnae be making matters worse. That's the earl, did ye nae ken?"

What did his being earl have to do with it?

Then Seth comprehended the reality of the vast chasm between himself and these ordinary working people. The young woman lashed out in her grief at the loss of her husband and provider, but the older woman feared how he might react, feared perhaps that offers of charity might be withdrawn in anger.

The older woman looked back at him. "Pay her no heed, Yer Lordship. It's her grieving. Nothing more."

"I know that. I'm sorry," Seth forced the words over his hoarse throat.

She offered a mute nod of her head before turning her attention back to the woman she comforted.

The older children remained huddled in the doorway, but the youngest looked up at him silently. Seth readily identified with the lost soul in those eyes.

It nearly made him weep.

He turned and walked stiffly out the door of the cottage toward the doctor who waited outside.

"Anything... anything at all the family needs. Just send word."

"Aye, I'll do that." The man placed a hand on Seth's shoulders. "Now, about ye..."

Seth shrugged and walked toward his horse. The doctor accompanied him.

"That was a nasty knock ye took to the head, and concussion is nothing to dismiss out of hand. I'd feel better if ye werenae riding back to Castle Glenuig, especially now that it is getting dark."

He knew the doctor was right. He felt half-dead on his feet but mustered enough energy to mount his horse and looked down at the medical man.

"I'll stay the night at Strathaird."

The man looked as though he approved the choice. "Good. I'll call on ye tomorrow."

Seth set off in the direction of the house. He squeezed his eyes shut, letting them water behind his lids to remove the grit.

There would be an inquest, of course. An examination of the building, its construction, and the materials used.

Seth felt sick to the stomach. If Roddy were beside him, he would be pragmatic and say that it was simply any empty belly complaining, but he knew better.

THE LOWERING SUN turned the windows of Strathaird gold, guiding his way. This would be his first night under its roof since he bought the house. He wished it could have been under less trying circumstances.

The butler and a couple of footmen met him by the entrance. It was clear that the news of the accident had reached here also. Seth hid a wince from the pain of his throbbing head as he dismounted.

"Tragic news, My Lord. Will ye be staying the night?"

Seth nodded and wished he hadn't. His head pounded.

"I am sorry yer stay here is nae under happier circumstances," the butler continued, "I understand from one of the villagers that ye put yer own life in peril to help that poor man."

"I don't feel particularly heroic."

Seth wished he hadn't seen the look of sympathy from the man, finally recalling his name, Jackson.

"I understand, sir."

Seth doubted it.

A BRANDY WAS left for him on the table in a small library where a fire had been lit. A bath was being drawn and a room prepared but, in truth, he could fall asleep in the chair he sat in.

He would leave here early tomorrow. Roddy would want a full accounting of the events.

Accounting.

Seth's heart sank even further. The cost to his purse would be tremendous.

The investment made in ironwork for the mill was a waste. He'd have to pay for the wreckage to be removed. Building anew would extinguish the last of his financial reserves. Worse, it would put him into debt, and that was something he wanted to avoid.

Still, getting credit on the strength of his title of Earl of Glenuig shouldn't be a problem.

But what if even *that* was taken from him?

What if his father revealed in his will that he was not a legitimate heir? It wouldn't have been the first time he'd been so threatened. It was one thing to be called a bastard, another to actually *be* one.

The more Seth thought about everything, the more tired and despondent he became.

He heard Fergus' widow's cries of despair. He heard his father's recriminations in his head, condemnation that told him he was miserable, useless, stupid. The inquest, of course, would add to his litany of faults and shortcomings paraded in front of everyone, including Ruby.

Marvelous. Just marvelous.

He must have fallen asleep because the next thing he knew was being shaken awake by Jackson.

Seth trailed behind him as meek as a lamb, climbing the stairs to the floor above and along the galleried landing he recalled from his first visit. Soft inviting light spilled out from the master suite and illuminated the brass plaque on one of the portraits' frames, catching his eye in passing and causing him to stop. The writing on the plaque was large enough for him to read without his glasses.

Lady Ruby McAllister.

Realization hit him in the gut, winding him.

Nurse Ruby Campbell.

For the first time, he *really* looked at the portrait. The flesh and blood woman he knew had matured from the girl in the painting, but there was no mistaking the identity. Seth found himself becoming lightheaded.

Some called him laird, but he was no one of consequence.

Why? Why did she sell Strathaird? Why did she become a *nurse?* And why was she nursing his father?

He swayed on his feet.

"He looks queer, should we fetch the doctor?" a footman whispered.

Seth mustered the last of his reserves to pull himself together.

"Sir?"

Seth looked into the worried eyes of Jackson, the butler.

"No. No doctor. Bath, then bed. I'll be fine by the morning."

CHAPTER SIXTEEN

R UBY'S RIDE BACK to Castle Glenuig was slower than the one out to the mill. It had been hitherto made in silence, and Ruby could no longer bear it.

"Lord Musgrave told me about his plans for the mill," she said.

"Aye, this setback will cut him deep. He's sunk every penny he had into the mill to show his old man up."

"What of Skye-Heath? Surely that will be His Lordship's to do whatever he wishes with it."

Roddy shrugged. "What the Lord giveth, the Lord taketh away. The old duke's been threatening for years to sell off Skye-Heath to make sure Seth doesnae see a farthing of it. He's even let it be kent that he'd give it to his bastard children and leave him with nothing."

Ruby straightened in the saddle. "He can't do that! Seth is his legitimate son and heir."

"Perhaps, perhaps nae. There's no proof the duke had bastard children, although Seth was told a time or two that he was one."

Ruby didn't pretend to hide her incredulity. The portrait of the duke as a young man hung in the house in London was the very image of Seth.

Roddy grinned at her. "I ken, I ken – plain as the nose on my face. His, too, if ye've noticed it."

"So, Seth lives under the belief that everything he has can be taken away from him with one word from his father?"

The jovial expression evaporated.

"Aye."

Her heart bled for him. As much as the duke had created financial hardship for her family, never once did she doubt her own father's love. Even when, toward the end, he became so lost in his own mind that he struggled to recall his daughter's name.

"So then, does Seth ken ye're Lady Strathaird?"

Ruby reined her mount to a rapid stop and breathed deep, afraid that if she didn't, she would faint and fall off.

"How –?"

"Ye're a very bonny lass in yer portrait, Miss Ruby McAllister. It took me a while to recall why yer face was so familiar to me. But it was yer face when Strathaird was mentioned earlier that put it back in my mind."

"You've been to the house?"

Roddy leaned forward to rub the neck of his horse. "Aye."

Suddenly, it was as though a veil had been lifted. Things which were shrouded in mist were now clear, just as they were after the fall of rain.

"Seth owns Strathaird..." she said, more to herself than the man alongside her. "That's why his mill is on the border."

Roddy nodded in silent confirmation.

"If he knows, then why has he said nothing to me?"

"Because he doesnae. I've been Seth's friend for twenty years, so ye'll be forgiving me for saying there are times that a man cannae see the nose in front of his face. But I'm thinking ye had no idea Seth was the owner when ye took on yer position as nurse to the old duke. Am I right?"

Ruby missed the fact the statement had not been phrased as a question. "I swear I didn't know! I did it to find out why the duke had defrauded my father in a business venture!"

There it was. Her confession. The truth laid bare.

But there was more than that.

Pinpricks coursed through her body. She faced Roddy.

"I want Strathaird back. I thought if I could make the duke admit what he'd done, he would settle the affair by giving me enough to buy back my home. I had no idea Seth was the new owner."

She waited for the censure, but Roddy said nothing, simply snapped the reins and set his mount into a walk, once more.

The rest of the journey back to Castle Glenuig was made in silence.

RUBY WATCHED THE thick, dark amber liquid lighten and turn a pale gold as she mixed it into the tonic water.

"Where were you this afternoon?"

The duke's voice was stronger, but she knew it was for show. Still, he insisted being out of his bed and seated in a chair that overlooked the grounds. Twilight cast a purple hue across the lawns, the trees on the edge of the estate darker still. The last of the direct sunlight struck one of the corners of the castle walls, painting a thin line of gold down its length.

"I was out, Your Grace."

The old man snorted out a scoff. "Well, that was bloody obvious, because you weren't here. Stop prevaricating, otherwise I'll think you have something to hide from me."

"When I'm not attending you, I would have thought my activities would be of little interest to Your Grace." Ruby kept her focus on the glass and the column of bubbles that rose from her stirring.

"Bloody balderdash! I rang for you and was told you had gone out with my son! That damned well makes it my business."

"I accompanied the earl because there was an accident at a mill. Men were hurt. I went to help."

"There, was that so hard? I might be dying, but I'm not a fool."

She handed the duke his medicine. His hand shook ever so slightly, but he downed the contents of the glass in one gulp.

"Where? What mill?"

"Not Skye-Heath."

The man set down the glass with a slam.

"I didn't ask where it *wasn't*, I asked where it *was*. Why are you lying to me?"

Frustration at holding her tongue for so long bubbled over.

"Because it's none of your business!"

The words were out of Ruby's mouth before she could stop herself. Now that she had said them, she couldn't bring herself to regret them. The duke's face sharpened. In fact, he looked good and angry.

She waited for the hot blast of his temper. Instead, his words were as cold as ice.

"You forget who you speak to. You forget that I am the duke. *I* am lord around here."

"Not for much longer," she uttered under her breath, but there was nothing wrong with his hearing.

His pallid face bloomed with color, pink, then red. Ruby wondered whether she had pushed him too far. What if he died now in high dudgeon? Instead, the duke seemed more alive than he had been for the last month.

"And won't you be glad of it then, my girl? You and that son of mine conspiring behind my back."

Ruby's back stiffened in indignation. Better that she bite her tongue. But the duke's faculties were so attuned that he noticed even that small gesture.

He leaned forward, pinning her with a hard stare. "While I still have breath in my body, *I am master*. Never forget who is in charge. I can *destroy* you."

Ruby raised her chin in defiance, somehow no longer afraid.

The duke noticed this, too. Oddly, a look of pride crossed his face before moving to the bed. He closed his eyes and lay back.

"Read to me."

She picked up the book of *Sonnets Pour Helene* and opened it at the bookmark. She read aloud.

In these long winter nights when the idle Moon
Steers her chariot so slowly on its way,
When the cockerel so tardily calls the day,
When night to the troubled soul seems years through:
I would have died of misery if not for you,
In shadowy form, coming to ease my fate,
Utterly naked in my arms, to lie and wait,
Sweetly deceiving me with a specious view.
The real you is fierce, of pitiless cruelty:
The false you one enjoys, in true intimacy,
I sleep beside your ghost, rest by an illusion:
Nothing's denied me. So kind sleep deceives
My loving sorrows with your false reality.
In love there is no harm in self-delusion.

By the time she set down the book, twilight had deepened almost to a gray – but not enough to light a lamp just yet. A retinue of servants soon entered the chamber to see to his bathing. She asked whether the earl had returned. A shake of the head was the reply.

The duke's nighttime routine commenced at nine o'clock sharp. And the servants moved with the efficiency of an army that took pride in their duties even if they had no love for their commander.

This next hour afforded her the chance to eat and rest in her room, perhaps even nap before returning to her overnight vigil.

She ought to welcome the respite. She was as exhausted by this one day as all the days on the road here. But if she closed her eyes, she would see the contorted features of Fergus as he suffered. She would also see Seth lying on the ground unmoving.

Unable to sit still, Ruby took her lamp and entered the adjoining boudoir that had belonged to Georgiana.

Without knowing why she did so, Ruby gravitated toward the wardrobe that held the white and gold dress. Tonight, it called to her. *Georgiana* called to her. This time without hesitation, she removed the gown from the shelf and held it up against herself.

How different things might have been – for father and son – if Georgiana Musgrave had lived.

In the duke's occasionally fevered mind, Ruby had become the voice of his late wife, and it occurred to her now that she really knew nothing of her.

To understand someone, one has to walk a mile in their shoes...

The urge to turn to the long looking glass behind her was so compelling that Ruby wondered whether Georgiana herself whispered to do so.

She drew close to the glass, the gown still held in front of her. It shimmered.

With one hand, Ruby loosened the pins of her chignon, letting dark curls tumble about her face. Georgiana's hair was light but that didn't seem to matter in that moment. Ruby raised her chin. The similarity to the young woman in the portrait was striking.

For several seconds, she was gripped by a nearly overwhelming urge to take off her own dress and put on the gown.

If she did, she would *become* Georgiana. She would see her staring back at her in the looking glass...

A deep, unaccountable sadness filled her with such a suddenness that Ruby wondered at her reaction. Was her sadness for Georgiana – or for herself?

She ripped her gaze away from the mirror to break the spell.

"Come now," she whispered to herself. "There is work to do."

She folded and returned Georgiana's gown to the wardrobe. She closed the door and rested her forehead against the cool wood a moment.

The melancholy lingered until it found a focus.

Seth needed to be here, at his home, where he could be loved.

Loved by *her*.

"I promise you Georgiana," Ruby whispered. "I will love him as he needs, as he deserves."

She set the light in the window. If Seth returned home to-night, he would know that someone was waiting for him.

DAYLIGHT THE NEXT day saw the duke in his worst temper yet. He railed at the slothfulness of the solicitor who sent word that he could not arrive until the afternoon. He complained at the slowness of the valet who was to dress him. In fact, he had venomous words for everyone who crossed his path.

Ruby considered what she might say to excuse herself from his excoriation but could think of nothing.

The events of yesterday still weighed heavily on her mind. If Seth had returned and seen the lamp she left in the window, he didn't stop to see her. She wanted to see him alone, not to confess as she had intended yesterday, but to give him comfort and take solace for herself. Was it selfish of her that she needed to feel his arms around her?

Now, because the solicitor could not attend the duke until the afternoon, the events previously planned for that time had been moved forward to this morning. That was another cause of her unease.

They were to visit Skye-Heath.

There, she would see the looms that used her father's invention. And no one would know that a good measure of the wealth the machines produced belonged to *her* by right of inheritance.

No one knew. Not even Roddy, who Ruby realized now was canny about so many other things, knew the full details of the business agreement with the duke.

Today would be as bitter as rue. She had failed her beloved father.

There was no doubt in her mind – and the doctor's, too – that the duke was not long for this world. And yet he hung onto life with the tenacity of climbing ivy. When he was in full voice, it was all too easy to believe him immortal, even in his diminished state. How long could a man go on?

Although the summer day had started off cool, it warmed up quickly. Nonetheless, the duke was rugged up as though it was early winter.

Shortly before ten o'clock, two footmen arrived to carry the duke down to the carriage. As they settled His Grace inside, Ruby observed her patient pale and taciturn, his mouth a thin line of concentration. She had given him a mild analgesic to keep the pain at bay and, for once, he didn't protest. That concerned her more than his earlier bluster.

Only then did she notice Seth. Frankly, the son looked no better than the father. His face was drawn and under his eyes were dark from lack of sleep. He was aloof, retreating so far inside himself it was difficult to reconcile the charmingly uncertain man she had come to love over these past few months.

And for the first time ever, the Earl of Glenuig was dressed as a man befitting his station. The navy-blue superfine fitted him beautifully – the jacket cut square across the shoulders and tapering to the waist. His breeches were buttoned at the knee with brass buttons that appeared to be embossed with a coat of arms. His black boots carried such a polish she might have seen her reflection in it.

She knew he expected people to see the clothes and not the man beneath. He wore them to hide his true self.

It was a ploy Ruby knew well. Hadn't she been doing exactly the same thing herself?

As she gathered her satchel with the duke's medicines, she caught a glimpse of herself reflected in a window and sighed.

She had beautiful gowns in her wardrobe; even the simplest of them was more flattering than this drab blue which had become her uniform. She felt like a servant.

And soon Seth would be a duke.

Despite Roddy's grim words, she didn't truly believe the duke would deny his son's inheritance. Soon, he would be expected to find a wife. Perhaps a very proper London wife. A titled wife. Someone of his equivalent station.

And that someone was hardly likely to be her.

Seth climbed into the carriage after her. Ruby dropped her eyes before he could seek them out, but she made the mistake of looking toward the duke who pretended to pull on his blanket. The man's hawk-like eyes watched her.

"We'll visit Skye-Heath first, Your Grace," Seth announced, rapping on the roof to inform the coachman.

"Your manners are very pretty today," the old man croaked. "Is it a special occasion?"

Ruby waited for there to be a rejoinder as there had been so frequently when the two men verbally sparred, but there was not one today.

She looked at Seth from beneath her lashes to find him cold and remote.

Ruby tugged a shawl across her shoulders and kept her attention on the view outside as, after a while, they turned down a long street lined with terrace houses. Through the tightly packed homes, gray sky blended with the gray stone.

The misery outside reflected the misery within the carriage, so she was only too pleased to escape its suffocating confines the moment it came to a halt.

While footmen settled the duke into the bath chair, Ruby took in Skye-Heath.

Up close, it was more impressive than she'd imagined. Built of gray stone like the workers' houses on the terrace rows, the mill was about four stories tall and, by her estimation, more than two hundred feet long. It sat alongside a tributary diverted to turn the water wheel that provided the power for the looms.

Over the sound of the flowing water was the unmistakable *clatter, clatter, clatter* of enterprise from inside the building. A delegation of three came out to meet them. The spokesman for the group was a man in his mid-fifties, hair turned to white. He had an open, friendly expression that sobered as they neared, as though he belatedly realized this was to be a formal occasion. He glanced to Seth, his eyes sliding past her before falling on the duke.

"It *is* a pleasure to have ye attend Skye-Health, Yer Grace. Ye will see a lot has changed in the ten years since ye honored us with a visit. Se–, er, His Lordship, the earl, has done a lot of good here since he came of age. No one kens textiles and milling better than he. 'Tis a pity he was born to be a nobleman."

If the duke spoke, Ruby did not hear it. The foreman turned an uncertain look back to Seth who stood as stiff as a statue.

"Thank you, Dougal," Seth answered formally. "We would be pleased to begin our tour."

The foreman frowned once more.

Ruby watched the exchange with a morbid fascination. She kept her hands folded one over the other, pressing the thumb into the palm of her other hand.

This was *very* wrong, like a musical movement played out of order. This should be a moment of pride, but it was anything but a happy occasion.

The noise of the working looms grew louder as they approached the building. They were given cotton to stuff their ears.

She caught only snatches of the foreman's words as they began the tour – he told them there were twenty-eight looms in this building.

"There were only fifteen when His Lordship took over the running," he yelled. "Mind ye, there are mills in Manchester bigger than this one, but none more efficient this side of the border. We regularly do three hundred picks per minute."

The sound became deafening as they approached the factory floor itself. Conversation stopped while they watched the looms in operation. Ruby focused on the one closest to her. The timber shuttle, pointed at each end and hollow in the middle to accommodate a bobbin, fired like a projectile through the warp threads which rose and fell on each pass.

She raised her eyes to look up at the head of the loom. Now would be the moment of truth. Ruby pressed her thumb into the palm of her hand once more. She frowned.

Punch cards? Where were the run of punch cards that would dictate the pattern? That was at the heart of her father's invention, and it was not here!

She scanned about, but could see them nowhere, not on *any* of the looms.

A bead of sweat formed on her forehead which pounded mightily.

Why would the duke go to all the trouble of drawing up a partnership agreement with her father if he never intended to use the invention?

None of this made sense.

She had no idea she was shaking until she felt a hand on her shoulder.

Seth looked down at her. He spoke, and she strained to hear him over the noise. Ruby concentrated on his reading his lips instead.

"You look unwell," he shouted. "It's the noise. I'll have Dougal take you to his office to recover."

Ruby nodded and followed the solicitous foreman. Her headache ebbed the further they walked away from the machinery.

Soon, they entered an office on the far side of the building. Dougal escorted her to a chair. Belatedly, Ruby realized the foreman had been talking to her.

"—noisy. Sometimes it takes a good hour or so at the end of a shift to get yer hearing back, and—"

Ruby interrupted the commentary and looked up at him. "Are they new looms?"

"Been the same ones here since I were apprenticed as a mule scavenger at the age of nine." Dougal paused and held up his right hand to illustrate his years of service. The third finger was missing. "Why do ye ask?"

"I was expecting… something that would make patterns."

"Like them Jacquard looms from France?

She nodded.

"His Lordship has been talking about them, but we ain't ever had them here."

He offered a small smile and a bow, apparently keen to return to his guests. He left her in the office alone. Her head started pounding again. Her last bit of evidence was gone.

If the duke had never used the invention, then the partnership would be null and void. Her entire reason for attaching herself to William Musgrave was gone.

CHAPTER SEVENTEEN

SETH WALKED ABOUT Skye-Heath like he was in a waking dream. He did and said all the right things, falling back on the manners and behavior drummed into him from childhood.

He didn't dare look at his father, no matter how much of him wanted the old man's approval.

His head told him there was nothing to complain about. The mill was well-run, the workers were paid well, the factory was as safe as he could make it.

Yet logic wasn't enough to ease the roiling of his gut.

It was all too easy to retreat within himself and play the role the people expected of him. Even so, Seth wasn't so caught up in himself that he didn't see Dougal's momentary confusion when he arrived dressed as he was, nor Ruby's cautious manner toward him.

But he could do nothing about that.

The tour ended. Seth thanked Dougal for his time, but the duke asked no questions and gave no praise, only a grunt of some kind that might be something, or might mean nothing. Who could tell?

THE ONWARD TRIP to the cemetery at St. Augustine's was made in silence.

Seth listened to his father's labored breathing as the old man accepted Ruby's ministrations without complaint.

He looked up at the sky. The overcast morning had turned darker still by the afternoon. There was a hint of rain in the air. Their visit – the very reason for the duke's return to Scotland – could not be a long one.

Seth dismissed the footmen, electing to push the duke's bath chair himself. That earned him a look of surprise from his father.

"Afraid I'll just leave you in the vault?" Seth asked.

He hadn't realized how menacing his tone of voice had been until he saw Ruby clasp her hands together as she was in the habit of doing when nervous.

"I might prefer that to your company," the old man replied. "I'll find more worthy examples of the Musgrave name in there than you."

Seth gritted his teeth and shoved rather than pushed the chair down the stone path to the mausoleum just as misting rain began to fall.

Now it stood before them – an impressive structure, he supposed, large and gray and telling everyone that people of importance were interred here. The door stood open. They had stopped at the gatehouse and announced their visit, and a man who'd hurried down to unlock the door stood discreetly under the shelter of a tree some yards away.

Seth felt a twinge of guilt that he'd only visited this place a couple of times in all the years he'd lived in Glasgow. He eased the chair up the three wide stone steps and sheltered under the portico before he noticed Ruby had accompanied them carrying a large umbrella which she had not yet unfurled.

Her standing in the rain made him feel guilty.

"Nurse Campbell, would you be so good as to wait in the carriage out of this weather?" he asked.

She looked ready to argue with him, but plainly thought better of it. Her expression was unreadable. Perhaps she was even angry at him, because she took the umbrella when she left.

Seth grabbed the handles of the bath chair once more and

pushed his father into the vault and toward the niche where his wife lay.

My mother.

Seth recalled the reason why he didn't often visit the grave – he never felt her presence here.

"I should confess that I took Mother's miniature after the funeral," he said. "I thought I deserved something to remember her by. I can't imagine you missed it."

The duke shook his head.

"I miss *her* every day," he whispered.

Seth winced and turned away.

Well, damn, you old man. Thank you for making me feel contemptible.

Eventually, Seth replied, "We have that in common, if nothing else."

Silence fell between them. Outside, framed in the open doorway, the mist was turning to a light drizzle.

The angle of the soft silvery light brought the embossing on the plaque into relief.

Georgiana Catherine Musgrave
1764 – 1795

Seth belatedly remembered that he ought to have brought some flowers. He stuck a hand in his pocket and came across his purse. He pulled apart the drawing strings and pulled out a new half-crown that glinted brightly in the filtered light.

He set it on the edge of the niche. A token to show that she was still remembered.

"She's begun to speak to me." The duke's voice was soft, half-embarrassed even, as though he were making a confession he wasn't comfortable with.

"Who?"

"Your mother."

Seth nodded, not trusting himself to say anything. He pushed down a frisson of irrational jealousy. Why would she talk to *that man* and not him? *He* could no longer remember his mother's voice.

He looked down at the sound of a sob. Once more, the powerful Duke of Auchen was a frail old man in his eyes, not an ogre. Compassion, contempt, and envy warred in him a moment. Honor won. He pulled out a linen handkerchief and placed it in his father's hand. The duke clutched it and brought it to his eyes.

His father wept unashamedly before him, a sign of weakness that, in his prime, he would have allowed no man to see.

Seth crouched down, resting an arm along the wicker edge of the bath chair. If it had been any other man, he might have touched a hand to the distressed chap's arm, but this was his father – a man unforgiving of any softness in others.

"What does she say to you?"

The duke took in a great gulping breath to compose himself, dropping the hand that covered his eyes to his lap.

Blue eyes met blue, the same hue being one of the many features which put to rest any talk about who his progenitor was. The duke regarded him cautiously, as though wondering whether the question mocked him.

But Seth was genuinely sincere. He *did* want to know – even if it was nothing more than the desperate fevered imagination of a dying man.

"I hear her close, as though she whispers in my ear, but I can never see her. She says I must make amends for my life if I want to be with her in the hereafter."

Seth found himself nodding, whether in agreement with his late mother or as a sign to continue, he wasn't entirely sure himself. This was the first time he could ever recall his father touching on matters in the least bit religious. Interesting that as one approached the end of one's life, thoughts arose of what may lie beyond this mortal veil.

Seth had a vague memory of the parable of the rich man and the beggar. The rich man in hell, forever in thirst and torment for his selfishness and pride. The neglected beggar, so hard done by in life, now had ease and plenty in the bosom of Abraham.

William Gregory Musgrave, Duke of Auchen, desperately wanted to believe in the promise of heaven as much as he was terrified of the prospect of hell. But, perhaps more than that, he despaired of never again seeing the woman he loved.

The old man clutched Seth's wrist with a bony hand. Seth leaned closer to hear his father over the sound of the drizzling rain outside.

"I have made so many mistakes in my life, and I have no time to atone for them all."

Seth said nothing. If his old man wanted comfort, or absolution, it was not his to give.

"If you're half the man you pretend to be, you'll take your warning from me and not make the mistakes I did."

He really couldn't leave enough alone, could he?

Seth rose to his feet.

"Believe you me, I have no intention of making the same mistakes as you."

I've made enough of my own...

With that bitter thought, he walked to the doorway of the mausoleum, looking out over the grounds. A hundred or so yards beyond, he saw a solitary figure standing at a small headstone. He recognized her from the set of her shoulders.

There she was, Ruby McAllister, Lady Strathaird. A woman he thought he knew, only to discover he knew nothing of the sort.

RUBY PICKED UP a pebble and held it in the palm of her hand, letting the rain pool there to wash off the dirt. Now clean, she put the token on her parents' headstone.

"Well, it's over, Papa," she whispered. "I was wrong. I was wrong about everything. But you knew that didn't you?"

She clutched the umbrella tight.

"That's why you hid the agreement. You knew your invention wasn't used."

The sound of the falling rain was her only answer.

So much time wasted in pursuit of useless revenge. The heat it stoked only carried her so far, and now, its fuel spent, left her cold and isolated.

What was she to do now? She was no better off than she had been six months ago.

Ruby laid a hand on top of the gravestone and bowed her head in a final prayer for her mother and father. She turned and looked at the ornate Musgrave family crypt.

It was time for them to leave. The solicitor was expected at four o'clock.

It was also time for her to consider her own future.

She made her way toward the mausoleum just as the bath chair emerged onto the steps. Ruby hurried to assist. The footmen dashed from the shelter of the coach to attend to their master.

Ruby stood at the crossroads of a decision. She could simply leave when her duty was discharged, saying nothing to Seth about her true intent. And, in time, she would be nothing more than a frisson of flirtation that he might halfheartedly remember when he was a duke.

Or she could tell him the truth, and he would curse her for being a gold digger.

Or she could tell him the truth and trust he would understand.

Of the three, Ruby hoped for the latter.

No longer could she deny the depth of her feelings for him. Seth Musgrave was the opposite of his father. He was a good man with a sensitive soul. The longer she knew him, the more she wanted to explore what there was between them, a passion that might deepen into something more profound.

Ruby climbed into the carriage and looked across at the duke, bundled up in his blankets, his head down, eyes closed. Clearly, this morning's activity had exhausted him and he slept.

Now would be the best time to salve her conscience. She had missed her chance last night, and there would be no opportunity when they reached Castle Glenuig.

Seth sat opposite her, his attention out of the window.

"I haven't been entirely honest with you," she said.

"Oh? In what way?" he asked absently.

"How I came to work for your father."

Seth laughed, then turned to give her his full attention. Her chest felt tighter than a bow string.

"I remember," he said. "I was there at the time. I plucked you off the street."

Ruby rubbed her hands nervously and pressed on. "I was there on a personal matter. I didn't come to be his nurse. I came to confront him over what he did to my father."

The look of faint amusement ebbed from his features and was replaced by a light frown.

"Go on."

Ruby took a deep breath to keep her voice steady. She made sure she looked him directly in the eyes. There was to be no misunderstanding.

"My father invented a means to improve the speed of pattern selection for the looms. After he passed away, I found documents that showed the duke entered into a contract to use the invention. He agreed to a partnership worth thirty percent of Skye-Heath."

Ruby saw Seth straighten in the seat. His expression became even more grave.

"I take it that no money was ever paid on it," he said.

Ruby shook her head slowly.

"I had come seeking redress from His Grace, hoping to force him to remember his signed agreement with my father. But none of that matters now. Today's visit confirmed something I've belatedly come to realize."

"That the looms at the mill do not use your father's invention?"

She fought a lump in her throat and nodded. She took in a deep breath and continued.

"So now I sit before you with my conscience clean. I am only what you ever imagined me to be, a humble nurse."

Seth leaned forward and took her hands in his. "I hope you know that you are much more than that to me."

She squeezed his hands in return.

"I fear you are being too kind, My Lord."

The look he gave her suggested so much more than that.

How she could fall into those eyes and stay there…

This was the man she had fallen in love with. Seth Musgrave, the ordinary man, not the Earl of Glenuig, not the future Duke of Auchen. Her heart beat more quickly.

"What plans do you have after… your current duty is fulfilled?"

"My cousin in a mantua maker. In London. She has offered me work."

Seth raised their joined hands and brushed a kiss across the back of her hand. Ruby fought a sigh, not successfully if the sparkle in his eyes was any clue.

"Don't make any hasty decisions," he whispered.

She nodded.

Her heart went out to him.

"And what of you? Your life will change as the new Duke of Auchen."

Seth squeezed her hands once and released them. He straightened in his seat, and peered out the window. Ruby looked, too. The carriage had just turned down the drive. She had no idea they were so close to home.

"Getting all you wish for is a blessing as much as a curse."

CHAPTER EIGHTEEN

SEEING THE SOLICITOR'S gig outside the front door soured Seth's stomach.

His few moments alone with Ruby were not nearly enough to help restore his mood.

Now, as if by some miracle, his father, who had slept for the bulk of their journey, was not just awake but exceedingly alert.

He really shouldn't have been surprised by his father's ability to rally. Perhaps the man had already been to the Pearly Gates and Saint Peter sent him back to earth with a flea in his ear.

The solicitor waited at the front door with not one but two clerks.

"Gentlemen, we weren't expecting you so soon," said Seth. "My father will need time to recover from his outing today."

"Don't talk about me as if I were not there! I am not deaf and I can well speak for myself!"

He cast his father a baleful look before addressing the footmen.

"Take His Grace inside. Nurse Campbell, does my father require anything before he sees his guests?"

Ruby dropped a curtsy, her pretty features contained behind a mask of stoic indifference.

"No, My Lord. If His Grace feels well enough, there's no reason why he could not attend to his visitors as soon as he is refreshed."

There – the stiff formalities over.

The solicitor smiled widely with the look of man who had already calculated his fee and found it substantial.

"Well, My Lord," the man beamed, "in that case, there are matters ye and I can attend to while we await the duke's pleasure."

Ruby bobbed a curtsy once and turned away. For some reason, Seth had the sense of being abandoned, just as he had as a child.

Irrational. Foolish. But there it was.

Mindful of the solicitor's waiting attention, he directed the man to the study. The two clerks followed dutifully, each bearing a large box. The older of the two juniors opened his and pulled out what appeared to be a ream of paper.

"As yer father is in failing health, there are a number of matters regarding the present running of the estate. These documents, witnessed here today, will give ye authority to act in his stead."

"That would presuppose me to be the heir," he said.

The solicitor blinked rapidly, as though Seth had suddenly take leave of his senses, but was too polite to remark upon it.

Seth huffed before taking a seat at his father's desk and reached inside the drawer for his spectacles.

And he didn't care what the damned man in front of him thought about them.

AT THE END of an hour of signing, Seth's hands ached.

Ruby's arrival was a welcome one.

"His Grace is ready for you, sir," she said to the solicitor.

Seth rose to his feet and watched the lawyer follow the footman and his two little lackeys follow right after him toward the library. Ruby looked prepared to turn away, too, leaving him in the study alone – something he could not bear to be right now.

"Walk with me in the garden."

He hadn't meant it to sound like an order but, apparently, she had taken it so because her shoulders squared and her posture stiffened.

"Please?"

At that, he caught a glimpse of the real woman behind the efficient nurse. The one who seemed to like him for the man he was, not for the title he so awkwardly carried.

She remained a couple paces away from him – a proprietorial distance – until they reached the walled garden.

Only then did she walk as an equal at his side, down the newly weeded gravel paths. The raised garden beds which had remained fallow for years were newly turned over ready for planting. This year, he'd ordered the gardener to give over more of the garden beds to vegetable planting. What the household could not consume would be distributed to the needy through the church.

It would be what his mother would have done.

"This was your mother's garden," observed Ruby.

Seth smiled, more to himself than to her.

"I've always felt close to her here. When I was very young, I would follow her out into the garden, and she would point out the different plants – not that I can remember them now. Mostly, it was just a feeling of peace, away from my father."

"Tell me about her."

Seth stopped. He looked at Ruby. How was it that she was beautiful at the moment? She had not changed or clothes or her hair. She wore no artifice on her cheeks or her lips. But he wanted nothing more than put color into both.

Instead, he only trusted himself enough to take her hand.

"What can I tell you beyond the unreliable memories of boyhood?"

"Still, they must be fond memories. Does it matter whether or not they're reliable if they give you comfort and make you feel close to her?"

Seth shrugged, the only thing he could do and still hold himself together. He moved on, Ruby still beside him, anchoring him to this time, this moment.

"I can understand a man being so besotted with his bride that he would do anything for her, including building this large, extravagant folly of a garden. I just can't reconcile that man being my father."

They strolled past another fallow plot right in the middle of the garden, diamond-shaped with a sizable plinth in the center. On it was a stylized globe of iron strapping, an armillary sphere, he remembered from his science lessons. an arrow piercing it through the center. It ought to be scrubbed and repainted; the engraved numbers were nearly impossible to see behind the rust. He would ask the gardener to see to it.

"Your father dreams of her. He talks of her in his sleep."

As distracted as he was by his internal musing, Seth didn't miss her softly spoken words.

"I know. He told me at her grave."

"He loves her still."

Seth turned his face toward the bitter gray sky and breathed in deep.

"Tell me, how does a man who creates all of this, showing himself to be of great refinement and sensibility, revert to being an uncivilized, hate-filled savage?"

"I don't know. But I believe your father hates himself most of all."

"He has an amusing way of showing it."

She squeezed his hand. He looked at her, her eyes glistening with unshed tears.

"Your mother would not want you estranged."

Seth caught the first tear before it left her lashes and folded her into his arms before he could see the rest.

Why did she shed the tears that ought to be his?

Ruby accepted Seth's embrace, and they stayed like that for long, long minutes.

"It's nearly over," she whispered.

Three simple words gutted him to the core. Because when it was over, she would leave.

Seth's arms tightened around her.

"I'm sorry," he whispered.

She could have no idea how deeply sorry he was.

Ruby raised her head, forcing him to look at her.

"You have nothing to be sorry for," she said. "We have both been dealt cards we did not wish. And it is our obligation to play our hand the best we can. It is easier for me. I can fall into an agreeable life away from here. You are the Earl of Glenuig, soon to be Duke of Auchen. You can never get away from your destiny."

Silence fell between them as they walked hand-in-hand, until Seth broke it with a question.

"Tell me, if the duke had acknowledged your father's invention, and given you recompense, what would you have done?"

"I'd have bought back my family home."

Seth felt his pulse pound in his chest.

"Where is that?" he asked, watching her reaction closely to see if there was any intent to obscure, to deceive.

Ruby hesitated, licked her lips, then swallowed.

"Strathaird."

Seth let out a long sigh. For him it was one of relief, but Ruby pulled her hand from his. She regarded him as cautiously as he had watched her, evaluating his reaction to the weight of the one word she had spoken.

Before Seth could say anything, Roddy appeared, walking toward them with purpose. His timing couldn't have been worse.

Ruby stepped away and seemed to withdraw from Seth right before his eyes, an invisible chasm opening despite the fact they were no more than two feet apart.

Roddy acknowledged Ruby with a nod before addressing him.

"The solicitor is done with His Grace. I thought ye might want to talk to him about setting up a trust for Fergus' family."

The ugly reality of the world outside had penetrated the sanctuary of the walled paradise. Would that he could stay here forever with Ruby, but duty... duty came first.

A touch to his hand stilled him before he could take off after Roddy.

"I'm here if you need me."

Seth searched Ruby's face again for a moment, watching her expression change like the sunset, uncertainty, reservation, then the rosy glow of tenderness. It was beautiful.

"Be sure to get some rest," she told him. As they walked away, she called out, "Roddy, make sure he looks after himself."

"Aye, that I will, Miss. Ye can be right sure about that."

A FOOTMAN ENTERED to light the lamps, followed by the butler who asked when His Lordship would be wanting supper.

"Now, thank you. Serve it here and bring a bottle of claret."

"But, sir, the dining table..." The man caught himself and swallowed his scandalized expression. "Yes, My Lord. Supper for ye and yer guest in the study and a bottle of claret. Yes, sir."

The man left. Roddy quirked his lips.

"For a man who doesnae want to be duke, it's sitting well on yer shoulders."

Seth wasn't in the mood for banter. He returned a wry smile and picked up a pamphlet Roddy had slid across the desk. It was an advertisement promoting a new method of forging iron. According to this information, it was a special process that created iron with virtually no carbon. They called it wrought iron. It was robust, easy to work with and resistant to rust. Most of all, it was strong. It was ideal for building.

"Habetrot can be rebuild better, safer – just as ye always wanted," his friend offered.

"If we rebuild."

Those three words had been rolling around his mind ever since he left Fergus' widow.

"Ye dinnae think we should?"

"I don't know if we *can*."

"Even when the insurance syndicate pays out?"

"I don't count chickens that haven't hatched. And I'm not waiting like some ghoul for my father to die."

"That doesnae leave us with many options."

Seth paused until he had Roddy's full attention. "I am considering a mortgage on Strathaird."

His friend's expression – surprise, then grim dismay – told him what he had begun to suspect.

"How long have you known Ruby's real identity?" Seth spoke the words softly, like taking a tentative first step onto the fens. He wasn't sure how firm the ground was though he trusted Roddy completely.

"Since the day of the accident," he said after a long moment. "I saw how she reacted when ye mentioned Strathaird, and then it occurred to me why she looked familiar – I remembered the portrait of young Ruby McAllister. So, I asked her, and she told me."

Seth closed his eyes a moment.

Damn me for being a shortsighted fool.

"I should have recognized her, too."

"In fairness, it's that nursing garb. It leads ye astray. She'd come up right bonnie in a proper gown fit for a lady."

Now there was a hint if there ever was one. But he wasn't prepared to confess the same thought had crossed his mind.

"You're soft in the head as well as the heart," Seth retorted.

"Be that as it may," Roddy continued. "Do ye really want to mortgage Strathaird?"

"I can't see we have a choice. It's either that or abandon Habetrot. We have no idea what surprises my father has left in his will, and I won't get the balance sheets for the ducal estate for at least the next few days to see the true state of affairs. He wouldn't be the first emperor with no clothes."

Roddy's expression closed. "I'll go along with whatever ye feel is best."

That was as good as disapproval in his eyes.

The thought of seeing the same look from Ruby was something Seth didn't want to think about.

CHAPTER NINETEEN

*H*E KNOWS NOW. *Seth knows who I am.*

Ruby attended to her patient with only half her mind on her task. Whether the duke knew of her inattention or not, she couldn't say. He appeared to be sleeping, propped up on his pillows. The long day appeared to have sapped the last of his reserves – or he could be foxing. Either was possible.

She looked at him once more, observing his pallor. His skin had taken on a distinct graying tone. The Duke of Auchen was as close to death as she'd ever seen him, and she didn't need a doctor to tell her that. Her father had the same cast in the days before *he* died.

The hatred she'd earlier felt for the man before her now seemed like it belonged to another person, a stranger she no longer recognized. In fact, she felt nothing at all, except a vague feeling of wishing for the whole wretched affair to be over.

Did Seth feel the same? Or did the strained relationship between he and his father make things more difficult? Did he think of it at all, given other concerns might weigh more heavily on his mind?

She extinguished one of the two lamps and turned the other down low so the room was cloaked in shadows. She sat heavily on the wing back chair beside the bed, leaned back, and closed her eyes. She let out a small sigh.

This afternoon in the garden was not the way she wanted to tell him of her claim to Strathaird. Strange that the revelation didn't surprise him as she thought it might.

Her portrait.

Like Roddy, he saw her portrait at Strathaird and put two and two together.

Did knowing who she was, that she'd deceived him as well as the duke by masquerading as a nurse, make a difference to him?

Ruby stared unseeing at the twilight view through the windows. She might have even dozed where she sat, because she started at the rap at the door and the golden lamplight that spilled in as the footman entered bearing a supper tray for her and His Grace.

Ruby lit a couple of lamps, just enough to see by.

The chef had done himself proud. A few moments ago, she would have forsworn an evening meal, but what was underneath the cloches smelled inviting.

The duke did not waken. Nor did he seem to be in any pain. She thought it best to let him sleep, and ate her own meal in silence, contemplating what her future might hold.

She didn't think Seth knew the truth of who she was when he'd asked her not to do anything in haste. She'd been afraid to look further at what his words meant then. Would they have the same meaning now?

The foundations had shifted.

In truth, as things now stood, she and Seth were worlds apart, destined for different futures. And what was their foundation anyway?

Hate brought them together. Did they have anything in common apart from that?

Her beloved Strathaird.

Unbidden, the thought of using his attraction to her to cajole for return of her home filled her mind for a moment. She shook her head violently, appalled and ashamed at the selfishness of the thought.

He'd bought her home not knowing the circumstances that came with its sale. He was blameless. The house was his by right and by deed.

Oh, how the fates conspired...

Would Seth let her see it again? If he knew how much the estate meant to her, could he be persuaded to let her live there as a tenant? After all, once he was duke, he would have houses aplenty to live in.

A tenant. In her *own* home.

Tears pricked her eyes.

Ruby halted them with a shuddering breath and sat in the semi-darkness alone to await the arrival of the Angel of Death to take the duke.

Even his vinegary observations would be welcome instead of the oppressive weight of silence that blanketed the room.

How much time passed, she could not say, but the night chilled her from within. She struggled to her feet and tugged her shawl tighter before approaching the fire, adding fuel and prodding the embers to coax them into flame.

A sudden loud keening wail caused her to jump and drop the poker. The sound was awful, like a portal to hell had been opened, the embodiment of all human suffering exposed within.

The tormented sound came from the duke, his back arched off his pillows.

Ruby rose gracelessly from the hearth and stumbled toward the apothecary box, her hands trembling as she prepared a draught.

"Your Grace? Sir! Wake up!"

His cries did not abate. She spooned the elixir into his mouth, the gurgling sound it caused no less alarming than the sound from a moment before. In desperation, she thought of something else.

"Uilleam! I'm here, I'm here..."

Whether it was the potency of the drug, or her soothing words, it seemed to have an effect on the man. His cries abated and his breathing slowed. The grimace lines around his eyes and mouth eased a little.

"Helen?"

The name was a whisper. If she hadn't been listening for it, she would have missed it.

"Shhh, my love. Not much longer. Soon, I promise. We'll be together." The words were soothing nonsense, but they calmed him enough. He sank back onto his bedding, seeming fully awake now.

And his eyes were wide open when he spoke again.

"Georgiana?"

She gasped. It was the first time she'd heard the duke call his wife by her Christian name. Her mouth dried instantly. There was no choice.

"Yes, dear?"

She spoke the words and paused. Which face of Janus would she see?

"Why can't I see you? Am I blind? Or is this my hell – to hear but never see you?"

"No, Uilleam. It is nighttime."

"Then why is there no lamp lit?" The duke's voice was calm, measured.

What could she say?

"I… I've just put the baby to bed."

"Our son." A statement, not a question.

"Yes." Ruby held her breath.

"I want to see you. Why can't I see you?"

And, at that, the great Duke of Auchen, the stern master of Glenuig, burst into tears like a child.

Ruby's chest tightened, clinging to the remnants of bitterness and resentment toward him as a bulwark against feeling pity.

She lost.

Her heart went out to him instead, filled with an overwhelming compassion for a man she did not even like.

Attempts to shake him awake and into the present proved futile. He called the name of the late duchess over and over again with increasing desperation which only increased Ruby's own. If only she could calm him! Then it came to her.

Perhaps there was *a way...*

What harm could it do to enact a little deception to ease his soul?

To the sound of the Duke of Auchen sobbing, Ruby entered the duchess' boudoir and headed directly for the wardrobe.

Ignoring her qualms about wearing the dead woman's dress, she watched herself in the mirror as she unlaced her own gown and poured the white silk over her body. Breathing out, she settled on her face the expression that she'd seen in the portrait in London – proud, but full of compassion and tenderness.

No longer did the looking glass reflect Ruby McAllister. The visage before her was that of Georgiana Musgrave, the Duchess of Auchen.

She went back into the duke's chamber and raised the lamp's wick only ever so slightly, as much as she dared.

Although the duke's eyes were open, it was by no means certain that he could see out of them. She took the man's hand and squeezed it.

"Uilleam... Uilleam. I am here."

The duke turned his head in her direction and blinked rapidly. His grasp on her hand tightened.

"Speak to me, so I know you are not a phantom."

Ruby knew a moment's panic. What should she say? What if he recognized his nurse and not his long-deceased wife?

"Uilleam," she whispered. "I'm here. I've always been here."

The old man's tears flowed once more. But this time, they were of joy. His face brightened, and she caught a glimpse of the hale and handsome man the duke had been before he succumbed to the ravages of his disease.

If, in his younger years, he had been as handsome and kind as Seth, then it was no wonder Georgiana fell in love with him, just as Ruby knew in this instant that she loved the duke's son.

His expression turned to awe. "You haven't changed, my

darling Georgiana. You're still young and beautiful as the day I wed you! But I am old and weak. Weak in so *many* ways. I've failed you, and I failed our son. In your lifetime and after you were gone. Oh! Had I known you watched over us, there are so many things I would have done differently. Can you forgive me?"

"You cannot ask forgiveness of the dead, Uilleam, only of the living."

The light in the duke's eyes dimmed. "It is too late to make amends."

What could she say to that? She squeezed his hand once more. "I pray for your soul, Uilleam. Speak to our son. Nothing else matters. Do not go to your grave regretting things you did not say to him."

The duke's eyes slowly closed, the grip on her hand loosened. Had she succeeded in bringing him comfort? Or had she frightened him to death?

Ruby eased her hand from his and ran into the duchess' room to remove the deception she wore.

THE SOUND OF weeping urged Seth faster along the hall. These were not the tears of a woman. He recognized the agonized cries as belonging to his own father.

Surely not. The Duke of Auchen was made of granite.

There was no ounce of tenderness in the man. And, yet, he had to own that at the mausoleum today, he did catch a glimpse of his vulnerability.

He opened the door gently. The room had fallen silent.

A figure in white hovered over his father's bed, dimly silhouetted by a low-burning lamp on a side table.

Gooseflesh crawled over Seth's body.

Damn his poor eyesight… not a specter; it had to be…

He blinked, and the figure disappeared in the blackness of the room.

A moment later, his father cried out once more. The sound of it cut Seth through. It was the sound of a wounded animal, a soul in torment. In a few steps, he was at his father's bedside.

The duke's eyes opened, his pupils wide and black.

"Father!"

The duke rallied, turning his head toward him.

"Did you see her? Did you see her, Son?"

"Who? Nurse Campbell?"

"No!" He seemed to realize he was shouting and lowered his voice. "Your mother, Son. Your mother was *here.*"

Seth patted his father's arm.

The man seemed to take the gesture and his silence for denial.

The duke took his hand and gripped it surprisingly hard for a man who was *in extremis.*

"Did you *see* her?"

The creeping dread filled him once more.

Who? The figure in white?

"Yes. I saw her."

The man's rigidly held posture eased, and he slumped against the mattress.

"Your mother... she was here. She has come to take me home."

Seth lowered himself onto the edge of the bed.

"I'm sorry," the duke whispered, and lapsed into silence.

An apology? For what? For dying? For a life ill-used? For him?

The silence continued.

Where is Ruby?

Seth rose to his feet and searched the blackness. He was about to go to the lamp to turn it up when he felt a tug on his hand and looked back down to his father.

"Seth... *Son...* forgive me."

The words slammed into his gut. He took a step back as though they had been blows. Never had he imagined those words coming from that man's mouth.

Seth's decades of resentment had come to a head at this moment. He could offer his absolution, and the Duke of Auchen could rest in peace – or he could withhold it and William Musgrave would know with his dying breath how much he was hated.

"I forgive you, Father."

To Seth's surprise, he found that he meant it and with that revelation, he felt a weight lift, a burden disappear. One of them anyway. "Go. Be with Mother."

A touch to his shoulder alerted him to Ruby presence. He breathed in the scent of lavender from her warm skin as she moved past him to spoon some liquid into the duke's mouth. After a couple of swallows, the old man's eyes slowly closed.

"He will rest easy," she whispered.

Seth nodded. Ruby returned the spoon and the bottle back onto the table that held the medicine chest.

"Has anyone else been in this room tonight?"

"Not since the footman brought supper."

Seth waited for Ruby to ask why, but she did not. And what could he say in return? That he had just seen the apparition of his mother? He couldn't rely on what he saw. But the duke was so adamant.

"My father told me that he saw my mother," he said.

Seth smiled then, and shook his head. Of course, she knew, he'd told her that. She was in the room with them. And the figure he'd glimpsed was obviously Ruby, despite the fact she wore a uniform of blue. The dim lamplight must have caught the white of her cap, and he'd imagined the rest in the gloom.

Ruby took a step forward toward him and, after a moment's hesitation, laid a hand on his arm. Seth was glad for her touch. He covered her hand with his own.

She looked up at him. "It's unlikely the duke will see the dawn," she whispered. "It was like that with my own father. His last words were to my mother, and she'd been gone five years."

Seth nodded his understanding. He looked over his shoulder

to where his father rested, chest rising and falling almost imperceptibly.

It all seemed rather final.

"You don't have to stay. I'll be here."

He turned back to the beautiful woman before him and lost himself in her eyes, grateful to the core of his being that she was part of his life. What would he do without her?

He stroked her cheek with his free hand. She allowed the liberty.

"I'll stay," he said.

Just before dawn, the Duke of Auchen breathed his last.

CHAPTER TWENTY

Three days later

RUBY WENT TO bed when it was dark and awoke when it was light. The natural routine of it still felt foreign after nearly three months of the reverse.

And yet living in these daylight hours, the world was brighter and more lively. A house which had been half-asleep for years bustled with activity as its occupants prepared for the lying in and the funeral of William Gregory Musgrave, the eighth Duke of Auchen.

In the airy guest room in which she had been installed, Ruby put away her plain navy-blue gown and prepared to don one in black. It was the gown she had most recently worn. The gown she had mourned her father in. How ironic that it would now be worn to mark the passing of the man she had perceived as her worst enemy.

As a hireling, there was no obligation for her to display her mourning, it was just that she was so damned tired of wearing blue that to wear the expensive, black lace-trimmed gown made a pleasant change.

It didn't do to think too deeply about how she felt about the duke. She had no love for the man. He had been downright nasty, and yet, it could be said that at the end, she understood him.

In understanding him, he was no longer the diabolical figure she had railed against, but simply a man. A flawed one who wasted much of the gift of the life he had been given. *That* was something to mourn, even if she couldn't bring herself to mourn the man himself.

How did Seth feel about his father's passing, she wondered?

On reflection, she set aside the black gown. She would be a hypocrite to wear it, so she reached for a simple sky-blue dress instead. It was the only other decent gown she had brought with her. She also styled her hair properly for the first time in months. No longer would she wear a white starched cap.

The Duke of Auchen was not the only one to die that night. Nurse Campbell had passed along with him. She would return to her real name and her title.

"Ruby McAllister, Lady Strathaird."

She spoke the words aloud and examined her reflection in the mirror.

The title was hers, even if her property would never be in her hands.

In the days since the duke's passing, Ruby had not seen Seth above a handful of times and, even then, only in passing. But she noticed a change in him. There was a distance in his manner as well as his expression.

She understood why.

So many people had claim on his time. There were the servants who ran the house, the workers at Skye-Heath, the great and good of Glasgow who wished to pay their respects to the late Duke of Auchen and to make themselves known to his son and heir – some to curry favor, others to gawp at the man who they'd been told over many years was feeble in mind.

Her heart ached for him. She wanted nothing more than to return to the moment of intimacy they'd shared in the private walled garden, to put her arms around him and give him comfort and allow her to draw strength from his embrace.

All of which made her aware of the impropriety of staying at

Castle Glenuig.

Could she even stay on in Scotland? It would be a reminder of her failure. A waste of months in which she might have found a cottage to live within her means of genteel frugality.

Returning to London held no more appeal. What would she do there other than assist her cousin, Francine? Ruby knew her cousin would welcome her back, and insist once more that she was still young enough to find a husband.

She pulled a face at her reflection. After five years of caring for her father, she'd never given much thought to marriage. And now the only man she could ever imagine herself with was the new Duke of Auchen – the very man who owned her beloved Strathaird.

What she wouldn't give to see her family home just once more.

Why not?

There was none to gainsay her, no one to miss her if she went there on her own. She was no longer a servant. It would be a walk of only a few miles.

She would do it.

She got as far as the landing when two elegantly dressed women – mother and daughter, she guessed – were ushered into the hall below.

"I'm *sure* he will remember us," announced the stout older woman, loud enough for Ruby to hear, "we *are* family, after all."

The young woman looked no older than seventeen. She was dressed to pay a call on a *very important person*, but carried herself with such unease that Ruby was left in no doubt she was there only at the instigation of her mother.

The old duke was not even laid to rest, and already the vultures were circling.

The older lady spied her at last, raising a gold lorgnette to her eye. Ruby felt the weight of the woman's scrutiny. She squared her shoulders and descended the stairs. The butler wore a slightly panicked expression.

"And who are *you?*"

A rival for Seth.

The wicked thought entered her mind unbidden but, once there, it would not be shaken. Ruby straightened her shoulders and continued down the stairs.

"Good afternoon," she addressed the ladies. "I'm afraid we haven't been introduced. I'm Lady Strathaird."

Ruby caught the butler's eyes lift in surprise – no, *shock* – at her use of a title, but he said nothing.

The older woman's lips thinned briefly. "Lady Millarstone," she stated. "This my daughter, the Honorable Miss Jeanette Millarstone. Were you acquainted with His Grace?"

Ruby knew the real question being asked.

"I am a friend of the new duke."

The girl turned red. Her mother pursed her lips tight once again.

And, as though he had heard his name, Seth emerged from the study, his head down examining the sheaf of papers in his hand. Sunlight glinted silver off the rim of his glasses.

He stopped, narrowly avoiding collision with the back of the butler.

SETH TOOK IN the scene before him. Three women, strangers to him, stood in the entrance hall.

No, not three – two. The woman in light blue he recognized.

Good heavens, Lady Strathaird – you're beautiful!

That thought he kept to himself. But he smiled at seeing the normally unflappable Banforthe looking unsure what to do. And Ruby looked ready to stand and repel all boarders.

That didn't best please the matronly looking woman.

He said nothing, but looked to Banforthe for an explanation.

"Lady Millarstone and the Honorable Miss Millarstone wish an audience with ye, Yer Grace."

The title grated on his nerves. He could not think of it and not remember his father.

"We're related... third cousins, you know... on your father's side. Naturally," the woman added hastily.

Should that mean something to him?

Perhaps it was to be expected that obscure relatives called. How was he to behave in such circumstances? They were here now. He couldn't very well send them away. But he didn't have time to entertain either.

"We're aware there's no mistress of the house and..."

Seth cut her off.

"I'm sorry. I don't have time to renew acquaintance at the present. But perhaps you'll stay for tea and keep Lady Strathaird company. Ruby, will you do the honors?"

If he didn't know her as well as he did, he would have missed the flare of the nostrils, the slight widening of the eyes that marked her surprise.

Surprise at what, exactly? That he recalled that her father was laird? Or that he had appointed her as hostess in his stead?

Equally, she might be angry with him. He had yet to learn all her moods. The idea of doing so lightened his own considerably.

With a bow to his erstwhile guests, Seth carried on across the hall toward the door that connected to a private morning room he and Roddy had taken over.

"Well!" Lady Millarstone huffed.

"Banforthe, would you please arrange for tea and refreshments to be served in the blue drawing room?"

Out of view of everyone, Seth allowed himself a grin. He'd relied heavily on Nurse Ruby Campbell over the months. Now, he intended to impose on Lady Strathaird to help him navigate this strange new world he inhabited.

Roddy looked up from his desk as Seth closed the door behind him.

"What's going on out there?"

Seth sat heavily in the chair opposite his friend.

"It turns out I have more relatives. Just one knock on the door by the Reaper, and they come out of the woodwork."

"Aye, and they've all come to pay their last respects to their dear, departed relly." Roddy's sarcasm was unmistakable.

"Such is the life of a duke." Seth shrugged and dropped the papers in his hand heavily on the desk.

"Shouldnae ye be playing host?"

"I put them in Ruby's capable hands."

Roddy's eyes gleamed speculatively. "Are ye intending on making her mistress here?"

"Perhaps, maybe, I don't know. But I do know she'd make a better hostess than me."

It was an unsatisfactory answer, but it was honest.

Roddy wisely changed the subject. "How fare the arrangements for the funeral?"

"Easy. When you agree with everything the bishop suggests, the details simply take care of themselves."

"That's something at least."

"That just leaves us with the inquest over the mill."

Roddy leaned forward, planting his forearms on the desk. "If it comes to it, put the blame on me."

Seth closed his eyes and removed his glasses.

"No. I won't let you do that."

"They might look for a scapegoat."

He squeezed the bridge of his nose. "Then we'll put the blame where it truly belongs – with me. I was the one who advocated for the use of cast iron. I was the one who fashioned the design. I was the one who failed to get Fergus out."

Roddy slumped back in his seat. "Yer title may nae protect ye if they decide Fergus' death is manslaughter."

"I wouldn't expect it to. I'll accept the verdict and mount no defense other than give an honest account of the events as they happened."

"The king may end the Duchy of Auchen."

Seth shrugged. "We live and serve under the prerogative of

His Majesty George III, King of the United Kingdom of Great Britain and Ireland."

"That will mean no land, no status, no income..." Roddy warned.

"I can live without the land and title. The funds would be handy, though." Seth thought adding a little bit of levity might lighten the grim expression on his friend's face. It didn't.

"That would leave ye with a mountain of debt, and Strathaird as yer only asset."

"I've given some thought in that direction, too. I want to deed Strathaird back to Ruby."

"Why nae just marry the lassie and have both?"

Seth smiled thinly. "You've just listed all the reasons why I should not."

⤜⤜⤜⤜

CASTLE GLENUIG WAS silent, yet Ruby was wide awake. It was about just after midnight as a guess. Just a week ago, she would have been preparing the duke a sleeping draught. The routine of it had become so ingrained that she couldn't go back to sleep.

Equally, her insomnia might be a result of the truly awful afternoon she'd spent with Lady Millarstone and her daughter.

Servants who were used to considering "Nurse Campbell" as one of their number were mildly bewildered at receiving instructions from Lady Strathaird.

The hesitation and uncertainty had not gone unnoticed by Lady Millarstone, which only served to fuel the curiosity of Seth's distant relation.

"I've been tracing the Musgrave family tree back to King Malcolm III," she said. "I don't recall seeing a McAllister in the line."

Ruby lifted the tea cup to her lips, pausing before giving an answer. "I am not a relative, My Lady. I am a guest of the duke."

"The duke? Which one?" the woman asked mildly.

"Both of them."

The look of surprise was worth the pain of suffering this woman's company.

"The current duke entrusted me with the task of helping nurse his father."

"Isn't that a role of a servant?"

"There is nothing servile about making oneself useful."

The young Miss Millarstone quirked a smile of amusement out of her mother's view.

Ruby had no qualms in making the older woman feel uncomfortable. It was clear she saw a chance to thrust her poor mousey daughter on the bachelor Duke of Auchen. And knowing of Seth's abandonment after the death of his mother, no "long-lost relative" should ever claim such familiarity, especially not one with such naked ambition.

"Tell me, how long has it been since you've seen the present duke?"

Such a blunt question was water off a duck's back to this woman.

"Well, as one would well know, the late duke was a difficult man... not for the want of trying did I wish to offer my family's devotion to the poor benighted boy. He will need the support of his family in order to walk in his father's footsteps."

"Why would you describe him as *benighted*?" Ruby knew she hadn't misunderstood. Lady Millarstone lacked the wit to be subtle.

As the woman set down her tea cup, Ruby waited for an answer to a question she'd clearly not prepared for.

"Well... I mean to say... *you've* spent time with him. I'm sure you've noticed that there's something... *amiss*." The woman punctuated the word with a tap of a finger to her temple.

"I beg your pardon?" Frost dripped from Ruby's every word.

Lady Millarstone's eyes widened in belated awareness of her error, her face paled, accenting the lines on her eyes and around her mouth which gaped open like a freshly caught trout.

"I... I..."

The daughter, who had hitherto remained silent, had a glimmer of mischief in her eyes as she spoke. "You will have to excuse Maman. She is under the impression that the Earl of Glenuig is an imbecile."

At that, Ruby had a newfound respect for the Honorable Miss Millarstone. There was a personality there quite separate from her mother, after all. She took a deep breath and slowly nodded her understanding, waiting to see where the girl went with the conversation.

"Of course, she naturally has Musgrave's wellbeing foremost in her mind," she continued, her tongue firmly planted in her cheek, "and who better to guard his welfare than his wife?"

Lady Millarstone was too obtuse to realize her daughter's ridicule of her. The woman shrugged her shoulders and resumed possession of her tea cup.

"It was no more than his father led us to believe," she said before her expression hardened. "Don't tell me that an adventuress like you has not had the same thought."

Even hours after the Millarstones' departure, the recollection still caused Ruby to flush as red as her namesake, indignant on Seth's behalf and equally embarrassed. Had she not inveigled her way into the Musgrave household under equally false pretenses?

She climbed out of bed, slipped on a robe, and lit a lamp. Perhaps if she walked the halls for a little while, her nerves would calm enough for her to return to sleep. Her path led her without conscious thought to the old duke's suite. She paused, half-expecting to see a familiar sliver of lamplight underneath the door.

William Musgrave lay in state in one of the ground floor rooms.

The door to his former quarters was not locked, and she opened it. She stood at the threshold a moment and breathed in deep. No longer did it smell of a sickroom. It smelled of beeswax and orange from furniture freshly cleaned and polished.

How odd that she should feel a sense of loss. Surely not for William Musgrave?

She went over to the windows and opened the curtain a sliver. A crescent moon, soft against the whisps of light clouds, stood proud over the woodlands that separated the estate from the River Clyde which flowed further downstream to Strathaird.

Her home... that was what she missed.

She closed her eyes. The chill through the window pane cooled her cheeks.

Tomorrow. Tomorrow she would go to Strathaird.

She shook her head.

No. It was the funeral tomorrow and the accompanying wake. Strathaird would have to wait another day.

And after that?

No. It was time to say goodbye to her dream of going home. In fact, tomorrow would be the end of so many things. She closed her eyes and squeezed them tight and allowed herself the tears she had denied for so long.

They were tears of relief as well as sadness, disappointment, and regret. But she could not bring herself to regret everything. Her father, God bless his soul, had been good at so many things. He'd just not been good at finance. If he had been, she would have had no reason to have sought out the old duke, and if she had not sought *him* out, she would never had met Seth.

In truth, they ought never have met. What to do now that the man they had both despised, but latterly pitied, was gone?

Her sobbing ebbed, and she took a deep, shuddering, cleansing breath.

What would happen on the morrow would be the world returning to its proper order. These past months were the aberration.

Ruby closed the curtain, the ducal bedroom in darkness save for the lamp she'd left on a table in the corner. She looked about her surroundings.

For months, she had played a ghost, and now *she* was haunting this room.

She allowed herself a small smile at the thought.

But her heart ached when she thought of Seth. The responsibility now on his shoulders had consumed all his days since his father's death. The demands on his time would only grow larger when he moved to London.

Not to mention the aftermath of the accident at his own mill site.

Through Roddy, she'd made inquiries after Fergus' family and asked if she might write a letter of condolence. She enclosed some coins, a mere token, but she could think of nothing else to do. Everything that could be done for them had already been put into place.

Had that only been a little more than a week ago?

Still no more tired than when she came in, Ruby considered what to do. Perhaps reading would send her off to sleep.

The passage to the stairs down to the library took her past another bedroom. A golden line of lamplight shone on the polished floorboards beneath this door.

Seth's room.

Ruby frowned. He ought not to be awake, he ought to be resting. There was much to do on the morrow.

She ought not have put her hand on the door handle.

Nor should she have turned it, nor pushed the door open.

But she did all of those things.

She hesitated at the threshold. Seth sat at a small bureau, a lamp illuminating the document he was working on. He was hunched over, intent on his work. He was not yet alert to her presence. She wanted to speak his name, but found herself voiceless, unaccountably close to tears once more.

She watched him shiver at the cool air brought in by the open door. He looked up, started, then took off his glasses.

"Ruby? What are you doing here? Is anything amiss?"

Her tongue was still lost, so she shook her head.

Seth left his place at the desk and joined her, touching a gentle hand to her elbow.

"You shouldn't be here," he whispered.

CHAPTER TWENTY-ONE

"'I COULDN'T SLEEP."

Seth's resolve to send Ruby away dissolved. He closed the door behind her and, with a gentle urging, guided her toward the fire in the hearth so she could warm up. He set his dressing gown over her shoulders for additional warmth.

"Please don't send me away," she whispered.

What could he do but enfold her in his arms? It felt so right. A storm may rage about them but, here, clinging to one another, they might find salvation.

"Good sense tells me I *should* send you away but, from what I hear of Lady Millarstone's opinion of me, good sense is in short supply."

"Wicked woman," Ruby giggled before tightening her arms around him. "I nearly tipped a pot of hot tea on her. How dare she say such things?"

Seth kissed the top of her head and stepped back a moment so he could see her face. "There will be more where that came from. Depending on the blackness of my father's mood, he would have told people in no uncertain terms that I was a cretin. Even if they were not inclined to take it on face value, my absence from society will have had people forming their own view."

The look of pain in Ruby's face was an odd sort of comfort. She cared for him. She knew him for the man he was, not what was said about him.

"The funeral will be a trial. They'll be looking for the signs of defect that saw me sent away. I expect the wake to be worse still, when the guests are not constrained by the sanctity of the cathedral, and have liberally imbibed the spirits on offer."

Ruby's hands curled into fists, gripping his nightshirt, though she did not seem aware of her actions. "The moment I find myself feeling pity for the duke, I discover that his perversity lives on in others, and I get angry again."

Seth breathed in deep. Her familiar lavender scent lit the flame of his desire. Yes, they had kissed before this. He'd tasted the passion that lingered on her lips but, now, in this midnight hour, each wearing nothing but nightclothes, his desire for her deepened.

He caressed Ruby's cheek and decided it wasn't enough. Her eyelids fluttered closed as he lowered his mouth to hers for a kiss that was rich in emotion – gratitude, delight, and a very healthy measure of lust.

Eventually, he broke away from her mouth, satisfied by the ragged breath he drew from her lips. Ruby threw her head back, presenting him with the column of her neck. He obliged with open-mouthed kisses until a line of gooseflesh appeared, accompanied by a moan, the sound of which went straight to his groin.

He'd never felt such desperate need. The temptation to take her into his bed was great. His body's growing insistence on this very course of action threatened to subsume his rational faculties.

"You can't stay."

Ruby didn't pull away. Instead, she rested her head on his shoulder and remained in his embrace.

"Lady Millarstone has probably convinced herself that I am your mistress; possibly your father's as well."

Seth offered an exaggerated shudder in response. In truth, mention of his father had dampened his ardor instantly. He pulled away, glancing at the half-finished eulogy on the writing bureau.

I come to bury Caesar, not to praise him. The evil that men do lives after them; The good is oft interred with their bones; So let it be with Caesar.

"Please don't send me away."

He took in what she wore, the form of her full breasts beneath a plain lawn nightdress in white peeked from beneath the blue brocade robe that was his. Black curls tumbled down her back. It was the first time he had seen her hair loose. Her lips were full and red from their kiss. And those eyes that looked at him as though they could see into the depths of his soul...

Ruby was *truly* beautiful.

The full realization came upon him with an urgency that took him by surprise. He'd already acknowledged to himself that her features were fair and her form pleasant, but this was more. She was everything.

"Your reputation..." she offered. It was a weak excuse. And she knew it. The look of disappointment damned him.

"I've presumed too much."

Seth sighed. He'd never done anything like this before in his life, had never even *considered* it.

"I don't know what life you had before you started nursing my father, or what you plan to go back to after the funeral. But if you stay with me now, it is not just for tonight. As you've probably guessed, I'm not a man who is fickle in his attentions. If you spend a night in my bed, it's not just a night, it's for always."

Her lips parted. The throbbing in his groin started again.

He remained where he was. The next choice would be hers. Part of him hoped she would leave. At least that would maintain the status quo. He could throw himself into his work, and he wouldn't know what it was to have a wife, a help-meet at his side, a woman he truly loved in his bed.

He wouldn't miss what he never had, right?

He watched Ruby's expression closely. She knew him as well as any woman had ever done. She knew what he was, and what he wasn't. By his own reckoning, the positives in his ledger would come up short. If he knew nothing else, he knew this: if she stayed, his heart would forever be hers.

Tears filled her eyes, making him feel worse, not better. But the pain of it eased as she returned to his arms.

"You're offering marriage?"

Yes... no...

In truth, he wasn't sure. He hardly knew his own mind at the moment.

"Do you know what you'd be giving up if you married me?" she continued. "The opportunity for a wife with a grand title, one who would open doors for you in London. Give you the life that should have been yours."

The thought had never before occurred to him. Consider it another example of his shortsightedness.

"All I know is I want you," he answered.

"Then let that be enough. Tomorrow, the world changes for both of us. You will be the Duke of Auchen, and I... just want one night where we are not our titles or other people's expectations. Just one night where I am Ruby and you are Seth."

He took the two steps to reach her side and pulled her into his arms. He lowered his lips to hers in a tentative exploration of her mouth. He determined to go slow, to savor every moment. He would give her what she desired.

Never before had a woman felt so right in his arms, like she belonged there. Too long he had hidden himself away from the world he had been destined to inherit. No longer. He would face his destiny with courage knowing this woman believed in him.

"You can't know how much I want to make love to you now," he whispered in her ear.

Ruby pressed herself closer to him, the full press of her breasts, the heat between her legs stoking his arousal.

"Then make love to me, Seth," she whispered.

His kisses were too potent for coherent thought to last for too long.

She ran her hands over shoulders made broad by physical labor. The play of muscles beneath the linen of his nightshirt reminded him of how strong he was. He did everything a man could to save Fergus' life. How close he came to serious injury himself. She closed her eyes and welcomed the feel of those arms around her.

"Here, you're shivering."

She'd hardly been aware of it. Seth led her to the step up into the rosewood four-poster bed. She climbed in, and he followed, urging her onto her side, facing away from him, and wrapped himself around her, his legs tangled around hers, his arms around her body from behind.

It didn't actually matter what he promised. Lying here with him like this was all that was right with the world. They could pretend nothing else existed outside these four walls.

Light kisses returned to her neck. She sighed and snuggled closer into him while his hands roamed freely across her flanks, along her waist and up under her breasts. The thin layer of fabric that separated his hand from her bare skin did nothing to dull the sensuous tension that lingered from where he trailed his hands.

She tried to reach behind her, to touch him in turn, but he would not allow it.

"Shhh... you came to me because you could not sleep. I'm going to help you relax." Not for a moment did his hands stop their exploration.

"This doesn't feel relaxing," she sighed, but it was not a complaint.

"What does it feel like?"

"Like... like the sun on my skin, but the warmth is coming from within."

"Concentrate on my touch, *mo leannan*."

My beloved.

Ruby did, and a restless yearning rose from within, made

more powerful by the fact she couldn't touch him. Instead, her fingers kneaded the sheets.

He centered his attentions on her breasts. Light passes with the pads of his fingers coaxed her nipples to stand proud. Everything he did seemed to have the singular aim of keeping her off-guard. She pressed back closer to him, feeling the hard erection against her buttocks.

His hips rocked, and she recognized the tingling ache between her legs as a sign of her own arousal. She stretched, tangling her legs between his. Seth palmed her breasts while he lined her neck with kisses which sent shivers through her.

It was not enough. She needed to touch him, feel him inside her.

"Please…" she moaned.

"Please?" His question was a tease. Ruby knew full well that he knew what she was asking with that one word.

"Seth." His name was a sigh on her lips.

His hands left her breasts, his left hand ran down her body to the hem of her nightdress and tugged. Their nightclothes tangled together, and she shifted to help him remove the final barrier between them.

She rolled onto her back. Seth rested on one arm, his eyes roving over her body, his face full of desire and longing. She reveled in his gaze and stretched once again, arching her back, presenting her breasts to him. He looked like a hungry man, and Ruby desired nothing more than he feast upon her breasts and upon her.

She reached up and kissed him, her own hunger unfulfilled. Open-mouthed kisses, raw and demanding, stoked her need for him.

"You're even more beautiful than I'd dreamed," he whispered.

Her eyes flickered shut as his head descended to one breast. She moaned with pleasure as his mouth enclosed her nipple, and his tongue coaxed it to stand hard and erect.

He dreamed about her.

"I've dreamed of you, too."

He lifted his head and blew on her aching nipple, making her shiver again.

"Really? Tell me," he asked before descending on her other breast to give it the same lavish treatment as the other.

She opened her legs. Seth settled himself over her, his firm erection pressing against her mound. The little bud of flesh between her legs ached to be closer to him. He teased her with light strokes while she ran her hands across his back, then up through the strands of his sandy-brown hair.

"Hmm?" he asked. She had all but forgotten about his demand that she tell him of her dream.

"No dream can compare to what you are doing to me right now," she said. "I want you completely, over me, through me, in me, until we are one."

He slid his hands down her waist to her hips where he held her still as he slid down the bed. His mouth descended on her clitoris, his tongue teasing it, teasing her, leaving her helpless against a rising sensation. His lips explored the most intimate part of her, and she wanted more – more sensation, more of him.

She brushed her own hands across her breasts. Still sensitive nipples hardened once more. She touched her breasts even more firmly to recall the hitherto unknown sensations Seth had just brought her.

Her restless yearning was now acute. The moment of her release hit in a flash. She cried out his name over and over, riding the wave of her orgasm.

Seth raised his head. There was a predatory satisfaction in his eyes which was both shocking and arousing once more.

"Please," she whispered.

"More?" he inquired.

Ruby shook her head and halfway sat up. She reached down toward him and took hold of his large, hard erection. He closed his eyes, his mouth open.

"Ruby."

She stroked him, tentatively as first, but with growing confidence as she watched his facial expression change. With one hand pressed to his back she urged him closer until he lay on top of her, his face close enough to kiss, which she did, all over.

Ruby dug her heels into the mattress and raised her hips until the intimate parts of them touched. She released his cock and rubbed up against him. Her second orgasm hit hard and fast.

"Take me, take me, take me..." she whispered over and over.

He entered her swiftly then stilled. She gasped with the suddenness of it. His hand reached up and stroked her hair tenderly. She saw him watch her closely, and how his gaze fixed on the round "O" of her mouth.

His pubic hair tickled her still-sensitive bud. She sighed as he lowered himself to her mouth for another kiss.

Her hips rocked once – from desire, from instinct, she couldn't say – but it was enough to bring him to the brink.

She matched his rhythm as though this had not been their first time together and opened her eyes to watch him, his eyes squeezed shut, his mouth, those full lips, parted in ecstasy, as another orgasm rose and crashed over her.

As it did, she vowed she would remember his face and this moment for as long as she lived.

She loved him with her whole heart and soul. She loved him.

Loved him enough to let him go...

CHAPTER TWENTY-TWO

SETH WOKE FROM the deepest, most restful sleep he'd had in months. Waking with Ruby in his arms was the world put to rights.

If he kissed her sleeping face, would she awaken to him as she had done last night?

His cock twitched, and he allowed his arousal build.

But he observed the soft light that limned the curtains, suggesting that morning had already arrived. He listened and could not hear the sound of servants, so he guessed it was still early.

Ruby stirred. He looked down, and she gifted him with a sleepy, feline smile. How he wished they could stay in bed all day and make love.

"Good morning," she whispered.

He bent down to kiss her, afraid that if he spoke, it would betray the emotion that bubbled beneath the surface.

She returned the kiss fully before pulling away, reluctance written on her face.

"I should go."

He nodded, halfheartedly.

In reply, Ruby tenderly stroked his face. That was almost more than he could bear. He took her hand and planted another kiss on her palm before getting out of bed. He found the tumble of nightclothes on the floor and untangled his nightshirt from it.

He placed Ruby's nightgown over his arm and turned to her.

She lay on one arm, her luscious breasts exposed. The way she looked at him appreciatively firmed his erection – and she knew what she was doing.

Minx!

He shook his head and smiled at her.

"Get dressed. I'll escort you to your room. You should be able to get a couple more hours of sleep," he said.

She got out of bed, accepted her nightrail, and slipped it over her head, covering her body from his view.

They walked to her bedroom door in silence, unwilling to break the spell. Words seemed so unnecessary after last night. In just a few hours' time, it would feel like a dream, and he would be faced with the cold reality of the day ahead – the day of his father's funeral.

All eyes would be upon him. It would be the first time he would be formally addressed as "Your Grace". And it would take him a hell of a long time to get used to being styled in the manner.

How much easier it would be with Ruby standing at his side. He could draw strength from her. To hold her hand, let her ground him when all eyes were on him. But he knew as well as she that this path was his to walk alone.

He gave her a lingering kiss, a promise of a sort, although a promise of *what* he could not say. She stepped across the threshold into her room.

Away from him.

He was surprised by how hard the sensation of loss hit him. He reached for her hand before the distance grew. He brought it to his lips and kissed it. Her eyes glistened before the lids closed for the briefest moment. She squeezed his hand, then swallowed against emotion of her own.

"What of you? Will *you* get some more sleep?" she asked, her voice hoarse.

He shook his head. "I need some time alone to clear my head

for today."

Ruby nodded her understanding. God bless her. Then the door closed, and the distance between them widened again to a gulf.

Seth drew a deep breath and returned to his room to quickly wash and dress. He glanced at the notes on his desk. He had hoped to memorize the eulogy and forego the need for his glasses.

Why?

If he needed them, he needed them. Others' opinions be damned.

He slipped the spectacles into his pocket, intending to go down to his mother's walled garden, the place only two other people would venture to look for him, and read through the eulogy there.

But something made him pause by his father's suite.

He stepped into the room and closed the door behind him.

It was strange, not seeing the old duke lying there. It had become just a room. The man's presence didn't linger. There were no reminders even that this was once his sickroom – all the apothecary bottles had gone, and the room had been thoroughly cleaned, ready for its next occupant.

Seth doubted he could bring himself to claim the suite as his. Not yet anyway.

He wrapped his hand around one of the mahogany posts on the tester bed and felt its solid form.

To imagine that his father talked him into believing he'd seen a ghost!

Seth had genuinely thought he saw *something* in the hours before his father's death. He hadn't dared tell Ruby. What would she have made of it? Of *him*?

No. He imagined it because of the power his father still held over him.

He left his spot to head to the door of the adjoining suite. Entering, he opened one curtain and early morning sunlight streamed through. Through the window was a view across to the walled garden.

Ruby and Roddy knew to look for him *there*. No one would think to look for him *here*.

He pulled back another curtain and sat at his mother's desk. He read over his notes again and again until they were imprinted on the back of his eyelids when he closed them…

The chime of the long case clock announced it was seven. Seth started awake. He'd put his head down on the desk for just a second and fallen asleep instantly. Now his eyes flew open and fell on the armoire. He sat up and looked at it. Its door was ajar.

Getting up, he approached in order to close the door, then changed his mind. He opened it wide instead, and a rainbow of fabrics was lit by the morning sun.

Seth looked about him, taking in the room that had been maintained but otherwise remained untouched since his mother's death. He shouldn't have been surprised that her clothes were still there, but he was. He lifted out a gown and recognized it instantly. The white dress with the gold trim was the one his mother wore to have her portrait painted – the one that hung in Glencoe House.

Nostalgia crashed over him like waves on the shore, threatening to drown him in a sea of emotion. He traced the embroidery on the ribbon, horses and apples. The Trojan Horse, the golden apples.

Mother as Helen of Troy.

He brought the fabric to his face to touch it to his cheek, as if to be kissed there by it as his mother had kissed him as a child. After so long, there could be little chance of there being a trace of her scent, but he breathed in deeply anyway.

A hint of lavender…

Ruby.

She was the only one he knew who wore the perfume and had been in this room. And, as if to confirm his suspicion, he found a strand of curly black hair at the neck of the gown.

A thought struck him, taking him by surprise.

Your mother, she was here...

Seth's mouth fell open a moment.

Then he laughed.

Indeed, she was *here, Father!*

So *that* accounted for Ruby's insistence on staying with the duke all throughout the night. She had somehow managed to persuade his father that his nocturnal visitor was the spirit of Georgiana Musgrave.

He knew he ought to be angry, but he couldn't even bring himself to be mildly annoyed with her.

Good for you, Ruby, if you caused the man to spend his last few weeks in reflection and repentance.

Still, it had done her no good when the real prize was not payment for her father's unused invention, but rather the regaining of her beloved Strathaird.

Well – perhaps there was something he could do about that...

RUBY SLEPT, AWOKEN at nine o'clock by a maid who brought in hot water and fresh linens. If not for the soreness between her thighs she might have imagined that last night with Seth had all been a dream.

She *felt* different, so she half-expected the world to be different, but the maid went about her usual business with brisk efficiency as Ruby washed and dressed.

Downstairs, the mood was solemn. From the top of the stairs, Ruby saw Lady Millarstone and her daughter had just arrived. The footmen directed them to the dining room. Ruby came down and found the only other inhabitant of the room was Roddy. He wore a fine gray woolen suit with a black armband announcing his status as a mourner. He had risen from his place at the table to greet the Millarstones.

Ruby watched from the doorway as Lady Millarstone cast her

eyes about the room, as if to find Seth hiding behind the cellarette.

"Help yer wee selves to some breakfast, willnae ye now?" said Roddy. "His Grace has asked me to express his regrets that he willnae breakfast with us this morning."

Lady Millarstone's dismayed expression was priceless. Ruby forced down an inappropriate smile and watched Roddy similarly try to master his composure. Miss Millarstone, safely out from her mother's view, simply rolled her eyes.

While the two women served themselves from the sideboard, Ruby took the opportunity to approach Roddy.

"Has he eaten?" she inquired softly. "I fear he won't take care of himself."

"Worry none about that, he's fine. He just needs time to clear his head."

"He said he same thing to me."

That earned her a brief speculative look before Roddy smiled, patting her on the arm.

"He's asked that I be yer escort. Dinnae worry – we two who ken him best, we'll be there for him. And, if ye dinnae mind me saying so, I am a friend ye can count on, too, Lady Strathaird."

The use of her title brought a bittersweet smile to her lips. She settled her hand over his and squeezed.

"Thank you."

RUBY STOOD WITH Roddy and the rest of the servants out on the lawns of Castle Glenuig as the pallbearers carried William Gregory Musgrave's casket to the hearse.

Seth, dressed in mourning black, followed behind.

The hearse's matched black horses stamped their feet and nodded their heads, making their black ostrich plume headdresses flare and sway, as the casket was placed inside. With a gentle snap of the reins, the hearse started the stately journey that would take the late duke to his final resting place.

Seth's expression was closed. His face was somber as befitting the occasion, but there was no grief etched into his features.

It was as though he had retreated deep within himself.

It was all too easy to imagine him as a lonely little boy, locking his true feelings away from his tyrannical father.

The temptation to leave her place among the line of servants and go to him was strong. She felt Roddy's steadying presence beside her. She glanced up to see that his attention, too, was focused on Seth.

They watched as he stepped into the ducal carriage which followed behind the hearse.

After the vehicles disappeared from view, the servants left in twos and threes to return to their duties and to prepare for the wake.

Ruby turned to Roddy. "You've known him a long time. How does… is he…?"

"Aye, I've kent Seth for fifteen years and he doesnae give much away, but he kens the job of work he's got to do and he's a man who'll do it to the best of his ability."

Ruby looked away and swallowed against a lump in her throat.

Roddy nudged her shoulder. "Come now, lassie, save yer tears for something really worth crying for. All we can do now is be there for the man. What say we be on our way?"

To Ruby's surprise, the church was filled with mourners. Most of the great and good of Glasgow were there. How many of them attended to pay their respects to the late duke, and how many wanted their first look at the new duke, she could not say.

Today, Seth resembled the man in the portrait in Glencoe House – the late duke in his prime – most closely. Austere, remote. Was Seth aware of his transformation?

She rose with the congregation to sing the first hymn.

It also didn't escape her notice that Lady Millarstone and her daughter managed to have themselves placed among the lead mourners, on the same pew as Seth. She had to own to a moment of jealousy.

Seth then rose to deliver the eulogy.

Ruby twisted a handkerchief in her hand. He had told her that many would be here today to see for themselves whether the new Duke of Auchen was an imbecile or not.

Now, she heard the whispers for herself from those around her.

Well, it can't be a physical deformity. He looks hale enough, and he didn't limp behind the hearse.

I heard the man has a terrible stammer.

It's more than that. They say he's feebleminded. It's really quite cruel to put him through something like this. Poor creature.

Roddy leaned across and patted her hand. He'd heard the comments, too.

The congregation went silent as Seth raised his face to them. "As many of you know, the late Duke of Auchen was known for his exacting standards," he began, then he reached into his coat pocket, withdrew his glasses, and put them on. "He didn't approve of weakness. He certainly didn't approve of these glasses."

A slight chuckle went through the mourners.

"The duke was more than his title. He was a husband and a father. As his son, I have come to understand both aspects better over the last months of his life.

"As a husband, he loved my mother dearly, and I'm sure he was thinking of her at the end."

Ruby frowned. Did Seth really just peer over his glasses and search the congregation for her face?

"As a father," he continued, "William Musgrave was an austere man with a will of iron and standards that were hard to live up to. Some would say, impossible."

Seth paused. He removed the spectacles from his face and placed them back in his coat pocket. Ruby held her breath. Roddy took her hand and held it. She dared a glance across at him. The man's posture was tense.

Surely this wasn't all he was planning to say about his father? Yet what more could be said that was kind to his memory, and was still honest?

"I learned his lessons, as well as the ones he did not intend to teach." Seth's words were softly spoken. Many in the congregation leaned forward to hear them.

"The greatest of these," Seth continued, "was to how to be my own man and not allow the vicissitudes of fate determine my future. If only he had mastered that lesson himself..."

His voice trailed off but he was not overcome with emotion. If Ruby had to pick an expression, she would describe it as thoughtful.

"There is not a man alive who does not have regrets. The greatest lesson is to die with as few unresolved as possible. Did William Gregory Musgrave succeed in this? As his son, I cannot give him a passing grade but it will be held to God alone to judge.

"But what of the man's legacy? He did not shy away from enterprise. In the Skye-Heath textile mill, he left a business which I have built upon and will continue to do so. In his duties in London, I look forward to advancing the interests of Scotland and doing proud to the name of Musgrave.

"I learned a lot from my father. The lessons he taught me, intended or not, I've taken to my breast. I hope my own legacy is as far reaching as his."

It was only after Seth returned to his pew that Ruby realized that not once had he looked at his notes.

Ruby let her tears fall, not for the old duke, but for Seth. She knew how much those words cost him, and the meaning behind them that most would never know. But at least now people would see what she saw – a sensitive, accomplished, whole and handsome man. Now a *wealthy* man, a duke.

She became aware of renewed whispering around her.

Well, I never expected anything *like that.*

Doesn't he speak beautifully?

He'll be quite the sensation in London. I wonder if Prinny has sent an invitation yet?

What's the name of Lord Batterley's eldest girl? I think there could be an advantageous match to be made there.

They would fete him, flatter him, and welcome him into the inner circle that he had been excluded from for his whole life.

She swallowed her emotions down.

One part of her was pleased for him. He deserved the honor and attention that was his due.

Another part of her mourned that the world they'd shared for such a brief period of time must come to an end.

CHAPTER TWENTY-THREE

S ETH DIDN'T REALIZE that one could be in two places at once.

It struck him as rather amusing. His body was here in the hall of Castle Glenuig at the wake for his late father. And yes, he was shaking people's hands, giving a nod of his head, and generally saying something appropriate. At least he hoped it was appropriate because, truth be known, he had no idea what he was saying.

His mind was in another place entirely.

He wasn't quite sure where, but it wasn't where it usually was. He seemed to be looking on quite separately, as though he were the ghost in the room, and those who spoke to him were speaking to someone who simply looked like him.

He searched for Ruby several times over the hours and, each time, found her in conversation with some Right Honorable someone or other, but he had not been able to catch her eyes.

How strange that he could feel so alone in a room full of people. Perhaps he could slip away, and no one would be the wiser? What he wouldn't give to escape into the walled garden for a while.

That thought had him search Ruby out once more. He would take her out to the walled garden, away from the well-meaning condolences, the vapid attempts by some to court his favor, and put his arms around her to be sure he held on to something real.

His mind ran with this fantasy. He would kiss her, even make love to her there in the warmth of the late summer sun. She would call out his name in ecstasy and *that* would reunite his body and mind, and his soul with hers.

Seth willed his body to move toward her, only to be intercepted by a smartly dressed old man who introduced himself as Magistrate Brian Halliwell and asked if he could speak to him in private.

The gravity of his expression and the knowledge that Magistrate Halliwell was to preside over the Habetrot inquest forced Seth to nod his head and direct the man to his study.

"My condolences, Yer Grace," he said when the door was closed behind him. "I have no wish to intrude on yer grief."

Seth allowed himself a private smile.

"Not at all, sir. Please, won't you take a seat?"

The older man slowly lowered himself in a chair. Seth took the one opposite.

"I've come to let ye ken there will be no need for a formal inquest," he said. "I have read through yer statement as well as the statements of the men who were there at the time, and also one on behalf of the widow. My verdict will be that what happened was an accident. Yer generous settlement on the widow brings the matter to a close."

Seth briefly closed his eyes and felt tension leach from his shoulders.

"Thank you," he said.

The magistrate stood just as slowly as he'd sat down.

"I'm glad to have brought ye good tidings today, Yer Grace. It is good to see the name of Musgrave live on."

Seth rose and shook Halliwell by the hand, but did not accompany him back into the hall. He needed a moment to himself to deal with the news.

He sank back into the chair and covered his face with both hands for a moment, then took a deep breath and raised his head.

Relief could not begin to express how he felt at that moment.

Not only had a weight been lifted, it meant he could begin anew.

He stood and caught his reflection in the mirror above the fireplace and started at how much he looked like his late father.

He was Seth Arthur Musgrave, the ninth Duke of Auchen.

He *was* the duke.

He squared his shoulders.

For the first time in his life, he didn't have to count everything down to the last copper. If he wanted something done, he could simply order it so, and it would be done. He would forge his identity beyond what he could accomplish with his two hands alone.

To wield such power was intoxicating.

There was another knock on the door. Seth bid the person enter.

He hoped it was Ruby. Instead, it was Roddy. Not quite the same, but at least a friend he felt comfortable with, rather than some stranger around whom he found himself on tenterhooks.

Roddy handed him an envelope, then helped himself to a measure of whisky. Seth didn't give the letter a glance until his friend made himself comfortable in the chair opposite. The envelope was addressed to the Duke of Auchen in florid handwriting.

"I didn't make a fool of myself today, did I?" he said, looking up at his friend. It was more a statement than a question.

Roddy took a sip and offered a sigh of satisfaction.

"Yer father knew his whisky..." Then he gave Seth his full attention. "Ye certainly didnae. Dinnae let yer guard down though, Man. Once they're getting over the condolences they dinnae genuinely mean, they're talking about the new Duke of Auchen, and how they can best curry favor."

Roddy hid a grin before getting up, pouring another glass of whisky, and setting it down at Seth's elbow.

Seth shook his head slowly before raising his glass in salute.

"Ah, so I am to be a sought-after Duke of Auchen, then?"

Roddy leaned forward in an exaggerated conspiratorial manner.

"It's nae the men I'd be worried about – it's the women. At least three of those titled ladies out there have ye married off already."

Seth returned a mock shudder.

Roddy raised his eyebrows and nodded toward the envelope that Seth had forgotten in his lap. "Are ye nae going to open the message?"

"Not if it is going to be one of those insincere condolences or a begging letter from 'fond' cousins that I didn't know I had."

"Look at the seal."

Seth looked at the missive properly for the first time. The paper was heavy and therefore expensive. The writing of the address was even and practiced. He turned it over. The seal on the back was gold and featured three feathers encircled by a crown.

The Prince of Wales.

Seth broke the seal and scanned the letter inside.

"Well?"

"I'm instructed to come to London for a private audience with His Highness."

"Prinny himself! Wait until word gets out. Ye're in the bon ton now, laddie!"

Seth accepted the teasing, and even managed to fashion a grin he didn't truly feel. It was one thing to know one's title and status, but quite another to balance such a mantle securely on one's shoulders.

RUBY WATCHED SETH exchange a few words with an older man and retreat into his study with him.

She pressed her thumb into the palm of her hand. She had been briefly introduced to the man and had overheard mention that he was the magistrate set to preside over the coroner's court.

"Lady Strathaird."

Ruby acknowledged Lady Millarstone with a nod of her head. This time, she remembered they were on the same social level. The woman would no longer make her feel like a fraud, an imposter in a lady's clothing.

"Do you intend to go to London with the duke?"

Ruby couldn't help a frown.

"London? What makes you think that His Grace is leaving Scotland?"

The woman laughed, catching the attention of Jeanette Millarstone who now approached them.

"Why, of course he's going to London. One would hardly refuse a command from the Prince of Wales."

Ruby's confusion must have been plain because the daughter spoke.

"Mother happened to see a messenger from London announce himself to His Grace's man of business," said the young woman.

Lady Millarstone interrupted. "As it so happens, I was planning to ask the duke if he could spare some of his precious time in sponsoring Jeanette's Season, given that we are related by blood. In fact, I think we should accompany him south. After all, we are bound for the same destination, and His Grace's coach would be much more comfortable for such a long journey, wouldn't you say?"

Trapped between the console table and the settee, Ruby was stuck. It became all too much. She spoke and damned the consequences.

"I wouldn't know, Madam," she said. "The last time I saw the coach, it had been turned into an invalid transport for the late duke. Just one large bed, really. Who's to say whether Seth will ever want to change it back?"

Lady Millarstone blinked uncomprehendingly. Jeanette hid a smile behind her fan.

Ruby took her opportunity to sidestep and make her escape.

She circulated the room once more before the servants began to clear the tables.

It was only then that Seth emerged from his office to accept the farewells.

She thought he might be tired after such a trying day, and yet he looked relaxed.

Ruby waited until the last of the guests, including the Millarstones, had departed before approaching him. The expression on his face was tender, and she longed at that moment to put her arms around him. But she said nothing until the last of the servants had departed.

"I saw the magistrate leave."

Seth nodded his head slowly in acknowledgement, but said nothing for a moment before reaching out his hand toward her. Ruby stepped forward to take it, her heart quickening as his fingers curled around her own.

He led her into the study and closed the door behind them.

"How do you fare?" she whispered.

"Surprisingly well, all things considered," he said, offering her a smile – a genuine one, not the face he showed the attendees of his father's wake.

He stepped closer. His soulful blue eyes watched her carefully, evaluating her expression as he enfolded her into an embrace. Ruby returned it fulsomely. They remained in each other's arms a moment before she realized this embrace was different. It was not a prelude to passion, rather one of relief and of comfort.

"The inquest is over. Halliwell will deliver his findings tomorrow," he said softly. "An accident. No one is to blame."

Ruby closed her eyes. She squeezed them tight and held Seth even tighter. She felt a kiss on her cheek and a long sigh eddied across her ear, sending a deep shiver through her. Memories of last night's lovemaking filled her thoughts anew.

Delicious shivers went through her at the thought of giving herself to him completely once again. He owned her forever, heart, body, and soul. There could be no other man for her but this one.

Seth settled another kiss on the top of her head and gently disengaged his embrace.

"I have something for you."

Was this a proposal? One part of her was thrilled with the thought. Another part, a little devil on her shoulder, warned against inflating her hopes, whispered it was more likely to be a small bequest, a token for service that all the servants had received from the old duke's will.

Yet another part said, *no, he needs time. Time to know what it is to be the duke. Time to divine if what he feels for me is real...*

Seth turned to the desk and sorted through some papers until he found what he was looking for. He looked at the envelope in his hand a moment before handing it to her.

Ruby opened it and removed the sheaf of documents with.

Written large on top of the first sheet were the words *Deed of Property.* Ruby read the rest of the writing there twice over to make sure she understood the right of it.

The deed to Strathaird.

She raised her eyes to find Seth watching her expression closely. His was impossible to read.

"But *you* own Strathaird."

Seth shook his head slowly.

"No. It's yours. It's always been yours."

"But... what of you? What of Habetrot?"

He shrugged.

Ruby waited for him to expand on the gesture, but he didn't. She looked at the deed once more, to make sure it was real, before looking back up at him.

"This is impossible. I can't afford to buy Strathaird from you."

"You don't need to. It's a gift."

Tears welled in her eyes. She glanced down once more. The text before her blurred. She hastily put the papers down lest her tears spoil the document. It was everything she had wanted – the return of Strathaird into her ownership.

Seth took her hand. He led her over to a chair and urged her to sit. He remained crouched at her side, keeping her hands in his.

"Ruby, I *know*," he whispered. "I know... about my father... the voice he heard was *you*."

She started, but Seth held her hands firmly. "The ghost in his room. That was you. Wearing my mother's dress."

She burst into tears. Seth pulled her forward into his arms. She sobbed so hard she couldn't draw breath to even say she was sorry. And it wasn't just for deceiving the duke...

"You did what you had to do, and I admire you for it," he continued. "You did what you had to do for your father and for your home."

Her tears became weeping.

Seth tightened his hug until her emotions subsided and she composed herself. Her throat was still constricted, but she managed to get out a few words.

"I don't know what to say."

Her offered a wry smile that kept her feelings off-kilter.

"Say you'll accept it. As payment, as recompense, as a token of my gratitude to you... a token of my love."

The first three things she could accept, but not the latter. Of the triad of voices that spoke to her just moments ago, one had finally won.

She pulled far enough away so she could see his face. It had grown more serious in her silence. His attention was solely on her eyes as though he were trying to see into her very soul.

Love.

How easy it would be to accept the word at face value. He might even believe himself in love with her, but whether he knew it or not, he was no longer the man he was when they first met.

He was now the Duke of Auchen. That changed everything; it opened doors and closed others.

She suspected Seth had not comprehended the full measure of expectations that would be upon him now – in terms of managing his late father's estates, certainly; for his own plans for

Skye-Heath and Habetrot, without doubt. But, for all the wealth and power a duke might wield, he was still the king's man and, as such, a duke did not, under any circumstances, marry a pretend nurse whose only claim to a title was from ancient custom. There were lairds a-plenty in Scotland, most of them without two farthings to rub together, and few of them were taken seriously south of the border – or north of it, for that matter.

No, the fitting wife for a duke would be a duchess or a countess. The Prince of Wales would expect it, and Seth would be unable to refuse. But she would not tell him that.

Ruby looked away, fishing a handkerchief from her pocket and bringing it to her eyes to wick away the moisture.

"You can't possibly do this."

Seth's brow creased. "Is it so hard to believe?"

"After knowing I took the position as nurse under false pretenses? That I impersonated your dead mother to try to manipulate your father?"

"I know *why* you did those things. You did it with honorable intent."

Ruby slowly shook her head. "No. I did not. I did it out of selfish intent. I did so in revenge."

The expression on Seth's face ebbed away. What was once warm and open was closed off, making him look so much like the man in the portrait in London.

His father.

"Was *everything* you did in service of your goal?" he asked. The words were softly delivered, but the meaning behind them was unmistakable.

There was no point in hiding it. She would tell him the truth and let him make his own decision, but she wouldn't unnecessarily blacken her own character. Ruby shook her head and swallowed.

"You have no reason to believe I'm telling the truth. I lied about being a nurse. I lied about my name. I lied to a dying man. But my feelings for you are true. I've never lied about that."

After a long, silent moment, Seth gave a curt nod and walked to the side table where he poured himself a whisky. He held up the decanter, silently offering her one, too.

Ruby shook her head.

"Hate brought us together," she said. "You and I – we both hated your father."

He huffed out a breath. "Hated. Past tense. I suppose there is no point in hating a dead man."

Ruby found an unasked-for glass of whisky pressed into her hand anyway.

"You stopped hating your father weeks ago."

Seth snorted. Ruby spared him a skeptical glance.

"You cannot tell me that you hated your father at the last. I shan't believe you."

His face flushed red. He turned away from her. Unthinkingly, she brought the glass to her lips. The scent of the whisky itself seemed intoxicating enough. She sipped the smallest measure of the spirit.

The tick of the mantel clock seemed suddenly very loud. It marked away the seconds until a minute had passed, and no other words had been spoken between them. Seth broke the silence at last.

"My father spoke of regret. He spoke of wanting to be reunited with my mother, and he said he needed to make amends. It was the beginning of a rapprochement between us. Are you telling me I cannot even trust the memory of that?"

Against her better judgment, Ruby took a larger sip of the whisky and felt the fire of it burn down her throat, setting her stomach ablaze. She gasped, and her eyes watered. It was a moment before she could reply.

"When we visited Skye-Heath, and saw the looms did not use my father's invention, I was bereft. Everything I had supposed was wrong."

"And yet you stayed. Why?"

"I stayed because… I found myself falling in love with *you.*

When your father believed in his delirium that I was your mother, I continued pretending to be her because I believed... I hoped... that if he treated you kindly at the end, that his passing would leave you with less regret."

She chanced a look in his direction and found the cool blue of his eyes meeting hers.

"We have declared love, but can we trust it?" she continued. "How can there be a solid foundation to a life together when so many lies have been told to build it?" She paused, then added, "When *I* have told so many lies?"

She picked up the envelope containing the deed to Strathaird and held it out to him.

"I cannot take your gift."

"You do not want it?"

Tears filled her eyes once more.

"Yes, I want it."

Seth's expression softened.

"Then accept it. I ask nothing in return that you are not willing to give... not even your love."

CHAPTER TWENTY-FOUR

October 1818

HOW HAD AUTUMN arrived so quickly? Ruby looked out over the familiar grounds of Strathaird, the wide expanse of lawn, the ancient trees whose leaves had turned the most magnificent of colors – fiery red, burnished copper, and a yellow so bright it seemed that it ought to be warm to the touch.

She accepted the footman's hand to assist her from the carriage.

She took a deep breath and glanced heavenward. The cloudless sky above was pale blue and perfect, just as she remembered. A gentle breeze carried with it the smell of decaying leaves, a tinge of wood smoke, even the hint of sweetness from fallen apples being reclaimed by the soil.

All of a sudden, she was ten years old, returning home after visiting with Frannie and her family. If she waited, she would hear the voices of her parents.

I have come up with a wonderful idea. I must write it down!

Well, best you do that now, Jacob, because we do expect you to join us at the table. Cook is already preparing dinner, and you know she refuses to serve a fine meal out in your workshop!

Ruby smiled at the memory.

Jackson, the butler, stood waiting, along with the dozen servants who cared for the house and grounds of Strathaird.

"It is a pleasure to have ye home, Miss Ruby," he said. "A most unexpected pleasure! Ye'll find everything is as ye remember."

She nodded and thanked him, then found a smile and a word of greeting for everyone, but still she was aware that Seth watched her, too. Still, she couldn't disguise her feelings at being *home*.

It was everything she wanted.

But why did her heart squeeze at that moment?

She knew. Strathaird wasn't *everything* she wanted.

She swallowed the errant thought down, but couldn't help being drawn to Seth's side – or perhaps it was he who joined her?

"Thank you for bringing me home," she said.

He nodded once, his expression unreadable.

"Show me," he said. "Show me Strathaird through your eyes."

She really wished he wouldn't be so kind and understanding. It was a knife in the heart with every breath. He would be leaving for London within days, and it would be months before he returned.

If at all.

Inside, she opened the library door and entered. The heavy curtains that covered the French windows were parted. There was a fire set in the grate. Trust Jackson to remember her habits. This was her favorite room in the house.

She felt close to both of her parents here. Her mother had used this room as her morning room. Her father could also be found here late in the evenings when his workshop became too cold.

This was where she'd discovered his loom invention and first learned the name of William Gregory Musgrave, the Duke of Auchen.

She thought it would be difficult to tell Seth about her girlhood at Strathaird, the warm family memories, the sadness following her mother's death, and how close she grew to her father in the years when it was just the two of them. How, even when his memory faded, there were moments like when he was telling stories of his past, in which her father seemed like his old self.

But once Ruby began the recounting, she couldn't stop. There was the bell system her father had rigged up to call the servants. Not a new invention, but something he'd insisted on installing – and improving – himself.

And speaking of bells, there was the clock her father had taken apart and put back together – included with an added set of chimes.

In her father's bedroom, Ruby showed Seth a large walnut double secretaire desk that stood strangely out of place among the pieces of fine, craftsman-made oak furniture in the room.

The desk had three full-length drawers at its base. Either side of the drop desk leaf were four small drawers which were only four inches wide, but they were deep.

On top of the desk, where a bookcase would usually be, was another set of small drawers on either side of a cupboard. The timber chosen was nicely figured, but not embellished with inlays as one might expect from a London cabinetmaker for a piece of this type.

"It's certainly an eccentric looking thing," Seth ventured.

Ruby laughed as she walked to the windows and drew back the curtain, allowing early afternoon light to spill across the room. "I think that's the kindest thing anyone has ever said about it."

He ran his hand across the surface of the desk.

"Still, it is a credit to your father. He was quite accomplished in the manual arts. The joints are very well done."

"My father wasn't necessarily the most skillful carpenter, but my mother was apparently taken with it," she said. "Normally, she preferred my father's inventions to remain outside the house.

But that's not all – this desk has eight secret drawers."

Seth whistled. He stepped back to examine the desk as a whole.

"If it was any other man, I would have my doubts, but since this is a piece made by your father, I have no difficulty in believing the claim."

He turned her way, his face brighter and more animated than she had seen in well over a month.

"I could guess at the location of some, but not all," he said.

This was a glimpse of the man she had come to know over the past six months, a man who had disappeared on the day of the duke's funeral to be replaced with a more reserved man, one who was painfully aware of his new situation.

"What of you?" he continued. "Do you know where all the secret drawers are?"

She shook her head. "My father refused to tell me. He made me find them for myself. I only ever managed seven," she added wistfully.

THERE HAD NEVER been any doubt in Seth's mind that he had done the right thing in signing over to Ruby the deed to Strathaird, despite the substantial financial cost. But today, walking with her through this house and having her point things out which would have passed him by unnoticed, only cemented the decision.

Was it any surprise he'd felt at ease here when he'd first come to inspect the place? An unexpected wave of longing had washed over him along with the realization that, for the longest time, he'd had no home.

Granted, he'd always had a place to live and, now, a very grand place to live. But it wasn't the same as a *home*, was it? A home was a place where happy memories were made, where the furniture and decoration served more than a practical purpose because each piece had significance, a tale, a history.

There was very little he had which had such a claim on him. But Strathaird and its contents had such a claim on Ruby, and it was right to return it to her.

He cast his eyes across the desk once more. He would never have dreamed that a provincial piece would conceal a single secret, let alone eight. Just as, when they first met, he'd had no reason to suspect Ruby had things to hide...

As much has his heart and ego were wounded that his declaration of love for her was not fully returned, he could at least now leave for London with an ease of mind, knowing he had done the right thing by her with regard to her home.

He looked back to Ruby.

It was hard to believe that just a few weeks ago, she was in his bed. He thought that was the beginning of something more... well, it didn't matter what he thought now, did it?

His eyes fell to a small movement of her hands. She pressed her thumb into the palm of her other hand. He'd noticed her do it often. It was, he believed, an expression of anxiety.

What if she was with child? His child? He wanted to make her promise to tell him if it were so. No child of his would face the stigma of being a bastard.

He pretended deeper interest in the desk, so he didn't have to look into her beautiful face and be rejected once more. The gulf between them that had emerged on the night of his father's funeral deepened. He didn't want to believe that her feelings for him were solely the result of the mutual antipathy for his late father.

Any port in a storm. Is that how you think of me, Ruby?

He knew if he stayed here in Scotland, he'd become bitter, and, after witnessing its destruction firsthand, he'd rather avoid his father's fate if it was all the same.

At least he was wanted in London – even if was at the Prince Regent's command.

She seemed to sense his thoughts. "When do you leave?"

Seth's hand stilled on the desk, but he couldn't bring himself to look at her despite the note of sadness in her voice.

"Day after tomorrow," he said. "I've sent Lady Millarstone and her daughter on ahead in my carriage. I'll ride for a day or two and see if I feel up to traveling in their company."

"It was kind of you to take Jeanette Millarstone under your wing," Ruby said. "She seems to be a nice girl."

"Unlike her mother," Seth muttered.

Ruby laughed. "You might say that, but I couldn't possibly – after all, Lady Millarstone's *your* relative, and she appears to have a singular plan in mind for the bachelor Duke of Auchen."

He turned to her and grinned, hopefully. "Then come with me. Save me from that woman's machinations."

To see his smile had returned sparked a flare of happiness that was quickly doused by melancholy when she slowly shook her head. Ruby's own expression faltered, turning grave, making her look more like the Nurse Campbell of old.

"Does Roddy not go with you?" she asked.

Seth headed toward the door. Surely he could manage if only he could he put a little space between them. They headed downstairs, back to the library. After a couple of minutes of silence, Seth felt obliged to answer her question.

"Roddy is staying behind. I've left him a bit of a mess to sort out. The ruins of Habetrot for a start. I've given him carte blanche to do whatever it takes to deal with it. Most likely, the best thing to do is salvage anything that can be sold and walk away."

"You mean to abandon Habetrot? It was your dream."

The maid arrived with the tea.

Seth sat on the settee opposite Ruby and watched her pour a cup for him and then one for herself while he considered his answer.

"It was the dream of another man."

"You are still that man."

Seth accepted the cup and shook his head.

"I'm not the man I was when I met you."

Ruby eyed him thoughtfully, as if trying to determine whether he jested or was in earnest.

"Don't give up," she said at length. "Not just yet. Give it time."

"It takes a wise man to know when to cut his losses."

She blinked rapidly, betraying her awareness of the second meaning behind their conversation. Turning her face away, she pretended interest in the spoon she turned around and around the cup.

"When... will you return?" Her voice revealed that she had not lost all tender feeling toward him – that was something, at least.

"Hogmanay, perhaps. But from what I understand, Parliament will be in session. and there'll be the expectation that I'll stay for the full Season, I suppose. Unless Jeanette receives a suitable offer, of course."

Ruby nodded before continuing, caution in her tone. "I am not insensible to the attachment we have formed over these past months, but I do not wish to it be an obligation. If you should... encounter a lady whom you feel would make a suitable duchess, I would understand. I..."

Her voice trailed off with finishing the sentence. She didn't need to. That was the problem. Ruby understood too much and nothing at all. Judging by her countenance, at least he could comfort himself with the knowledge she was not completely unmoved by his impending departure.

The clock struck four. Seth used the distraction of it to set down his cup, get to his feet and call to have his carriage made ready. He should go now before he made even more of a fool of himself before her.

As much as he fought against bitterness, the sweet poison of it was already in his veins. Now, he couldn't wait to be away from it. He bitterly rued the pride that caused him to stake everything on Habetrot simply to cock a snook at his father.

Months ago, he'd cursed the man for the need to leave Glasgow for London. Now, he was tempted to curse the woman he loved for forcing him to go there alone instead of with her at his side.

She stood at his side now, but in parting.

He watched his carriage draw up at her door.

It shouldn't end like this, Ruby.

He kept the thought to himself.

She spoke. "Would I be welcome to write?"

The very fact she asked the question, along with the quavering note of uncertainty that accompanied it, thawed a little of the ice he felt forming around his heart.

He bent over her hand and pressed a kiss there.

"I'd be honored, Lady Strathaird."

Her hand squeezed his tightly in return for a moment and, if he was not much mistaken, she blinked away tears.

Good, if she suffered half as much as he did now.

He regretted the thought, even as it brought him cold comfort.

The footman opened the carriage door. Seth strode toward it. He would be like Lot and escape the brimstone. He would not look back like Lot's wife to become a pillar of salt.

His carriage pulled away.

They said time healed wounds. Would adding hundreds of miles distance help the ache in his heart? How long should he wait for the woman he loved to love him in return?

CHAPTER TWENTY-FIVE

London
November 1818

S ETH TAPPED HIS foot restlessly.

Of all the amusements he'd been offered thus far in London, musicales were the ones he preferred. Not that he was a particular acolyte of Euterpe, the muse of music, but it was the only activity where he was obliged to do nothing but sit and applaud politely at the end of each piece.

It was one of the few times he could be guaranteed time alone with his own thoughts, without the interruption of servants and various callers, the well-wishers, the merchants, and the various men of business all of whom told him that their business was of the utmost importance and needed to be attended to at the earliest opportunity.

He had to confess as to being unsure what a duke was supposed to do, but his experience over the past three months had seen his day begin at nine o'clock in the morning for the first business appointment and end at two o'clock the following morning after the attending a ball, a soiree, a concert, a play, or other such activity that he was told by his new secretary was *"absolutely obligatory, Your Grace"*.

God only knew how he'd be able to keep up such a schedule

when the Season *actually* began.

When his head hit the pillow, he slept the sleep of the dead. At least back in Glasgow, running the mill, he could leave at seven o'clock, spend a few hours at the pub, and be in bed by ten ready to start fresh again at eight of the morning.

Add to that the fact he hadn't even known he *had* a secretary until he'd arrived at Glencoe House, but there they were – a new secretary and a new valet, appointed by the Prince of Wales himself.

What an uncomfortable first meeting *that* had been. Seth shook his head at the recollection.

It was clear the Prince Regent had been under the same impression as everyone else – that the new Duke of Auchen was feeble in mind and body – and he had done nothing to hide his surprise on their meeting.

"You're not at all as your father had us believe."

Seth had bristled. "I have spent my life confounding my father's opinion of me, Your Highness."

At that, Prinny had barked out a laugh.

"Me, too, Musgrave! Me, too."

Nevertheless, the Prince Regent's original opinion of him was revealed in his choice of aides for the new duke – the secretary and the valet. Initially, the two servants conspired together to carefully manage Seth's life to the point that all he had to do was to say "yes" or "no" to carefully crafted "choices" that gave the illusion of control, but whose outcomes were preordained to be the "right" ones.

It took a week for them to realize they didn't have to talk to him in words of no more than two syllables, and another month before they dropped their condescending tone altogether after fully appreciating that they weren't dealing with an idiot.

Seth grinned at the memory, happening to glance in Lady Millarstone's direction as he did. As though she had some kind of sixth sense, the woman turned his way, giving him a mild frown.

Ah, a faux pas. One did not smile during recitals.

Noted.

Seth sobered his expression, gave the good lady a brief nod of acknowledgement, and turned his attention to the program.

For all that the woman was annoying, she was a stickler for etiquette and protocol – at least most of the time – and that made her a useful barometer of sorts.

While he was confident his manners would suffice in most circumstances – he knew how to treat a lady, after all – there were, he decided, some arcane rules that were some kind of shibboleth to identify the lower classes who dared make an appearance in the higher ranks of society.

So, in the end, Prinny's choice of men to carefully "manage" the Ninth Duke of Auchen turned out to be fortuitous after all, and Seth accepted their coaching with as much good grace as he could muster.

The first lesson was that one never speaks of business. Oh, one might discuss the land in terms of the quality of the grouse shooting or the stocks of fish on one's country estate, but never about *working* the land – let alone any other industry that put food on one's table or clothing on one's back. Such things were beneath the notice of a gentleman, let alone an aristocrat.

Now secure in the acceptance of the Prince of Wales' favor, Seth found himself with a never-ending list of invitations to parties over the past few months, and there was no getting around the expectation that he would dance. When it came to the country-style dances, he managed creditably, but he'd never learned the formal and court dances, so he sat them out.

But far from harming his reputation, it only seemed to en-hance it. The more he regretfully shook his head in response to looks from hopeful young ladies, the more interest they seemed to take in him.

He tried not to hate himself for the fact that he looked twice at every woman with jet black hair, hoping it might be Ruby.

It had gotten to the point that, at many of these soirees, he ended the better half of the night in the card room with the men.

Not that he was a gambler. Far from it. But the activity served to mask his unfamiliarity with all the social airs and graces, and his card game was good enough to hold his own to finish the night with a few coins extra in his purse.

Actually, these evenings did serve him well – he was beginning to learn who truly held the levers of power in this city.

Thus far, he was content to endure the openly curious speculation of the men and suffer the coy glances of women who whispered behind their fans. The more they learned about him, the more *he* learned about *them*.

It wasn't the first time he had to navigate a world so different to the one he had known. It had taken some time to get used to working at the mill. But, unlike working at the mill, he didn't imagine that in business in the city he'd have to use his fists. No, the weapons here were more subtle – but could wound no less deeply.

The musical piece came to an end. Seth followed along with the applause and pretended to read the program while he continued to retreat deep into his own thoughts.

He felt Roddy's absence keenly. His friend had acute powers of observation, as well as good sense. How he missed the man's counsel. Still, he'd done the right thing in having him go manage his affairs in Scotland. There was no one he would trust more to keep him appraised of Skye-Heath's business, or to wrap up the misbegotten affair that was Habetrot.

The failure of that venture cut deep, but perhaps it was meant to be. He was passionate about the possibilities of increasing production and promoting the safety of the workers, and Habetrot was intended to be a model of both. And yet it was also born of a desire to be a success and rub the old man's nose in it.

He'd harbored so much bitterness against the man. For so many years, that hatred had fueled him, made him get up when he'd been knocked down – physically and metaphorically.

But what happened when the hatred was gone? What drove him then? Frankly, he didn't know.

Something thrummed within him, a recollection of the conversation he'd had with Ruby at Castle Glenuig when she rejected his pledge of love.

Could a love conceived in bitterness be healthy and survive?

The past six months had been a blur. He hadn't considered the consequence of being an earl, let alone becoming a duke. Everything had come upon him so suddenly that he'd had precious little time to think.

No, better that Habetrot be consigned to history. He had nothing to prove – *correction*, he had no one to prove it to. As owner of Skye-Heath, instead of merely being its employee, he could make the changes he wanted there.

But while here in London, he was trying his damnedest to fit in. What did it say about him that the most reliable of his acquaintances were two relatives whom he hardly knew?

But, due to his position, there were some men with whom he was acquainted. Even then, they treated him cautiously, like an outsider, nodding politely and pointing him toward Members of Parliament and the men seated in the House of Lords who would be grateful for a financial contribution to advance his ideas for protection for industrial workers.

However, making laws was one thing; encouraging mill owners to see the benefits to their ledgers of a safer workplace was quite another. It would require an enterprise successful in both before people truly took notice.

Once again, the people around him applauded and he absently did the same.

"Woolgathering again, Your Grace?"

Seth pulled his thoughts together and turned to the Honorable Miss Jeanette Millarstone, noting belatedly that, all around them, people were leaving their seats to make their way to the ballroom for the next entertainments.

"Was I that obvious?"

"Only to me," she said kindly. "But you do find these affairs to be quite the bore, don't you?"

Yes. No.

Before he fashioned a correct answer, Jeanette snapped open her fan to disguise their conversation.

"I think you and I understand each other better than we think."

"You're not enjoying your Season, Miss Millarstone?"

She offered a brief shrug of her shoulders.

"Maman is pushing me forward to every eligible man in London. And just like a general planning a battle, she has identified you as a most promising target."

"I'm flattered."

"You shouldn't be."

"Any gentleman should be honored to have a young lady of quality take an interest in him."

"Very prettily said, and if I believed you genuinely meant a word of it, you'd turn my head and make my mother a very happy woman indeed."

There was a sparkle in her light brown eyes that let him know she was teasing him. Seth smiled, a genuine one this time.

"Isn't it unladylike to doubt a gentleman's word?"

Jeanette smile broadened.

"On the contrary, it is a lady's duty to be utterly skeptical of a gentleman's word, especially when she knows he is actually in love with someone else."

The allusion to Ruby ended his taste for bantering with this young woman. He moved to leave when Jeanette placed her fan on his arm.

"Wait. Please, Cousin."

He paused. The family connection between the Musgraves and the Millarstones went back four generations and was a tenuous link at that. Why did she raise it now?

"I know my mother is keen on a match between us but, as kind and forbearing as you are, I do not love you."

Despite the fact that he'd became a little kindly disposed toward the girl during their short acquaintance, her bluntness did put a slight bruise on his ego.

She continued, "I want time to enjoy my Season, to meet people, even perhaps to find a husband of my own choosing."

"That's completely understandable," he commented wryly.

"I'm glad we understand each other because you are under no less pressure than I to wed. I've seen the way other girls and their mothers have set their caps at you, and it will only get worse when the Season begins in earnest."

"That does seem to be an inevitable consequence of being paraded on the marriage mart."

"Don't you see? It doesn't have to be. Not if you truly love Lady Strathaird."

Seth couldn't hide his frown, but the girl went on.

"Do forgive me if I speak out of turn, but I do not believe I am mistaken, nor am I mistaken in my belief that she has an equal regard for you."

Seth rose to his feet and looked for an escape – the garden, the cardroom, hell – even the dance floor with his two left feet would be welcome now. He had spoken to no one about his feelings for Ruby, not even to Roddy and he'd be damned if he was going to speak of them to some *debutante*.

"I regret that I have to bring this interview to a close, Miss Millarstone," he said tightly before offering a short bow and heading out to the balcony. He pushed his way through the French doors and found he hadn't realized that he was close to breaking into a sweat until he'd taken a deep breath of the cold night air.

How wrong Jeanette was. How desperately wrong.

He welcomed the distance between himself and Ruby. Hadn't she made it plain? Strathaird was really all she ever wanted, and any feelings she might have had for him were a misbegotten folly as a result of their mutual hatred for William Musgrave.

Seth walked deep into the gardens, mindful of keeping away from a couple taking the air. He came to a halt at one of the terraced gardens and rested a hip against a railing. He breathed in deep, picking up the scents of burning tobacco, damp soil, and the soft berry sweet fragrance from the pale pink flowers of the potted viburnum nearby.

Damn it! It had been months, and he could still see her face in his mind's eye, those full pink lips and large brown eyes, still feel her soft skin beneath his touch.

Even his dreams betrayed him, recalling memories of their lovemaking that were so vivid that he woke the next morning with an erect member and a bitter disappointment.

In two months' time, it would be Hogmanay. It had been his intention to go back to Scotland and mark the New Year there, but he couldn't. Not yet, not until he could be finally free of her.

Furthermore, until he could be free of Ruby in his heart and his mind, he would not commit to another.

And he certainly did not want to let his own unfamiliarity with the customs of the *ton* leave some girl and her family believing he was entertaining a proposal when all he was doing was being polite and pleasant.

The delicate scent of the viburnum suddenly gave way one more cloying – gardenia, orange blossom, and something else he couldn't determine.

"Your Grace," a husky feminine voice greeted him.

Seth recalled the face and the figure – displayed admirably, he had to admit, in a low-cut evening gown of shot silk, silver and pink, a combination artfully enjoined to set off perfectly coiffed blonde hair. But for the life of him, he couldn't remember the lady's name.

"Good evening, Countess." Thank goodness he could remember her title, at least. "Have you lost your escort?"

The beautiful woman smiled at him as though he'd said the wittiest bon mot.

"I feel the chill," she said. "Do you not find it brisk this evening?"

A question of that type was a command, an obligation for

him to remove his warm jacket and lay it over the shoulders of an inadequate dressed female who didn't have the sense to bring a wrapper.

And, as a gentleman, he did the chivalrous thing for – Beatrice Rowlands, Countess of Engelton, his memory finally supplied.

"Thank you," she said in that husky voice that suggested sex and sensual delights. "I dare say you don't feel the cold, coming from Scotland."

Seth fought a shiver. "No, My Lady, you are quite correct."

"Fascinating! I've not been to Scotland although I understand it to be a very romantic place."

If she asked about Scotsmen and their kilts, he'd take back his coat, and she could freeze to death.

Fortunately for the lady, she did not ask, although she did manage to slip her arm through his as they made their way back to the house.

"Do you intend to stay for the whole of this Parliamentary session?"

"At this stage, yes, unless some pressing business takes me home."

"Edinburgh's loss is our gain, then."

"Glasgow."

"I beg your pardon?"

"Glasgow. A city that will soon grow to be one of the most important in the empire."

"I see."

Seth was pretty sure she didn't.

In his estimation, Glasgow had potential – textiles, shipbuilding, and more. His city could be as famous as Manchester, the name a byword for quality and industry.

He safely returned the lady to the warmth of the assembly room. Their absence had not gone unnoticed. Yes, he could imagine what it looked like – a return from an assignation. Beatrice gave him a knowing look after she disentangled her arm from his and shrugged off his coat. Obviously, this is what she had intended to happen.

From across the room, the Earl of Runcorn gave him a nod and a look of approval, and it was balanced by the dark glare of disapproval that Lady Millarstone cast his way.

"I should like to know more of Glasgow. Would you consider paying me a call, Your Grace?"

Some mischievous imp deep in his soul leaped to life, dancing with the idea of displeasing Lady Millarstone even more. And should word get back to Ruby via Miss Jeanette, then so much the better.

Seth bent over the countess' hand and kissed it. "The honor would be mine."

The woman squeezed his hand once before letting it go. "And the pleasure mine."

The gong rang, announcing supper. The Earl of Runcorn approached while Seth searched for Lady Cynthia Renshaw, the woman he had drawn to escort to the table.

He didn't mind Runcorn. He was an engaging character who'd gone out his way to make him feel welcome when he was so obviously a fish out of water.

The man jostled his shoulder while pretending to look out for his own lady to escort.

"Well, you've drawn yourself a winner's hand, old boy," he said. "The countess doesn't usually make such a bold move in front of an assembly."

"If I didn't know better, I thought she was a courtesan," Seth answered under his breath to limit the spread of their conversation.

"Close enough. She's been a merry widow for the past five years with a taste for the younger man, although she did make an exception for Prinny once, I believe. Many of the ladies of the *ton* despise her, but they are keen to know every minutiae of what she wears and every detail of who she's seen with. If she's picked you as her lover for this Season, then you're a lucky man in more ways than one."

"She's a beautiful woman, and difficult to say no to, but why do I feel like a fly to her spider?"

Runcorn raised his head, finding his partner for supper and setting a wide smile for the girl's benefit, before saying under his breath, "I wish you all the best of it, Musgrave. At least you know where you stand with her."

CHAPTER TWENTY-SIX

December 1819

Dearest Ruby,

I read your letter twice to make sure I understood it in full. That you are again in full possession of Strathaird seems nothing short of a miracle. I can scarcely believe that the new Duke of Auchen should make you a present of it and ask nothing in return.

You'll forgive my bluntness, of course. I know you are well of age and not naïve in the ways of the world, and know as well as I, that men – even those who own the title of gentleman – often attach strings to their acts of altruism. As my uncle's granddaughter, I do feel as maternal toward you as though you were one of my own girls.

Since I can only read between the lines that you have written here, I simply have to conclude that you are nursing nothing more serious than a bruised heart over Seth Musgrave's absence.

You've shown remarkable restraint by only mentioning him the once in your letter. I am not so insensible that I fail to recognize you will want news of how he fares in London. From what I have seen, he is friendly, not exactly diffident, but reserved. This appears to have served him very well so far.

The truth is the man has become quite the sensation this

Season. A duke, unwed, wealthy by all accounts, and hand-some – I do think that you did me an injustice by not more fully describing him in your letters – a novelty, as he is completely unknown in this circle. He is always the first to receive invitations which has done his young charge no harm at all. She was sponsored almost immediately at Almack's.

She's not exactly a diamond of the first water but winsome enough when she is out of the clutches of her maman. What a delightful woman Lady Millarstone is. (You may take that in whatever way you wish!) I should tell you that she almost created a scene at Countess Cunyinghame's dinner party the other night when she overstepped herself in relying on her somewhat tenuous connection with Musgrave. From the way she spoke, one would believe her to be the duke's mother – or mother-in-law, which is more to the point.

Do not stint in your reply to me. I will want to know everything that goes on with you. Are you truly content being at Strathaird on your own? Your father was such a larger-than-life character. His presence must surely be missed. I urge you to find some other enterprise beyond the estate to occupy your time. I trust that you are not too lonely without a ready supply of suitable companionship. It is not too late to journey down to London. Due to Lady Asquith's patronage of my services – I've outfitted all four of her daughters – invitations to parties and balls are never in short supply.

Do write soonest, dear Ruby.

With deepest felicitations,
Your cousin Francine.

P.S. I have included some sketches of some of the most stylish creations seen in London thus far. If you do not intend to travel, you could have something similar made and be the most modish female in Glasgow. You always had a good eye for the latest trends and what is au courant.

Ruby read over the letter three times before setting it down on her dressing table and picking up the fashion plates. Although it had traveled the length of Great Britain, the paper still smelled faintly of the sweet creamy scent of gardenias.

She smiled. Receiving a letter from Frannie was always a joy, as though her dearest friend were sitting beside her sharing the latest on dit.

The waistlines were dropping, Ruby noted. More obvious was flounced petticoats adding more fullness in the skirt which were now being decorated with more elaborate ruffles and tucks.

With the defeat of Napoleon, it seemed the nation was in the mood to celebrate.

I wonder if Seth's paying attention?

The management at Skye-Heath would benefit to know of such things and set their weavers to work on producing the best fabrics for the fashions.

The thought of Seth paying close attention to the mode of ladies' dress made her smile, but the reaction was soon followed by a wave of longing that surprised her.

He'd been gone three months now. It should have been long enough to overcome any lingering tendre she felt. And yet, she found herself thinking of him at the oddest moments, imagining his reaction to the demands and strictures of the rarefied world he now inhabited, wondering what he thought of the wonderful entertainments London offered.

How she wished she was there with him, seeing London through his eyes, sharing the experience with him for the very first time.

Stop this! Stop this now! That way lies madness, and you know it.

You did the right thing letting Seth leave. He could never be truly happy unless he had a chance to experience the life and privilege that should have been his since birth. What would it have been like to arrive there tied to a provincial nobody?

Ruby swallowed against a lump in her throat.

Doing the right thing should have been easy. So why did it feel like her heart was breaking?

At first, she had been successful in distracting herself from thinking of Seth. Her days were filled with the demands of the estate, and she enjoyed being involved with the management of it.

But more and more recently, her thoughts had turned back to Seth.

Frannie was right, she would need more occupation than Strathaird provided on its own. She considered her current "amusement" – relocating her belongings to the master suite of the house. Satisfying, but hardly exciting.

And, in truth, an estate like Strathaird did not require attention every minute of the day. She'd started inventing things to occupy herself, and that was why she found herself in her father's bedroom claiming the quarters for her own.

She regarded her father's double secretary desk. If she could find the key, she could make use of it herself.

Perhaps she could even find the elusive eighth secret drawer.

A tap at the door distracted Ruby's thoughts. Wendy, her maid, stood in the threshold.

"Beg pardon, mum, but a gentleman's here to see ye."

She was expecting no visitors today. Unbidden, her heart leaped.

Seth!

Ruby dismissed the thought. He was four hundred miles away enjoying the glittering parties and balls, reveling in the attention that was his due as the Duke of Auchen.

She thought of him often. Not every day – but not too far from it. And in the time he had been gone, she had received two letters from Frannie, but none from him.

Despite his assurance that letters from her would be welcome, she had not yet plucked up the courage to write to him.

No. If he *really* wished to continue their friendship, he would have to make the first move.

Still, a visitor was still a visitor. Ruby examined her reflection, then pinched her cheeks to give them a little color before going downstairs.

Her visitor was not Seth, but a face just as familiar.

"My dear Roddy!" she greeted him with unfeigned delight and a hug. "It has been too long! How do you fare? What of Skye-Heath? Any news regarding Habetrot?"

A grin split his features.

"Well, lassie, that's as full and grand a welcome as I've ever received! In order, my answers are 'fine', 'prospering', and 'would ye like to see for yerself?'"

Ruby blinked rapidly trying to work out whether she'd actually been given the answers to questions she sought.

"Really? You're going out to the mill site?"

"While the weather is still fair, I thought ye'd might like to ride out with me, and I'll share all my news."

Did that include word from Seth? Ruby bit her tongue and forced the errant thought down.

"I should be delighted to ride out with you."

RUGGED UP AGAINST the lowering sky, she rode with Roddy toward the woods that bounded Strathaird's lands and led to the site of Habetrot. Winter had bitten deep. It had stripped the trees of all their leaves, their silver branches lifted heavenward in naked supplication. The earth smelled loamy. The ground was soft beneath the hooves of their horses as a result of recent rain.

Just to the right of the path was an ancient stone-walled barn. Once, it had held the winter feed for the cattle and sheep. But in more recent years, it had become where her father hoarded broken bits and pieces from both the house and the estate.

Roddy brought his horse to a halt so Ruby stopped, too.

"I've a confession to make and an apology, too, Lady Strathaird," he said, making her wonder at his formality. "I'm afraid I took it upon myself to make use of yer barn for getting some of the bits and pieces from Habetrot out of the weather. I'm very sorry."

"You don't have to be, just as long as you stop calling me Lady Strathaird," she smiled. "What have you put in there?"

Roddy proceeded toward the barn. Ruby followed.

"My father would prevent the servants from throwing away anything remotely useful," she said as they went. "He would swear to Mother that he had gotten rid of it, but it ended up here where she never went. Occasionally, he'd even surprise us and actually find a genuine use for something which ought to have been long discarded."

As they approached, Ruby saw the barn now held more items that might have been discarded. Lengths of iron, too large to fit fully inside protruded from the open door. Riding closer, she recognized among the piles the twisted and broken beams that took Fergus' life and nearly Seth's along with it.

Then, Strathaird had belonged to Seth, and the barn was not so far from the edge of the estate, so it would make sense for him to use it then. And as far as she was concerned, they were welcome to use it now.

"What do you plan to do with it?" she asked, bringing her horse to a halt and dismounting.

"It's of no use to us now, but it can be melted down for something. The scrap merchants can take it, and we'll at least make a few bob back."

Ruby peered inside. Beyond where the beams lay, the barn was filled to the brim with bits of old household furniture, broken pieces of farming equipment, bricks, timber, and more.

Roddy eased his way past a plough missing several of its tines and a cart with a missing wheel and splintered axle.

"Best ye stay there, lassie. I dinnae think I'm the only creature lurking about back here," he said.

Ruby wrinkled her nose. "Then you'll forgive me if I don't follow you."

He barked out a laugh and continued to look around. "Do ye have any use for all this old junk? I could ask the men coming for the beams to take it away, too – there might be a bob or two in it for ye as well."

"It's hardly worth hanging on to, is it?"

Roddy emerged and gave her an evaluating look before turning to their horses. They mounted and continued toward the river.

"A barn's a useful building," he said, "an empty barn even more so…"

Ruby knew Roddy well enough to know that he didn't say anything he didn't mean – and much of what he said bore significance. She leaped on the comment.

"You have some scheme in mind, don't you?"

He said nothing until they stopped by a tumble of stones at the edge of the derelict mill site.

They walked around in silence. The stream that would power the looms chortled as it bubbled over the rocks and into the river. If she listened, in the distance she could hear the bells of ships making their way up the Clyde to Glasgow.

Truly, this *was* an ideal place for a mill.

"Do you think Seth will ever rebuild Habetrot?" she asked.

"The man would be daft nae to, but he's nae exactly been in his right mind lately."

Ruby nodded, then bent down to pluck one of the small daisies which had begun to spread over the ground. *Bellis perennis*, she reminded herself. She and her childhood playmates had made chains of them, and she wondered at the pretty white-petalled, yellow-centered flower's ability to bloom, forgetful of the season. Drawing a deep breath, she asked the question.

"Have you heard from him? A letter perhaps?"

Roddy lightly shrugged.

"Aye, a short note confirming I was authorized to draw credit from his bank… to do whatever was needed here."

Roddy paused. She noted the quirk of his lips and a twinkle in his eyes.

There was a further question being begged, so she asked it. "And what do *you* think is needed here?"

"A mill. Seth wants to walk away, but it'd be a damned shame if he did. There was nothing wrong with his plans for the building, just a bit of bad luck. We've nae used up all the capital set aside for this. We could rebuild and have the mill finished by the beginning of next autumn."

Something quickened inside her. Ruby looked back over the site, and no longer saw an empty field. She could see the water wheel and a chimney, a lazy line of smoke issuing from it like a beacon to draw men and women to work. A mill that was prosperous, safe, and with plenty of work. And a garden memorial for Fergus, so his family would know he had not been forgotten.

"Do you really think it could be done?" she asked, making no secret of her excitement. A prosperous village was what her father wanted. And now, as Lady Strathaird, she had responsibility for the tenants and the villagers.

Roddy grinned, obviously pleased to see her enthusiasm matched his own.

"To really make it work, we'd have to have looms that could produce cloth faster and better quality," he said. "I always had a hankering to try something like Jacquard's loom with his hole punch card business."

"Like my father's invention…" said Ruby.

"Yer pa didnae happen to leave some detailed plans lying about, did he?"

"How I wish!" Ruby laughed. "I imagine my father gave William Musgrave the plans and kept none for himself. I expected see the process being used in Skye-Heath. I was shocked to see ordinary looms."

"We found a drawing when we were clearing out an old warehouse, but it was nae detailed enough for us to make plans out of it. We could experiment. Get a couple of weavers to work with an engineer and figure it out and build a working model. It would be cheaper than paying a fee to the Frenchman to use his."

This! This was how she could repay Seth for his generosity. This was how she could ease her conscience over her deception of both dukes.

She had been so blinded by her hatred of the late duke that

she justified her own actions and ignored her father's culpability in leaving Strathaird encumbered with debt.

She saw a new way forward.

She would pay Seth back for his generous gifting of Strathaird and approach him anew as Lady Strathaird. He would get to know *her*, not Nurse Campbell.

She prayed that with the air clear between them, he would fall in love with the woman she was and not the one she'd pretended to be.

"Take the barn," she said. "Get rid of everything that is not of use to you. Start Habetrot there until the real mill is complete. I still have a sum of money left from the sale of Strathaird."

The more she spoke, the more weight seemed to lift from her shoulders.

"After all, it is Seth's money, what he paid my solicitor for it. It's only right that I invest it back into something that he is passionate about. Oh, Roddy, this *will* work. I know it will! Habetrot will be the most famous name in Scottish textiles. The finest gowns in London will be made from the finest silks made right here."

"Do ye think ye're getting a bit ahead of yerself?" Roddy's grin belied the question.

"No! Not at all! We can do this!"

Ruby told him about her cousin who went by the name of Madame Francine Dumont, one of the most sought-after mantua makers in London.

"All it would take is one fashionable duchess to wear a garment of material made by Habetrot, and every woman in London would want one in just that fabric."

Roddy's eyes softened.

"I ken why ye're doing this, and there's no need."

Ruby's smile stumbled.

"I'll invest because I wish to."

"And nae out of guilt?"

She could not own that her motivation wasn't that, in part.

Neither did she want to admit that as being the truth. She looked down and considered her answer.

"I am in Seth's debt, and I do not wish to be," she said.

"'Tis nae a question of debt, lassie. The man loves ye."

She squeezed her eyes tight against the prick of tears.

Ruby raised her head, needing to see Roddy's face. The man was a friend and he knew Seth better than anyone.

"I know he loves me, and I love him, too... but given everything that went before, so is the potential for hate."

Surprise, then confusion clouded Roddy's features.

"I never want him to wonder whether I love him simply out of gratitude for restoring Strathaird to me," she explained. "I don't want him to believe he loves me because I was kind to him when he experienced so little kindness in his life."

Roddy's look turned to pity, and she couldn't have that.

"Seth has every right to enjoy the birthright denied him so long," she continued. "And I want my conscience clear. To have no further secrets between us, and no misapprehensions. If we are to love, it will be as equals; on a true and solid footing.

"Most of all, I want him to love me and not Nurse Campbell."

CHAPTER TWENTY-SEVEN

January 1819

Dear Ruby,

You surprised me once when you announced your plans to confront the Duke of Auchen about "stealing" – your words – your father's invention. And here you are surprising me again about going into business with his son.

I have to own that the notion is an intriguing one, so I will not create suspense but tell you plainly that you can count on my involvement. The promise of preferential access to the latest colors and textures from the mills of Skye-Heath? It is impossible to resist.

But do tell me more about your plans for this new mill, Habetrot. How do you plan to scale production to compete with the mills of Manchester?

In the meantime, I send you more watercolor sketches of the most fashionable of this years' Incomparables as well as swatches from fabrics I've only ever been able to procure from France and Italy. Replicate these at lower cost, and your investment in Habetrot mill will reward you tenfold.

I should point out, for your edification, one repeated face among the most fashionable. Beatrice Rowlands, Countess of Engelton. She is an outstandingly beautiful woman with impeccable taste in everything she does.

Unfortunately, she is not part of my clientele, but if your mill can produce fabric fine enough for this beautiful creature, I will design a wardrobe for her that will set the trend for the Season to come. Women across England will be seeking out your fabrics – and my designs, of course!.

You did say in your last letter that M—knows nothing of your involvement in Habetrot? What makes your scheme so irresistibly serendipitous is that your duke has been squiring the countess around town for the better part of a month.

I've included a clipping from a recent newssheet, so you can see for yourself what a splash they have created.

"Good news all around, wouldn't you say?" Ruby handed Frannie's letter to Roddy who skimmed over the contents and paid greater attention to the pieces of fabric that accompanied it.

He hadn't noticed that her enthusiasm was forced. Of course, she was glad her cousin saw merit in their plan and offered her full-throated support – that *was* the plan, wasn't it?

Seth had found another.

The depth of disappointment she felt surprised even herself. What reason had she to feel sorry for herself? Wasn't he experiencing all she had ever wanted for him – recognition, his rightful place, and a beautiful titled woman on his arm that he could make his duchess?

That was what love was, wasn't it? She wanted nothing but the best for him. She loved him. She loved him, so she let him go.

"Aye, I reckon our boys can make fabric as fine at Skye-Heath as this if we're talking wools, but these silks of yer cousin's… it could be done, but in Habetrot's first year with new looms and weavers, it'll nae be easy. We're still clearing out yer old barn. That will house three treadle looms, but it'll be slow going."

She drew a deep breath, thankful that Roddy seemed unaware of her inner turmoil. Now, he was a welcome distraction.

"We need my father's invention to truly compete with the larger mills, don't we?" she asked.

"I willnae lie to ye, lassie, it would give us an advantage."

Ruby took another cleansing breath and squared her shoulders.

"Then we will look again for the plans," she averred. "Every nook and cranny of Strathaird will be searched, and if I have to turn my father's desk into kindling, I will do it to make sure they don't lie in the mysterious eighth secret drawer!"

There, that's what she needed, another distraction, another dragon to slay. Anything to stop herself imagining Seth holding another woman in his arms. It made it worse to actually see a representation of the woman in Frannie's fashion plates.

Blonde hair, fair complexion, an Incomparable indeed. The familiar tentacles of resentment and jealousy wended their way around her heart. She fought them. She had no claim over Seth. She was glad he was free to live and love as he chose.

If only she could make herself believe that were true…

"So where shall we first look?" asked Roddy.

The sound of rain beating against the windows made the decision for her.

"My father's desk," she said.

Roddy inclined his ear to the sound of rain and grinned. "I was hoping ye'd say that. I dinnae fancy a turn outside."

"THE FIRST THREE were easy to find," Ruby announced.

The writing slope dropped down on its hinges like a drawbridge. Ruby pulled out two small interior drawers on either side of the writing space and set them aside.

"Ah! The drawers dinnae go all the way into the back of the cabinet," said Roddy.

Next was also in the interior of the desk. In the center was a cupboard. Ruby opened two little doors with ivory knob handles and reached into the back. She slid the back panel upwards to reveal another void.

"The next two were also obvious – *if* you knew my father and how he thought."

Ruby closed the drop front and reached up to the top left

corner of the secretaire. She pressed on a decorative panel. A semi-circular drawer hinged out. Its twin was found on the right-hand side.

Long familiar with the piece, Ruby pulled open a drawer underneath the fall front and pressed a brass button up inside the drawer.

"I heard a click but I didnae see anything move," said Roddy, who make it clear that he was enjoying himself.

Ruby felt like a salon magician doing tricks. She raised a finger, then, with a flourish, indicated back to the desk. She lowered the front fall slope and eased up a rectangular piece of mahogany in front of the interior fittings that held a space about the size of a glove box.

"That's six, but where are the other two?

"I discovered the seventh by accident. Will you help me remove the lower drawers?"

Ruby stepped aside while Roddy pulled out three heavy drawers.

"There is another sliding panel right at the back. The front drawer supports lift out, otherwise it would be impossible to reach in to the back."

"So why did the laird create such a piece? If ye dinnae mind me saying so, there's a touch of madness about the whole thing."

Ruby wasn't in the least bit offended. She'd pondered the same thing often.

"I really have no idea, other than he wanted to prove it could be done."

"Well, I suppose there's something to be said about that. Shall we see if we can find the other drawer?"

After an hour, Roddy shook his head.

"Well, I cannae find it. And if ye cannae ken where it is…" Roddy shrugged, leaving the rest of the sentence unsaid.

"I've made a thorough examination of the cabinet above the desk, too," Ruby said, "that would have been the most obvious place to add another compartment."

Roddy frowned and scooted under the desk. Ruby offered him a puzzled look, then heard a click.

"Did ye hear that?" he said.

"I did."

"The light caught something, and I thought it might have been another one of those buttons. Can ye see if anything opened?"

Ruby examined the front of the secretaire again and found nothing.

"What about the sides or the back?"

Ruby was about to announce her defeat when she noticed the back panel standing slightly proud of the rest of the cabinet. She pressed it and it clicked back into place.

"I think I've found it. Press the button again."

Roddy did so. The panel moved ever so slightly.

"It's heavy," Ruby warned. She held the solid piece of timber in place as Roddy scrambled out from under the desk to help.

"I've got the weight of it," Roddy announced. "I'll ease it out, ye feel behind."

Excitement thrummed through her.

This had to be it! The space between the back of the cabinet and outer panel was wide enough to hold documents. Plans for his masterwork, the modern punch-card loom.

Ruby reached her arm between the wall and the back of the secretaire, stretching her fingers, hoping to find something, *anything*.

"Well?" Roddy asked, his voice hopeful.

Ruby squeezed her eyes shut and reached further until her fingertips brushed the other side of the void.

"No, nothing." Disappointment weighed every word. "I thought the plans for the loom would surely be here."

Ruby stepped away and slumped down on a dressing stool.

"When Strathaird was sold, I went through all of my father's papers and found the contract with the old Duke of Auchen. I searched everywhere for any plans, any illustrations, anything I could use to prove my claim. I even searched his workshop. I'm sorry, Roddy. I think the loom plans are lost."

Roddy reassembled the desk without comment. She could sense his disappointment, although he was too much of a gentleman to say so.

"What about the outbuildings?"

"You mean the chicken coop? Because that is the only other place, aside from the barn, that hasn't been inventoried thoroughly."

Jackson, the butler, came to the door and addressed Roddy.

"Excuse me, sir. There are a couple of workmen who have come up from the old barn and wish to speak to ye," he said. "They await ye in the kitchen."

Ruby looked at her father's desk once more. Now she knew all its secrets, and she was left only with was a sense of disappointment and finality.

She admired Roddy's optimism, but she could no longer hold on to the dream. She had given up so much for it – just like her father. Perhaps they were more alike than she previously supposed.

Her father had become obsessed, losing touch with everything other than the world of his inventions. It consumed his time and attention before it also devoured his health.

Hadn't she done the same thing herself with respect to Strathaird?

She ventured downstairs. No doubt Roddy would be needed to further address business matters, and she wanted to say goodbye to him.

He emerged from the back hall at a brisk pace.

For one horrible moment, she feared another accident. But this time, his face was bright and animated.

"My men have found something. Ye'll want to see it."

Ruby blinked. She was missing something.

"You mean in the barn?"

"Aye, get yer walking boots on."

Roddy refused to say anything more on the mile walk to the barn. The cold air gave extra impetus to hurry to their destination.

Lamps and braziers created a warm golden glow that beckoned them close. Around them was strewn detritus but, as Ruby got closer, she could see that even the piles of rubbish had some kind of order to them.

She paused at the entrance to the barn, surprised by what she saw. This was the first she'd known the floors were actually paved with stone instead of packed earth as she had assumed. More than that, the space was so clear that she could see the walls. Lamps lit the underside of the thatched roof and, for the first time, Ruby could see there was a mezzanine to another level.

"Ye'll be wanting to come this way, My Lady, Mr. McClane," said the workman who'd accompanied them back from the house. As they walked down the barn, the man spoke.

"There's a big room back here. We seen this thing in it covered with a huge canvas, so we lifted a corner. We could see that it was made of wood so I told the lads to bring an axe and hack at it. But when I pulled off the sailcloth, I thought it looked all right; not like the broken rubbish. Then one of the men said he recognized what it was, and I should fetch ye right away."

He stood back and let them enter the wide door to the space beyond.

Ruby put a hand to her mouth to stifle a gasp.

In the yellow light of the lamps hanging in the room, she took in the tall wooden frame, quickly identifying the heddle frame and harness connected to two lengths of timber treadles. Also in place were the rollers for the cloth roll-takeup, the warp beam let off, the platen…

It was a loom. But more than that was the superstructure at one side – a timber frame which held a series of laced-together cardboard punch cards which would be drawn up and over the weaving frame, past the batten and down the other side.

Her father's vision stood there before her.

"Oh, Roddy…"

She looked to her friend who simply stared, open-mouthed.

"It looks like yer father built himself a working model of his invention. This is the loom like the picture we found at Skye-Heath."

"So, we did right in keeping this thing?" the worker asked.

Roddy clasped the man by the shoulder.

"Ye done good, laddie!"

Ruby turned away and walked out of the barn before emotion got the better of her. She sought out a quiet spot, out of the way of the workmen, and fought back tears.

Joy, disappointment, grief, pride all warred for a place in her mind. Joy that the search for her father's invention had not been in vain; disappointment that he never spoken of it; grief that he was not here to see it come to light; and also pride that his finest invention would now be used as he had envisioned.

The only thing which would have made this moment better was if Seth had been there.

Habetrot was *his* vision, as the loom was her father's.

Did such a thing interest him now that he was Duke of Auchen?

Ruby imagined him to have become a dandy, his mode elegant and refined in dark blue superfine – the type Skye-Heath produced so well. His knowledge of fabrics would ensure that his clothes – immaculate linen shirts, exquisitely tied cravats and expertly tailored coats – were cut to display his fine physique.

She dismissed the thought almost immediately. She would not believe that London could change him so much in so little time. But how well did she really know him and how this countess was reinventing him?

"There ye are!" called Roddy. She wiped under her eyes before turning to face him.

"What are ye out here? Get yerself by the fire." Roddy gestured to a brazier.

Ruby went with him, the warmth most welcome. "I just

needed a moment. Seeing my father's invention at last left me a little overwhelmed."

"Well, I can tell ye, it's a gem," said Roddy. "Seeing how yer father integrated the punch cards into a standard vertical loom makes it easier for our men to make another like it – two, in fact. "Three looms to get us started here in yer barn while we get to work building the grand mill Seth always wanted."

"Have you told him about continuing with Habetrot?"

"I'll tell him in my next report to him. May as well – he'll see it for himself in the itemized expenditures. But that's nae due until the end of March."

There was a gleam in his eyes that lit a spark in Ruby. It burned away the sadness, leaving only hope and a plan.

"In that case, as a new partner in Habetrot, I'd like to make a suggestion," she said. "We *don't* tell him about our plans. We go to London ourselves and *show* him with fabric made on Habetrot's own looms."

CHAPTER TWENTY-EIGHT

London
February 1819

"DARLING, I THINK we should hold an occasion."

Seth inwardly groaned. He hated how Beatrice called him that. Worse was the woman knew it, too, and did it deliberately. But still, he played along because if there was any consolation at all, it was in witnessing Lady Millarstone's expression turned to granite.

"What occasion are you thinking of?" he asked.

"I've taken an interest in your young relation, Jenny."

"Her name is Jeanette," Lady Millarstone bristled.

Seth glanced over at Jeanette who hid a smile as she leaned forward to place her tea cup back on the small table before them. He and Lady Millarstone may have no fondness for this game, but Jeanette was proving to be a great sport in all of this.

And that being the case, the young woman *ought* to get something out of it, at least.

"Are you suggesting an event in Miss Jeanette's honor? A ball perhaps?"

Beatrice's eyes gleamed, a slow smile spreading across her features. He'd guessed upon the right answer, it seemed.

"What a capital idea!" she said. "You will need a hostess, of course. A bachelor duke cannot possibly arrange such a thing on his own."

Indeed, that was true enough.

"And you, *my dear*, would do me the greatest honor by providing such a service," he agreed.

"*Darling*, it is *I* who would be honored to provide *any* service you wish."

Lady Millarstone spluttered, setting down her cup with a rattle, her face turning puce. She looked like a volcano ready to erupt. Jeanette's eyes widened in a pretended display of innocence, but Seth could tell the girl knew a double entendre when she heard one.

For the better part of four months, he had been a willing fly to the spider as he had joked with the Earl of Runcorn. He allowed himself to be Beatrice's, on her terms, confident that by summer she would have moved on. He had to confess it was mutually advantageous to squire a beautiful, intelligent woman to the finest events in London. She had smoothed his entry into the Beau Monde – if she had accepted him, then they would accept him.

Why not use it to his advantage? A spring ball in early May, one of the last before Parliament recessed for the summer season. And he liked Jeanette. She was a good egg. It wasn't her fault she was saddled with an odious mother.

He would even stand a dowry for her to see she was properly launched into society. Lady Millarstone would swallow her complaints for that, he was sure.

But just to make certain, he asked.

"You would have no objection, Cousin?"

Her smile was brittle, but at least her face had become a more normal hue. There, that would finally put paid to any lingering ambition the woman had of making her daughter his duchess.

"You are very generous, Your Grace," she said between gritted teeth. "Jeanette, tell the duke and countess how grateful you are for their notice of you."

Jeanette gave her thanks, first to Beatrice and then to him, her expression one of genuine surprise and gratitude.

No doubt, Beatrice would use the occasion for her own ends, an excuse to order new gowns to make sure she ended the Season being talked about, and her style being emulated by the new Season of debutantes.

Seth hated the thought that he was becoming jaded with London with only four months of exposure. There was still a lot to explore and experience in Europe's finest capital, and he had not even scratched the surface of it.

But even with the glittering spectacle of the London Season, he found himself thinking of the change of seasons in Scotland.

If it was cold, there would be the chance of snow instead of rain up in the Highlands with some beautiful days to go hiking. The hunting was also exceptional with deer coming down from the mountains to forage. The meals of venison and freshly caught salmon could not be matched anywhere else in the kingdom.

He wondered what Strathaird looked like in the winter. Beautiful, he imagined. What might Ruby be doing? Perhaps walking through the woods around the edge of the estate, with the lightest touch of frost on the ground. The White Cart would be flowing, the waterfalls would be a delight to see.

He would be walking with Ruby at his side, her hand in his. She would turn to him, and—

"Darling?"

Seth blinked. The woman in front of him did not have raven-haired tresses, she was blonde, and that was a disappointment.

He raised his eyebrows in mute inquiry.

"Do call for my carriage. We have the theater tonight."

Seth did as she bid and, a few moments later, Beatrice joined him in the hall, slipping her arm through his. They strolled a few steps before she paused, turning to him, stepping closer until her body touched his.

"Are you going to kiss me goodbye?" she asked, her voice husky.

He wouldn't own to being a man if he wasn't tempted. Who wouldn't be? His eyes grazed her lips, and he felt the first stirrings of arousal. He disengaged her arm from his, but retained hold of her hand and kissed the back of it.

"You are an unusual man, Seth Musgrave," she whispered. "I thought I knew you, but I see you have some secrets I need to prize from you."

"Some things are better kept as secrets, My Lady," he said. "I wouldn't want you to tire of me so soon."

The flattery did its job. Beatrice traced his cheek with a gloved hand and gave him a warm smile.

"Until this evening."

He escorted Beatrice to her carriage and waved to see her off.

"Jamieson, have my horse saddled," he said to the groom.

After so long in feminine company, where conversations contained a wearisome undercurrent that forced him to remain alert to its meaning, he needed to be outdoors, doing something to expel the restless energy that had built up over the morning.

He would ride out to Hyde Park and consider what he would say in an overdue letter to Roddy.

Should he come straight out and ask how Ruby fared? Would that be placing his cards too firmly on the table? He had never spoken to Roddy about his feelings for Ruby, but the man was no fool.

So why did he hesitate? Did he want to hear from Roddy that not only was Ruby doing well, but thriving without him? Would that let him off the hook?

He indulged Beatrice because it was easy. She had no expectations of a commitment, and he had no expectations beyond that he was simply this Season's diversion. What harm would it do to engage in a little *affaire de coure*? It certainly would be a mutually beneficial relationship. They would part on good terms by the end of summer, and she would move on to the next crop of young eligible bachelors. And as for him? His reputation would be enhanced, and his status assured.

No longer would people speculate that he had some defect which was the reason his father kept him out of society. It would go a long way to prove, not only to his peers but to the world at large, that he was not feeble in mind or in body. He would carry the title of Duke of Auchen on his own merits.

As Seth rode out past the gate onto the main road, he considered what he might write.

Dear Roddy,

Thank you for the last set of accounts, although I have to confess not running through the numbers as I normally would. Your summary was thorough and everything I needed to know.

Still, I cannot help thinking that we were on the right track with Habetrot. Cast iron is too brittle for large clear spans such as a factory framework, although wrought iron has shown promise.

But I have heard talk from one of the Lancashire MPs that a Mr. Richard Roberts is considering using cast iron for the frame looms. If we can create greater output without a cost to quality, we could better compete with the mills of Manchester. I am convinced that the more innovations of this kind will see the number of mills in Britain vastly grow in number, and the cost of goods fall.

Would you be so kind as to get McDermott to send a few bolts of our finest silk-wool cloth to me. I have finally reached a détente with Lady Millarstone. She will stop throwing her daughter at me, and I will pay for a ball in her honor in May. Given Miss Jeanette's coloring, I would suggest the lotus pink.

Now, I do recall Lady Strathaird mentioning that she has a cousin or an aunt or something who is a dressmaker here in London. Would you happen to recall the name? If not, it is of no matter.

In truth, I have not written to Lady Strathaird as I do not know how well any correspondence would be received. My neglect of you both has not been deliberate. I have two watch-dogs appointed by the HRH himself and whose chief aim is to

*keep me out of mischief by ensuring that every hour is carefully
orchestrated and managed.*

*My approved outing is a ride in Hyde Park and, even then,
I have a groom in attendance, although he knows me well
enough by now to ride some yards back.*

*I confess at last to a better understanding of my father or at
the very least appreciate the wellspring of temper, as I've seemed
to have inherited it, too.*

*This came as a revelation when I arrived in London to take
possession of Glencoe House.*

*But that is not the only surprise (I can only wish I could see
your face as I tell you) – my father had written to the butler and
the estate manager, along with his bank and the board of
White's commending my admission. The letters were of recent
authorship so I can only conclude that he'd dictated them to the
solicitor who dispatched immediately.*

Seth ended his mental dictation. There was so much more he
could say, but he wanted more time to think about it before he
committed his thoughts to paper.

His return to the house had his nerves jangling. It wasn't just
the long trip which left him feeling spent, it was the memory of
his prior arrival there all those months ago when he was primed
for a fight with his old man.

And once more, he'd had to fight for his reputation as a man
worthy of the honor of being a duke. So far, it was a fight he
appeared to have won. And once again, he'd done it alone.

Without conceit, he could point to his achievements. He had
not been dealt a perfect hand in life – and others had it much
worse – but there was something to be said for not allowing the
past to dictate the future. Wallowing in self-pity was the quickest
road to hell he could imagine.

Still, he wanted to understand more about his father – not to
dig up his corpse and bury it over and over again – rather to
better understand himself. Did the apple fall far from the tree?

His secretary seemed content enough to give him a few hours

on his own each day to go through his father's papers. So far, he'd compiled a few journals and letters, and had made a start, based on the earliest of those letters – the ones he exchanged with his mother.

There is so much I never understood about my father, Roddy. Now, as I go through his study and his papers, I begin to see him as he truly was – not a monster but a man. A deeply flawed man, a hurt man who lashed out like a wounded beast, careless of those in his orbit.

So where did that leave him? His driving ambition for more than twenty years was to prove himself to his father. And now he had succeeded. He had achieved everything that a man is said to want – wealth, prestige, honor. Every whim and desire could be catered for.

A man could live a very easy life with what he had.

So, why did that not feel like enough?

His eyes drifted across the park to see a man hoist a toddler up onto his shoulders. He reached out to his wife then, to aid her up from the bench, and they walked together, hand in hand.

Something wealth cannot buy.

The sight filled him with a touch of longing. Once, he might have been that little boy. More than that was seeing the child's mother and father stroll contentedly together, clearly happy in each other's company.

Family.

It was something he ought to consider.

As duke, he would be expected to marry and produce an heir, of course.

When he was simply Seth Musgrave, working man, mill manager, he'd only had his charm and conscientiousness to commend him, he thought wryly. Now there was no shortage of willing women attracted by his wealth and title as much as any other of his limited attributes.

But it would not be soon. Being with Beatrice bought him time he desired to adjust to the new world he was now a part of. Perhaps in a year, once he felt on firmer footing, he would consider it. Still, he couldn't imagine there would be much joy in selecting a bride from the cattle yard that was the marriage mart. Checking over the livestock, researching the pedigree, testing for temperament, and then hoping one has made the right decision because an unhappy marriage was a miserable life sentence to endure.

Seth wheeled his horse around to head home, nodding politely to people who seemed to recognize him, but who he couldn't recall at all.

Being married to the right woman, on the other hand, would make him the richest man in the world. He should start giving the matter some thought.

What did he want in a wife?

He ought to stop deceiving himself now. He knew.

The example that resolved itself in his mind's eye was Ruby.

Could he be so lucky and find that another like her existed?

CHAPTER TWENTY-NINE

London
Late March 1819

"E XPLAIN IT TO me again, because I cannae see where yer thinking's at, lassie."

Ruby glanced at her companion as they strolled around Berkeley Square on the cold and crisp afternoon. Roddy rarely got irritated at anything, so far as Ruby could tell. But he appeared to have reached the end of his patience with her.

She had to make him understand. He could not intervene on her behalf with Seth. To do that would ruin everything.

"Dearest friend," she said, "I know you have only our best interests at heart, but Seth is not the man he was back in Glasgow. How could he be? He is the Duke of Auchen and that comes with expectations that Seth Musgrave never had."

"Bah! Ye should have gone to Glencoe House like I said in the first place, and all of this stuff and nonsense would be over with."

"And put Seth in an uncomfortable position if he was seriously courting the countess?"

"He doesnae love her."

"You don't know that, and neither do I."

"All I ken is that he *was* in love with ye when he left for London."

"Then consider this, would you have society think that Seth has installed a mistress in his house?"

Roddy huffed.

"Then this is the only way. I will not be an obligation to him as the Millarstones have been. He has to see me as Lady Strathaird, a future Duchess of Auchen, not as simply a one-time lover."

Ruby felt Roddy's arm stiffen, the man coming to a dead halt on the path. She looked up at him to see what expression he had at that revelation. It seemed it was shock, quickly replaced with pity and sadness.

"Och, what have ye done, lassie?"

"I refuse to feel regret for what we did. But now do you understand why I simply cannot just go to his door?"

"But ye're nae... ye ken..."

Yes, she did know. The possibility of being pregnant hadn't even occurred to her until she'd reached that time of the month, and when it proceeded as normal month after month since, it was no longer of concern.

Ruby shook her head.

"If the Duke of Auchen is going to meet and fall in love with Lady Strathaird," she said, "it's going to take time."

She stepped forward, obliging Roddy to fall into step with her.

"We have a plan, remember?" She patted his arm and continued. "No matter what happens between me and him, Seth has to fall in love again with the dream he had for Habetrot."

Roddy seemed relieved to be on safer ground. "Ye can leave that with me. 'Twas a stroke of genius ye had to produce ribbons using the punch card technique. I've nae seen it done before."

"It also means Skye-Heath and Habetrot aren't in direct competition. And to see the expression on Frannie's face when we showed her materials – you'd have thought all of her Christmases had come at once!"

Roddy laughed. Ruby breathed a sigh of relief, his censure of her apparently over.

They'd also reached the end of the park. They turned and walked under the bare branched plane trees through Berkeley Square once more.

"Still, it's nae going to be easy to keep from him that ye're in London."

"Soon. I promise you. Lady Asquith and her daughters are going to a recital tonight, and I'll be accompanying them. According to Fran, Seth and the countess always attend on Wednesday night. And the following Friday night there is the Countess Ilfracombe's charity ball. There, I hope to receive a formal introduction."

Roddy shook his head. "A formal introduction to a man ye already ken."

Ruby braced herself for another argument, but none was forthcoming, just one long sigh.

"Far be it from me to even try to ken the ways of women. But ken that I love the both of ye and will do everything I can to make ye both happy."

Roddy escorted her to Frannie's door, located in a fashionable section of Bond Street.

"Then it will most likely be tonight."

She squeezed his hand. "Trust me. It will work out for the best."

RUBY FOUND HER cousin in the cutting room, supervising a girl, aged about fourteen, on marking up a piece of muslin that would become a pattern piece.

Frannie looked up over her half-rim glasses. She smiled at Ruby, giving her apprentice additional instructions then leaving her place.

"You won't believe who I saw today," she said, steering Ruby to the drawing room where she received visitors.

"The countess."

"Which countess?"

"*The* countess."

"Beatrice?"

Frannie nodded. "She saw the sketches for Jeanette's gown and decided that she wanted me to design something for the Duke of Auchen's spring ball."

"Oh, Fran! That's wonderful!"

"I didn't expect you to take the news so well."

Ruby shrugged. "You told me you always wanted to design something for her, and how good it would be for business. Why wouldn't I be glad?"

"Well, yes, I told you all of that before I knew you were still in love with Musgrave."

"Both things are true. The countess leads fashion here in London, we both know that. And a commission from her will have your seamstresses employed for the next three years."

"I should have spat in her eye!"

"Frannie!"

"Well, I should say that if the Duke of Auchen has any sense at all, he will prefer you over that... that... made up tart. If not, then it will take more than spectacles to deal with his shortsightedness."

Ruby hugged her cousin tight.

"With you and Roddy in my corner, I could hardly lose."

The embrace was returned then Fran pulled away. "There is something else you should know. The ribbon you brought with you from Habetrot, the one with the elaborate design with gold-colored thread running through it? The countess spotted it and wanted it immediately. She has ideas. Some very *specific* ideas."

Ruby knew the ribbon. It was on a dark blue ground with gold leaves and soft pink flowers. It was the finest, most elaborate work the weavers had ever done. And Ruby had wanted it for herself.

She would be lying to herself if she didn't feel a stab of jealousy that this woman wanted to take it from her, as perhaps she had taken Seth.

She quashed the thought before it could take root. Then another occurred.

"Then let her have it. It doesn't matter."

"But that was for you! You told me how much you loved that design."

"What is one piece of ribbon? Do whatever the countess demands, make her the finest creation she can conceive of! You will make her an utter sensation, and I will have the satisfaction of knowing I am just as responsible for that fine gown. Every sale made afterwards is coin that comes back to me."

"I will have to start over with your gown," Fran warned.

"Then let me show you the ribbon I next prefer. The one with the turquoise blue ground and the diamond shapes in silver."

Her cousin's face lit up. "Not a color I would have chosen for you at first, but I do think it is very pretty. I shall give some thought to it. I will not have my cousin, a future duchess, be upstaged by a mere countess!"

SETH SET DOWN his glasses and closed the ledger book.

"Skye-Heath is certainly doing well. I have to confess that I miss being there every day. There is something to be said for seeing yards of thread being turned into yards of fabric to be turned into hundreds of gowns," he said to Roddy. "You know, every time I paid a compliment to a lady, I found myself paying more attention to her gown than her. I'm sure that some of them thought me quite peculiar."

Seth noted that Roddy still held himself to attention. Was there something he missed?

"I have some news for ye," he said.

Immediately, his heart sunk.

It was about Ruby.

She was married.

Seth held his breath and prepared himself for the worst.

"I havenae been honest with ye."

"About?"

"Habetrot."

What? Not Ruby?

Seth turned his chair to give Roddy his full attention.

"Go on."

Roddy told him the story right from the time he'd left for London. The desire of the men who would be employed to rebuild, the discovery of the punch-card loom in a barn at Strathaird, and Ruby's suggestion that Habetrot fashion elaborate ribbons and trimmings.

He ended the tale by handing over a foolscap card with three-inch lengths of ribbon stitched onto it. There were a dozen in all – ivory and silver brocade, colorful wildflowers, even the Musgrave tartan in royal blue, green, orange, and yellow.

"It's nae yet profitable, but we have faith it will be... um, especially now that Ruby's cousin has seen it."

"You've been to see her? Madame Francine?"

"Aye."

It was on the tip of his tongue to ask about Ruby, but he did not.

"Ye're nae mad at us for going against yer orders?"

"All of these were made on Habetrot's looms?"

"Aye. And in record time. What would take a month to produce normally, we can do in a week. When we finish rebuilding the mill and put in the power looms, what used to take us a week, we can do in a day."

Seth shook his head. Roddy's smile faltered.

"Ye're nae pleased?"

"Overwhelmed is what I am. And Ruby...?"

He let the end of the sentence trail off. He didn't really know what he wanted to ask. How did she feel about being in business and seeing her father's invention – once dismissed and thought lost – now producing as fine work as this? Did she ever think of him?

"*Darling!* There you are! Surely you and your man aren't going to discuss business all day. We'll be late."

Beatrice walked into the study as if she were already the mistress of Glencoe House. Seth glanced across to Roddy to see his steady, practical friend stare at the woman in – shock? Awe, perhaps? – before recovering himself.

Beatrice had that effect on everyone she met. She was, Seth reflected, a force of nature.

"Countess, I would like to introduce you to my man of business from Scotland, Roddy McClane."

"An honor to meet ye, My Lady." Roddy bowed.

"My, my – are all men from Scotland so handsome?" she gushed. "I really *must* travel north one day."

Beatrice didn't stop to see whether her flattery had any effect on Roddy – which it didn't – because her eyes immediately fell onto the ribbon sampler.

"Why, I saw something similar to this only today," she said, looking up at Seth. "That little mantua maker you selected for Jeanette had lengths of this ribbon. I had no idea ladies fashion fascinated you so."

Seth knew there was a tease in the woman's voice, but he wasn't particularly in the mood to play along.

"As it so happens, I own the mill that made this."

Beatrice was astute enough to discern the edge to his voice.

"A man of business as well as rank. I stand corrected," she said.

It was as much of an apology as she was ever going to give. Still, everything about her annoyed him right now, and he couldn't quite put his finger on the reason why. Before she could say anything further to ruin the appeal she held for him, he determined he'd best send her away.

"Go to the deSilva recital without me tonight. I've business to conclude here."

"But *darling*! We promised to dine with the Lanchesters afterwards."

Seth didn't recall making such a promise, but he had allowed Beatrice control over his social calendar, thus ensuring Jeanette received an invitation, too. Well, tonight they would just have to survive without him.

There must have been something that resembled his bastard father in his expression because Beatrice looked uncertain a moment. She gave Roddy a sidelong glance before dropping a small curtsy.

"Then I hope your business concludes well, Your Grace," she said and exited the room.

There was a silent count to five before Roddy spoke.

"*That's* the harridan ye've been squiring about London?"

It was the wrong thing to say.

Seth surged to his feet.

"That's enough out of you. I'm not going to justify my choice of women."

Unlike Beatrice, Roddy knew when to back down. Or perhaps not. He had the better of Roddy by a good four inches, but the man squared his shoulders. And, for the first time in all years they had known one another, there was a look of contempt on his friend's face that was directed at him.

"Has London turned ye into a fool, man? What are ye doing cheating on Ruby with that—"

Seth held up his palm to stop Roddy from slandering Beatrice's character. He knew what she was. More importantly, *she* knew what she was. And even so, what was said of her didn't begin to scratch the surface of *who* Beatrice really was.

"Ye're in love with Ruby still. There's no use denying it."

Roddy's more conciliatory tone wasn't enough to stop the raw agony of a barely healed wound from coursing through him.

"It hardly matters whether I do or I don't," he spat. "She was the one who rejected me."

Seth didn't hide the pain from his voice or his face. He wanted Roddy to see it and know that he suffered. If his friend was going to be her champion, then best he knew the truth of it.

"I was too blind to see that Ruby only wanted one thing – her beloved Strathaird," he continued. "She was honest with me about that, at least. Did you know that I all but begged her to come with me to London?"

"Dinnae judge her too harshly. She had good reason and I agree with her. But she loves ye, I can tell ye that for nothing."

Seth harumphed, the heat of his anger cool, leaving nothing behind but ash.

"She has an odd way of showing it."

Roddy drew a deep breath. "There's something I need to tell ye now," he said.

Seth slumped back into his chair. "Is it really the time? I suddenly find myself not in the mood."

"Better now since ye're in a bad mood, because it cannae get worse."

"Are you sure?" Seth growled.

Roddy folded his arms and shrugged, clearly not caring if Seth got angrier or not. He continued, "Ye dinnae own all of Habetrot."

"The *devil*, you say! Who gave you authority to sell off part of *my* company without informing me?"

"*You* did. When you told me to do whatever I needed to deal with Habetrot."

Dear God. What an addle-witted idiot he'd become.

Who was this mystery partner Roddy had saddled him with? Seth stared into his friend's face looking for the answer. Then it came to him…

Ruby.

The sound of her name on his lips sent an answering call to his chest.

Roddy nodded once in confirmation. "The woman put up her own money for the building works. And since we found a scale working model of her father's loom, and she let us copy it, I figure her stake in Habetrot to be thirty percent. I brought the contract deed with me. I thought ye could sign it now and get the matter over with."

At that, Roddy pulled out a deed of arrangement from a sheaf of papers on the desk and shoved it toward him.

Seth was at once aghast and in admiration of his man of business.

He didn't need his glasses to find Ruby's name and her feminine signature on the deed. He added his own without hesitation.

This was one way to keep her close. If she no longer loved him, she at least *believed* in him.

In us…

There was something about seeing their names side by side that made him desperately wish for one short moment it was a marriage contract he signed. Then he remembered where he was.

"How is Ruby?"

Does she mention me at all?

"I ken ye need a wee dram of something," said Roddy, rising and crossing to the tantalus.

Seth shook his head.

"Ruby is well. She wishes ye well," said Roddy, pouring them both a whisky. He paused as though wondering what to pick and choose to tell him. That was never a good sign. "Her cousin sends her all the news from London, including those newspapers for the ladies about who's seen with who and what they are wearing."

"So. Ruby knows of Beatrice."

Roddy simply nodded as he made his way back to the desk, but Seth felt the need to explain himself. "It's not everything the newssheets make it out to be."

"It very rarely is." Roddy shook his head, put Seth's whisky glass down, then slapped him on the shoulder, announcing, "C'mon, end yer moping, man. I didnae get to see much of London when I were last here with ye, and now that ye're the duke, I expect to be shown the town, and I fancy to take in a concert. Ye can introduce me to yer fancy friends as a laird, and ye can make it up to yer countess."

Seth quickly signed the duplicate copies of the contract and passed them back to Roddy. The idea of a distraction appealed greatly.

"Beatrice is not my countess," he grumbled.

Roddy laughed. "Glad to hear it, man!"

CHAPTER THIRTY

R UBY LEARNED QUICKLY how easy it was to elicit information from Lady Asquith and gain an invitation to the concert tonight at the home of Baroness deSilva.

As it happened, the lady was quite the devotee of the countess and was not at all displeased to see a budding friendship between her son and the countess' protégé, Miss Millarstone, who just happened to be a relation of the Duke of Auchen.

And, with Fran having provided a generous discount for the outfitting of all four daughters, Lady Asquith was quite amenable to adding one more – the dressmaker's cousin, newly arrived from Scotland – to their party.

That was all Lady Asquith knew about Ruby McAllister, *Lady Strathaird*, and it was all she cared to know. Anything which drew attention to their party – and the marriageability of her four daughters – was all to the greater good.

That suited Ruby just fine – she only hoped that her nervousness was put down to the excitement of attending an evening's entertainment and not some other cause.

Tonight, she would see Seth for the first time in more than six months. They had spent more time apart than they had in each other's company and, in all that time, her news of him came through his letters to Roddy or the newssheet gleanings Frannie sent her way.

Now was the time to see if Seth's declaration of love had stood the test of time. As for her own heart, she was certain. She loved him. Had always loved him, which is why she had to let him go, to find his own way in the new world he inhabited as the Duke of Auchen.

With a closed fan in the palm of her hand, she could not press her thumb into the palm of her other hand as was her habit. Instead, she gripped the fan tightly and waited for the majordomo to announce them.

Once inside the ballroom, Lady Asquith gathered her daughters like a hen with her chicks.

She nodded to her left. "Oh, there's the Earl of Castleford and his wife, what a handsome couple they make. How on earth he was able to make it up to her after leaving the poor girl at the altar all those years ago. Oh, well, I suppose it is all water under the bridge now."

Then she gestured to her right. "Girls, the Earl of Runcorn is one you should definitely try to make the acquaintance of. Isn't he handsome? And with a good fortune, too!"

The Asquith girls looked about dutifully, and Ruby did likewise. "Oooh, look! There's Count Armand Danger," Lady Asquith continued. "He's enough to make an old woman like me swoon. Yes, yes!, Try to catch *his* eye. He may be born French, but his family comes from the *highest* pedigree."

Name after name was mentioned along with vital statistics – name, rank, and income. With the targets identified, and a plan of attack agreed, Lady Asquith sent her daughters out like a general sending out troops, not to kill, but to charm and to conquer.

Ruby was fully convinced that if preparation alone was enough to make a success of the marriage mart, the Asquith daughters would all be betrothed by the end of spring.

That left Ruby standing alone at Lady Asquith's side.

"Should we see who we can find for *you*, my dear?" she said. "Apart from the Duke of Auchen, I don't know any Scotsmen."

She found a smile and gave it to Lady Asquith. "I am so new

to London, it is enough to simply enjoy the evening for what it is."

"Ah, well, I suppose it can't be helped in your case." By now, Lady Asquith was distracted by the arrival of more guests – perhaps there were better prospects for her daughters among them.

Ruby, too, watched for new arrivals and, as the time for the concert drew near, she knew one thing was for certain. The Duke of Auchen wasn't one of those in attendance.

The Countess of Engelton was among the later arrivals, but she came alone. She was older than was depicted by Frannie's sketches – closer to fifty than to forty, by Ruby's critical estimation.

But her precise age mattered little because the woman had a presence that was undeniable, drawing all eyes to her, female as well as male.

Indeed, the woman walked in as though she was the queen herself. Their hosts for the evening, the Baron and Baroness deSilva, immediately broke off their conversations and made their way to countess to thank her for attending.

If she was at all disappointed that she had not walked in on Seth's arm, it was impossible to tell.

Ruby weighed her up, and found her lacking nothing. It would be so easy to be envious of this woman; beauty, poise, presence, and wealth she plainly possessed in abundance, and something about the way she carried herself said everything she did was for her own pleasure.

"I thought it was you! I knew I couldn't possibly be mistaken!"

Ruby started from her consideration of the countess and turned to see Jeanette Millarstone approach.

It was clear the London Season was going well for her. Her face was lively. How did Frannie describe her? *Winsome.* Yes, that was the word.

"I take it your mother isn't here tonight."

Jeanette laughed. "How did you know? No, Maman has a cold, so Lord Asquith agreed to escort me."

His name was spoken with a most attractive blush to the young woman's cheeks. There came with it the temptation to tease, but Ruby didn't quite know the young woman well enough to make comment on the possibility of her having a beau.

"Does Seth know you're in town?" Jeanette asked.

It was a small shock to hear his name so familiarly spoken. For so many months, the love she nurtured to her breast remained unspoken. She was not even sure Fran understood the depth of her feelings.

"Shall we take a turn about the room?" Ruby suggested. It was much easier to release agitation by walking and so to avoid any opportunity for accidental eavesdroppers. Ruby took Jeanette's arm in hers, and they strolled around the hall.

Ruby was aware of eyes on them as they promenaded the room. The pretty young debutante in a peach and cream-trimmed laced gown was a known feature, it should appear. Ruby knew that she, too, presented a fashionable figure – thanks in no small measure to Fran. Her gown this evening was periwinkle blue, cut square across the bodice with small puffed sleeves. The skirt was of the latest circular style, its shape held by rope sewn into the hem, and decorated with a double layer of flounces.

She'd kept her jewelry simple – pearl earrings and a matching strand at her throat.

"I thought I'd keep my visit to London a surprise. I came down to see my cousin," said Ruby, pleased that every word was the true, if not *exactly* the truth.

"The mantua maker! Seth told me she was your cousin. She is a very clever woman, indeed, to have turned out Lady Asquith's daughters so well on such a small budget."

Ruby inwardly sighed relief. She was on safer ground with fashion.

But the relief was short-lived.

"He's usually here with Countess Engelton." Jeanette nodded

her head in the woman's direction. "Maman doesn't much care for her, but she has had to swallow her pride since it was her idea to have Seth throw a ball in my honor. I think she has finally given up on making me a duchess."

"I saw you with young Lord Asquith tonight. Is he to be your conquest?" Ruby teased.

"We are simply *friends*," she said. Ruby almost believed her if not for the slight coloring of her cheeks once more. "He is pleased that his sisters have a friend who is somewhat sensible."

"I can see the Season has been good for you," Ruby observed. "If you'll forgive the observation of a stranger, you've grown confident in your own opinions. It is lovely to see. A man of quality would be honored to have you as his wife."

Ruby felt Jeanette squeeze her arm in silent thanks.

"Perhaps, now that you are here in London, you might find someone for yourself," Jeanette ventured.

"Not if he plans to take me away from Scotland. That is where my home and heart lie."

SETH CRANED HIS neck and fought the urge to adjust his cravat as his valet took his sweet time in arranging it *just so*. He hated being late. It put him at a disadvantage. Being on the back foot was something he'd fought his whole life against.

The fact that he was assured that punctuality did not count as a ducal virtue did his mood no good at all. The fact that he was obliged to spend the rest of the evening with the Lanchesters, following the deSilvas' concert, was a further irritation he could do without.

He was tempted to absent himself from the evening altogether, and would have done so except Roddy seemed particularly keen to attend.

He would make his apologies to Beatrice and go as meek as a

lamb to supper with the Lanchesters and be agreeable to whatever she wanted to do afterwards – which usually involved being in her bed until morning.

By the time he arrived, the familiar strains of Bach's *Brandenberg Concertos* filled the house. The footman opened the salon door and peered about, obviously looking for a way to seat a distinguished guest without disrupting the performance of the small orchestra.

"Do not trouble yourself. I am content to remain standing until the intermission," Seth told the relieved footman.

Not only was he content to remain standing there, thus unseen, he actually preferred it. Here, he could be himself and just *be* without being acutely aware of having his every move judged like he was a performer up on that stage instead of just being a man. Wealth and privilege was a poor marker of a man's worth. Surely his character had to count for something more?

Seth joined in the enthusiastic applause at the end of the movement. After a moment, one, then another of the audience got up out of their seats.

The first to reach the back of the room was the Earl of Runcorn. The man had a minor reputation as a member of the fast set – vapid, superficial – yet Seth knew there was a depth to him that one only got to know away from the crowds, and he liked the man even for his faults.

"Good evening, Musgrave!" The greeting was friendly with an edge of a smirk that left Seth in no doubt that the earl knew he engaged in a bit of flagrant familiarity. "I've been meaning to ask you about property in Scotland. I'm considering a bolt hole; somewhere quiet with good shooting."

Seth nodded along. "Then permit me to introduce you to my man of business, Roddy McClane."

Roddy bowed.

"If anyone knows of anywhere to rent or buy between Glasgow and Edinburgh and further north, he's your man."

"My Lord," said Roddy. "I am at yer service."

"Very good!" Runcorn declared. "Are you chaps engaged after the concert this evening? A group of us are planning to try out luck at The Lyon's Den."

Seth shook his head in regret. "I have another engagement."

"Ah, yes. I did see Beatrice here tonight, looking ravishing as usual."

Seth didn't enjoy what the tone implied. Roddy's expression only added to his chagrin.

"If the offer holds, My Lord, I would be honored to join ye. I always wanted to try my luck in London," Roddy said.

Runcorn looked delighted. "By all means! Scottish money is as good as any other."

Seth excused himself from the conversation. Beatrice would expect him to search her out. He headed to the refreshment table for a couple of glasses of punch. He procured the drinks and scanned the crowd. Beatrice should not be difficult to find – just look for a coterie of swains.

Coterie? Was that the right collective noun? He wasn't sure.

"Your *Grace!*" Only two words uttered, and he knew their owner before he even turned to face her.

Lady Asquith.

"I was beginning to despair of your attending tonight."

Seth found a polite expression and fixed it. There was something to be said after all for being claimed by Beatrice for the Season, and that was it put him off limits to ambitious debutantes and their mothers. It was the unwritten rule – one which Lady Asquith determinedly ignored.

"Always a pleasure to see you, Madam," he said mildly before indicating down to the two full glasses in his hands. "But if you'll forgive me…"

Lady Asquith refused to take a hint. "There is someone I wish you to meet."

He suppressed an inward groan. Not one of her daughters. He'd already met the quartet and, as pleasant as they seemed to be, he was not at all interested.

"It's a countryman of yours... oh, no, that *can't* be right."

The woman looked about, the object of her interest clearly being absent.

A lucky escape, he thought ruefully.

"Don't you go away. I'll be right back."

Seth ignored the order and searched around for Beatrice. He found her deep in conversation with a distinguished man with a distinct military bearing. They'd not been introduced, but Seth knew him as Colonel Hoddleston.

With glasses in hand, Seth made his way toward them. He was within six feet when Lady Asquith called out once.

"Your *Grace*, I've found her!"

He rolled his eyes and turned. Lady Asquith clutched the arm of a young woman who was being dragged from a conversation with a young man.

"This is her! You're both Scottish, so I'm sure you have *lots* in common. Come on, my dear," she chided the younger woman with ebony hair and a graceful figure.

The woman turned. Seth felt as though he'd been struck by lightning.

"Here he is, the man I've been telling you about."

Her eyes met his and widened in recognition.

"Your Grace, I'd like to introduce you to Ruby McAllister, Lady Strathaird. Ruby, my dear, I'd like to introduce you to Seth Musgrave, the Duke of Auchen."

Ruby's eyes never left his.

"Your Grace..."

Her voice was pitched low and aroused him more than two words ought to.

She curtsied, looking more beautiful than any woman had a right to.

He drank in her face, artfully made up to show off her fine features. The gown she wore was expertly made for her by, he assumed, her cousin.

The only resemblance she bore to Nurse Campbell were

those rich, brown eyes.

A thousand questions gathered at his lips.

When did she get here? Why had she not come to see him? Did Roddy know?

Of course, Roddy knew. The bastard. *They'd be having words about this.*

"Darling, how clever of you to bring refreshments!"

Beatrice smiled at him as if she knew all his secrets and accepted a glass from his hand. "Come meet Colonel Hoddleston. He has a most interesting tale to tell about India."

He wanted to tell Beatrice to be silent. Ruby wore an unsettled look on her face. He grabbed her hand before she could leave. Ruby squeezed it in return.

"It was an honor to meet Your Grace," she said. "Perhaps we will meet again soon."

CHAPTER THIRTY-ONE

RUBY'S HEART SANG.

True, Seth had been shocked to see her, but not unpleasantly so. In fact, judging by his pained expression when the Countess of Engelton called his attention, he did not want their first meeting to end.

She squeezed his hand in mute reassurance. They *would* see each other again.

"Roddy knows where to reach me," she said.

Seth nodded at that before allowing Beatrice to claim him.

"Well, that was a fortuitous first meeting!" Lady Asquith exclaimed. "It was almost as if you already knew one another."

"We do... that is, the duke and I were previously acquainted in Glasgow."

"Well, I *do* feel like a fool!"

"Oh, no, My Lady. Never that. You have done me a good turn. There was the distinct possibility that the duke wouldn't remember me at all."

"How *wonderful*! You will put in a good word to the duke for my girls, won't you? Between you and Miss Millarstone commending them, I'm sure they'll gain the notice of the right people."

Ruby assured Lady Asquith that she would do her best, her attention now on observing Seth with Beatrice on his arm.

Her heart swelled. Seth looked every inch the dashing duke. He had taken his birthright and embraced it fully. She was delighted at how well he was received. He had done this on his own. He'd shown them the man he was, not who his father made him out to be.

And as for Beatrice, well, she *was* the type of wife one might expect a duke to have. They made a fine couple despite the difference in age. Not a few people had remarked on it tonight already. She turned away and swallowed against the pang. She should find her seat for the second part of the concert.

Roddy approached, a wide smile on his face.

"I saw ye two," he said. "Like Romeo and Juliet."

Ruby burst out laughing. "They ended up dead, you know."

Roddy grinned, undeterred. "Seth's given me a message for ye. He has another engagement this evening, but he wants to call on ye tomorrow."

"Tell him I look forward to his call. At St. James' Park, by the lake at eleven o'clock."

"A PLEASANT DAY to you, Miss."

Ruby smiled, recognizing the voice. She looked up from the book she was reading. Across the way, Fran glanced up from her easel and gave her an encouraging smile.

"A good day to you, Your Grace."

Seth gave little away in his expression. Watchful perhaps, even curious.

"A pleasant day for a walk, perhaps?"

They both glanced to the sky. It was gray, and there had been a rain shower an hour before this.

"Yes. I've not seen all the gardens. Anticipating spring is such a lovely time of year, do you not think?" At least Seth appeared to be playing along.

"Fran, do you wish to accompany us on a stroll?"

Fran put down her charcoal. "I wish to finish this sketch of the lake. Do go on without me."

It was theater. They all knew it, which is why Ruby giggled as Seth muttered, "Thank goodness for that" under his breath.

Still, it wasn't until they were some yards away that he spoke.

"Well, here we are."

"Indeed, although I'm not sure what you mean by 'here' or 'we'. Where are we?"

Ruby witnessed a flash of irritation.

"Stop it, Ruby," said Seth. "We're not strangers. Do you forget how you came to me and shared my bed? Was there nothing between us then?"

Ruby knew his choice of words was deliberate, and the memory of being naked in his arms caused her cheeks to heat. He noticed. A look of satisfaction appeared on his face.

Ruby licked her lips and marshaled her thoughts rather than linger in *that* moment.

"There *is* a lot for us to talk about. Habetrot for one."

"Thank you." His short answer was a surprise. He quirked a smile at her own bewildered expression.

"I thought you might be angry. You told Roddy to dispose of it, but he... *we*... we couldn't do it. We both saw the tremendous potential, especially once we found my father's loom. You were right, it should be done."

"I am not like my father. I have no trouble admitting when I am wrong. I was surprised, yes, but when Roddy showed me the ribbons and the other notions Habetrot could produce, I was delighted. I *am* delighted. Your father's invention means it is only right you should be a partner in the business."

They walked on past the far end of the lake.

"I didn't want you to think Strathaird was all I wanted."

"What is it you want, Ruby?" His voice was soft, but there was an edge to it. A dangerous edge. Only now did she notice they were completely alone.

"I've always believed in you," she said. "The man you are, the man you are capable of being. That's why I invested. That's why I let you go when you declared your love."

Seth shook his head and came to a stop before a bed of tulips just a few weeks away from blooming.

"Help me understand, Ruby, because, God help me, I don't."

She took his hand to draw his attention back to her.

"You needed to discover the man you are on your own. Seth Musgrave the man is brave, strong, passionate, thoughtful, and intelligent. But what of the Duke of Auchen? What is *he*?"

"I'm still the same man."

"You cannot honestly say becoming duke has not altered you." She watched Seth consider her words carefully, weigh them.

"Your father took away your worth and status," she continued. "You fought for everything you had. Now you have it all. What any man would desire."

"Not everything."

Ruby's heart tumbled a few beats, but she pressed on.

"Then there was me. I was full of hatred, deceitful when we first met. It doesn't matter my justification. It colored everything. It affected us. Your father, even in his grave, still had the power to come between us because of my choices."

"We can't change the past."

"But we can change the future. We carried on an affair in the darkness, under deception, but now… if you, that is…" She could not continue. A blush heated her cheeks, and she looked away.

"Why, Lady Strathaird, are you hoping I'll pay you court?" His playful tone buoyed her spirits. Seth tugged on their clasped hands and drew her closer.

"I want us to fall in love with each other anew," she whispered.

"*Do* you want a courtship?"

Ruby nodded her affirmation, afraid that if she spoke her voice would break.

Yes. A courtship – a romance unclouded by the taint of old enmity.

Seth sensed her emotion and did not press for a verbal answer. Instead, he brought her hands to his lips.

"My Lady will have all she desires."

IT WAS OVERCAST above but, for Seth, it was as though the clouds had parted, letting in the warmth of sunshine.

She loved him.

She may not have said as much in words, but they needed no words. She'd shown him time and time again in what she did. How was it that she could see so clearly what he could not?

He understood now, as heartbreaking as their parting had been, it was necessary. Now, he could show her another side to him, the better man he'd become, all because she loved him.

A courtship? Hell, he'd give her everything. He'd given her Strathaird. All he had to give now was himself. And he was going to make damned sure he was worthy of her.

The first drops of rain began to fall as they approached the bench where Fran was hastily packing her easel.

"Ladies, my carriage is at your disposal, as am I."

For once, Seth didn't think. He allowed himself to simply enjoy the moment and, since the day had turned to drizzle, he suggested lunch at one of London's finest establishments.

Seth was fascinated by Ruby's tale of finding the working punch-card loom after fearing all sign of it was lost. He was impressed at her and Roddy's decision to set up in the barn to begin with – it was small scale but high quality to establish Habetrot with a reputation for fine work. The conversation naturally fell to fabrics and fashion.

Fran insisted on hearing all about Skye-Heath and Habetrot, learning more about the mills' capabilities, and the plans to produce a wider range of cloth to meet the demands of a growing merchant class who were developing a taste – and the money –

for the finer things.

"How clever of you to decide on ribbon," said Fran. As an aside, she revealed how she started as a lacemaker under the tutelage of a French émigré. "Do you think your looms could make lace? Imagine yards and yards of it produced on these mechanical devices. Do you think it would be possible?"

"I can't see why not," Seth replied. "If we can harness steam to drive engines, then anything seems possible."

Considering his lunch companions, he decided he'd be hard pressed to know when he had enjoyed feminine company as much as he had now with Ruby and Francine. They were smart, intelligent women who forced him to stay on his mettle, not because he was in danger of being deceived, but to keep up with their constant probing of the possibilities this new technology offered.

And what a fortunate man he was that Ruby had chosen him to love...

A page approached.

"A message for Your Grace."

Seth gave the boy a coin and took the note. He didn't have his glasses with him, but the signature was clear enough.

Beatrice. Oh...

He pulled out his pocket watch. The time read half-past three. He'd forgotten all about a whist party he was supposed to attend.

"What's wrong? Not bad news?" Ruby asked.

"No, just an appointment I've forgotten."

"Oh, dear. We've monopolized so much of your time, Your Grace," said Fran.

"Not at all, I've truly enjoyed it. Come, let me take you home since the weather has turned foul."

"No, you go. Do not trouble yourself on our account. Fran and I will conduct a few errands in this part of town and hire a cab."

Seth rose and gave a slight bow. Fran, bless her soul, also rose from the table and excused herself, giving Seth and Ruby precious moments alone.

"I wish I could see you later, but I have long-standing plans for tonight and tomorrow night."

Ruby touched his arm.

"*Beatrice.* I understand, you need to speak with her."

"You can be assured that despite what the newssheets say, it was never a serious attachment between us."

"You need not explain. There is nothing to apologize for, nothing to forgive, although I cannot tell you how glad I am that she does not hold your heart."

He picked up Ruby's hand. He would have kissed her there and now had they been truly alone.

"You own my heart. I am your servant."

"Seth, my love..."

"I will send you a message as soon as I'm free."

He called for his carriage and settled the bill. As much as he hated to, he had to put thoughts of Ruby aside and attend to the business of breaking off with Beatrice. He didn't imagine it would be easy.

He recalled his diary. He would head home to Glencoe House and pen a note apologizing for his absence. He was due to take Beatrice to the theater tomorrow night. He would send another note to beg an audience before the engagement.

He forced himself to endure the opprobrium of his secretary for the breach in etiquette with equanimity before sending him on an errand to have a jeweler call on him on the morrow. It was then that Roddy decided to join him in the library.

"Well, ye ken how to put a household in disarray. Yer secretary, Jeeves, has been having conniptions."

"His name is Jervis."

Roddy shrugged and went over to the table, pouring them each a large tumbler of whisky. Seth accepted the glass, noting a question was written large on his friend's face, but that he did not ask the question.

Seth left the man's curiosity unsated until he could bear it no more.

"Did I hear ye call for a jeweler? Does that mean what I think it means?"

"I'm offering for Beatrice."

Roddy exploded. "Ye're the worst of all bloody fools!" A few more curses left the man's lips before Seth could no longer contain his laughter, nearly doubling over with it. Roddy's ire ebbed to a simmer.

"Bah! Ye're a wicked man, Musgrave. Ye almost killed me with a heart attack, ye blue-blooded bastard."

"Ruby and I will be engaged within in the next few weeks. We are starting anew – a proper courtship and, by God, a proper wedding."

The jeweler wasn't just for Ruby. The Auchen family jewels, which had not been worn, not even seen in public, since his mother died, would soon belong to the new Duchess of Auchen.

And as for Beatrice? He knew well enough that a mere bauble wouldn't be enough to buy her off. Her pride was worth more to her than a mere piece of jewelry. That, she had aplenty from her late husband and various lovers alike.

He knew the bargain. The countess chose her "companion" for the Season, and it was she who chose when the end of the liaison came, not he.

Seth had no doubt she would let him go early, however. The novelty had to be wearing off, surely. The only thing to be negotiated was how much she would extract for the break in their contract, notwithstanding its unwritten state.

He called his secretary and asked for a list of the invitations that had come across his desk.

Until this moment, he'd allowed Beatrice to set his social calendar. But now, he would begin to make those decisions himself.

He owed it to Jeanette to continue with her debut so that had to go ahead. But one way or another, he would favor events of interest to Ruby especially occasions that permitted him to introduce the woman he intended to marry to London society.

Memories of their kisses and stolen moments recalled themselves. Memories of the night they'd made love. What he wouldn't give to have her in his arms right now. In his bed.

A *courtship*. Ruby asked for a courtship, a public courtship, and he willingly granted it. Moreover, he wanted that for her, for *them*. But still those carnal delights beckoned. What might it be like to seduce the woman he was going to wed?

He looked forward to finding out...

Seth looked back at the list of invitations. There was just one major event on the calendar that he needed to manage carefully with Beatrice – his spring ball.

The countess had pulled out all the stops. Even the Prince of Wales had it on his calendar. The Duke of Wellington, too. She would not relinquish ownership of that without argument.

THE BEJEWELED BOX stood on the little table between them unopened. Perhaps it was better that way, Seth mused. The garnets in the piece inside perfectly matched the coloring of her face right now, although he knew it would be suicidal to tell her so.

"No. I forbid it. I will not be thrown over before the end of the Season, just because you've found some fancy."

"I will not sleep with you again."

Beatrice regarded him with something akin to contempt.

"Do you think I care? Go make calf-eyes at your lady love, it matters nothing to me, but know this – I made your reputation, and I will have my due. The spring ball, in which I have invested so much time and my not-inconsiderable influence, will be hosted by you with *me* at your side.

"Furthermore, I have already accepted a number of invitations on our behalf, and you will attend them with me until such time as I choose."

Seth swallowed his anger and his pride. What choice did he have? That Beatrice had been instrumental in easing his way into society could not be doubted. Without her sponsorship and contacts, it would be doubtful that Jeanette would have had such a successful Season, and he conceded the value of her influence on his reputation. Without her, half of London might still imagine him an imbecile.

He would not fight her on this.

"Agreed. But our attendance together will be only the public events already announced, and no more. I will also be seen with public with Lady Strathaird, and proudly so. Moreover, you will greet her with the courtesy due my intended."

Beatrice raised an eyebrow at the last, but then the anger left her face and her mask of beauty returned "These are *all* the conditions you wish to impose?" she asked.

Seth nodded once. "The spring ball? Yes, we will host it together. By my estimation, that will be our final engagement. You may be assured you'll never hear a word against you from me – as long as you promise to do the same."

Beatrice looked thoughtful, as though considering the offer. With a nod of her own to Seth, she reached for the jeweler's box and opened it. The garnet and diamond bracelet had set him back a pretty penny.

He watched her examine the piece, then fasten the clasp over her wrist and examine it once more. She raised it toward him, as if for him to see it on her wrist also – then slapped him hard.

His cheek stung. But he did not react. She swept past him out of the drawing room and into the hall where she was completely transformed into the elegant Countess of Engelton once more.

Seth rubbed his cheek to obscure any remaining handprint, and followed after her, accepting his gloves and hat from the butler.

He didn't know how much the fellow had overhead, but it

was enough for him to give Seth a commiserating look. The man had probably heard it all before.

Seth found himself considering the Bible. Jacob labored for Laman for seven years only to be given Leah instead of Rachel as his bride. But he did not give up. He labored another seven for Rachel.

Seth could bide his time. It was only six weeks until the spring ball.

CHAPTER THIRTY-TWO

"THE COW! HOW dare she set such terms?"

Ruby watched Fran rail, violently stabbing a pin into the hem of a gown. Between Seth's ire and Fran's anger, Ruby could remain calm. She glanced once again at the short note she'd received from Seth.

Of course, there *had* to be a reckoning. A woman like Beatrice had to at least be *seen* to hold the upper hand always. It was the source of her allure and her power.

In recent weeks, whenever she and Seth had attended the same functions, he was attentive enough to notice her, but not so much as to cause anyone to question her reputation. Any surprise the *ton* may have had about her sudden appearance, and Seth's attention could be explained away as simply that they were both Scottish.

To most observers, Seth and Beatrice were still the couple of the Season. He paid the correct amount of attention to her one would expect of a gentleman, but Ruby saw clearly there was no affection between them, no tender regard. It was all a performance.

As for Seth's manner with her? Ruby found it wonderful and maddening by turns. He was not making it easy. A secret caress here, a lingering touch there. She'd even given in to stolen kisses out in the gardens. It was impossible to deny him because it would be denying herself.

There was something thrilling about conducting a clandestine affair with one's own betrothed.

"And to think that I have to make that woman's gown for the ball," Fran continued to grumble. "She's already demanded first choice of the best fabric and trim I have. I should leave the gown full of pins to spite her."

Ruby burst out laughing at the thought.

"As satisfying as that would be, it would do your reputation no good. Deliver your best work to Beatrice. It is what we always planned. And, as you are always at pains to say to your clients, each woman is her own unique canvas. You'll just have to create a different work of art for me."

"I've already started."

"May I see?"

"No, you most certainly cannot! Not before fitting. Now – the gown you are wearing to the theater tonight. I've added some Habetrot ribbon to a dress you already had. Not too much, just a trim around the sleeves and the bust. It helps that the gown is relatively plain. It's enough to draw a little bit of attention. I chose it to match the sapphire collar of your mother's."

"Thank you."

"Are you nervous? You'll be spending an entire evening with that she-wolf."

"I won't be alone."

"Do you think Lady Jeanette and Lord Asquith are enough protection?"

"You forget Colonel Hoddleston."

"Humph! It wouldn't surprise me if the countess tried to fob *him* off onto you!"

"The colonel is a very nice man and, from what little I know about him, he's not the type to be 'fobbed' upon."

"Still, don't turn your back on her."

DESPITE HER WORDS of assurance to her cousin, Ruby was only

too keenly aware of the tension in the air as she and Jeanette, in the company of Lord Asquith, arrived at their box. They milled about outside, waiting for the senior ranking members of their party arrive.

She glanced into the balcony and out into the theater beyond. The curtain was closed, but there was a performance happening nonetheless. Like an actress on cue, Beatrice appeared alongside Seth with the colonel a step behind. Before she reached them, Beatrice stopped to speak to the party in the box next door.

Ruby sought out Seth. Their eyes met. He smiled and offered a small nod, which might have been addressed to the three of them, but Ruby knew it was directed at her. She smiled back, but not before Beatrice witnessed it. She reached behind her to claim Seth's arm and draw him into her conversation without once looking in his direction.

The move was clearly territorial. The countess would have her pound of flesh from this arrangement it would seem.

Many other women would be jealous and angry at such a proprietorial display, but Ruby worked on finding the right amount of disinterest for her expression – for Seth's sake as well as her own. The Countess of Engelton was on borrowed time, and she knew it.

Ruby and Jeanette curtsied while, behind them, Lord Tarquin Asquith bowed as the ranking members of the party entered first. Seth and Beatrice commanded the front seat where they could be seen by others in the balconies as well as the crowd in the gallery below. Ruby was escorted to her place by Colonel Hoddleston with Jeanette and Lord Asquith seated beside them.

The seating arrangement lasted only until the end of the first act. During the brief intermission, Jeanette and Tarquin spotted friends and wanted to watch the rest of the play in their company. Part way through the second act, Beatrice excused herself.

A few minutes later, the colonel did likewise.

Seth glanced back to her and left his seat to sit at her side.

"Well, look at this. Alone at last, Lady Strathaird," he remarked dryly.

"Do you think Beatrice and the colonel...?" she whispered.

He shrugged then reached to take her hand. "If so, it is a recent development."

"I wonder what they're up to," she said.

"Perhaps something like this," Seth suggested, drawing a finger down her cheek, bringing her close enough to kiss. It was a long unhurried one, tender and arousing.

Hidden in the shadows, there was something undeniably naughty about it. She liked it very much.

"Spring cannot come soon enough," he said. "Marry me tomorrow."

When he touched her in the way he was doing at that moment, it was impossible to refuse him. Their lips met again. He coaxed her mouth open and explored it with his tongue. She returned it, giving measure for measure. His hand lightly touched her breast, fingers trailing across the satin of her gown until her nipples budded, sending a bolt of desire through her.

His lips left hers to begin a tender assault on her neck.

"A summer wedding," she said. Seth ended his lovemaking, much to her disappointment.

"Do you mean that?"

The seriousness of his tone surprised her. She turned to see his eyes and took hold of both his hands.

"Are you proposing marriage?"

Seth's face broke into a grin. "I'm making a hash of it the second time around, aren't I? You wanted a courtship, the culmination of which is I get on bended knee in a flower-strewn arbor on a sunny afternoon. Would a proposal mid-seduction in the box of a theater be acceptable?"

"Yes."

Ruby held her breath in response to Seth's reaction. Silence tumbled a few beats.

"I love you," she said. "I loved you from the start. I was afraid I had lost you."

Seth took her face in both hands and kissed her once again deeply. It tasted of passion, joy, thankfulness and a dozen other nameless emotions. When it ended, Seth's forehead rested against hers.

"You are the only woman who has understood me, who made me see who I was capable of being. Your love is a precious gift that I will strive a lifetime to be worthy of."

Tears of joy started to well, but before they could fall, Seth wicked them away with his kerchief. His kiss now was soft.

"A summer wedding, you say?"

It was exactly the *right* thing to say. Ruby stifled a giggle and took a deep breath to compose herself.

"A summer wedding. In Scotland," she said.

"Consider it done. A honeymoon in Paris, and then Venice – a working holiday."

She lifted an eyebrow in mute inquiry.

"To see what the fashionable are wearing abroad. We both have a business to run, you know."

Ruby knew his comments to be a tease, a sliver of light and levity after so much of their time together had been dark and serious. She could match his teasing tone.

"Or perhaps we could lock ourselves away at Castle Glenuig and not emerge until autumn."

"Do you think that one season in bed would sate the hunger I have for you?" The low timbre of his voice sent goosebumps through her. "A lifetime is barely enough."

Before she could answer, Seth took both her hands in his and bowed his head to kiss them.

"The six weeks we must wait before making our betrothal public will disappear in no time at all. Until then, we can plan," she said.

Seth raised his head and kissed her. "Oh, I plan to do much more than that."

Before Ruby could wonder how much of a seduction they could get away with in the fleeting time they had, she heard

Jeanette giggle and Tarquin's low tones behind the curtain at the back of their box.

Ruby sat up straight and smoothed down her skirts. She expected Seth to return to his own seat, but he did not. He simply sat up and continued holding her hand. The curtain parted, and the young couple entered.

"Cousin!" Jeanette addressed Seth in a loud whisper. "We have news!"

She turned to Tarquin expectantly. "Ah, Your Grace, I have..." the younger man began, "that is..."

Ruby lowered her head to hide a smile.

"Jeanette has consented to marry me... with your approval, naturally."

"It's not my approval you should be seeking," Seth answered, his warm expression belying the apparent disapproval in his words.

It was only then Jeanette noticed that she and Seth were holding hands. The girl's eyes widened. Ruby held out her free hand to draw the girl near.

"Does this mean...?" she asked. Ruby freed her hand from Jeanette's and put a finger to her lips. "We are not ready to announce just yet, but soon."

Jeanette leaned forward to hug her. "I get to call you my cousin, too! I couldn't be more delighted."

"When do you intend to have an audience with Lady Millarstone?" Seth asked Tarquin, taking command of the conversation.

"Tomorrow. I would be grateful to have your support," said the young man. "I know Jeanette's mother places great stock in what you have to say."

"I suppose that is one way of putting it."

"One way of putting what?"

The rear curtains parted once again, admitting Beatrice, followed by the colonel. She looked at the four of them, particularly noting the fact that Seth and Ruby sat side by side.

"My, this is a party," she said, looking directly at Seth. *"Dar-*

ling, what did we miss?"

"Another reason to celebrate. The spring ball will be to announce an engagement."

Ruby saw Beatrice's face turn stony. Animation of her face added so much to the illusion of youth in the countess. Now, she looked her age – older perhaps.

"Whose?" Beatrice asked stiffly.

"Lord Asquith and my dear young cousin, of course!" Seth replied.

Beatrice's face came to life again, and her focus now fell on Jeanette and Tarquin.

"Then I am delighted for the both of you. The ball, of course, will also be an excellent opportunity for your sisters. They have yet to accept any proposal, have they not? I'm sure that will change."

THIS TIME, GLENCOE House was not the foreboding edifice Ruby remembered from her first visit. The large building that backed onto the Thames seemed different. But why should that be? The day was as sunny as it had been a year prior. The house itself had not changed. The grounds, which she could see through the gate, were still immaculately kept.

The difference was only in her mind. After all, the only thing which had changed was that she was riding through the gates as a welcome guest, not walking in as an outsider plotting a scheme against its owner.

It seemed she was the last of the party to arrive. The Asquith family was already there, judging by the hubbub of lively conversation that came from one of the downstairs drawing rooms.

She had spent a month at Glencoe House as a nurse and had never been in this room. It was decorated in whites and yellows – an airy room to match the sun outside. Through the French doors, the Asquith sisters, along with Tarquin and Jeanette, played croquet while their mothers sat on wicker chairs shaded from the sun. Seth and Roddy stood aside and watched the young people play.

It was Seth who noticed her arrival first. He approached and bent over her hand.

"I see that I'm late," she said.

"No. On time. It's the Asquiths who are early. The daughters are whirling dervishes. I wish well any man who marries any one of them."

"Has Tarquin spoken to Jeanette's mother?"

"He has, and she's delighted – especially since I've given my approval, for what little it's worth. And, if she is delighted, her husband will be also. From what I understand from Jeanette, her father is very much a man who wants to keep the peace with his wife."

"Oh, dear."

"I think I might call on him when we return to Scotland. A show of moral support, if you will," he grinned. "There are a lot of relatives that I've only just become aware of, and so many of my father's acquaintances who I briefly recall from the funeral. They will expect a visit."

"An invitation to a wedding will do it, I'm sure," Ruby teased.

Seth took her hand and urged her to walk with him toward the rose gardens.

"This is the first time you've been to Glencoe House since coming back to London. Does it bring back bad memories?"

"No, it simply brings back memories. What of you?"

"Fewer than I thought, the truth be known. The two men, my secretary and my valet, that Prinny forced upon me have barely given me a minute to myself since I arrived."

"Will you keep them on?"

Seth flashed a cockeyed smile. "They might be unbearable sticks-in-the-mud, but I've grown rather fond of them actually. They know more about being a duke than I do."

Ruby laughed. "Then we ought to keep them on because I know even less about being a duchess."

"Then that is a project to keep them happy – find my bride a lady's maid."

"And a secretary. I must have a secretary of my *own*. I imagine I shall be entertaining in equal measure to my husband."

Seth took her into his embrace for a kiss. She did not know whether the rest of the party could see them and, frankly, she did not care. Surrounded by the sounds of birds in the trees and the scent of newly blooming roses, Ruby savored this moment.

She was released from Seth's embrace.

"Tell me what you would like to do with Strathaird."

Ruby blinked. She'd not given it much thought. It was hers. But home would soon be Castle Glenuig. She was the last of the McAllister line, but Strathaird should still remain in the family. Having risked it all to get it back, the thought of selling it would break her heart.

"Castle Glenuig and this house are entailed, are they not?"

Seth nodded. "Only Skye-Heath is not."

"Then I would like to keep Strathaird for our second born. Or for our daughter to keep in her name and benefit from the income."

Seth grinned. Ruby frowned.

"What amuses you?"

"That you're thinking of our children already."

She blushed and looked away. Seth took her hand and drew it up to his lips for a kiss. The sound of laughter and cheerful banter from the Asquith sisters reached them.

"Children…" said Seth. He thought back to the man he'd seen in the park, carrying his child upon his shoulders. "As many as you'd like. A family filled with love and siblings, so they will never have a childhood as lonely as mine."

"I love you," she whispered.

"My heart and my love are always yours."

CHAPTER THIRTY-THREE

IF RUBY CONSIDERED Glencoe House different when she visited two weeks ago, now, today, it was utterly transformed.

What had seemed to her to be a quiet house – more mausoleum than mansion when the old Duke of Auchen lived – was now a riot of color and noise, and the ball was still hours away from starting.

Colorful blooms filled vases. Chandeliers were fully lit, even in the middle of the day, sending shards of rainbow light onto the floor.

"Well, I have to give the countess credit," said Fran. "She knows how to put on an event."

Ruby could only nod in agreement. "Let me assure you that I jest not when I say I am making notes."

Seth had given Ruby a suite with two rooms; the second would be for Fran's use as a fitting room, not only for Ruby but also the Asquith sisters.

They followed the footmen in their colorful, formal livery as they carried the first of four trunks up the stairs to their rooms. A maid awaited to assist with the unpacking.

"At last! I get to see the dress you fashioned for me," Ruby exclaimed. "I cannot believe I let you talk me into having all the fittings with a blindfold on!"

"I wanted it to be a surprise," Fran said firmly. "Every eye will be on you."

She turned her attention to the maid.

"That one there, the one covered in the blue muslin – hang that in Lady Strathaird's room. Have Lady Asquith and her daughters arrived?"

"No, Ma'am, I don't believe so."

"That would be so. They'll arrive at the last minute, all at sixes and sevens," Fran muttered to Ruby before addressing the maid once more. "Please take these gowns to their room."

The maid did as directed, nearly hidden under swathes of fabric.

"Four of my girls will be here after the shop closes for the day. Two will look after the Asquith girls, and one each for Jeanette and the countess. I intend to be your lady's maid for tonight."

Ruby hugged her cousin.

"You've already done so much for me."

"Nonsense! Stop it, or you'll make me cry. I am just as grateful to you, you know. I'll be the dressmaker to the most fashionable duchess in all of England and Scotland."

There was a knock at the door. Another maid bobbed a curtsy at the threshold.

"Madame Dumont? His Grace says he believes he has what you are looking for, and wishes for you to join him at your earliest convenience."

"Seth?" Ruby asked. "Why does he wish to speak to you?"

"Ask no questions, I'll tell you no lies, dear cousin. You settle yourself here. I shall be back presently."

Ruby had little choice but to do as she was told. She wandered into the suite. It was larger than she expected and sumptuously appointed, the centerpiece being a large four-poster bed. The coverlet and curtains were a brocade of grassy green and gold. She wandered to the window to investigate the noise outside. From the window, she had a view down to the river where three barges were anchored.

Fireworks!

Below her, workmen were hanging festoons and lanterns, ready to be lit at dusk, all under the direction of the countess herself. The fact that the Prince of Wales was attending was truly a feather in her cap. She had put much thought and effort into the Duke of Auchen's spring ball.

Ruby quietly smiled to herself. The countess was not the only woman capable of surprises.

A few moments later, Fran returned with a small casket.

Ruby eyed it with open curiosity.

"What do you have there?"

"Something very special."

Ruby stepped forward to take the box. Francine was quicker and held it out of reach.

"Patience, dear one, patience. You'll find out what's in the box soon enough. In the meantime, I believe you should take a stroll in the rose garden."

"I believe you are unreasonably bossy."

Fran would not be moved and simply pointed at the door, a grin on her face.

With Fran occupied, Ruby went downstairs, deciding to take a shortcut into the garden through the bright and cheery yellow and white drawing room.

No sooner had she entered than the French door opened and Beatrice came in. The woman seemed surprised to find the room occupied.

Ruby curtsied.

"Countess, this *is* opportune. I was hoping for a few moments of your time," she said.

Beatrice raised an eyebrow.

"What matter concerns you, Lady Strathaird? I can only spare you a moment." The countess was pleasant but watchful, no doubt waiting for a jealous word or catty remark.

"I shall be brief then," said Ruby. "I want to thank you."

The older woman blinked a couple of times, clearly bemused.

Ruby used her faltering to continue.

"For everything you've done for Seth."

Beatrice nodded over to a yellow and white striped brocade settee.

"Sit with me a moment, Lady Strathaird, and permit me to recover from my shock."

Ruby went to the settee and sat. Beatrice joined her.

"I know," said Ruby, "*we know*, that his entrée into society would not have been as smooth if you had not taken him under your wing. His success this year is all *your* doing."

Beatrice bowed her head a moment, clearly collecting her thoughts before raising her head again and pinning Ruby with a direct look.

"Surely *you* of all people do not underestimate the man himself," she replied.

"I do not," Ruby answered. "I know the type of man he is, and the type of man he is capable of being. He needed you to help show him what he could become here in London with the full weight and import of his title and his heritage.

"That's all I wanted to say." Ruby rose to her feet then paused. "Oh, and to hope and wish that you receive everything you want from this evening."

Beatrice's expression softened, and Ruby caught an unexpected glimpse of the woman behind the polished façade. "I must say, that is very kind of you to say, my dear. Not many brides-to-be have thanked me for being the making of their husbands. In fact, very few speak to me at all."

"I can well imagine. Not many women *would* feel comfortable speaking to their husband's former lover."

"And it doesn't bother *you*?"

Ruby offered a half-shrug of her shoulders. "It is what it is. Seth and I had parted. I had no claim on him. If I had come to London to find him happy and in love with another, then I would have wished them both well."

"Despite your broken heart?"

"Despite my broken heart," she nodded.

Ruby looked toward the door and swallowed against a lump in her throat.

"Well, I'll leave you, Countess. I've taken up enough of your time and doubtless you have many more preparations to make."

"Wait."

She looked back. Beatrice got to her feet and moved ahead of her toward the door.

"I always knew Seth's heart lay elsewhere from the beginning. And, after tonight, rest assured he will be yours completely once more."

The countess departed. Ruby returned to the couch and sat down, exhaling a long breath.

The words she'd said where unrehearsed, but she meant them. She bore the woman no ill-will. She knew there was more to Countess Engelton, and she wanted the woman to know it. It was clear she had her reasons for doing what she did year after year, Season after Season, but what they were would have to remain a mystery.

RUBY MADE HER way to the rose garden, only half-surprised to find Seth there also.

"Banished from your own house, Your Grace?" she said airily.

"Then we are to be exiles together it seems, Lady Strathaird," he answered. Ruby fell in step with him as they continued down the path.

"It was always my philosophy to leave those who know what they're doing to their tasks. So far, I see nothing amiss with tonight's preparations. And you?"

Ruby shook her head. "Beatrice has done a superlative job."

"That's what I supposed." Seth found a seat overlooking the Thames. They sat in the dappled shade of the tree overhead. "So, there is nothing for us to do but to enjoy each other's company. Besides, I think a respite from both Lady Asquith and Lady Millarstone, is in order."

Ruby giggled. "Can you not see them coming over for tea often?"

"Yes. But not while I'm here." Seth grinned to soften his words. "I'm still getting used to demands on my time which are not of my making. I imagine it is all *expected* of being part of the aristocracy."

"Do you regret it?"

"What do you mean?"

"There was a time you believed that you weren't your father's son."

"Ha! I fear I am far too much like my father. If I had been a by-blow then my life would have been no different to the one I had made for myself. But would I have been enough for Lady Strathaird?"

Ruby rested her head on his shoulder.

"For you, I would have remained Nurse Campbell if you wished – for richer or for poorer."

He put his arms around her and kissed the top of her head. She settled into his embrace.

"Before long, we'll say those words before a priest," he said. "Until then, I hope you will save at least a couple of dances for me tonight."

"NOW YOU MAY see it." Fran removed the cover from the gown with a flourish worthy of a stage conjurer.

Ruby's breath caught in her throat. She was aware her eyes were wide in her face and her jaw dropped. She had never ever seen anything as fine.

The gown was plaid, the colors of green and blue intersecting with the bands of yellow and orange.

That in itself was a bold statement, but the embellishments were works of art in themselves.

The gown was wide across the shoulders with a gold watered silk fabric festooned along the neck before being carried down onto the short, puffed sleeves.

The skirt, too, was of the most fashionable style, falling from the bust in a more structured shape. Around the hem, a double row of twisted gold satin ribbon had been sewn, similar in style but narrower to the one which decorated the neckline.

"Are you pleased?" Fran asked.

"Thrilled! Speechless!" Ruby stammered out.

"There is something else… do you recognize the tartan?"

Ruby shook her head. Fran's grin grew bigger.

"It is the Musgrave tartan. It's made on Skye-Heath looms, but only ever for the family. Roddy brought a bolt of it down from Scotland with him."

Ruby brought a hand to her lips and blinked away the tears that threatened to spill over.

"Ah! None of that! Your eyes will be red, and that will not do. What the countess does not let you say in public will now be announced for the whole world to see."

"And Seth? Does he know?"

Fran shook her head. "It will be a surprise for him also."

Fran aided her into the gown. Out of habit, she closed her eyes as the stays were fastened. Tonight, Ruby wore her hair up in a chignon. She opened her eyes when Fran settled in a comb of ostrich feathers in gold, orange and blue – picking out the colors of the plaid.

"You'll turn me frightfully vain. I cannot stop looking at my reflection."

"And there's more. Your intended gave me permission to look through the Auchen family jewels." She reached for the box and drew out its contents. "It is not the most expensive piece in the collection, but I knew it was the piece you had to wear tonight the moment I saw it."

Ruby knew she had never seen the like, a *collier d'esclavage* – a strand of three gold chains linked together by blue enamel jewels. The first and third strands were styled in the form of leaves, the middle one as forget-me-not flowers.

Linking them together in three places – in the hollow of the shoulder and center above the bust – were gold disks decorated in stylized foliage of blue, green, orange, and yellow against a white ground.

The colors of the Musgrave tartan.

"I look like a duchess," she breathed.

"Even more than that. Tonight, you will look like a woman in love."

A maid came to the door to ask for Fran. One the seamstresses attending the Asquith girls needed her mistress' guidance.

"That will be Tilly. If that girl argues whether something is red or puce just one more time…"

Ruby waved her cousin off, pleased to have a few minutes on her own. Strange that she would be so nervous. She was no artless young girl attending her first ball, but it was the first with Seth, the first time she would dance in his arms.

The first time she would see what her life would be like as the Duchess of Auchen.

Another knock on the door broke her reverie. It was Jeanette, looking beautiful in the lotus pink gown, delicately trimmed with a spray of pearls at the waist.

It was just perfect for her coloring.

"Excited by tonight?" Ruby asked.

"Can one be excited and terrified at the same time?" Jeanette asked.

"I hope so. I feel the same way."

Ruby reached out her hand, and Jeanette took it.

"I've never thanked you enough."

"Whatever for?"

"I was very much under my mother's thumb back in Scotland, but you saw something in me."

"I saw what already existed – a intelligent young woman who only needed the encouragement to spread her wings."

Jeanette blushed prettily at the compliment.

"I trust Lady Millarstone is not too disappointed that you are marring a *mere* lord, instead of a duke?"

The girl laughed. "Her ambition was thwarted the minute we saw you. In fact, I expected you and Seth to wed before we left Glasgow. I worried that Seth had lost his mind after taking up with Countess Engelton here in London. But the gown you wear! Musgrave tartan, if I am not mistaken – dare I hope for a happy announcement?"

Ruby squeezed Jeanette's hands. "Not tonight. This is to be yours and Tarquin's moment, but soon."

SETH GLANCED AROUND the room and spotted Jervis. The man was a stickler for etiquette and had been drilling him endlessly for months on the "right" way to do everything. Now, as he and Beatrice prepared to receive the Prince Regent, the man could have no complaints at how his master conducted himself.

And yet, despite the honor bestowed by the Prince Regent's attendance, there was only one person Seth wanted to see and, so far, he had yet to spot her.

"Musgrave, you've done quite well already for yourself. I knew you had potential the moment I saw you."

Seth bowed to the Prince Regent.

"You're too kind, Your Highness."

The man gave him a speculative grin before addressing Beatrice. She dropped a deep curtsy.

"Madam, you excel yourself every time I see you," he said. "We must make sure we see more of you next Season."

"As Your Highness desires," she answered.

Seth knew the Prince Regent's words would be known by all by the time the receiving line finished, just as Beatrice intended. Perhaps she was losing her taste for callow youths and had set her sights a little higher for next year.

Still, after tonight, Beatrice would be out of his life for good. There was only one woman who filled his thoughts now.

Over the increasing noise and hubbub of the crowded ball-room, Seth clearly heard Ruby's name announced, and he turned.

What he saw took his breath away.

Never had Ruby looked so ravishing. And the gown! He recognized the plaid and had no doubt of its origins.

Roddy, you magnificent bastard. Thank you.

This afternoon, Seth had allowed Fran to have her pick through all of the family jewelry, and he'd wondered why she had passed over the rubies and emeralds in favor of this smaller piece.

Seeing it on her, he knew why Fran had chosen it.

"Your Grace."

Ruby's greeting carried with it an aware smile. She knew the effect the gown, that *she* had on him.

"You look very fetching tonight, Lady Strathaird."

The compliment came from the countess.

Ruby curtsied to the woman who possessed the remarkable ability to smile and speak at the same time.

"Remember, my little love birds, there is a promise you are not yet released from until the end of the night."

CHAPTER THIRTY-FOUR

DESPITE BEATRICE'S WORDS, she did not make undue demands for Seth's attention. Nor, to his relief, did she go out of her way to make things difficult for Ruby. In all, it seemed a very mature way to end an affair – such as it was.

He had to admit that the countess was an experienced social campaigner, recalling names and titles as though she had simply memorized Debrett's *Peerage of England, Scotland and Ireland* for entertainment.

So, he did what he had done in the six months of her company, and that was to listen and give her the attention and courtesy which was her due. Funnily enough, he also found himself enjoying Beatrice's company tonight as much as he had on their first meeting.

He thanked God and the heavens above that Ruby was not the jealous type. She knew his heart was hers, and she'd allowed him to do what he needed to successfully end the arrangement he had with Beatrice.

Whenever he looked for Ruby in the crowd, she was well engaged in conversation or taking part in the dances. Whenever their eyes met, she smiled at him, letting him know in her own way that everything was fine, and that she was having a good time.

For the first time since arriving in London, Seth was beginning to feel like his old self and be at ease in company. How simple it was to fall back on protocol and general etiquette to ensure their guests were enjoying themselves and that the guests of honor – Jeanette and Tarquin – were especially feted.

He had grown in confidence in his position as duke. He had spent so long determined to be nothing like his father, he'd neglected to consider what kind of man he *ought* to become.

Tonight, he became aware of how much he owed to both women.

Now, dancing was well underway. One drew to a close, and Seth sought out his dance partner for the next. This would be his first dance with Ruby this evening. It wouldn't be his last.

He spotted her in conversation with a group of young ladies, a couple of the Asquith girls among them. Their conversation stopped as he approached, Ruby's back to him.

"Good evening, Lady Strathaird, I believe the next dance is ours."

Ruby turned, and he remembered why he'd fallen in love with her in the first place. The delight on her face, the love in her eyes held him in thrall. She offered him her hand, and he kissed it.

There might have been a sigh from the small party around them, but they didn't exist as far as he was concerned. All that mattered was the woman in his arms. His eyes never left hers as the dance brought them together and then apart. Every touch was significant. The color on Ruby's cheeks was more than simply the exertion of the dance.

"Do you enjoy fireworks, Lady Strathaird?" he asked.

"I do, Your Grace," she answered as she turned full circle around him. "I seem to recall one particular evening."

He did not misunderstand her meaning, and he felt the stirrings of arousal.

"There is a particular vantage point where the view is likely to be especially good," he said, his eyes taking in every movement, every expression. He watched her lips part and the desire to kiss her right then and there nearly overthrew his common sense.

The dance came to an end all too soon, but not before he had whispered instructions to meet him on the gallery landing at half-past eleven.

That left a better part of an hour and a half to build anticipation.

Seth looked for Beatrice, but did not see her amongst the revelers. She would be expecting him to show some attendance to her. Perhaps she was taking some air out in the gardens. He got as far as the path to the rose garden when he spotted the silvery shimmer of her gown. She sat alone on one of the stone benches.

"Good evening, Beatrice. It is not like you to be here alone," he said.

She looked up at him and smiled.

"What makes you think I'm alone?"

Seth laughed and dropped a kiss on the top of her head.

"I couldn't imagine that for a second. Shall I leave you?"

"Not just yet." Beatrice patted the bench beside her. "Come, sit beside me a moment."

He did as she bid.

After a moment of silence, listening to the celebrations at the house, Beatrice spoke. "I like your Ruby. She is a woman worthy of being the Duchess of Auchen."

"I hope I am worthy of being her titled husband."

Beatrice patted his knee. "You will be. You are."

"Thank you." He hesitated before continuing. "I don't know what you appreciated in me when I first came to London, but I was a man lost. My title felt like a fraud, that I was wearing another man's clothes. The fact that tonight is a success and my acceptance here in London has been assured is in no small measure thanks to you. You have smoothed the way, helped me make connections. Even the fact my cousin's daughter is celebrating her engagement here tonight is all thanks to you."

"The pleasure has been mine." Her hand returned to squeeze

his knee, but Seth recognized the gesture as a playful one. "You have been one of the most thoughtful of my lovers."

Seth heard the sound of heavy footsteps crunching on the path toward them. A man approached, alone, his figure a silhouette against the lights from the house.

He and Beatrice glanced up, but the man passed them by without comment and continued on his way into the gardens.

Silence fell once more.

Seth cleared his throat. "There is a question I have never asked, and tonight I must. Why did you not marry again after the earl died?"

Beatrice smiled thoughtfully. "I could give you the answer that I have given to others – I married young and, now widowed, I wished to fully sample the gardens of sensual delights."

"And the truth?"

"I loved my husband dearly. When he died, I was certain that I would never love again. That such love only came to a few and to those it did, just once in a lifetime. My lovers have been distractions, a physical consolation. I cannot deny it has been a mutually beneficial arrangement."

"But you *could* marry again if you wish."

Beatrice rose from the bench and cupped Seth's cheek, giving him a quiet smile.

"You and Ruby give me hope."

She looked away. Seth wondered whether she was blinking away tears. Her hand fell from his cheek. Beatrice walked away into the rose garden without once looking back.

BUTTERFLIES DANCED AROUND Ruby's stomach. She put a hand there wondering if she could feel them.

She waited in the upper gallery alone. No, not *entirely* alone. While none of the guests were in this part of the house, she did see the occasional servant, most of whom dutifully ignored her presence, although one or two had done a double take, recognizing her as Nurse Campbell despite her expensive gown, coiffed hair, and jewels.

She paced the gallery landing as she had done a year earlier, examining the portraits of the Musgrave family dating back to the reign of James the Sixth of Scotland, who the English knew as James the First.

She knew their features well, the eyes and the reddish-brown hair in most of their likenesses. Once more, she walked down the line of portraits, stopping at the portrait of William Gregory Musgrave.

What an enigma he was.

She nursed him for months, but she could not say she knew him.

"Do you remember his demand for the lawyer after visiting my mother's grave?"

Seth stood only a few feet away. Ruby had been so lost in her thoughts that she did not hear him approach. Now he stood as she did, examining the large portrait of his father.

The firmness of the jawline and the color of the eyes were the same, yet she knew Seth had many of his mother's features as well.

"I remember," she said.

"I thought the old man was going to change his will and cut me out. It turned out he was opening doors for me in London – bank accounts, clubs, lines of credit from bakers to tailors, letters of introduction calling me his *much-loved* son. I still don't know what to make of it."

"And we will never know, not in this lifetime. All we can do is learn the lesson of leaving hate and bitterness behind."

Ruby stepped into Seth's embrace.

"I love you," he whispered.

"I love you, too," she replied, resting a head on his chest, savoring the warmth and the scent of cinnamon and patchouli.

"I promised you a view of the fireworks," he said.

"I thought that was simply an excuse for us to be alone."

He grinned. "That, too."

He led her to the end of the hall where she took one last look at Georgiana Musgrave, William's Helen of Troy, the woman who'd managed to bring out the last vestiges of decency in Seth's father.

They rounded another corner down a short hall that opened out into a schoolroom nursery.

"And here's another enigma. I found all of my childhood toys here," said Seth. "I would have thought the old man had gotten rid of them years ago."

A loud bang, followed by a series of pops told her the fireworks had already started.

Seth took her hand and led her into a smaller room, the nursery bedroom which had a large window that looked out over the gardens and an unimpeded view of the river.

She leaned against Seth's chest. He slid a hand around her waist and drew her closer, so her back was against his chest.

Explosions of reds, yellows, oranges and whites filled the night sky while fountains of golden sparks seemed to come up from the river itself.

His lips on her neck made her close her eyes.

"Have I told you how beautiful you look tonight?" he whispered.

"Not in so many words," she answered.

"Who needs so many words when I can show you instead?" he whispered. "Will you promise me you'll wear that gown for our wedding?"

"I certainly will not," she answered. "It is bad luck for the groom to see the bride in her gown before the wedding."

"Does it matter?"

"It matters to Fran especially when she has already spent a number of hours on a wedding gown already."

Seth chuckled. The warm eddies of air filled her ears and the electric shock of desire sent goosebumps everywhere.

"Then I eagerly await the unveiling. I love you, Ruby, and a lifetime will not be long enough to show you the many ways I do."

Ruby turned around so she was fully in Seth's embrace. She didn't need to see fireworks when there was heartfelt desire and immeasurable love in the eyes of the man before her.

She opened her mouth to say something, but couldn't think of the words to say that would fully express what was in her heart. But she didn't need them. As though he read her thoughts, Seth lowered his mouth to hers for a sweet and sensual kiss.

No words were needed when there was love.

EPILOGUE

Glasgow
June 1821

SETH HEARD THE skirl of bagpipes even before the carriage came to a halt in front of a sizeable brick building on the banks of the White Cart.

Before the doors opened, he looked to his wife and grinned. His beautiful Ruby, and on her lap, their much-adored son, Jacob George William Musgrave.

Seated opposite them was Roddy, the most steadfast friend a man could have. Beside him sat his wife Aileen, and their son Iain.

Six months separated the boys in age but already they were shaping up to be lifelong friends, just like their fathers. Brothers, though not by blood.

His heart swelled at the applause which broke out when he emerged from the ducal coach. It continued as Ruby alighted, then Roddy and Aileen. Two nurses who had arrived earlier came forward to help manage the children.

Seth stared at the large three-story brick building before him.

Habetrot – just as he envisioned it. Complete at last.

Ruby reached for his hand and took it. She knew without asking that he needed her grounding presence beside him.

"Somehow, it still doesnae seem real," said Roddy.

"It's real enough to me," said Aileen. "Ye should be right proud. All of ye."

Seth followed the pipers to the door of the mill, acknowledging with a nod and a smile, those men and women who worked at Skye-Heath and Habetrot who cheered the procession.

In many respects, the official opening of the mill was merely a formality. Habetrot had been operating from this building for a couple of weeks now. Today was about acknowledging the workers who had turned his vision into reality.

There, in the crowd, he was heartened to spot Fergus O'Donnell's widow who came with a posy of flowers to lay at the plaque acknowledging her late husband.

There were more surprises. Lord and Lady Asquith, Tarquin and Jeanette, had come up to Glasgow especially. They brought news of Lady Beatrice Rowland, Countess Engelton, who had finally accepted a proposal of marriage from Colonel Hoddleston.

Seth gave his speech, not from prepared notes, but direct from the heart.

It was a carnival atmosphere around the grounds of the new Habetrot Mill. In addition to the pipers who welcomed the Duke of Auchen's party, there were musicians for dancing, games for the wee ones, and an al fresco feast under a bright red marquee.

Much anticipated was a football match between the men of Habetrot and Skye-Heath, a healthy, but friendly rivalry between the two mills that had grown over the past twelve months.

Later in the day, he and Ruby managed to find some moments alone.

"I've been thinking about Strathaird," she said.

"What about it, my love?" he asked, drawing her into his arms.

"We spoke of it being the inheritance for a younger child," she said.

"We've been busy with the construction of Habetrot, but I've not forgotten. Why do you raise this now?"

Ruby offered an enigmatic smile, took his hand and placed it over her quickening belly.

"You're certain?"

Ruby nodded.

Seth knew the expression "a heart full to bursting". Over the past year and a half, he experienced many of those moments and was grateful beyond measure for each and every one of them.

How much more room there was in one's heart when bitterness, enmity, and hatred were driven out in favor of love, joy, and contentment.

The greatest of these is love.

And no truer word was ever spoken.

THE END

Sonnets Pour Helene Book I: IX
The other day you saw me, as you passed by,
While I was above you on the stair: you turned
Your gaze, dazzled my eyes, my soul so burned
At finding myself the focus of your eyes.
Your glance entered my heart and blood, just like
A flash of lightning through the clouds. I burned
Hot and cold, in a lasting fever, well-earned
By the mortal wound of your glance's piercing flight.
If your fair hand had not made a sign to me then,
White hand that makes you a daughter of the swan,
I'd have died, Helen, of the rays from your eyes:
But that gesture towards me saved a soul in pain:
Your eye was pleased to carry away the prize,
Yet your hand rejoiced to grant me life again.

About the Author

Elizabeth Ellen Carter is an award-winning historical romance writer who pens richly detailed historical romantic adventures. A former newspaper journalist, Carter ran an award-winning PR agency for 12 years. The author lives in Australia with her husband and two cats.